Gauging the Player

Book 3 in The Playmakers Series®

BY G.K. BRADY

This book is a work of fiction. Names, characters, places, and incidents are the product of the author's imagination or are used fictitiously. Any resemblance to actual events, locales, or persons, living or dead, is coincidental.

ISBN 978-1-7332763-5-1

Cover design by Getcovers
Edited by Jenny Quinlan, Historical Editorial
Proofread by Word Servings
Trefoil Publishing

Contents

Chapter 1 ~ There's a Hitch in my Skate-Along 1
Chapter 2 ~ Etta James is Alive and Well in Denver 8
Chapter 3 ~ You Meet the Darnedest People at Strip Clubs ... 22
Chapter 4 ~ Of Vampires and Pancakes 32
Chapter 5 ~ Because Everyone Needs Social Media 41
Chapter 6 ~ Sisterhood Doesn't Require Pants 49
Chapter 7 ~ Flow with the Go 57
Chapter 8 ~ There's a Football Game Going On? 69
Chapter 9 ~ Tell Me Sweet Little Lies ... Please 80
Chapter 10 ~ Game Time 90
Chapter 11 ~ If Wishes Were Wings, I'd Crash 100
Chapter 12 ~ Crush, Crush 109
Chapter 13 ~ Game On 117
Chapter 14 ~ Careless Whispers 126
Chapter 15 ~ Stuck in the Discovery Channel 136
Chapter 16 ~ Spectral Visions 147
Chapter 17 ~ Shall He Do Her? 153
Chapter 18 ~ Is It Hot in Here, or Is It You? 163
Chapter 19 ~ I'm Not Shy 172
Chapter 20 ~ What's Passed Isn't Past 184
Chapter 21 ~ Making Beautiful Music 191
Chapter 22 ~ Phantom Shadows 197
Chapter 23 ~ Red Light, Green Light 205

Chapter 24 ~ I'm Going to ... Dillon? 213
Chapter 25 ~ Parenting 101 217
Chapter 26 ~ You Know What They Say About Assuming 225
Chapter 27 ~ Wisdom Is an Elusive Pearl 234
Chapter 28 ~ Claiming a Stake 239
Chapter 29 ~ Deep Into That Darkness Peering 248
Chapter 30 ~ Grabbing a Gear on the Stick Shift of Life 255
Chapter 31 ~ Reveals and Reasons 265
Chapter 32 ~ Nice to Meet You, Rod Serling 272
Chapter 33 ~ And This Is Why 279
Chapter 34 ~ Big Sister Knows Best 285
Chapter 35 ~ The Long Good-bye 296
Chapter 36 ~ The Holy Grail 303
Epilogue 313
Acknowledgments 322
Author's Note 323
Other Books 324
About the Author 325

Dedication

To my dear friend Sue, love's eternal optimist—may you find your second Gage in this lifetime. To all those who have loved and lost too soon.

Chapter 1

There's a Hitch in my Skate-Along

Late January

D*rop the damn puck already!*

Gage Nelson gripped his stick across his thighs. Poised and taut, he deliberately placed the blade of his stick on the ice, mirroring his opponent's stance, keeping his eyes glued to the puck in the linesman's hand. *Drop it, drop it, drop it!* He waited. Normally, he had patience in spades, but right now it was as hard to find as meat in a frozen pot pie.

Tonight his team, the Colorado Blizzard, faced Boston. For the most part, he respected all the NHL teams—but not Boston. He *hated* Boston. He also hated that they were owning his team on home ice, thanks to his poor play. Fortunately, it didn't show on the scoreboard. Yet.

Not one usually distracted by anything beyond the rink glass, he had to remind himself, for the fifty-sixth time, to forget about the blond with the long curly hair sitting in the stands. Was it her? He hadn't been able to get a close look all night, though he'd sure tried his damnedest.

Forget about her and focus, doofus.

The other center in the faceoff circle growled out a taunt—another part of the game Gage usually had infinite patience for—and though he didn't catch everything the guy said, it was enough to make him flinch and draw his blade back too early.

"Premature again, meat sack," his opponent chuckled under his breath. "Just what your last girlfriend said. Or was it your boyfriend?"

The linesman tossed Gage out of the faceoff, and he glided backward, making room for his right winger, T.J. Shanstrom, to take his place. Shanny side-eyed him. Gage easily read what was written on his teammate's face despite the bright arena lights bouncing off his visor. He had to be thinking something along the lines of, *What the fuck, Nelson? Three times in one period.*

Yeah, contrary to what Gage's family yapped at him, he was *not* perfect. Hopefully, his mom was watching and would finally understand he could be off his game. Way off.

Darting his eyes toward the stands, he went into another crouch, waiting for the puck drop. Before he dragged his eyes back to the play, he glimpsed the blond in question laughing at something the guy beside her said. He'd absently scanned the stands when he'd taken the ice for warm-ups, and that's when he'd caught sight of her and his game went off the rails. He hadn't been able to keep his mind—or his eyes—off of her. And now something unidentifiable jolted through his bloodstream.

Watch the puck. Keep it simple. It's all about the game. Nothing else.

Watch. Puck. Get. Puck. Skate.

Put. Puck. In. Net.

T.J. drew the puck back, winning the faceoff, but Gage missed corralling it. The other team picked it up before he could get his stick on it, and their line flew toward the Blizzard net. A three-on-two breakaway. *Damn it!*

He dug in, turning on the turbos. Normally, he could overtake anyone on skates, but he was a step behind. His D-men backed up. A smooth give-and-go between the opposing forwards. The puck landed on the winger's tape. Gage dove from behind. Swept his stick in front of him. Caught the guy in the skates. The player went down hard. Crashed into the Blizzard net. Took Wyatt, the Blizzard goalie, down with him.

A whistle blew.

Wyatt sprawled on his back on the ice, looking like he was frozen mid-snow angel. The net had come off its moorings when the Boston player ended up in the back of it. As said Boston player untangled himself from the netting, he spewed a spate of choice words at Gage, who was picking himself up off the ice.

Gage didn't need to look to know the orange armband was in the air—the one around the ref's arm—and a penalty was being called. On him.

Shit!

He stood up fully, relieved when Wyatt got to his feet, seemingly unhurt. The goalie adjusted his cage and gave Nelson a quick "it's okay" head jerk.

The ref pointed at Gage and signaled the infraction. "Number six, two minutes for tripping!"

The Blizzard team captain, Dave Grimson—"Grims"—whacked Gage on his calf. "Could've been worse, Admiral. At least he didn't get a penalty shot. Take your two minutes and get your head right. Me and the boys will kill this off."

Admiral. Somehow Gage had been labeled with the moniker in San Jose, and like many incongruous nicknames, it had transferred over to Denver when he'd been traded two years ago.

He skated to the sin bin with a headshake. The penalty box wasn't a spot he normally visited. The door closed behind him as he stepped inside and sat on the bench. He sucked in a breath, watching his team, now a man short, trying to keep Boston off the scoreboard. Fiddling with his helmet, rearranging his gear, he tried to look as nonchalant as possible while fans yelled and banged on the glass surrounding him. Lots of words of encouragement peppered with the occasional "You suck!" rang around him. In other words, standard fare.

Penalties were part of the game; normally, they didn't bother him. *You go to box, you feel shame.* But the blond was only three rows back, getting an unobstructed view of him serving his sentence. It occurred to him that if *she* could get a good look at him, *he* could get a good look at her. He stood up and faced her way, pretending to adjust his elbow pads. That's when he realized it wasn't Lily. Just someone with hair like hers. The pang of disappointment threw him off balance, his synapse relays as wobbly as one of his mini-mite players learning to skate.

He sat down hard and pigeonholed his bothersome thoughts to ponder some other day. It was time to focus on the penalty kill finishing up on the ice. His eyes traveled to the game clock—thirty-seven seconds left in his minor penalty.

Go, boys!

They did, but with only ten seconds to go, Boston scored a power-play goal. Gage came out of the box, and the same jerk center skated toward him. "Thanks for the gift, Nelson." He gave Gage a little shove with his stick as he went by.

Gage was no hothead, but he'd reached his limit. The evening's frustrations, his inability to keep thoughts of Lily caged, fused together and boiled over.

That's it!

He took a few strides and shoved the asshole back. The guy rounded on him and laughed. Before Gage could react, someone crosschecked him from behind and flattened him on the ice. He popped up, wheeled, and faced Boston's heavyweight—Cal Beaumont. Their quasi-enforcer, a giant of a grinder with feet made of stone and fists to match. The guy also had three inches on Gage and about thirty pounds.

"C'mon, you little pussy," Beaumont taunted as he threw down his gloves.

Gage shook his own gloves, but before he could rid himself of them, T.J. skated in front of him, blocking his access to Beaumont.

"Out of the way, T.J. You're third man in."

T.J.'s gloves were off in a nanosecond, his fists cocked. "Not this time."

The audience went into a frenzy, screaming for blood as T.J. and Beaumont, two massive men, sized each other up. Another Boston player grabbed Gage around the chest and hauled him backward. Each player on the ice had hold of an opponent as though pairing off for a dance. But all eyes were fastened on the main attraction: the showdown between two evenly matched titans. That is, they were evenly matched in size and fighting experience, but T.J.'s playing ability was light years beyond Beaumont's.

Beaumont threw the first punch and missed, but T.J.'s answering blow connected. Fists flew between the two like Rock 'Em Sock 'Em Robots. The fight was over in seconds, leaving both men winded but upright. The home crowd went wild, raining down cheers and shrill whistles.

A short while later, Gage and T.J. *both* sat in the box, matched by two Boston players on the opposite side.

The crowd roared, and Gage snapped his attention to the jumbotron, where T.J. and he were on full display as they sat in the box. The camera moved to the two Boston players serving penalties, and the crowd booed. Back and forth it went.

"Take a bow, Admiral. You're tonight's entertainment," T.J. chuckled as he inspected his chin strap.

"You shouldn't have jumped in," Gage groused. "Not on my account."

"You were on your way to getting your ass kicked. I couldn't let that happen, now could I? *No* one messes with my center." T.J. part-laughed, part-growled. "Besides, who else is gonna set me up for all those sweet goals I've been racking up lately?"

Embarrassed he hadn't fought his own fight—he'd never been a fighter, but still, he should've taken his own licks—Gage hid his unease with a well-timed grunt.

T.J. grabbed a water bottle and squirted water in his mouth. "What started it?"

"They were doing a lot of chirping out there." Lame answer, but it was all Gage had at that moment.

"Well, next time pick on someone your own size."

"I'll keep that in mind next time one of their players pisses me off," Gage said dryly.

T.J. turned and gave him an appraising look. "Guys don't normally get under your skin. What's really eating you tonight anyway?"

Gage lied. "Nothing."

"Yeah, right," T.J. said with a chuckle.

Gage had known T.J. long enough to know he wouldn't push. They'd become buddies when they'd been traded from the Bay Area together. Gage had been in shock, and T.J. had helped him navigate Denver and the choppy waters where Gage had landed after the surprise trade.

Though Grims was the captain and wore the *C* on his sweater, T.J. wore an *A* as alternate captain because he'd become the heart and soul of the team. Gage wore the other *A*, and while he was beyond honored, he was still scratching his head over why they'd given it to him in the first place. "Because you're the perfect guy for it," he'd been told. Yeah, right. Perfect he wasn't. As for wearing the *A*, he suffered from impostor-itis, like he hadn't earned the right yet. Sure, he was a decent playmaker, but he didn't have Grims's swagger or T.J.'s bruising presence.

Further proof that they overestimated him lay in the result of tonight's game. It ended with a Boston win, which translated to a checkmark in the Blizzard's loss column—a loss Gage draped around his shoulders like the damp towel from his post-game shower.

Exiting the players' area, he fell in beside T.J. Natalie, a pretty, willowy brunette, greeted them with a wide grin. T.J. slid his arm around her waist and pecked her lips. Beside her, their two dogs—Ford and Deke—wagged and whimpered at the sight of T.J.

"Nice fight," she said to T.J. "I'm glad to see your lips didn't get hurt." She gave Gage a sly look. "Hey, you."

He bent and ruffled each dog's neck. "Hi, Natalie."

"Just ignore him," T.J. said. "He's beating himself up for the loss tonight."

Natalie scrunched her eyebrows. "And he's doing this why?"

T.J. shrugged. "Who knows? It was a team loss, but he seems to think he did it alone. Pretty impressed with his ability to affect the outcome, I'd say."

"Walking right here, guys," Gage huffed.

Though talking to Natalie, T.J. wagged his head at him. "See what I mean?"

"And he's usually so cheerful," she said. "I'm not used to Grumpy Gage. I prefer Happy Gage." She sent Gage a wink, and he flashed her back a grin.

Seeing T.J. with his wife always brought a smile to Gage's face. After all, he'd helped get them together. Who knows how long it would've taken them to find their way to each other if he hadn't taken charge that one disastrous night a few springs ago?

"Join us for dinner?" Natalie ventured.

"No, thanks." He was on the verge of saying, "I'm just gonna head home," but she said it for him. Yeah, he was *that* predictable.

Holding up his phone, he added for good measure, "I've got some family stuff to take care of."

Natalie's expression shifted to one of concern. "More trouble at home?"

"Always."

As she and T.J. peeled away, heading for their car, she called over her shoulder, "Let us know if you change your mind."

With a wave, he said, "Absolutely." They both knew he had no intention of taking her up on it.

He climbed into his Porsche Panamera 4S and watched them for a few beats. With a headshake and a smile, he drummed his thumbs on the steering wheel. Should he call his mother now and get it over with? Listen to her complain about his sister, his grandma, or whatever drama had her riled up this time? Or wait until he'd recharged his reserves?

Putting aside the looming conversation, he let his normally equable mind travel to the other female force agitating it: the woman who'd sneaked out of his bed in the middle of the night six long months ago, and who'd been haunting his thoughts ever since.

Chapter 2

Etta James is Alive and Well in Denver

Six months earlier

Gage peeked around a pillar, watching the band warm up. Could tonight get any worse? He'd been in a perpetual state of flight-or-fight, evading a very enthusiastic bridesmaid named Blair. Somehow the lady had concluded that, in addition to escorting her up and down the aisle, his groomsman duties included a bedroom interlude. Which it absolutely didn't.

But in addition to this irritation, a musical tragedy was about to assault his ears. He could practically hear nails scraping down the chalkboard, and his neck hairs stood on end.

From center stage, the band had just proclaimed the first dance would be Etta James's "At Last." The announcement had come from what he could only presume was Etta's stand-in, and Gage slumped inside. This woman was too slight to produce the sort of singing power that placed her anywhere close to an *amateur* blues singer, let alone one of Etta James's stature. He'd seen far too many bad blues acts to know she needed at minimum an extra fifty pounds—along with a few inches—on her small frame to do the piece reverent justice.

He checked his disappointment and braced himself for the underwhelming singer about to butcher one of his favorite songs.

For the hundredth time, he questioned whether he'd made the right decision in not bringing a date. Unfortunately, he knew no one well enough to feel comfortable asking in the first place. Not that he'd looked since landing in Denver a year ago. It was events like this that made him miss Sarah. He was a banana split with no banana. She'd been his plus-one countless times, but she lived over thirteen hundred miles away in Seattle. Damn, he missed her! They'd been one another's crutch for occasions just like this one, and now he was one crutch short and pegging around in circles. Why hadn't he thought to fly her in?

Gage's musings were overridden by a breathy purr coming through the sound system. "Please welcome Mr. and Mrs. Shanstrom, everyone," the singer announced.

T.J. and Natalie stepped onto the dance floor and double high-fived. Around them, applause and whistles rose to a deafening level as T.J. gathered Natalie in his arms. So much happiness shone in T.J.'s eyes that Gage felt a pang. Not that he wanted Natalie. Sure, she was perfect for his buddy, but his envy centered on the fact T.J. had found that rare person he trusted with his heart. What the three generations of romance-reading women who'd raised Gage would have called "The One." In his teenage years, he'd inevitably countered the term with a loud scoff and an exaggerated eye-roll, if for no other reason than it was expected of him.

Gage raised his Woodford Reserve to his lips and sipped while the singer commandeered the mic. *Girding my loins here.*

A hand tapped his shoulder, and he startled.

"Whoa, dude. Easy." His teammate Hunter McMurphy guffawed, his hands up in surrender.

On high Blair alert, Gage scanned the crowd. "Thought you might be someone else. Where's your girlfriend tonight?"

Hunter shrugged. "She couldn't make it." He shamelessly eyeballed a trio of women hovering at the edge of the dance floor and smiled wolfishly. "But don't worry about me."

Dick.

A familiar, haunting strain began, jerking Gage's attention back to the band. Beside a violinist, the guitarist adjusted his guitar strap.

Nice Strat. Hope he knows how to play that thing. What Gage wouldn't give to be home right now, working over the strings on his own guitar.

He squeezed his eyes shut, hoping it would stave off the carnage about to befall his ears.

A voice, sultry and soulful, resonated through the speakers. He lifted one eyelid, disbelieving what he was hearing. Words declaring that her lonely days were over seemed to pour from deep within the woman's diminutive form. Where she kept that voice, he had no idea. He opened the other lid and searched for a sound engineer or some proof she was lip-syncing but found nothing.

He darted another look at the stage. The singer lowered herself into a semi-crouch, her eyes shuttered. Bringing her voice with her, she rose, unfurling as though the song worked its way up from her toes to her throat, emphatically belting out that she'd found a dream and a thrill. The lyrics, delivered with so much heart, sent a thrill through *him*.

Transfixed, Gage fastened his gaze on the singer laying her soul bare and locked out the rest of the crowd, a silent apology rolling around in his head. *Totally underestimated the power of her vocals. But how can such a small person sing like she's got the lungs of a walrus?*

The song came to an end, people clapped, and Gage reentered his body. Beside him, Hunter's shrill whistle pierced his eardrums. This was followed by a guttural growl. "Fuck me, I want a piece of *that*!"

Gage flinched. Ah, to have a T-shirt that boldly stated "I'm NOT with Stupid" would have been priceless in that moment. The guy was twenty-five—same as Gage—with all the maturity of a twelve-year-old.

The keyboardist began a soft tune, and the singer warmed up her vocal chords on the next song, Christina Aguilera's "Beautiful." She seemed to feel every word, every note, to the depths of her being.

More songs followed, and his curiosity was so piqued that when Blair surprised him with a hug from behind, he was totally caught off guard. Rather than flee, he gave in and accompanied her to the dance floor to get a closer look.

Mere feet away, the singer belted out another Etta tune, "I Just Want to Make Love to You." Gage roamed his eyes over her, taking in light eyes—*Blue? Green?*—and long curls that floated around her heart-shaped face in a golden froth, skimming ivory shoulders bare of anything but the straps of her red dress. The dress hugged her curvy figure. If her voice hadn't sent chills zipping along the race track that was his spine, her body alone might've done it.

Shapely calves narrowed to shapely ankles and feet encased in sky-high heels, emphasizing strong, lean legs. His mind vaulted to wondering if those legs were insured, like Tina Turner's. They should've been because they were lethal. Then his mind took another herky-jerky detour, like Mr. Toad's Wild Ride, and an image of those legs wrapped around his neck bounced through his brain. He quickly wrestled it under a virtual mat labeled "Neglected Need."

Blair chose that moment to snake her arms around his waist and pull him into a grinding hug. Though his virtual mat was a lumpy, bumpy mess for all the Neglected Need stuffed under it, he disencumbered himself from her hold, saying he needed to hit the head. He hated like hell to lie, but he loped in that direction nonetheless and stepped outside. His gaze caught on Beckett Miller, the best man, who sported an empty pink baby carrier on his chest—and rocked a pink baby in his arms.

Miller's eyebrows inched up his forehead when Gage stepped up beside him and said, "I'm being chased by an octopus. Can I hang out with you two for a while?"

Miller chuckled. "Sure."

Babies were a mystery to Gage—he had zero experience—and he bent down to get a closer look, hovering his finger by her cheek. She latched on to it, wiggling frantically as she tried to draw it into her gooey mouth. "What's her name?"

"Elayne, after my mom. We call her Layne, though."

"She's got quite a grip."

"Yeah, she'll make a good golfer, won't you, sweet pea?" Beckett cooed to the baby.

The singer walked out, startling when her eyes landed on them. "Oh. I didn't realize anyone was out here."

Gage straightened in a flash.

"I was keeping my daughter away from the noise," Miller said.

"Not that your singing is noise," Gage interjected, side-eyeing Miller, who smirked.

Eyes fixed on Layne, the singer came closer, a beautiful smile lighting her face. "How old is she?" Despite the four-inch heels, she was small. Gage wasn't big like Beckett—guy had a few inches on him—but beside *her*, he felt like a giant.

"Seven months and ten days." Beckett spewed a litany of facts, and Gage suppressed an amused eye-roll. *Proud papa.*

During a lull in the exchange, Gage stuck out his hand. "I'm Gage Nelson, and this," he tilted his head toward Beckett, "is Beckett Miller."

Curious eyes bounced between them. "Are you hockey players too?" No fangirling in her tone. Nor had she offered up *her* name.

"Yep," Beckett said. "Gage plays for the Blizzard, and I'm with Arizona. And if you'll excuse me, I think it's time for a diaper change." He pushed his glasses up the bridge of his nose and made a stink face.

After he left, Gage turned to the woman. "Do you watch hockey?"

She shook her head, and her curls sprang like silk coils. "I don't have time to follow sports. So are you a friend of the bride or the groom?"

He chuckled. "Both."

Tipping her head at him, she arched one blond eyebrow. "Sounds like there's a story behind that smile."

"There is." Gage already knew *that* story. He was far more interested in learning about the woman in front of him. "How long have you been singing?"

"Professionally, not for a while, but I guess I've been singing all my life."

"Do you always sing the blues?"

"The blues is my favorite, but usually it's classic rock."

Big blue eyes—the color of the Pacific Ocean off Point Reyes. He bobbed his head. "You handle them all well."

She blushed. It was a pretty look on her creamy skin. "Thank you," she replied in a voice that belied the resonant pipes harbored within her body.

Surprising gratification danced in his stomach, setting off a chain reaction. His pulse picked up speed, his collar tightened, and his mind raced through what to say next. Small talk wasn't a language he spoke fluently. He usually kept to himself. When he had something to say, he did it without dressing it up. Just sort of threw it out there. Not that he was rude, at least not on purpose. Right now, though, he found himself wishing his tongue had a shiny silver coating.

On the verge of launching into the righteousness of the blues—and enumerating his favorite blues artists—he was interrupted when Hunter ambled out.

"Hey, pretty singer," Hunter said. "You're awesome!"

Gage detected a slight flinch before she dipped her head and plastered on what appeared to be a stage smile. "Thanks, um ..."

"I'm Hunter." He extended his hand, and when she slipped hers into it, he raised it to his lips. "And you are?"

Gage's thoughts swung from a disgusted *Seriously, dude?* to a grudging *Smooth move.*

Her eyes darted to Gage before returning to Hunter, and she hesitated before saying, "Lily."

"Are you staying here tonight?" asked Hunter. The venue was separated from a B&B by a stand of pines with walking paths leading from one side to the other. Though Denver was a mere hour away, some guests, including Gage, had chosen to spend the night at the B&B.

"Yes. The bride and groom offered to put us up so we didn't have to travel back to Denver tonight."

Hunter smirked. "Well, I'd love to see more of you tonight when this shindig's over." The comment wasn't even directed at Gage, but slime dripped from Hunter's words and made Gage's skin crawl.

Just then, the guitarist emerged, his head on a swivel. Scandinavian-featured, he was tall and blond with a trimmed reddish beard. He frowned when his eyes landed on Lily. "C'mon. We're up." He gave Hunter and Gage a disapproving perusal.

"Well, it's been nice chatting with you both." Lily seemed unruffled by her annoyed bandmate.

"Same," Gage called to her back as she walked away, her hips swaying alluringly.

Though she couldn't see him, Hunter waggled his eyebrows. "See you soon, Lily."

Once she was out of earshot, Gage turned to Hunter. "You and your girlfriend obviously have an open relationship. How do you do it?"

Hunter shot him a puzzled look. "What?"

"How do you compartmentalize? I'm not sure I could mentally put aside the woman I'm involved with while I'm coming on to another one. Or wrestle *my* jealousy when *she's* hooking up with other guys."

Striking a *WTF?* look, Hunter grumbled. "It's *not* an open relationship."

Gage widened his eyes dramatically. "Oh. The way you were acting, I thought ..."

Undaunted by Hunter's growing scowl, Gage continued. "So it's a one-sided thing. But don't you sometimes get confused, you know, mix up their names or their, ah, preferences?" Gage kept his voice in neutral, acting for all the world as if he were conducting a scientific survey, his tone belying his annoyance with Hunter's unmitigated display of douchebaggery. He'd met the girlfriend, and she seemed nice—and probably not on board with Hunter's antics. Not that it was Gage's business, or that he was an expert, but he'd had a front-row seat to the fallout from his dad's infidelity and the effect it had had on his mom. She'd never recovered.

"I mean," Gage kept on, "there has to be some kind of disconnect, right? Is that something you teach yourself, or does it come naturally?" Just because Gage wasn't normally a dick didn't mean he didn't have it in him.

Understanding flashed in Hunter's eyes. "Fuck off, Nelson." He stormed away.

Gage lobbed an oh-so-innocent-sounding, "Sorry, dude. Inquiring minds wanna know," after him.

Hunter responded with a one-finger salute over his shoulder. The thought crossed Gage's mind that instead of heading straight for his room after the wedding, he might need to run interference for lovely Lily.

After saying good night, the bride and groom retreated to their private getaway. Gage gathered up his suit jacket from the back of a chair, his boutonniere limp and brown around the edges—a metaphor for how he felt—and headed toward the B&B.

Guests crowded a gathering room beside the foyer. His attention caught on blond hair, and his alert system zoomed into red-line territory when he spotted Lily. She seemed to slide along the back of a couch as though she were skittish prey inching away from a predator. Which she was. Hunter—*Ha! Appropriate name*—was advancing, his gaze flicking south of her chin.

A shrieking giggle made Gage's spine go ramrod straight. "There you are!" Blair hurried toward him, full wineglass in hand.

Oh shit.

Like a desperate passenger seeking a plane's emergency exits, Gage cast about for an escape route. His eyes caught on Lily's gaze fastened on him. Something he couldn't explain flared between them. An electrical arc sent jolts through him, connecting them. Did she feel it too? In that moment, he read her silent plea to save her.

Blair pulled his arm to her chest. Lily looked away, and the spark died on the wire.

"Hey, Blair. Thought you'd turned in." He attempted untangling himself, but her tentacles were determined. It wasn't that he minded the feel of soft breasts. No, he didn't mind at all. But this particular pair were attached to someone he didn't want to encourage. His mind zip-lined through various ways to extricate himself.

Across the room, Lily's gaze found his again, and she inclined her head toward a wine bar set up on the veranda. Pointing at her wineglass, she addressed Hunter, then pivoted away.

What's she up to? Gage decided it would be more fun to find out than stay where he was. He politely shucked Blair's grip. "I'm going to grab myself some wine."

"'Kay. Hurry back." Her wolfish smile reminded him of Hunter. If he'd had the time, if he'd given a shit, he'd have introduced them—they'd make a perfect couple.

Gage strode to the veranda, glimpsing Lily rounding the corner out of sight. When he caught up to her, she was empty-handed, poised by an inconspicuous door that led outside.

"I'm sorry," she whispered. "He was coming on a little strong. You looked like you could use an escape too."

"She's not my date," he blurted.

"I didn't think so." She arched an eyebrow at the door. A small smile tipped her lips as she twisted the doorknob.

His heartbeat kicked up a notch. "Right behind you."

As they walked out into the cool night air, it occurred to him he was no longer fatigued. Actually, he was buzzing. Prickly heat on crack.

"We made it!" She looked up at him, her big eyes reflecting twinkly lights strung between the trees, and she laughed. Her laugh had a tinkling quality to it, soft and high, sounding nothing like her throaty, body-rocking voice.

They strolled along a crushed-stone path amid the trees. He cleared his throat. "I'd like to apologize for Hunter's, ah, behavior."

"No need. I'm used to the Hunters of the world. Are you friends?"

"Strictly teammates."

"Did you always want to be a hockey player?"

One corner of his mouth quirked. "No. I wanted to be a surfer."

"A surfer!" she laughed. "From water to ice. And hockey won out."

"It pays better." *Important when you have others depending on you.*

"So you actually surf?"

"Did. My contract doesn't allow it, so it's been awhile."

"Where are you from originally?" she asked. "I don't hear an accent."

They were walking in a loop and would soon be heading back the way they came. "Born and raised in California. My mother *and* grandmother taught English, which might have something to do with it."

"That explains it—and the laid-back vibe." The smile in her voice was evident. "But the way you speak reminds me of a professor."

"Is that good or bad?"

"All good."

"Ah. That'd make Grandma and Mom happy. Shall I quote you a little Shakespeare?" He paused when she giggled, holding back his own embarrassed laughter. Shakespeare was *not* his typical come-on—not that he had one.

"You quote Shakespeare?"

"Just the usual stuff. 'First thing we do, let's kill all the lawyers.'" Tossing dignity to the wind, he covered his heart with one hand and threw his other arm to the sky—which was when he noticed Hunter peering out the door they'd escaped through. Hunter didn't seem to have noticed them—yet.

Gage kept his voice low. "I think we're about to get busted."

Lily grabbed his sleeve. "Not if I can help it." She angled toward the back of the building, hanging a sharp right before coming to a stop at the foot of a dim staircase.

His grin broke free. It was the most fun he'd had all night. "Where does this go?"

"I'll show you, Professor." The poor light didn't hide the mischief playing in her eyes.

He swept his hand and gave a bow in a grand gesture. "Lead on."

Following her shapely calves up the stairs, he was surprised when she stepped through a door into the hallway leading to the guest rooms.

"Side entrance," she declared.

His room was only several doors away, and he pointed at it. "My room's right there."

"And mine's right here." She lifted her chin, indicating the door beside them.

Despite his best efforts to keep it in check, heat pooled in his gut, radiating through him. "Ah" was all he could muster. An awkward few beats passed while he debated how to ask for her phone number. "Will you be here for breakfast in the morning?"

She nodded. "I hear the food's fabulous."

Tongue in knots, he searched for something, anything, to say. Sadly, he came up empty. "Well, I'll just ..." He jerked his thumb over his shoulder. *I'll get her number tomorrow.*

Her breath hitched. "I have a full bottle of wine in my room. Interested in sharing a glass?"

The invitation caught him off guard. Did he want to join her? *So much.* He really liked her. Which was the same reason he bobbed his head toward his own door, stammering, “Uh, it’s probably best ... I should go.”

Her features pinched together. “Oh. I shouldn’t have presumed. Do you have someone?”

“No!”

Her eyes flew wide. Yeah, he’d been a little overzealous in his response.

“What I mean is, I’m not attached. To anyone. At all. Haven’t been, well, attached ... in a long time. Ever! Hockey comes first. Well, that’s not true. Family first. Then the game.”

Amusement crept into her expression. “You’re not what I expected,” she said, bringing a halt to his geyser-like sputtering.

I’m not what I expected either. He usually had no problems maintaining his composure around women. Apparently, this one was special.

She canted her head and smiled. “You’re different.”

A breath fled from him as he corralled his inner middle-schooler. The blame for acting like a babbling idiot, he decided, lay squarely on the attraction electrifying the atmosphere between them. That had to be it.

Fortunately, he recovered and, with a wink, said, “My mom calls it ‘being special.’ But I suspect she was soft-pedaling the truth all those years.”

Another giggle escaped Lily—now *she* sounded nervous. “You sure you won’t come in for a few minutes?”

His stomach turned a few flips while his mind ran through various scenarios. Not one of them included him leaving. *What could it hurt?* They could enjoy a drink and talk about music—without Hunter or Blair butting in. *Then* he’d ask her out. Maybe dinner next week.

Besides, a glass of wine might settle his jangling nerves.

“I’d really like that,” he said.

“Good.” She punched a few buttons on the door’s numeric pad, and he could’ve sworn her hand trembled. The lock clicked, and she pushed the door open.

The room was dim, illuminated only by the gauzy glow through a window, and he took in a small table flanked by two chairs, a fireplace, and a four-posted bed in shadows.

Grasping his hand, she pulled him in after her. It was small and soft, nestling nicely in his own. A mere foot separated them, and he caught her fragrance on the air—flowers, rain, mystery. Moonlight peeking through the window reflected frost-like in her hair.

She motioned toward the seating area. "Wine's over here. There's a private deck where we can sit and talk. Maybe look at the stars?"

He nodded his agreement and tracked her with his eyes as she uncorked the bottle and poured dark wine into two glasses. Grabbing the half-full bottle, he opened the deck door for her and followed her outside, where they settled into cushy chairs.

"Here's to the blues." He clinked her wineglass. A small smile curved her lips as she took a baby-bird sip.

She set her glass down and tugged at a fine gold chain around her neck that caught the moon's luminescence. On the chain was a plain gold ring she slid up and down absently. "Are your mother and grandmother here in Denver?"

"No, they're in the Bay Area. I have a sister, Sarah, who lives in Seattle."

"Do you see them often?"

A lump rose in his throat, and he coughed it back down. "I carve out time as often as the schedule allows. The off-season is a lot more flexible, though I still have camps, training, and other obligations."

"And your dad?"

"Not in the picture. He and my mom split when I was a kid, and he's got a new family in Oregon."

"Do you see him?"

They were moving into a prickly pear patch, where he didn't like going. "We trade the occasional obligatory phone call. 'Obligatory' applies to both sides." *And it's awkward as hell.*

His dad hadn't been bad to him and his sis, just uninterested. Opposite of how he treated their step-siblings. When he thought of his dad, a blank avatar came to mind. A placeholder. Add to that how he'd broken Mom's heart, and Gage had no reason to change the current dynamic.

He lifted his wineglass and gulped, suddenly aware he couldn't take his eyes off her. "What about you?"

"My mom and dad live in Florida, and my sister, Ivy, and her husband are in Denver. I spend lots of time with them. I guess you could say Ivy's my best friend." She seemed to consider him. "Are you close to your sister?"

"Sarah's my best bud, although she constantly gives me crap." A chuckle rumbled in his chest.

"That's what sisters do best."

"Well, Sarah's always done one hell of a good job at it." Another fortifying sip. "Back to you. You used to sing with the band, but not so much anymore?"

"I rarely sing in public these days. I only sang at the wedding because Derek needed a vocalist, and I knew the songs. Though I gotta admit, it was fun to be out there again."

Gage recalled the guy's glare. "Is Derek an ex?"

"Ex-bandmate only. No other sort of ex."

"And he's not your brother."

"No." She let out a sigh. "We've known each other a long time."

Something in her tone told him the subject was closed, and he let it go. "Ah."

She paused to top off his glass. Jeez, had he polished his off already? He was buzzing like a live wire. This woman was putting him off his game. Assuming he had a *game* ... which he didn't.

"So what do you do when you're not singing?" He took another sip.

"I volunteer, I do web design, and I'm a social media consultant."

"So, like, you help clients post on Twitter, Instagram, Facebook, other sites?"

She straightened, as if she were on a job interview. "Yes, exactly. I work up campaigns for them. Sometimes I execute them, and other times the client takes over."

"Ah. And what kind of volunteer work?"

She slid the ring along the chain more intently. "Grief counselor."

Her words seemed to punch out of her, and something told him to tread carefully. "Oh, wow. That's gotta be tough."

A slow sigh escaped her. "It can definitely be challenging."

They sat in companionable silence, sipping wine and staring at the sky overhead. The air around them was filled with buzzing and chirping. When she began shifting in her seat, he finished off his wine. "I should probably go." He stood, gathering up his glass and the now-empty bottle, and led her back into the room.

He opened her door and paused, facing her.

"You're really sweet," she said.

He told himself to go with it—right after he reminded himself he needed to leave. But he wasn't doing a good job listening to the last bit, distracted as he was.

When she rose up on tiptoe, ran her hands up his chest, and cupped his head, he didn't resist—didn't want to. Instead, he let her draw his mouth down to hers, telling himself he'd finish the kiss, *then* leave.

Her lips were soft and sweet; he lingered.

She pulled back, her lips hovering near his. "Please stay," she murmured.

Another kiss, deeper this time. Who initiated it, he couldn't say. Didn't care.

She let out a little mewl. The electrical charge that had been wreaking havoc inside him ratcheted up in amperage. He encircled her small frame in his arms and toed her door closed behind them.

Chapter 3

You Meet the Darnedest People at Strip Clubs

Present day, still at the arena

Staring through the Porsche's windshield into the nothingness of the arena's darkened parking lot, Gage startled from his memories back to the present when someone tapped on his window. Jesus, how long had he been sitting here letting his mind amble along its winding path?

He lowered his window, and Travis, the team owner's son, gave him a shit-eating grin. "Hey, Nelson. We're headed to the Sapphire Club, and you're joining us."

Gage had no interest in going to a strip club. "Kinda tired after the game."

"Too bad," Travis said. The guy's authority came solely from his last name, and he sure knew how to throw it around. Gage would have to be careful how he played the demand dressed as an invite.

Behind Travis stood a few Blizzard players whose facial expressions told Gage how they felt about being roped into Travis's reindeer games. Judging by the width of their grins, Wyatt and

Hunter were fully on board. Quinn Hadley looked as uncomfortable as Gage felt.

Shit, why didn't I go to dinner with T.J. and Natalie? Hell, why didn't I just drive out of the parking lot while I had the chance?

"No choice, Nelson," Travis barked. "Get your ass out of your car. My limo's waiting."

"Besides," Wyatt piped up. "You owe me after tripping that squid into my net. Nearly took my fucking legs off."

Gage suppressed an eye-roll. *Goalies.* With a long-suffering sigh, Gage shut off his engine, locked his car, and trudged after the frat boys.

Lily Everett pulled in a huge breath and swept her gaze clockwise, taking in every expectant face watching her from the circle—except for Brett, who might mistake it as a sign of interest on her part. Brett was grasping at straws, grasping so he could breathe, and her heart ached for him, but she couldn't—wouldn't—travel down the path he was heading.

"Thank you all for coming tonight. I get how hard this is, and I love that you participate and support each other." She paused a moment to gently beat her fist against her heart. "I'm always so awed by your courage and your compassion."

A chorus of thank-yous and we-couldn't-do-it-without-yous came back at her.

"Lily," Eva said, "my daughter's visiting next week, so I won't be here."

"Feel free to bring her, Eva. Maybe she'll benefit from our time together." The woman nodded and gathered her purse.

"I'll see the rest of you next week," Lily announced, "and, as always, if any of you needs to talk, you have my number." *But not you, Brett*, she refrained from adding. She'd been dodging him too much lately as it was.

Rustles and murmurs sounded as a half-dozen people stood from their chairs. Lily glanced at her phone, shocked that it was already ten thirty. Tonight's session had been more gut-wrenching than usual, making her relive some of her worst memories, and she was drained. A hot bath and bed awaited, and she yearned for both. Maybe a glass or three of wine would numb her so she could send her thoughts back to her mind's dusty storage locker and leave them there.

She cringed inside as Brett approached in her periphery. Fifteen years her senior, he was a recent widower whose only mission seemed to be to find his next wife. Lily understood—sort of. At least, she understood that feeling of loss, that gaping, unfillable void, just as she understood he was trying desperately to fill up the hole in his soul. But his approach—to replace his lost spouse—wasn't one Lily could relate to.

"Lily, um," he cleared his throat, "I wondered if you had a few minutes to talk now, maybe grab a cup of coffee?"

Hopeful eyes lit on her, and her heart squeezed. "I'm sorry, Brett. I need to finish up some notes and lock up, then head straight home. Maybe you can call me tomorrow if you still need to talk, or," she lifted her chin toward the others, "maybe someone else is looking to grab a cup too?"

The look of disappointment on his face made her feel like a class-A heel. He was lonely; he was lost. But they'd talked and talked since he'd started attending months ago, and she just didn't have it in her tonight. She wasn't his salvation. Hell, she hadn't even saved herself yet. Maybe never would. She'd hoped helping others through their own grief would be her catharsis too, but she often felt as though she were sliding backward instead.

Brett hung his head and nodded, then followed the others out the front door. Lily locked it and went into the back to use the restroom. When she came out, she peeped through a window, unnerved to see him standing in the parking lot, his back to her, as though waiting for her.

Well, shit!

She did have notes to write, but she'd planned to do it at home with soft music playing in the background—and that glass of wine.

"Looks like you're doing it here," she muttered to herself.

And that change of plans was also unnerving because of the late hour; this was not the greatest neighborhood at night. Limited funding for the volunteer operation being what it was, the small office was plunked beside a strip joint. A high-end strip joint, but nonetheless, patrons got rowdy.

She'd take her chances with the strip joint.

An hour later, she took another look at the parking lot and blew out a sigh of relief when she didn't see Brett. She shut off the lights, let herself out, and locked up. Surveying her surroundings, she headed toward her car.

A figure made a beeline for her.

Gage crossed the parking lot to the sidewalk, breath steaming the air in front of him. Behind him, garish lights blinked in the dark.

Where the hell was the Lyft driver?

He scanned the cars, his neon-pink-sign radar on high alert. He checked the icon on the real-time map again. The car seemed to be stuck in the same position it had been stuck in six minutes ago.

How did I end up here again? Wrong place, wrong time. All because Travis the Troll wanted to play BMOC and strut in with a contingent of hockey players. Now that he had what he wanted—namely lots of dancers' attention—Gage could finally escape his intoxicated teammates *and* Travis.

He double-checked the Lyft's position. Ah. Only *five* minutes away now, he thought dryly. What the hell was the hold-up at eleven thirty at night?

"Hey, Admiral!" Quinn hollered behind him.

Gage turned and eyeballed his linemate trotting over to him. "Run out of money for another lap dance?"

Quinn shook his head. "That wasn't me getting the lap dances. I was just making sure Hunter and Wyatt stayed out of trouble."

"And now?"

"And now I don't give a shit. I just wanna go home." Quinn shrugged. "If they get in trouble, it's someone else's problem. I'm tired of babysitting those idiots. I was hoping to catch a ride with you to the arena."

As Gage was opening his mouth to reply, his attention snagged on a woman with long curly blond hair talking to a guy in the adjacent parking lot. He squinted to get a better look. Her arms were crossed, and she seemed to be leaning away from the guy. Nothing threatening, but she looked uncomfortable as hell. He took a few steps in their direction.

"Nelson, where are you going?"

"Just need to check on something. Keep an eye out for a white Altima with a pink Lyft sign. That's our ride."

Gage increased his stride. As his focus sharpened, his breath caught.

"Lily?"

The woman lifted saucer-wide eyes to him, and the dude, a forty-something, swiveled his head, surprise all over his face.

"Uh, hey, Professor," she squeaked. "How's it going?"

Gage pointed at the man. "Is he bothering you?"

A few inches shorter than Gage and obviously not in good shape, the guy took a few steps back. "I-I just wanted to be sure she got in her car safely," he stuttered.

Confused, Gage looked between the two. Lily's expression bordered on alarm—whether it was caused by the dude or her seeing him, he had no idea. He made a snap judgment call and addressed the dude. "I'll make sure she gets where she needs to go. You can take off."

The guy scrambled away and hopped into a car, though Gage hardly registered it for being hyper-focused on Lily. His heart pounded in his chest.

"You are Lily, right?" He didn't need to ask. He'd recognize her anywhere.

She seemed flustered. "Identical twin?"

"Nice try." *Shit, she still wants nothing to do with me. What the hell did I do?* He blew a forceful breath through his nose, his mind careening like one of Disneyland's spinning teacups. *Where's she been? Why did she take off?*

Behind him, Quinn called, "Lyft's here."

Gage spun, which was when he noticed the guy was still sitting in his car, eyeing him warily. Was this guy playing guard dog? "You take it, Quinn," he shouted back.

Quinn saluted and grinned. "Admiral, I expect you to behave yourself and be at practice on time." There was no mistaking Quinn's repeat of one of Gage's worn caveats. In his own defense, however, any guy wearing the *A* needed to act the part with his teammates—even if it meant keeping their asses out of trouble at strip joints.

Gage watched as the Lyft pulled away. To Lily, he said, "Do you want to go somewhere so this weasel leaves you the hell alone?"

"He's not a weasel. He's just ..."

He arched his eyebrows. "So you want him following you?"

She shook her head.

"This your car?" He pointed at a gray Toyota Highlander beside her.

"Yes. Could I give you a ride somewhere since yours just took off?" Her eyes darted back to the dude, and she waved at him as if to say, "You can leave now."

"That would be fantastic." He followed her to her driver's side door, opened it for her, then retreated to the passenger side and clambered into the seat, but not before shooting a glare in Weasel's direction. Weasel seemed satisfied—or defeated—and pulled away slowly.

Good. Because right now all of Gage was zeroed in on his goal: to find out where this woman had disappeared to last summer and why. The incident still grated on him, and he wanted to spout the speech his bruised ego had cobbled together that gray morning when he'd woken up alone. Emotions ran a four-hundred-meter relay race inside him. Shock, anger, curiosity, more shock, wounded pride.

As they waited in charged silence for Weasel to merge onto the road, the front seat—hell, the interior of the whole damn car—felt like an ion storm was brewing. This was different from the electrical rope he'd felt tethering him to her that heady night, though no less powerful.

To his consternation, her fragrance drifted his way and slung him right back into her soft bed, the one in which he'd awoken naked that morning, drifting in a sea of warm contentment, coming to in a fuzzy, leisurely cadence. When he'd reached for her, the sheets beside him had been cold, empty.

He'd called to her, only to be crushed by disappointment. All she'd left behind were the empty wine bottle and a note with his name scrawled on it.

Dear Gage,
Last night was magical. Thank you for making this girl feel special.
Wishing you a wonderful life.
xo

Hoping he'd missed something—like a way, *any* way, to contact her—he'd reread the note several times. The message could have easily said, *Hey, thanks for the use of your dick*. In the end, that had been what it was about, hadn't it? Only sex. Well, amazing sex, but nonetheless, he'd let himself get worked. Used. Notched into a bedpost.

The incident had been a valuable reminder of why he didn't date. Women viewed him in one of two ways: he was either a bottomless bank account or a rock-it-all-night-long fuck. And yeah, he *could* rock it all night long, but he preferred to share with the right woman. And the right woman—one interested in what was behind the pro hockey player façade—wasn't among women he typically met.

His attraction to Lily had dazzled him, hoodwinked him into believing they had a special connection. A connection worth exploring, that went beyond one night.

But he'd been wrong.

She cleared her throat. "Looks like he's gone. So where to, Professor? Or is it Admiral?"

Gage snapped back into the Highlander's stifling atmosphere. "Blizzard Arena, please."

As she guided her car onto the street, silence shimmered between them, so thick he could almost touch it. Though he reined in the urge to steal glances at her, her rigid posture behind the wheel insisted on floating in his periphery.

Finally, he side-eyed her. "Why did you sneak out that night?"

Though she kept her eyes focused ahead, her expression softened. "Well, technically, it was morning."

He gave his forehead a dramatic slap. "Ah. Of course. That makes all the difference in the world."

"I left you a note."

Gage was in no mood for cute. He blew out a breath that sounded like a cross between a deflating balloon and a seal's bark. "Maybe we should take this conversation elsewhere?"

Her features morphed into panic-stricken.

He raised his hand. "Don't worry. I'm not the least bit interested in a repeat of last time."

A confused look replaced her alarmed one. "Right. Because you're hanging with strippers. Silly me," she muttered.

"You've got me all figured out, haven't you?" he snapped. And immediately regretted it.

She shot him a dagger or two.

I guess I sounded a little harsh. In a softer tone, he said, "Sorry. Look, last summer you told me I was different. But now I'm lumped in with a faceless, nameless group of guys, even though you know little about me. That doesn't seem fair."

A few more quiet beats went by, and an overwhelming, inexplicable need to defend himself reared up. He sighed. "For the record, strip clubs aren't my thing. A guy way up on the food chain told me to babysit my teammates. Didn't have much choice."

At a stop sign, she turned to him and offered an apologetic smile. "Sorry for the snark. I just assumed hanging out at strip clubs was what hockey players did in their spare time."

"You know what they say about assuming." Though it was dark in the car, he caught her eye-roll. "By the way, how come you were in that parking lot so late? Was that guy a ... date?"

She flinched. "No. I run a weekly meeting in the office building," she said softly. "It ran late, and Brett was concerned for my safety. I think."

He wiped his palm along his thigh. "Yeah, I can see that." Suddenly, his mouth took off before his brain could catch up. "There's an IHOP on our way. Why don't you let me buy you a cup of coffee for giving me a ride?" *What am I thinking? Is IHOP really the place to continue this discussion?* Not only did he want to figure what had happened, but part of him itched to tell her off too.

Gage had claimed his grandmother's philosophy as his own: anyone entering his life's orbit started out with a virtual stack of chips. Over time, a person's behavior dictated whether chips were added or subtracted from their pile. His grandmother, for instance, had accumulated enough to fill dozens of warehouses to the brim. Likewise, his mother's and sister's stashes were in positive territory. Other people, though, not so much. Like Lily. He'd shortened her stack six months ago.

Yet here he was, inviting her to coffee instead of clearing the air right here, right now. *Go figure.*

"Does that coffee come with a carafe full of questions?" she chirped.

He swiveled his head. "Why? Have something to hide?"

She didn't skip a beat. "Doesn't everyone?"

The vehicle lurched to a stop at a red light when she hit the brakes too hard.

A thought that had been turning over in his mind since last July nudged him. "Are you ... were you in a relationship when I met you?"

"Of course not! What do you take me—Never mind!" she barked.

Relief spiked in him while he simultaneously winced. "Sorry, but people aren't always open." His mind leapt to Hunter, whose girlfriend had dumped him after catching him bare-ass naked with someone else. "And not all relationships are monogamous either."

"Ha! And here you are getting on my case about lumping *you* into a category." Was she mad? Or just throwing sarcasm his way? He couldn't tell.

The light turned green, and she surged the SUV forward. She was muttering under her breath, though he couldn't make out any of the words. *Mad. Got it.* And now he felt like a tool for making her mad.

For some unfathomable reason, he really wanted that coffee, but his hope was disappearing quicker than a plate of bacon on a team breakfast table.

IHOP's glaring signs a few blocks away caught Gage's eye. In an attempt to lighten the moment, he let out a conciliatory chuckle. "Touché. Hello, Pot. My name's Kettle. Truce?"

Her shoulders dropped from where they'd been hugging her ears.

He puffed out a long breath. “Look, I didn’t mean to offend you. Can I buy you that coffee and make up for being an assmunch? I promise not to push for answers you don’t want to give.” Ah. And now, for some other unknown reason, he was giving her wiggle room.

She took her time answering. “Truce. And yes, you can buy me a coffee.” A hint of a smile sounded in her voice. “So what do I call you? Professor? Admiral? Gage? Blues Boy?”

Blues Boy. She remembered. That’s worth a chip. His smile hitched a little higher. “Whatever works for you.”

A sudden, unexpected twinge of giddiness caught him off guard, but it was quickly swallowed up by the voice echoing between his ears. *Danger, danger!*

Chapter 4

Of Vampires and Pancakes

Lily's heart hammered so loudly she was sure Gage Nelson could pick out the sound of it slamming against her ribcage. Oh Lord! Why hadn't she U-turned out of his life the second she realized who was striding toward her SUV? What were the chances she'd run into him again? In the parking lot by the Sapphire Club, of all places! At eleven thirty at night! Although, she was grateful to swap him for Brett. *I think so anyway*. Not that Brett was being stalkerish—he seemed genuinely concerned for her safety. Problem was, he'd started talking and didn't stop. He was just ... so sad, and she'd felt guilty wanting to get rid of him. The whole scene had been sucking what little energy had remained in her tank, and she'd been grateful to escape.

Suddenly, though, energy wasn't a problem. Here she was, all pins and needles, about to have coffee with a man she'd never planned to see again in this lifetime. A man she'd run from last July, who was looking for an explanation. Who was in her effing car, so close she could touch him!

Emotions whirled at high speed, making her insides slosh and slide like mud. Embarrassed to see him, distressed at the same time because of the memories he dredged up of their time together. The crushing guilt she'd felt when she'd woken up beside him. How could she have let herself get so carried away that night?

She stole a sidelong glance at him. He was as handsome now as he'd been then, despite the badass scowl he'd been sporting since the parking lot. Trimmed blondish-brown beard over a square jaw. Sandy-blond hair with a clean-cut line across his muscular nape. Sculpted neck on powerful shoulders that matched the rest of his rock-hard body. Beautiful blue eyes. And those oh-so-masculine hands that had done wonderful things to her that night. Things she'd dreamed about—to her horror and shame.

Why had she zeroed in on Gage in the first place? Because singing in front of people after such a long absence had transported her back in time, back to when Jack had still been alive and onstage with her. All the warmth, the feels, the *energy* had overwhelmed her, and she'd been floating on a cloud. When she'd looked at Gage across the room and felt that inexplicable connection to him, want and desire and longing had conspired and clubbed her over the head. Finding out he loved the blues as much as she did had drawn her in closer. Add to the mix that he wasn't a smooth talker and he'd sucker-punched her with sweetness, and she'd been drawn closer still.

The final "gotcha" had been his infectious smile that had struck her like lightning. Open, inviting, generous. Yeah, that had been the final nail.

And later, how he'd made her feel—he seemed to understand everything she needed without her even realizing it. He'd worshipped her, treated her like a cherished treasure. Not a one-night fuck.

Maybe that very intimacy had made waking up beside him worse. When she'd come to, when the evidence of what she'd done had confronted her, guilt had come flooding in. The memory sent a flare of shame up her spine.

Was coffee with him now a good idea?

I have to make amends. The thought she might have made him angry, or worse, that she'd hurt him, mortified her. She'd never considered that possibility as she'd sneaked around, gathering up her clothes, praying the entire time he wouldn't wake up. She'd fled her own room in a panic, and as the sun had crested the horizon, she'd gone to Jack's grave, where she'd fallen on her knees and begged his forgiveness.

The hollowness it had carved in her had been unbearable. Not something she ever wanted to repeat.

Those she counseled often asked how long one mourned the loss of a loved one. Her answer was always, "The timetable is as unique as each individual. There is no one-size-fits-all, and the length of time varies." Yet when she compared herself to many she counseled, her process seemed stalled. Was she stuck in a quagmire? No, she simply had more to work through. Maybe she'd never get there. *Grieving is different for everyone.*

Gage's deep voice snapped her out of her thoughts. "The turn's up ahead." He stared out the passenger window, apparently lost in thought. Was he revisiting that night too?

Doesn't matter. It will never be repeated. Period.

She coasted into a parking spot and turned off the engine. Gage hopped out of the car. Before she could gather her coat and bag, he was opening her door and helping her out. *Of course he is.*

Time for a distraction. "How's your season going so far?" she asked as they made their way toward the restaurant's entrance.

"Aside from not being in first place in our conference, it's going well."

"I see you were part of the all-star game last weekend. That looked like fun. What an honor to have been chosen, huh?" *And I voted for you at least ten times, every single day.*

"I was a last-minute substitute when someone else went down with an injury. I thought you didn't have *time* to follow hockey."

Was he sporting a smirk? Going for more nonchalance than she had in her arsenal, she shrugged. "I like to keep up with the hometown teams. It makes for good conversation starters. You know. Rah, rah!"

Truth be told, she'd submerged herself in the sport ever since the wedding, learning different nuances of the game. She had yet to fully understand offsides, but she'd get there eventually.

A hostess grabbed a few menus and walked them to a booth in back.

Once seated, Lily stared at the menu for several beats before Gage reached over and turned it right-side-up for her. "Breakfast menu's in the front, beverages in back," he said helpfully.

While her cheeks flamed, his posture seemed to ease.

Her gaze returned to the menu, a soft focus while her mind whirred. "Um, so I read that you're an alternate captain, and you're leading at something. Not penalty minutes, I hope." She faked a tsk.

He ran his index finger over his whiskered chin, covering the raised line of an old scar—one she'd familiarized herself with last July.

"Not penalty minutes," he said matter-of-factly. "I lead in faceoff win percentage."

"Out of the entire league?"

"Yep."

"What else are you good at?" *Oh shit, Lil! I can't believe you just said that.* Head back down in the menu, she cringed because she *knew* color stained her skin right now, and it wasn't pretty. She wore every emotion on her face, and each one seemed to have its own corresponding hue along the red spectrum.

He surprised her by thumping his palm against his heart. "Ouch! Guess I didn't leave much of an impression last summer." Though he dropped his voice to a mumble, she thought she made out, "Unlike the impression *you* left on *me*."

Her pulse shot into overdrive, making it hard to pull in a breath, while her cheeks fired up a shade or two on the embarrassment scale.

A waitress appeared with a carafe of coffee. "Ready to order?"

"Give us a few minutes?" Gage asked with a smile as he twiddled the corner of the menu. Once she was gone, he filled their cups. "Steering back to hockey, I'm also the points leader on our team, but that's because I have great linemates. Without them, my numbers would look a whole lot different."

"Sounds like you're being too modest."

"Nope. Quinn's got a wicked wrist shot, and T.J.'s been tearing it up all season. He makes a lot of room for me on the ice, plus he's got soft hands."

She frowned. "T.J., the bridegroom? He has soft hands?"

He chuckled. "Yes, that T.J. And the expression 'soft hands' refers to his great puck-handling skills, not smooth skin." He sipped his coffee. "For the record, I have no idea what his skin feels like, nor do I want to know. But we have great chemistry. I set 'em up, and he and Quinn bang 'em in."

A smile tugged a corner of her mouth. "So you're a playmaker."

"You really *do* follow hockey."

Busted. She sipped her own brew. "Like I said, I pay attention." *Especially when I watch NHL Network and hang on the hockey pundits' every word about a certain hockey player I met last summer.*

No lie, her stomach did a weird flutterbug dance move anytime Gage's smiling mug shot was plastered on TV, or—her favorite—whenever they featured a clip of him doing something jaw-dropping. She'd seen *lots* of those. One video showcased him skating with the puck while wearing an opposing player like a cape draped on his back. Somehow he'd managed to keep the puck on his stick and pass it through a forest of legs, placing it perfectly on the blade of his teammate's stick. All the teammate had to do was shovel it into the net. And afterward? A ridiculous celly—yep, she was learning *all* the lingo—where he threw himself against the glass with a Tarzan yell. So hot!

God, was she nursing a sex hangover after all these months? Pathetic.

IHOP was packed, which meant getting seated quickly was either a massive stroke of luck or divine intervention. Either way, Gage took it as a sign. Of exactly what, he had no idea because he still wasn't clear why he was sitting here. Well, if he were honest, he did know why: He wanted answers, damn it! The fact that she was fucking gorgeous had nothing to do with it.

He glanced over his menu at Lily, who was busy studying her now-right-side-up menu. Her curls floated around her head, spilling onto her shoulders like an abundant halo. He tried not to think of wrapping the silk coils around his fingers, instead scanning the crowded restaurant. "Do you ever wonder what people do for a living? I mean, look around. Are they *all* leaving bars, or are they getting off work and enjoying breakfast before they head home? Or maybe they're vampires and this is the middle of their day. They're out for lunch."

Her lips tipped up. "Vampires must get tired of the all-blood diet. They probably enjoy a healthy stack of pancakes and bacon from time to time." She ducked her head back to the menu. "Some of the patrons *could* be hockey players who've worked up appetites. They don't feed you at gentlemen's clubs, do they, Professor?"

Weary of metaphorically returning to the Sapphire Club, he released an exasperated breath. "Gee, with the way you keep bringing that up, a guy might think you're envious." He decided to indulge an urge to needle her. "Ever been inside a strip club?"

Sparkling blue eyes rose to his. A bright, blotchy pink was working its way up her neck to her otherwise blank face.

"If you're curious," he continued, "I could take you sometime, even though I generally avoid them." *Needling's one thing, but why the hell am I inviting this girl to a strip club? Out of my ever-lovin' mind.*

Eyes back on the menu, she lifted her coffee cup to her lips. "That's okay, Professor. I don't need to satisfy my curiosity. I've performed in one before."

Did not *see that one coming.* "You're a ..." *What's the PC term?* "An exotic dancer?"

A spew of coffee, followed by a cough she covered with her fingers. "No! I meant I performed *music* in one once."

Relief flooded him. "Ah. I knew that."

"No, you didn't," she laughed.

The waitress appeared, pen poised over her pad, saving him from sticking his foot further down his throat.

"Ladies first," Gage deflected.

Lily arched an eyebrow at him. "I have no idea. I thought we were just having coffee?"

"Guess I worked up an appetite after all." He sent her a wink and turned to the waitress to order chicken and bacon cheddar waffles and a large orange juice. "And this," he circled his finger over the table, "is on me."

"You *did* work up an appetite," Lily mumbled. With a sweet smile, she ordered Swedish crepes, a side of bacon, and a strawberry milkshake. When the waitress was gone, she turned the smile on Gage. "Thank you. For breakfast, I mean."

"Of course. My pleasure. In fact, I wanted to buy you breakfast that morning, but you left before I got the chance to offer." *Might as well just get it out there.* "Why *did* you leave?" Taking a sip of his coffee, he watched her with curiosity over the rim of his cup. Would he finally get his explanation?

She tugged out the gold chain he'd forgotten about and slid the ring up and down.

"Was I snoring?" he persisted. "Did I do the crocodile roll one too many times and steal the covers?" *Though I recall very little of covers ... or sleeping, for that matter.* He hesitated a tic before asking the next question. "Was I that bad?" He lifted the carafe and topped off their coffees.

If it were possible, her face instantly went a brighter shade of pink. "No! None of the above! You were ... It was ... I really enjoyed our time together. It's just ... my life's, um, complicated."

He wagged his head back and forth. "Whose isn't? Look, when I woke up ... I really wanted to see you again." *No point in soft-soaping my disappointment.*

Directness, he'd found, was usually the quickest way to the truth. Maybe it was part of his makeup after years of being raised by a mother whose approach to communication was of the let's-tiptoe-around-the-elephant-in-the-room variety. Lots of confusion and frustration had given birth to a just-say-it-like-it-is approach.

"You're seeing me now."

Apparently, dodging was more Lily's style. Sitting back, he glanced at their reflections in the window. "Six months later," he muttered.

Hesitation flitted across her face. "So, um, do you have a steady now?"

"Nope."

She slipped the chain back into its hiding place. "Friends with benefits?"

Wow. Bold much? Was it any of her business? No, but he saw no reason to hold back, so he let his irritation bubble to the surface.

"Why? Thinking of applying for the job? Sorry, but I'm not accepting applications at the moment."

Another self-conscious flush colored her very pretty face.

While he'd thought about her a lot since July, he'd forgotten just *how* pretty she was. "Sorry. That was a douche thing to say. No, no friends with benefits. Hockey comes first."

"I thought family was first." She tipped the creamer into her coffee.

She remembered that too. The thought wrapped his heart in a warm blanket. Another chip. "Yeah, family's first."

Lily beamed at him, startling him into silence as he took it in. A few moments of coffee-sipping quiet later, their drinks arrived with an apology from the waitress for the delay—a delay Gage hadn't even registered. He took a gulp of his orange juice to soothe his suddenly parched throat.

Lily slid her milkshake in front of her and dragged the straw through a mound of whipped cream that reminded him of a miniaturized Mount Evans.

"How's the milkshake?" he ventured.

"Mmm, delicious. Thanks again for breakfast." Her Pacific Ocean-blue eyes twinkled. Was he reading the same conspiratorial look she'd given him before they climbed the back stairs to her room last year? Yeah, he could totally get sucked in again. *Damn.* He'd meant to give her a piece of his mind, and if he wasn't careful, he'd wind up giving her a piece of himself. *No, can't afford it.*

"It's the least I can do to pay for your time tonight."

She crinkled her nose. "You make me sound like a hooker. Or one of those strippers."

He laughed out loud. "Well, if that's the case, you really should be over here in my lap."

"A lap dance?" she snorted.

Not that he'd actually wanted—much less bought—a lap dance tonight. "No worries, 'cause if you were to give me one, I couldn't touch you. So all things considered, much tamer than the night of the wedding."

If the color of her cheeks was an indication, his remark had thoroughly embarrassed her, which gave him a little lift of satisfaction. She excused herself and headed for the ladies' room, and he watched her the whole way, grateful her coat no longer hid her curvy ass. He told himself to knock it off.

Around him, diners buzzed in quiet tones, and plates and glasses clicked and rang. He sipped his orange juice, once more surveying the restaurant, though not seeing beyond the haze of his own thoughts.

His grandmother had taught him that if he followed his moral compass, it would take him in the right direction. He'd always tried to do just that. But could he apply that piece of wisdom to this situation? Things were usually pretty black-and-white, but Lily was blending the two into befuddling gray.

Chapter 5

Because Everyone Needs Social Media

Minutes later, Lily was walking back toward him, hips swaying softly side to side. He took in this view fully too, and when his gaze locked on hers, another zap of current jolted through him.

A gleam lit her eyes as she sat down and wiggled into her seat. "So what *do* you do for entertainment? Do hockey players get much downtime during the season?"

She drew her shake toward her, closed her mouth around the straw, and sucked, hollowing her cheeks. On autopilot, the tip of his tongue darted out and swiped his lips. He tried to corral his mind and not let it wander to how good it had felt when that mouth had done similar things to *him* that night. In fact, he needed to stop thinking about that night altogether.

Sadly, his talking-to fell short, evidenced by the rocket in his pants maneuvering itself into position for takeoff.

He cleared his throat. "I love live music, especially in the smaller venues. Have you ever been to the Soiled Dove Underground?"

"I *love* that place. They have the best blues and jazz acts, and the atmosphere is so intimate. I've spectated way more than I've performed there, though." A giggle escaped her, and he glimpsed the sixteen-year-old girl she must've been.

"How old are you?" he blurted. He could feel his mother's virtual slap to his head. Or maybe that was Grandma's. He could never tell.

Lily put on a scandalized expression. "Isn't that rather personal?"

He cocked an eyebrow. "Seriously?"

She cleared her throat, then finally managed, "I turned twenty-five early last month."

"There's another coincidence." Not that he was keeping track. "We were born the same year. I just turned twenty-six."

"Really? When?"

He pulled out his phone, glanced at it, and looked back at her with a smile. "Twenty minutes ago."

Surprised eyes caught his. "Oh! Happy birthday! What are you—?"

"Excuse me, do you play for the Blizzard?" a pretty woman interrupted. Behind her, four other women giggled.

Sitting up, Gage plastered a polite smile on his face. "Yeah. Hi, I'm—"

"Gage Nelson!" she squealed. Over her shoulder, she threw a "Told you!" to her companions. "You're my favorite player in the whole league! You should totally be MVP this year!" She practically bounced in place. He would've argued that he wasn't anywhere *near* MVP-worthy, but it would've taken longer, so he merely said thank you and hid his embarrassment while she gushed about how awesome he was.

"Do you mind if we get some pictures with you?" she asked. Now they were all waving their phones.

He flicked his eyes to Lily, who seemed to be watching intently. Though used to fan attention, he couldn't say he was fond of the interruptions to his private time. But fans were the reason he got to play a game he loved for a living and get paid a ridiculous amount of money for the privilege. As his grandmother was fond of saying, a little graciousness would carry him a long way.

"Do you mind? It'll just be a sec," he said to Lily with an apology in his tone.

She shook her head. "Of course not."

After too many pictures to count—and a few autographs—he begged off, and they finally scooted away.

"I expect that comes with the territory," Lily said. "Does it happen much?"

He shrugged. "Not as much here as in San Jose, which is fine by me."

"Do they always fondle you like that?"

"Fondle me?"

"You know. Grab your arms and chest. I'm pretty sure one of them had her hand on your butt."

He coughed out a laugh. "I'm pretty sure one of them did too." A sigh escaped him. "Fans are the most important part of the game, but sometimes ..."

"It must get old. The lack of privacy, I mean. Not the part about getting groped by five pretty young women."

"Actually, not every man enjoys being groped by strangers, even appealing ones. Present company excepted, of course. Though I wouldn't classify you as a stranger at this juncture, nor would I call what we did 'groping.'"

Yeah, he was having trouble letting that night go.

Her cheeks pinked again, turning the color of her milkshake—strawberries-and-cream—and she cast her eyes down. He liked that he could get under her skin like she was getting under his.

The mystery of what made her life so complicated reared up. But before he could ask, servers appeared and deposited their orders. He attacked his food, eager to do something besides swim in a whirlpool of confusion and frustration stirred up by the woman sitting opposite him.

An idea flared in his brain as he shoved down a bite of waffle. "Are you still doing social media consulting?"

She nodded.

His idea began to grow wings. "Do you ever handle fan mail?"

"I can. What are you thinking?"

"I get a lot. More than I have time to deal with. Sarah used to take care of it for me, but since she moved away, my fan mail's tripled. I've been toying with hiring a PA to do it for me, but I haven't had time to interview anyone. Besides, the thought of a stranger knowing *all* my personal business has zero appeal."

He stacked his empty plates and leaned forward, resting his forearms on the table. "The organization wants us to connect with fans, and social media's the most efficient way to go about it. I mean, those ladies were only five fans. I could reach exponentially more—and skip the groping."

Lily's plate was still half-full, and she pushed at the crepes with her fork. Her features suddenly brightened. She dropped her fork, rummaged around in her purse, and pulled out her phone. She tapped her screen, studied it for a beat, then thrust the device at him. "This is you, right?"

He squinted, studying the small screen. "Yep."

She pulled the phone back. "I've looked at your social media, what there is of it, and no offense, but it's kinda uninspired. You have all kinds of hockey celebrity cred you could be using to your advantage."

This statement floored him. "Wait. You've been on *my* social media?"

She gave him a sheepish look. "I might've taken a peek after we met last summer."

That warmed him all over. "So you're talking about me doing social media on top of what the team does?"

Her eyes were doing that sparkle thing again. "Yes! People could get their daily Gage Nelson fix directly from *Gage Nelson,* without the Blizzard filter."

"Trust me, my life's not that interesting."

"I can promote all kinds of things fans would find interesting. Do you have a dog?"

He shook his head. "Just a stray cat I feed whenever he comes around."

"What's his name?"

"I call him Hobbes." She gave him the scrunchy I-don't-get-it face, which he returned with an exaggerated eye-roll. "*Calvin and Hobbes*? The cartoon strip?"

"Um ..."

"Kid with a pet tiger, and he's always getting into trouble? It's a classic."

"I vaguely remember. I'm more of a Prince Valiant kind of girl."

"Because he's a knight, or because of his awesome bowl cut?"

She burst out with a laugh. "Oh, it's totally the hair. As for Hobbes, I could post a picture of you—it would look like you're the one posting—cuddling Hobbes. Fans would eat it up. Or of you sitting on your couch, with the cat in your lap."

Without him noticing, the waitress had removed the plates and swapped out coffee carafes. "Hobbes and I do *not* cuddle. Besides, what's the point?"

"You do charity work, right?"

He nodded.

Her face lit up, growing prettier by the second. "Think of the exposure for those organizations. Pictures of you hanging out with kids, relaxing with first responders, whatever the cause. The public *loves* that stuff, and they'll want to get involved because they see this hockey hunk—that's you—doing it, and they want to emulate you." She glanced at the phone again. "Your last post was in June?"

Carafe in hand, he tipped fresh coffee into their cups—though he didn't need any more caffeine in his system—and gave her a nod.

"You don't post, but you've got twenty-two thousand followers!" She began bubbling over. "You've got a ready-made audience dying to hear about you."

When he didn't respond—he was still processing her calling him a hockey hunk and that people wanted to hear about him—she said, "Tell me about the kinds of volunteer work you do."

He blinked. People always made such a big deal out of his community work, but it *wasn't* a big deal. Not to him. The really big deal was the fortitude of the patients, their families, their friends. Witnessing their struggles was invariably awkward, but it was a privilege. And the fawning over what *he* was doing just embarrassed the shit out of him because it shone a spotlight he wasn't comfortable standing in—it wasn't about him. He was just a small actor on a huge stage in these people's lives.

Staring at his full coffee cup, he spun it in small increments. "I visit hospitals. See kids, cancer patients."

Cup poised at her lips, she blew softly across the coffee's surface. "Those are set up by the team, right?"

"Yes, but there are some things I do on my own, like helping out with a sled hockey team." When she frowned, he explained. "They're guys with a variety of disabilities that keep them from standing upright, hence the sleds. I also sponsor a group of mini mites."

More tapping, and she passed the phone back to him. "This is an example of the work I do. That's the band's website. If you hit the icons, you can check out their Tweets, Instagram, Pinterest, their Facebook page."

Even on the small screen, the professional caliber was obvious, and it bowled him over. Not what he'd expected ... just like her singing. Maybe she wasn't the only one stuffing people into pigeonholes. He hit the white bird in the blue box and landed on the band's Twitter account.

Gage handed back her phone. "Impressive."

She dipped her head. "Thank you." Her cheeks were shiny and pink again. "I enjoy it. It's creative and fun."

The waitress materialized by their table, and Gage lifted his chin at Lily. "Another milkshake?"

"No. I'm full, thanks." Her plate wasn't close to empty. "I should get home," she added once the waitress had handed him the bill and moved on to the next table.

After paying, he followed her to her car and opened her door before climbing into his seat.

"Next stop, the arena," she said.

"Yep."

Where they had fallen into a spirited back-and-forth at the restaurant, a stilted silence now commandeered the air between them. Thoughts buzzed through his head like a swarm of wasps surprised out of their mud palaces by a water jet. While he hadn't gotten everything off his chest, the need to do so had lost its urgency, replaced by a humming that brought to mind a rambunctious electrical current. He told himself it had to do with her organizing and answering his fan letters, saving him time; with improving his PR; with her managing his social media which, before tonight, he'd been blissfully unaware he needed. And while he wasn't yet convinced he needed it, he couldn't deny the spark in his belly that hadn't been there mere hours before.

Not good.

That spark was the result of two forces dueling one another inside him: aggravation and enchantment. He had a decision to make, but he still didn't have the answers he needed to make that decision. He found himself wanting more time to solve a mystery he wasn't sure he could pinpoint. Like being armed with one puzzle piece and an array of boxes to match it to before he could hope to work the puzzle. Did he *want* to solve the puzzle sitting beside him? *Treat it like the game. Don't overthink it.*

The round-domed arena loomed, and she flipped on her blinker.

He motioned toward the players' parking lot, guiding her to his vehicle—the only one in sight.

After pulling alongside, she killed the engine. Overhead lights illuminated the car's interior. Her hair glowed pale gold as she turned in her seat and faced him. "Look, I'm sorry about the way I left that night. I never should've—"

"It's done," he said blandly. "Though I am still curious why you found it necessary to run away. I'm the one who did the walk of shame."

"Some walk of shame!" she scoffed. "What was it? Fifteen feet?" She paused, tucking a strand behind her ear. "For the record, I'm not in the habit of taking men to bed. That night was an aberration for me."

"Ah. I get that a lot from women I overpower with my charm." *Not.*

She tilted her head, letting a smile show through. "Sarcasm aside, I'm sure you do. Also, for the record, I don't recall you putting up a fight, Professor."

"You caught me in a moment of weakness. Look, how about we just forget that night?" *Like I can forget.* "I'd like to see what you can do PR-wise, so let's hit restart. You're the consultant, and I'm the potential client you're trying to sign. Dazzle me."

"Strictly business?"

He drummed the dashboard while he regarded her. "Strictly business, though I'm still not convinced I should hire you in the first place. And we haven't even discussed money yet."

"Tell you what, Professor. I'll do the job for free the first month and give you a chance to evaluate my work. If I don't up your followers by another thousand, then no harm, no foul. If I *do,* then you'll hire me for three months. A win-win with little risk to you. What do you say?"

A strange, fluttering sensation danced in his chest. Maybe it was a warning that the risk was, in fact, quite high. "I'll think about it."

Amusement flashed in her eyes as she raised her hand. "No hanky-panky. I swear."

He almost laughed out loud at the old-fashioned term his grandmother was fond of using. *"I'll let you borrow my car, but no hanky-panky in the backseat, young man!"*

"All right," he said. "I leave tomorrow—make that later today—and I'm back in a week. Let's see what you can do in that time."

She broke out in a triumphant smile that gave his heart an unexpected squeeze. "You're on, Professor."

"I'll need your number." *Ha! I'm finally getting it six months later.*

As it rolled off her tongue and into his contacts, his stomach executed a few back flips, bumping into the chicken and waffles. Maybe that meal hadn't been a good choice.

Minutes later, she was gone, and he sat in his Porsche and texted her. *This is my private cell number. Best way to reach me. Text me back when you're safely home.*

Lily: *I will, Professor.*

Gage: *And don't text while you drive.*

Elation two-stepped through his entire body. He'd found her! But a somber inner voice put a kibosh on the good feels.

"Strictly business. No hanky-panky," he muttered aloud. Never mind that his body had ideas of its own whenever he looked at her, leaving him in a constant state of semi-discomfort. Yeah, he'd probably have to work on that.

Chapter 6

Sisterhood Doesn't Require Pants

Lily walked into her quiet home. Dead quiet. Especially in contrast with IHOP's noise and brightness just a short while ago.

She launched a playlist over wireless speakers and flipped on hallway lights. Music played in the background while her eyes traveled over framed photos lining the walls. The rogues' gallery, she and Jack used to call it. But tonight, instead of walking past, she stopped and studied them. Pictures of Jack as a baby. A boy. A shaggy-haired teenager playing guitar. The man he became: a young Chip Gaines lookalike with a devilish smile.

From the day she'd met Jack, Lily had known he was her future. The man she'd grow old and rickety with. Her everything. People said there was no such thing as love at first sight, but she was living, breathing proof they were wrong.

She ran her fingertips over pictures of them together: singing in the band; reciting wedding vows; opening gifts beside a pathetic Charlie Brown Christmas tree; holding Daisy when she was a newborn.

Lily's gaze traced Jack's awed expression as he stared at their baby. As if on cue, "Have I Told You Lately"—their favorite song and a duet they'd performed together countless times—drifted from the living room. A shaky laugh became a sob, and Lily folded over at the waist, covering her face with her hands. The familiar ache stabbed her chest, followed by the inevitable anger that came rushing up from her gut. Fists clenched, she righted herself. *Life isn't fair!* She hadn't had enough time with him! Where were the other three kids they were going to have? The house they were going to build? The trip to Fiji they'd take on their twentieth wedding anniversary? Her dreams had all died along with him.

Was she just tired, or had seeing Gage Nelson whipped up a vortex of guilt, grief, and isolation?

Wiping her wet cheeks, she padded to her little girl's room, but the lively pinks and purples did nothing to lift her heart. She only seemed able to focus on the pictures of Jack grouped on Daisy's dresser and the pink toy guitar propped in a corner—the guitar he'd bought when Daisy had been born five years ago.

The eerie silence closed in around Lily. An ever-present shroud when Daisy was away, it was just as oppressive late at night when Daisy was there and sleeping. As tempting as it was, Lily would find no escape from the crushing quiet in a half bottle of wine tonight. Between consuming a gallon of coffee and holding up under Gage's blue-eyed scrutiny, she was too tightly wound to lie down. Throwing wine into the mix would guarantee a fitful doze at best.

Instead, she launched herself into her go-to therapy for bringing order to her world whenever it wobbled on its axis. She gathered up her bucket of cleaning supplies and scrubbed her two toilets to a high porcelain sheen. Next she attacked the gas range. After that, the counters. With an inner headshake, she acknowledged that her little house took the brunt of her topsy-turvy emotions. It was always spotless. Apparently, a state of calm was a nirvana as elusive as the proverbial pot of gold the damn leprechauns were constantly moving on her.

After placing a load of laundry in the washer, she glanced at the microwave's digital clock. Three thirty. Way too early to call her sister.

In need of another distraction, she opened her laptop at her kitchen table. No better time to build a file on her new client. She skimmed over the endless positive praise heaped on by coaches and teammates—it was obvious Gage Nelson had mad ice skills. Besides the many accolades, however, Gage—aka “Nelsy,” “The Admiral,” and God-knew-what else—seemed to be a model citizen. No compromising photos; no drunken escapades; no bad-boy behavior; no supermodels. Zero dirt. Zip. Nada. Was he really that wholesome? No one was. *Especially* not a pro hockey player. After all, he hadn’t hesitated when she’d invited him to stay that night, turning their time together into—as Ivy so quaintly put it—an epic fuckathon.

Guilt swelled inside Lily again over her lapse. Even she agreed with Ivy that she needed to stop beating herself up. What was done was done.

She detoured back to her new client, and her jaded self scoffed at the notion Gage didn’t sleep around. He probably practiced sex as devotedly as he practiced hockey, if the experience he’d shown in her bed was any measure. Maybe he was good at being discreet. She was inclined to give credit to a dynamite PR person who knew how to bury bad press, except Gage didn’t have a PR person. Well, he *hadn’t* had one.

As her fingers tapped away, what little she discovered bolstered what she knew of Gage Nelson: he was smart, funny, and successful. Adored by fans and hockey pundits alike. Add polite and self-deprecating, and he was the perfect man. Never mind that he was also hotter than a pizza oven. Which begged the question: Where were his conquests? The puzzle drove Lily to mine deeper for women whose names had been linked with his. At first, she found nothing, but then she stumbled on a picture of him looking dapper in suit and tie—not unlike the night she met him—his arm draped comfortably over bare shoulders belonging to a slender brunette with sparkling blue eyes and hair like rippling silk. The woman’s head rested on his chest with a familiarity that gave Lily an unexpected jab. Where had that come from? She decided to let the question go, instead returning to her investigation that was growing more fruitless with each stroke of the keyboard.

The closer time crept to six o’clock, the more it seemed to decelerate. Still on the indecent side of early to be calling, but Lily would bust a gut if she held out any longer. Taking slow, deliberate steps, she filled a water glass and plopped her butt back down before swiping her phone screen. Her older sister picked up on the second ring.

"Oh good!" Lily breathed. "You're up."

An exaggerated yawn on the other end. "Barely. What's going on?"

"So ... you remember the guy I met last summer? From the wedding?"

Ivy's tone took a one-eighty into wide-awake and hyperactive mode. In other words, Ivy mode. "The hot hockey player you did? *That* guy from last summer? Did you finally look him up? Jump his bones and shake more rust off your poor, neglected caboose? Oh, please tell me you did, Lil." An inhale. "I'm fixing myself a cup of coffee, so start talking."

"I didn't *do* him," Lily hissed. Why had calling her sister seemed like a good idea?

"No, he did *you,*" Ivy hooted. "Like, three times!"

"Twice!" He'd only had two condoms with him.

Heat rose from Lily's stomach, engulfing her chest, her neck, her entire face. She'd shared *way* too much information with her sister about that night. When would she ever learn not to supply Ivy with ammo?

The distinct slosh of pouring coffee sounded in the background. Ha! Like her sister needed the caffeine. So much already flowed through her system that she'd bleed coffee if she were wounded—probably a habit she'd never break as long as she kept her wacky nurse hours. An emergency room nurse married to an EMT, no less.

"Admit it, Little Sis," the coffee addict said. "It was the best damn thing that's happened to you in a loooong time. I was so proud of you! I was cheering from clear across town."

"Yeah, and I can *still* hear you."

"Okay. Back to the good stuff, namely Pucking Hot Hockey Guy." Her sister let out a noise that Lily presumed was meant to be a tiger growl but more closely resembled a cat coughing up a hairball.

"Pucking Hot Hockey Guy? Seriously?"

"It's what you've reduced me to since you won't tell me his name." A noisy slurp. "I keep picturing some big Russian dude named Sergei who's sporting a monobrow, by the way."

Lily dropped her forehead into her cupped palm and stifled a groan. "This is precisely why I am *not* telling you his name. I'm regretting kissing and blabbing as it is."

"Telling me doesn't count as kissing and blabbing. Besides, you are the *last* person to blab about a romp. Hell, you're the last person on this planet to actually romp. You do understand humans have sex because they enjoy it, right? It's not just about procreation."

"I saw him last night," Lily blurted. "Actually, I just left him a few hours ago."

A long beat of silence was followed by a squeal. "Omigod. Hyperventilating here. No, I'm good. Was it as hot as last time? How did you hook up with him again? Deets, Lil! Oh, sweet baby Jesus, it's January thirty-first, and my little sister already got laid! Happy New Year!"

"Ivy, stop! We didn't *hook up*. By sheer coincidence, I bumped into him outside, er, in a parking lot." No need to give her sister the exact location—it would just turn into more ammo Ivy could fire at her later.

"Oh shit, Lil! You plowed into him? Did you damage his car? He's probably got a really expensive car. All those guys do."

Four years her senior, Ivy reminded Lily of a tornado: lots of wind blowing stuff around and causing general mayhem of the batten-down-the-hatches variety. When the chips were down, though, Ivy was as steady as a flat tide.

"No, I didn't hit his car. He saw me and ... stopped to say hello." Lily filled her sister in on breakfast at IHOP.

"So you guys ate breakfast? That's it? No sexcapades?" Ivy's tone was shot through with disappointment; Lily almost felt sorry for her. Almost.

In spite of herself, Lily laughed. "No, just talk." Nor was Lily planning on anything more. Furthermore, in the off chance she wanted to rekindle their fling, he'd closed that door tighter than one leading to a vacuum-sealed meat locker, judging by his chilly vibe. Not that she could blame him for his obvious resentment over her exit last summer. Funny thing about that, though. She'd been surprised by his reaction because it was, after all, a *guy* move—sneaking out before the awkward wake-up scene. Not that she had personal experience, but she'd listened to other women lament.

And a handsome pro athlete like him? His nights *had* to be filled with oodles of opportunities to execute the "guy move."

Lily grudgingly admitted—to herself only—that Ivy was right on one score. Being with Gage had reminded her that her lady parts still functioned normally, even if her heart didn't. And the *real* deal hadn't matched the fantasies that had fueled her for years—it had blown them away like the buildings in the final scene of *V for Vendetta*.

She shook her head to dislodge her dirty thoughts.

Her sister's voice jolted her back to reality. "There's no such thing as coincidence, Lil. This was *meant* to happen. So no horizontal bop for you *last* night, but you're seeing him again, right? Please tell me you are. Your vibrator called and begged for a night off."

"God, you're ... That's ... Ugh!"

"Just calling it like I see it. And you know I'm right. Your tied tongue always gives you away. So when do you see him again?"

"How do you know I'm seeing him?" Out came Lily's chain, and she slid the ring over its smooth links.

"Because I'm your big sister. I know all, I see all."

Lily let out a sigh. "I sorta talked my way into being his social media expert, so I've got some work to do for him this next week." A high-pitched noise, like a deflating balloon, came from the other end. Ivy was emitting a long, reedy squeak of delight. "It's strictly business, Ive."

Lily stifled a niggling doubt about that declaration. If she repeated it enough, maybe it would take root and spread until a canopy of belief sheltered her.

"Ooh, better wear the *sexy* underwear, Lil. Shit. You don't *have* any sexy underwear." A coffee cup clattered on the other end. "Okay. I have a plan. You need to go shopping, and I'll come with."

"Last summer was ... a mistake. I got swept away in the moment. It's not happening again."

The phone rattled with indistinct muttering, which sounded suspiciously like cursing.

"Memories don't keep you warm, Lil. Come on. At least think about it. This guy might be perfect for you. I mean, you don't have to fall in *love* with him. Keep it light, fun. Just naked times between the sheets. Treat it like practice. Sharpen your skills. And just think! You could score hockey tickets and take your favorite sis to a game or two."

Even though Ivy couldn't see her, Lily shook her head vigorously. "I can't do that."

"What? Take me to a hockey game? Why not?"

"No! I meant I can't just sleep with him. That's ... I can't. Besides, who says he'd sleep with me again anyway?" *No hanky-panky. "You caught me in a moment of weakness. I'm not accepting applications."* Lily recoiled inside from the sting.

"Pfft. He's a guy. Correction. He's a *player*, which is a polite way of saying fuckboy. They'll sleep with anyone, anytime."

"Gee, you're really making me feel good about myself here."

Ivy scoffed. "You know what I mean."

Lily glanced down at the ring at the end of her necklace. "It won't work. The guilt is ... it's not worth it." Her stomach turned over, just like it had when she'd awakened beside Gage and realized what she'd done.

Ivy's voice took on a soothing quality. "You're my baby sister, and I love you." Lily braced herself for the "but" that came next. "But Jack's been gone over four years now. It's like you're stuck in your grieving steps—somewhere between despair and guilt—and you can't get yourself unstuck. Don't you think it's time to move on? There's nothing wrong with being attracted to another man. It's natural."

The fresh rise of tears stinging her eyes surprised Lily. The anguish was raw, stealthy like a thief. A thief that sneaked up on her and stole breath from her lungs.

"I *can't* move on." Lily hated the quaver in her voice. Hated how pitiful she sounded.

"Maybe you need to join your own group again or at least take a listen to what you tell others. I mean, I know your people love you, but I don't understand how you can counsel them if you haven't gotten to a place you're trying to guide *them* to."

Lily wanted to shout—if only she could breathe. It didn't help that Ivy was poking another of her sore spots, the one that told her she was an impostor.

Ivy went on. "Hell, your house is practically a shrine to Jack. Maybe you should take down some pictures, get his clothes out of your closet so you don't see them every day. I'll come over and help you box everything up and—"

All of Lily screamed, *No, no, no!* "You don't know what it feels like, Ivy," she cried. "You still *have* the love of *your* life. And Parker adores you as much as you adore him." When Ivy had married Parker Wilde, Lily had nicknamed her I.B. Wilde. It suited her to a tee.

Just as she had adored Jack and he had adored her. This perfect man—once *her* perfect man—had owned her heart. In fact, he'd taken up every part of it, making it impossible to let anyone else move in.

"Lil, you're a beautiful young woman with her whole future ahead of her, and I'm not just saying that because you're my sis. What you had with Jack was wonderful, but is it just the tiniest bit possible you've built him up into something more than he was?"

Heat clawed its way up Lily's throat. "Not fair, Ivy."

"No? Neither is what you're doing to yourself. Or to Daisy."

They hung up not long after. Utterly spent, Ivy's words haunting her, Lily bundled herself under her covers and started up her DVD player. And like Anna Crowe in *The Sixth Sense*, Lily tortured herself with every press of the rewind button as she watched an old clip of Jack playing guitar.

Chapter 7

Flow with the Go

Gage parked his rental car and strode toward Skyview's covered entrance, scanning the parking lot as he went. He eased slightly when he entered the lobby and spied the middle-aged, rotund woman behind the receptionist's desk. "Evelyn?"

Brown eyes rose to meet his, recognition dawning. She broke into a wide smile. "Gage! My goodness, it's been ages since I last saw you. Is this a quick visit, or are you here for a longer spell this time?"

He returned the receptionist's smile. "Just a quick visit between games. The team gave us the rest of today off, so I came as soon as I could. How is she?"

A cloud seemed to pass behind the woman's eyes. "Overall, she has more good days than bad." Her expression brightened once more. "Once she lays eyes on you, though, I'm sure it'll be the very best day."

If she recognizes me. On autopilot, he nodded.

Evelyn waved him toward the elevator. "Go on up, hon."

On the two-floor ride, he braced himself—just as he'd been doing since he'd figured out the timing for this stopover.

But he wasn't prepared for what he saw when he walked into the one-bedroom apartment. He skidded to a stop and blinked at the scene before him.

His grandmother, her wiry frosted-gray hair standing on end as if she'd stuck her finger in an electrical socket, was dressed in a puffy winter coat and snow boots, though the temperature in the room had to be at least eighty degrees.

He couldn't decide what shocked him more: the fact that the coat gaped open, revealing that she wore only her bra and a pair of men's trousers, or the sight of her standing behind a strange man seated in an armchair while she dabbed something on his bald head.

Jesus, I just landed in the Twilight Zone. Unbidden, the theme song ran through his head.

The man looked up and gave him a weak smile and a little wave. His grandma was so enthralled with whatever the hell she was doing that she didn't give Gage so much as a glance. Humming with gusto—Gage was pretty sure the tune was "Hey Jude"—she inspected her work and applied more of what appeared to be light blue paste.

"Grandma?" he croaked. No answer. He cleared his throat. "Grandma? What are you doing?"

When she still didn't acknowledge him, the man craned his head toward her, nearly taking a finger in the eye for his trouble. "Donna? Someone here to see you, sweetheart."

Sweetheart? Gage gawked at the man. Who the hell was this interloper, and should Gage be showing him the door? Or should he be grateful his grandmother seemed to have a friend? Before Gage could choose which reaction to go with, she looked at him and lit up. "Paul?"

Gage's heart nearly caved. Paul had been her husband—Gage's maternal grandfather—before he'd died years ago.

Gage gulped down his dismay, hoping it would fill the crack in his heart, and took a step forward. "No, Grandma. It's me. Gage."

She frowned, confusion clouding her sky-blue eyes, a half-dozen furrows waving across her forehead. Though the lines were deep, her smooth skin glowed a soft pink.

The man swiveled his head between them. As Gage got closer, the smell of spearmint tickled his nose, which was when he realized the paste she'd been anointing her friend's head with was in fact toothpaste—as evidenced by the half-squeezed tube of Crest she fisted in her other hand.

What the actual ...?

Gage reached out to button her coat, but she recoiled, her eyes widening with panic.

"Donna," the man soothed, "is this the grandson you're always bragging on?"

Specters seemed to shift behind her eyes. Those eyes widened as if cognizance was slowly dawning, like a heavy veil lifting. "Gage?"

"Yes, Grandma." He fought to swallow around the puck-sized lump forming in his throat. "It's me." *Do I hug her? Shake her hand? High-five her? What do I do?*

She ran her free hand up and down his arm, and her face radiated with pride. "I was at your game! Did you hear me in the bleachers? You were the best player out there. But then, you always are. I'm so proud of how you skated right through those defensemen and roofed that puck! I swear they were still picking up their breezers long after you scored." She sang out, "He shoots, he scores!"

He swiped the back of his hand under his nose, suddenly reduced to an awkward ten-year-old. "Thanks, Grandma."

"And the way you laid out that punky Bennett boy!" She flapped a hand at him. "Way to show him, honey."

A moment passed before he processed the name from youth hockey days. Ah. So he wasn't ten after all, but thirteen in her fragmented mind.

His relationship with his grandma had always been a close one, a special one. Whether it was because his mom was constantly working her ass off and Grandma was the caregiver he defaulted to as a kid, or whether it was because they simply had a unique connection, he had little idea. Didn't matter. It only mattered that the bond had been there, even if she didn't remember it.

He pulled in a cleansing breath and reminded himself that at least she knew who he was, even if she'd lopped off thirteen years. *This is about her, not you. Just go with it.*

Grandma moved to hug him, and he took a step back, pointing at her coat. "Ah, Grandma, I think you missed a few buttons."

"What?" she shrieked and glanced down at herself. "Oh, Lord have mercy, where is my head these days?" She began fumbling with the buttons. He reached out to help but snatched his hand back, caught in a surreal world suspended between past and present. One where her past was the present. The present where she'd recoiled earlier when he'd tried to help.

Stomach cinching into knots, he stuffed his hands in his front pockets to bide his time, his eyes drifting to the bald man he'd forgotten was sitting there. Kind eyes crinkling, the man offered him a head tilt and a knowing smile.

Still messing with her buttons, Grandma erupted in a laugh. Gage laughed along with her, if for no other reason than to keep himself from crying.

The old man stood, surprising him, and extended a bony hand covered in skin that resembled parchment. "My name's Oscar. I'll clear out so you two can have some private time. But first I wanted to say how happy I am to meet you. Your grandmother never stops talking about you and your sister."

Out of habit, Gage accepted Oscar's hand and shook. The man's grip was unexpectedly strong. "Donna is so proud of you," Oscar said. "Her memories might be a little hazy, but on that score, she's crystal clear."

If it were possible, the puck-sized lump swelled in Gage's throat, making it hard to breathe. Haphazardly fastened, Grandma focused bright eyes on him, seeming not to notice Oscar's departure.

"Gage, are you done with your homework, honey? I have some fresh-baked cookies for you. I just have to find where I hid them. You can help me." Her smile, warm and indulgent, was different from the one he'd grown up with and loved so much. This one was lovely but had a vacant quality, as if part of her soul was missing. God, how he longed for her real smile—the one she used when she was trying to be stern and they both knew she could bust out laughing at any moment.

With a break in his voice, he took her hand in both of his. "I did finish my homework, Grandma, but I can wait on the cookies for now."

Hours later, Gage sat at his mom's kitchen table, hands wrapped around a cold coffee cup, an unseeing stare focused outside the bay window on the glossy green leaves of a camellia bush.

His mother stood at the sink agitatedly clattering dishes, rambling through a convoluted apology that was simply a cover-up for hurt feelings.

"Honey, if only I'd known you were going there first, I would've met you. Or you could've come here and I'd have taken you there myself. You shouldn't see your grandmother alone in her ... current state. If only you'd told me your plans ahead of time."

"Sorry, Mom," he said absently. The wind ruffled the camellia plant, separating a few bright pink petals from its abundant blossoms. "I ended up getting free before I'd planned," he white-lied, "and thought it would be easier to head there first on my way here."

"Well, next time, Gage—"

"What's the big deal, Mom? I can handle it."

She seemed to grow more flustered. "Yes, but sometimes your grandmother ... I know you were only trying to save me trouble—you've always been thoughtful like that, unlike your father—but really, you could have called and, like I said, I'd have met you there and softened the blow for you."

Point taken, Mom. For the fifth time.

So much for Gage's attempt at covert operations. Between the shock of his grandmother's condition—which he was still trying to compartmentalize—and his mother's droning, guilt-tripping reproach, he swore off future secret maneuvers to visit Grandma on his own. For now.

Mom had been complaining about Grandma going downhill fast, getting loopier by the day, but his mom thrived on drama. While he admired her and loved his mother with all his heart, he was convinced that if life grew too serene, Nola Delaney Nelson would simply invent a crisis. So he'd mistakenly assumed her reports about Grandma had been exaggerated. Obviously, he'd been wrong, but he wasn't about to confess that tidbit to his mother and give her more reason to shoot him scowls.

He pushed out a breath. "It's okay, Mom. She finally recognized me, and it turned into a good visit," he repeated for the hundredth time. His knee bounced with irritation. Time to deflect. "So who's Oscar?"

A dramatic sigh accompanied a roll of her eyes. "He's a resident on the independent living side. His wife was in memory care, and he used to visit her daily. She died several months ago. Now he hangs around your grandma, treating her like a queen."

"Which she deserves," he interjected.

"Gage, honestly, sometimes you are so naive." She pointed a potholder at him. "This is why you have to be so careful about picking the *right* girl—one who won't try to take advantage of you."

This familiar tack in the conversation always frustrated him. He was a grown man, for God's sake, capable of *picking the right girl*—assuming he was looking to pick one in the first place. "What does Grandma's, uh"—*What do you call an eighty-something who hangs out with your grandmother?*—"boyfriend have to do with my love life?"

Her eyebrows drew together in a frown. "So you *do* have a love life? When did this happen?"

"I don't have a love life, and even if I did, it would be none of your business." He gave her a half-smile to soften the truth of the statement.

She turned back to her dishes. "Well, I say he treats her *too* much like a queen. And he's only been widowed a short time! Where's the decency in that? He's after something."

Gage scoffed. "Like what? She has no money." *He* paid for everything—for his grandma *and* his mom. Had ever since he'd started drawing bigger paychecks. "Maybe the guy's just being nice."

Mom turned away to check a baking casserole. "Men can charm women into doing whatever they want," she said over her shoulder. "Just like your father."

Oh boy, here we go.

While she ran through her usual spiel about the evils of men—not him, he was perfect, she was always quick to add—he slid his phone from his pocket for a quick glimpse at his Twitter account. Lily had been working magic, and his followers were up by nearly six hundred—not that he really cared about the numbers. No, the real fun was in Lily's texts, and his spirits got a boost when he spied a new one.

Lily: *Did you see the latest count, Professor? The mooney-eyed picture of you as a bantam getting Gretzky's autograph racked up another 80 peeps! We're on a roll. With butter.*

He stifled a laugh. His mother was still talking, and God knew she'd take his laughter the wrong way.

Sweet! he fired back. Then he added, *Not sure where you're mining the old photos, but they're perfect. Keep up the good work.*

Yep, despite his misgivings, he was impressed. The old pictures, combined with Lily's clever messages, were pure wizardry in Twitter World, and the week was only half gone.

Lily: *Looks like someone might be hiring someone soon.*

Another laugh tickled his chest. Though he couldn't put his finger on why, he was actually relieved she was hitting it out of the park on their so-called competition, even if he still wasn't convinced he needed the social media presence she was drumming up for him.

Gage: *Let's not get ahead of ourselves.*

Lily: *Spoken like a true professor. All I ask is that you please wait until I've handed in my completed assignment before you grade my paper.*

A dirty picture popped into Gage's head and shot straight to his groin. He refrained from sending a reply about bending her over his desk and spanking her bare ass if her work was subpar. *Where in the actual hell did* that *come from?*

The slam of the oven door reminded him he was in his mother's kitchen. He jerked to attention, feeling as though he'd been caught doing something truly cringe-worthy, like when he'd been fourteen and she'd busted him in his bedroom with a well-worn, pilfered porn magazine.

Back in full consciousness at her table, heat blazed his cheeks; he shifted his sitting posture. By the time his mother turned around, her head shaking and her lips moving as she carried on, he'd returned to a who-cares, crossed-arm pose.

"... terribly wrong," she yammered as she peered out the kitchen window. He had no idea what she was talking about. "Oh!" she suddenly exclaimed. "Look who just pulled up!" With a squeal of delight, she scurried to the front door and threw it open. "Jessica! What a surprise! Gage is here. He'll be so happy to see you." Mom shot him a look over her shoulder.

Surprise, my ass.

He stood and offered a limp wave to the woman on the other side of the threshold. “Hey, Jess.”

Jessica swooped in and beelined for him, arms wide, smile lighting her perfectly made-up face. Yeah, she’d always cleaned up well.

“I’ve missed you, Gage.” She pulled him into a fierce hug, her fragrance rolling over him. He’d probably smell of her all night.

Gingerly, he rested his hands against her back and gave her a light squeeze, his mother smiling approvingly in the background. Jessica pulled away, cradled his face in her hands, and stared up at him with what he could only describe as wonder. Then she pecked his lips and breathed, “I’m so happy you’re back, even if it’s just for tonight.”

Automatically, he gave the answer expected of him by both women. “Me too, Jess.”

“Jessica, I’m just about to pull dinner from the oven. You’ll stay and eat with us, won’t you?” his mother said sweetly.

Jessica’s blue eyes brightened. “Thanks, Nola. If it’s not a bother …”

“No bother at all. Afterward, maybe you kids would like to take a drive over to Half Moon Bay and stroll on the beach. It’s going to be a beautiful night to talk over old times.”

With an inner sigh, Gage resolved himself to the hijacked evening and put aside pleasant thoughts of a curly-haired blond tweeting machine.

On his way to morning skate the next day, he picked up an incoming call.

“Sar-bear!”

“Seriously?” his sister scoffed. “You’re what, twenty-six now, Waffle-Butt?”

He snorted. “It’s good to talk to you too.”

"Well, I got your text and had a few minutes. I figured it'd be easier to talk instead of texting freaking *War and Peace*."

"Agreed. And good timing. I'm driving to the rink, which means I've also got a few minutes."

"So what's going on?"

"When was the last time you saw Grandma?" Gage told Sarah about his visit the day before.

"Shit, I just saw her a few weeks ago, and she wasn't *that* bad. But maybe I saw her on one of her better days. How's Mom dealing with it?"

Gage blew out a breath. "Same as usual."

"In other words, with lots of drama."

"She let me know how unhappy she was that I saw Grandma without her."

"Yep, our mother, the control freak."

Gage chuckled. "I take it she's still trying to pick out a husband for you?"

"Not since I moved up here." Sarah's tone was unmistakably triumphant. "It's a lot harder when you live nearly a thousand miles away."

"Yeah, you always said I'd be better off moving away. I didn't believe you until I got traded to Colorado." He ducked his head to check a freeway sign. *One more exit.*

"So you're finally comfortable in Denver?"

It occurred to him he *was* finally comfortable in his new city. "Yeah, I like being there. No lie, I never thought I'd get used to the change, but now that I am, I realize how much I like the autonomy. *Especially* after being home for a night."

Except I miss Grandma. But she's not Grandma anymore. I'd miss her even if I was home.

Sarah clucked. "I'm guessing that you too are grateful Mom's not butting into your business, plotting out your entire future."

Gage let out a wry laugh. "My being gone hasn't gotten me off the hook. She made sure I saw Jess last night."

"Oh? And how did that go?"

Was he picking up on a hopeful note in his sister's voice? *Well, shit!*

"About as expected. Mom was doing everything she could to push us together."

"Mom might not be wrong about that one, Gage." Sarah's voice had grown solemn.

"Really? You're on Mom's side?" A sinking feeling bloomed in his chest.

"Call it being on Jessica's side. She's always been perfect for you, Gage. She's the Barbie to your Ken, even though you haven't realized it yet. And I know for a fact she thinks you're it for her."

Not this again. Gage puffed out an exasperated breath. "Everyone thinks she's perfect for me. Except me! She and I already went down that road, and it didn't work. She knows that. I know that. Besides, I think you're overplaying her feelings in this. We're just friends."

"Okay, okay, don't get your tighty-whities twisted," Sarah soothed. "Selfishly speaking, I always hoped you two would get back together. She's one of my best friends, and—"

"You forget we weren't ever *together*. Dating for a couple of weeks doesn't count." Gage guided his car down the off-ramp toward the arena. "Hey, Sis, I'm almost there. I need to cut this short." Truthfully, he had a few more minutes, but he wanted out of the awkward convo.

"Okay, Little Bro. Go score some goals!"

"Yep. Take care, Sar-Bear."

"Love you, Waffle-Butt," she giggled.

Waffle-Butt! Shit, would he ever live the nickname down? A smile tugged his lips before his mind wandered to Jessica Phelan.

Once upon a time, Jessica had carried a torch for him. He'd thought he carried one for her too, but the flame had fizzled shortly after they took it beyond the friend zone. Which puzzled him to this day. If he were a normal red-blooded male, he'd still be drooling over that woman. She was gorgeous, smart, sophisticated, and had a body that could muddle a man to the point he'd walk into oncoming traffic. In high school, he'd been one of countless guys who'd welcomed her guest appearances in their wet dreams.

So what was wrong with him? What had changed? Had it just turned into a case of "been there, done that"? Maybe sleeping with her, finally having his fantasy come true, had exposed him for the shallow, callous bastard his mother always referred to when she railed on about "men."

And if Jess was the closest he'd ever come to falling for someone? Sure, he was only twenty-six, but what if he never found that special someone, the one his buddies described as the woman who made you want to do your best, be your best? That made your mind blank out all other women? The one that made wherever you lived *home*, whether it was Denver or Tampa or Detroit?

Ah, well. Time to pull his head out of his ass and screw it on straight. Morning skate and tonight's game awaited.

He parked in the arena lot and glanced at his phone. Two texts blinked. His pulse picked up, and his fingers twitched when he saw that one was from Lily. He opted to read the other one first for the sake of delayed gratification.

Beckett Miller: *Trying to get a head count for our Super Bowl party this Sunday. You in?*

Gage began typing his answer when an idea struck, so he paused to read Lily's text.

Lily: *Just checking in to see how you're doing in sunny Cali and if you've had a chance to look at your likes today? You are rockin' it, Professor!*

As he read her words, he pictured her bright blue eyes glimmering with mischief. Eyes he was looking forward to seeing when he got home. Eyes that belonged to the woman he was about to hire as his social media manager.

Gage: *Seems I'm on the hook to hire you. I was invited to a Super Bowl party at a friend's on Sunday. Super casual. Interested in coming with and we'll work out the details?*

Holding his breath, he hit send before he could change his mind and delete the message. What would he gain if he didn't put it out there?

His phone chirped almost immediately, and he let out the breath, only to suck in a fresh one in anticipation of her answer.

Lily: *Sounds like fun. Where and when?*

His stomach broke out in a happy dance. *How about I pick you up around 3?*

Lily: *How about I meet you there?*

A logical response he aimed to counter. *Pretty sure they live in a gated community. Better if I come get you.*

He had no idea where Beckett and his wife lived, but he'd plead ignorance if it turned out not to be behind a gate.

During the several minutes it took for her to reply, Gage's mind ricocheted between what an idiot he was to the super genius he'd be if she said yes.

Lily: *Okay, then. Let's confirm deets Saturday?*

He pumped his fist and growled, "Yes!" *Wile E. Coyote Super Genius!*

Gage: *Sounds good. Till Sat.*

Thank God he'd been able to hide behind the texts because he sounded way cooler in print than he felt. As he RSVP'ed Beckett—*I'm in with a plus-one*—he spotted T.J. walking toward the arena. Gage cracked his door open. "Hold up, Shanny."

He climbed out of the car, grabbed his gear, and fell in beside T.J. "So you and Natalie going to Miller's party Sunday?"

"Yep. You?"

"Yep."

"Alone, I assume."

Gage kept his voice even, corralling the excited answer ready to burst from his lungs in a shout. "Nah."

He found a measure of satisfaction when T.J.'s eyebrows climbed his forehead. "Seriously? You're bringing someone? As in, someone with tits and plumbing that'll accommodate yours?"

Gage suppressed a laugh. "Yep."

T.J. smacked his arm. "Good job, Nelson. You're showing an interest in something besides hockey. Didn't know you had it in you."

Just needed the right motivation. And there it was. In a heartbeat, *no hanky-panky* drifted into the sky, where it vanished like mist in the clouds. He didn't dare contemplate whether or not this was a good idea.

Chapter 8

There's a Football Game Going On?

Lily sucked in her stomach and smoothed her baby-blue cashmere sweater over her waist—for the tenth time. She pivoted for a side view in her dresser mirror and groaned—also for the tenth time. Flattening her stomach made her boobs stick out. While that wasn't necessarily a *bad* thing, she didn't want to broadcast the wrong message to the man picking her up in ten minutes.

"Strictly business," she muttered to herself.

Spending the past week trolling the Internet for information about Gage Nelson had her struggling to keep him rooted under the "client" label. Somehow the man kept stepping outside his assigned compartment, toeing the "drool-worthy" category, and to her consternation, her libido was betraying her. Just as it had last July.

She gave her reflection a disapproving glare as she gave the clingy sweater two thumbs-down. She yanked the garment over her head, shimmied out of her jeans, and snatched up a cobalt dress draped over the edge of her bed. As she was about to pull it over her head—this would make the third time she'd tried it on—she paused to admire her new purchase, the lacy teal bra and matching panties she'd picked up without Ivy's help ... or knowledge. Even to Lily's critical eye, the set fit her well. Not that anyone would know because "anyone" wasn't going to get a glimpse. It was just a boost to make her feel pretty under her clothes.

Damn straight. She nodded at herself.

"Shame" by Elle King played in the background, and Lily hummed the words as she settled the dress over her hips. With a strut and a spin, she vamped in front of the mirror, stopping short with a critical assessment. Yeah, she looked good, *but* "super casual" did not equal "flouncy dress" at a Super Bowl party. And now she'd wasted three more precious minutes.

Back in front of her closet, she perused her choices, ignoring the section devoted to her old stage attire. *Definitely not casual.*

When was the last time she'd had such trouble deciding what to wear? Normally, she picked an outfit and rocked it with confidence—a knack she'd developed after years of being onstage. So why was she devoting so much time to dressing for her ... business meeting? Business meetings didn't cause her stomach to pitch like it belonged to a silly fangirl squealing over the lead singer in a boy band.

Ugh!

Her eyes landed on a subdued green leather jacket, and she pulled it off its hanger. While she dragged the jeans up her legs once more, her mind took a detour back to her new client.

Questions had been circling in Lily's head over the brunette in the photo. Who was she? If she was a celebrity—and with her stunning looks, she certainly could have been—she wasn't a well-known one. What was she to Gage?

And who else was hiding in his closet?

Which brought her to: Why the hell did it matter? *Because any good PR person worth her salt needs to know of any liaisons that could bite her client in the butt, of course.*

Lily blew out a breath that lifted the curls off her forehead. Gage was her client. Nothing more. Well, except a one-night stand. But that was in the past. Forgotten. Buried.

Right?

Lily kept her gaze pointed straight ahead as she stood beside Gage in front of humongous arched double doors. Mentally, she patted herself on the back for her perfect wardrobe choice. The green leather jacket over a white tank top was conservative yet trendy, finished off with dark-wash skinny jeans and suede ankle boots.

Gage, dressed in hiking shoes, jeans, a blue-striped button-down, and a black peacoat—all of which he wore extremely well—stretched in front of her and pressed the doorbell. She caught a mixture that was part-woodsy, part-leather, and all fresh man. The same scent that had greeted her when he'd helped her into his seriously nice car. Trying not to sniff the air like a bloodhound on a hot trail, she focused on the bells gonging inside the home.

How long was the line of women waiting to get a turn at Gage Nelson anyway? Was she about to meet some of his "fan" club?

The door opened, revealing a tall, good-looking man Lily recognized from the wedding. He pulled Gage in for a bro hug. "Nelsy, glad you could make it."

Gage canted his head toward her. "Beckett, you remember Lily?"

Beckett's eyes seemed to brighten with recognition. "Right. The singer at T.J.'s wedding. Nice to see you again. Come on in."

"No baby carrier today?" Lily ventured.

He laughed as he closed the door behind them. "Not today. She's down for her nap."

"Layne, right?"

His eyes widened. "Yeah. Good memory!"

Just then, a woman about Lily's size appeared, and Beckett dropped his arm around her shoulders. She was pretty in a girl-next-door kind of way, with waving auburn hair that curled on her small shoulders. But the most noticeable thing about her was her huge belly.

"Gage, you remember my wife. Lily, this is Paige, but I call her Andie." Beckett caressed his wife's stomach absentmindedly.

"When are you due?" Lily asked.

"Due for what?" Paige quipped, flashing a broad smile that showed off a dimple.

Oh shit! I know better than to ask that question! When Lily's mouth fell open, Paige grasped her hand in both of hers. "Sorry, Lily. Bad joke, but I couldn't resist. I'm due in late April."

Beckett chuckled. "We're pretty sure she got pregnant the night of T.J.'s wedding. Must've been your singing, Lily."

Paige slid him a sidelong smirk. "Or somebody insisting there was only one way he could fall asleep, only to keep me up all night."

He shrugged unapologetically. "As I recall, *I* was the one who stayed up all night." He winked at his wife, who'd turned a pretty shade of pink.

"TMI, Beck." She turned green eyes on Gage and Lily. "Let's get out of the foyer, shall we? Party's in the back."

Aw ... they're cute! A pang of envy dug its claw inside Lily. *Could I have that in my life again?* Just as swiftly, her inner voice told her no, that wasn't for her.

As they fell in behind the couple, Beckett dropped back. "Wanna see my man cave-slash-garage, Nelsy? T.J. and the guys are already out there."

Something uncomfortable waved through Lily. As used as she was to entertaining, chitchat with strangers ranked in the top ten of her least favorite things to do. Being onstage was more or less a one-sided conversation, with the microphone acting as a barrier. And if the awaiting crowd included some of Gage's past playmates?

The better to learn about him, Lil.

Before she could muster her stage face, Gage's deep, soft voice surprised the hell out of her.

"I'm dying to see this car collection I've heard so much about, but Lily doesn't know anyone here. Let me get her squared away first, and I'll check it out later, if that's okay."

Lily's entire body uncoiled a notch. She hadn't been aware how tightly she'd been wound.

"Fine by me," Beckett replied. "Andie, I'm just gonna duck in and see if the guys need anything."

"Okay, Beck," Paige called over her shoulder as she took Lily's arm, linking it with hers, and steered her farther down a hallway toward music and a growing burble. Such a natural, easy, comforting gesture. So homey. “I’ll introduce you,” Paige said with that winning smile.

They stood on the threshold of a huge family room filled with leather couches and a handful of ... women. Beautiful women, whose heads turned toward them. *Oh shit, I’m meeting Gage’s harem.* Some gazes bounced between Lily and Paige, while the rest seemed to land behind them ... no doubt on Hotness himself.

“Everyone,” Paige announced, “this is Lily, a phenomenal singer and Gage’s date.”

No, no! Not his date. This was business, though Lily couldn’t correct Paige at this moment. That would be rude.

A round of feminine “Hi’s” chorused, sprinkled with a few “Gage’s,” as his warm, reassuring hand pressed into the small of her back. A pair of curious brown eyes fixed on her from across the room. They belonged to a familiar woman whose mouth hung open and whose gaze traveled between Gage and her.

Incoming. Girlfriend number one?

Making her way toward them, the woman’s gape transformed into a warm smile when she reached Gage and pulled him into a hug.

“Hey, you,” she trilled. “T.J. said you’d be here.” Then she turned her smile on Lily, who developed a shameful urge to slink away when she recognized the bride from July. Without the wedding dress, she hadn’t recognized Natalie.

Gage cleared his throat. “Hey, Nat. This is Lily Ev—”

“Yes, I know! You sang at my wedding, and you were wonderful!” Natalie clasped Lily’s hand in both of hers and shook. Her eyes returned to Gage. “So how did you two, um ...”

Did Natalie know about that night? Not unless Gage was the kiss-and-tell type, but the label didn’t fit. Still, Lily felt a tomato stain oozing up her neck, and she began talking just as Gage did. Their words tumbled over each other like an overflowing, gurgling stream. Paige’s and Natalie’s eyebrows scrunched in unison as they looked from Gage to Lily and back again.

Though their mixed voices were a garble, they both spewed the same message, which equaled, “We’re not together.”

Lily’s face had to be the color of a roasted beet by now.

“Sorry. I just assumed ...” Natalie said.

Gage gave her a friendly wink. "You know what they say about—"

"People who assume," she finished for him, dismissing him with a wave.

Gage's hand slid from Lily's back to cradle her elbow, and she felt an urge to lean into it. Something told her he would hold her up, and an electrical surge connected him to her for an instant.

The room returned to its chatter, and Paige pointed out drinks and munchies before tottering over to a few guests.

"Drink?" Gage asked Lily.

"White wine, please, if it's available. Otherwise, water's good."

"I gotcha. Natalie?"

Natalie held up her mostly full beer bottle and shook her head. Gage excused himself, leaving Lily and Natalie in a shared awkward bubble. It was then that Lily noticed Natalie was a good four or five inches taller—because damn if she didn't seem to be looking down at her, inspecting her as though she were a bug under a microscope she wanted to pull apart with tweezers.

Lily took a calming breath, telling herself this woman was obviously important to Gage, and her scrutiny—uncomfortable as it was—was natural. She also found herself wanting Natalie to like her.

Okay, Lil. This is your chance to learn about the man under the hockey helmet. There be nuggets to mine! In her head, a pirate growled, "Arrr!"

Lily resisted the urge to tug out her chain and twiddle. Instead, she ventured, "So how long have you known Gage?"

"Almost two years now." Natalie's features seemed to soften. "Forgive me, but we're not used to seeing Gage with anyone unless one of us wives or girlfriends has twisted his arm into a blind date." She paused to sweep her hand around the room, indicating the women scattered throughout. Then she leaned in conspiratorially. "To my knowledge, those have *never* worked out. One and done."

Lily blinked. *Okay. False Assumption Number One bites the dust: These women are his teammates' SOs, not lovers.* The thought gave her toes an unexpected lift. Then she embraced False Assumption Number Two: he didn't hook up with their friends. But logic cautioned her about possible False Assumption Number Three: he hooked up with them once, like he had with her.

A random flashback popped into her head, threatening to combust her pretty new panties. Despite what he'd said, was he at all tempted to sleep with her again?

Where did that come from?

She buried the images deep. *Focus, Lil, focus!*

Just then, a strapping, curly haired man came up behind Natalie and snaked his arms around her waist. Mumbling something about amber, he nibbled her neck, and she broke into a fit of giggles.

"T.J., stop! I'm talking to Gage's date."

T.J. did stop—abruptly—raising his head to survey Lily with unabashed curiosity. "Oh wow. He *did* bring a date," he said as though said *non*-date wasn't standing two feet away.

Seriously? Are they all lying, or is a Gage Nelson date-sighting rarer than spotting the Loch Ness Monster?

"I'm not ... we're not ..." Lily stammered.

Natalie turned in her husband's arms, whisper-shouting, "They're not dating."

He gave Lily a skeptical grin, then a light seemed to wink on. "Hey, do I know you?"

Safer ground. "I sang at your wedding, though I wouldn't expect you to remember. You were a little preoccupied at the time."

The grin widened. "That's it! Sorry I didn't recognize you at first, but you're right. This one had me *preoccupied*. Like now." He cinched Natalie close and bent to her neck with a playful growl.

"T.J.!" she shrieked. "PDA!"

"Oh, you want *more* PDA? Happy to oblige."

Self-conscious, Lily darted her eyes about, landing on Gage, who'd been waylaid by a blond woman and a man in a wheelchair. In one hand, Gage fisted a beer; in the other, a full glass of white wine. Mid-speak, he captured her eyes with his and smiled. Then he pointed, and the man and woman turned their heads toward her and smiled too.

A tendril of warmth tapped her on the shoulder, which was when she remembered she'd felt the same way when she'd been with Gage last July. Before she'd freaked out and sprinted away.

Guilt shivered up her spine right before the unhappy remembrance of everything she'd had and lost with Jack suddenly swelled, wrenching her gut. A cleansing breath pushed the tears away. Her eyes continued sweeping the room, and the romantic inside her feasted on the warmth surrounding her. The ever-present practical side of her, however, wilted—her shot at love had come and gone.

"So," Natalie interrupted Lily's ping-ponging emotions, "have you been keeping busy with the band?"

Lily took in the sight of T.J. cuddling his wife from behind, his expectant eyebrows raised, matching his wife's expression. Two people in sync, behaving like one unit.

She coughed, giving herself a moment to recover. "No, your wedding was the first time I'd appeared in ages, and I haven't been onstage since then. That was my life full-time long ago, but things change." *So long ago*. "Now I freelance as a social media consultant."

Their befuddled faces spurred her to continue. "Oh, you're probably wondering about ... Gage and I ran into each other about a week ago and spent time talking. He decided to up his social media game and hired me to help him out."

As a matter of fact, they'd ironed out the details during the first ten minutes of the car ride over. He'd been very agreeable to her terms. It occurred to Lily the man was just downright agreeable. So much so, she'd overlooked the fact the Millers did *not* live in a gated community and Gage hadn't needed to pick her up. Yeah, she was content to let that one slide.

Lily rushed on. "That's the reason he brought me today. To give me a peek at his world and to meet his hockey family, so to speak."

Natalie nodded. "I assume you'll attend a few games too?"

Before she could answer that they hadn't discussed it, Gage stepped beside her, handing her the wineglass. "Yeah, she's definitely coming to some games." He glanced down at her, his expression devoid of any guile. "How about Tuesday night? I can get you a seat. More, if you want to bring your sister and her husband."

"And they can sit with us in the family section," Natalie added with glee.

By now, the man in the wheelchair had rolled over, the pretty blond riding in his lap. They both beamed at Lily. The woman extended her hand. "So you're Lily? Gage was just filling us in. I'm Carla, and this is my husband, Mark."

Mark's hand shot out. "Nice to meet you, Lily." He jerked his chin at Gage. "Dude, I'm not gonna lie. I was beginning to worry about you. I mean, being the best fucking center on the planet isn't all there is to life. Glad to see you're turning to the dark side and shedding your Shaolin monk lifestyle. Plus, she's really hot and makes a nice addition to our club. Good job, bro. You can stay." Looking directly at Lily, he gave Gage a few pats on the stomach that had Gage flinching. "*Love* this guy," Mark added.

The women seemed to stifle snorts. Gage scrubbed a hand down his face, his chiseled cheekbones burning red. "Filter, jackass?" he croaked.

T.J. burst out with a laugh. "He *has* no filters, Nelsy. Mark, you've been watching waaaay too much Deadpool. You are *not* Wade Wilson."

"True," Mark agreed. "I'm much better looking than Wade *or* Ryan Reynolds." He turned to his wife and puckered. "Right, babe?"

Carla offered Lily an apologetic smile. "Mark's an acquired taste."

"And I taste really fucking good! Just like—"

Carla covered his mouth. "I never know what's going to come out of this thing. Sometimes I swear it has a life of its own." She moved her hand away. "Are you going to behave?"

"Not a chance! But that's why you love me." He tilted his head and puckered again. "C'mon, gorgeous. Give us a kiss, or you'll hurt my feeling."

"Your *one* feeling," Gage chuffed.

Carla pecked her husband's lips and turned to Gage. "Will I see you in class tomorrow? Maybe you could bring Lily?" Her gaze slid to Lily.

"Carla teaches yoga," Gage explained.

"You do yoga?" Lily blurted.

"I have lots of athletes in my classes," Carla answered for him. "Ever tried yoga?"

Lily took an extra-large sip of her wine. "Um, yes. Love it, when I have the time."

"Lily's a social media consultant," Natalie interjected. "She's working for Gage."

A woman with dark hair and red-rimmed glasses approached the group, her big brown eyes focused on Lily. “Did I hear something about social media? Are you looking for new clients?” She offered Lily her hand. “I’m Katie, by the way. I work for Anderson Homes—which is really Paige—and so does Natalie.”

“And social media is a job neither of us handles. Not well anyway,” Natalie added with an apologetic shrug.

“No, we all suck at it, but Paige keeps saying we need to get it going. Maybe you and she should talk?” Before Lily could open her mouth, Katie called out, “Paige? I think we found your girl. Lily’s a social media expert.”

An unmistakable “Oooooh” drifted from the kitchen. “Be right there.”

In the car hours later, Gage side-eyed her and seemed to wince. “I hope you had a good time. Some of those folks can be overly—”

Lily let out a laugh. “I enjoyed meeting them all. Even Mark.”

“Really?” No mistaking the disbelief—or relief—in his voice.

“Really. They all seem nice, down-to-earth.” And she meant it.

Lily gazed out the window, replaying the day. She’d gone to the party to gain insight into the intriguing mystery that was Gage Nelson. Along the way, she’d picked up a new social media client, a yoga class, and seats to a hockey game. Gage had opened up his world to her, and his “inner sanctum” had wholly embraced her.

She’d also come away with a new PR angle to play up: the sled hockey team Mark belonged to and that Gage, T.J., and Beckett coached in their spare time. It turned out R-rated comments weren’t the only bits of his conversation Mark didn’t rein in. He also didn’t hold back when it came to singing the praises of the three guys who made the sled team a thriving endeavor.

Everything about Gage seemed straightforward, out in the open. No romantic entanglements or baby mamas lurking in the recesses of his celebrity, waiting to strike at the most inopportune times. *What you see is what you get.*

Except he had slept with *her* right after meeting her. He might not have secrets, but he couldn't be the dateless wonder his friends painted. After all, he'd known just what to do to open floodgates she hadn't been expecting to have opened that night. The man was obviously not celibate. But did that automatically make him a player? Not that it was any of her business if he slept around. He was entitled. Still, he didn't come across as that guy.

They came to a stop at a red light. She felt his eyes on her, and she glanced over. He gave her a hesitant smile, and, as natural as you please, raised his hand and threaded his fingers through her hair before tucking it behind her ear. His fingertips ghosted over her jawline.

The intimate move shocked her. It was both unexpected *and* exciting. She found herself yearning for more, but a lash of guilt laid her open. He must have seen something on her face because his smile slid away. "Sorry," he said. "I shouldn't have done that, Goldilocks."

Goldilocks? She kind of liked it, especially in his deep baritone, yet it too was uncomfortably familiar. A shimmy squirmed up her spine.

The light turned green, and he turned his eyes to the road, his hands firmly on the wheel. While her heart thudded in her ears and her mind frantically searched for the right words, she stole a few glimpses at his strong profile.

If she was going to be spending time with this man and his friends, she needed to get everything out in the open, set expectations before ... before what? Before he fell for her? *Pretty impressed with yourself,* her inner self scoffed.

No, he wasn't going to fall for her. Besides, it would never work out.

It's strictly business.

Gage turned into her neighborhood, and she jolted. The moment of truth was on her; so was dread. She screwed up her courage.

"Professor, there are some things about me I need to tell you."

Chapter 9

TELL ME SWEET LITTLE LIES ... PLEASE

No sooner had Lily begun her confession when her eyes caught on the Ford F-150 in her driveway. *Too late.* Her breath snagged. She slid her eyes toward Gage, who seemed blissfully unaware of the ball bearings careening around in her gut—the ones she could practically hear clinking as they rolled blindly into each other.

He glided his Porsche to a stop along her front curb and peered over her head at her lit-up house.

"Someone here? I don't recall seeing a truck in your driveway when we left."

She drew in a long, bracing breath. Why was what she had to tell him sucking the air from her lungs?

"Actually," she began in a raspy voice that she paused to clear, "someone *is* here. That's part of what you need to know. Do you remember me telling you at IHOP that my life is complicated?"

He switched off the ignition and swiveled his head toward her. "Yes, I remember."

"Well, one of the things that makes it complicated is in my house at this moment."

Though she couldn't make out their color in the dim interior of his car, she could see the shimmer in his eyes as they lasered in on her. He watched her expectantly, still as marble. She wasn't even sure he was breathing.

On second thought, it wasn't what she was about to tell him but his *reaction* making her as skittish as a mouse in a roomful of ravenous cats. Why? "So I have—"

His gaze bounced above her head just as she heard her front door slam. With a muttered curse, she turned toward the source of the noise. That source was stomping down her walkway toward them.

"What the—?" Gage uttered just as Derek reached her window.

She cracked the door open, and Derek peered in. Though his scowl was firmly fixed on Gage—who seemed to be returning the glare—Derek directed his question to her. "Everything all right here, Lily?"

Of course it is! Do I look like it's not? Suppressing an exasperated eye-roll, she said, "Derek, this is Gage Nelson. Gage, this is Derek Everett. You might remember him as the guitarist from our band? Derek, would you please give me a minute? I'll be right in."

He hesitated before bobbing his head, and she softly latched the car door and watched his retreating back. Heart slamming against her ribcage, she pulled in another breath—which was quite the feat, considering all the air had been vacuumed from inside the car. She faced Gage.

If she thought his look was intense before, this one could have burned a hole through her. "That could have gone better," she ventured.

"He has the same last name as you."

"Good observation. And this is why you're the Professor." Her joke fell flat, judging by Gage's unwavering stare. Twiddling her fingers in her lap, she met his eyes squarely. "Derek is my brother-in-law."

Gage's eyebrows knotted together. "Why is he here? And more importantly, what makes him your brother-in-law?"

Once Gage knew her whole story, she might never see him again. And while she wanted the work, something deep down dreaded losing their tentative friendship. This revelation surprised her even as she fought to keep her heart from wobbling and crashing off its axis.

"He's here," she replied steadily, "because he's watching my five-year-old daughter, Daisy."

Gage's head jerked as though he'd been punched in the face, though he didn't break his gaze.

Another lungful of courage—*Why didn't I drink more wine?*—and she rushed on. "I was married to Derek's brother, Jack, who's Daisy's father. Derek's here because he also has a daughter—her name is Violet—who's two years older than Daisy. Derek and Vi's mother aren't together, and he and I take turns watching the girls to help each other out. He had Daisy at his place today to play with her cousin, and he offered to watch her while I ... while I went to the party with you because I told him it was business."

Oh my God. I sound like such a slut.

She drew her bottom lip between her teeth and waited.

Gage stared out the windshield. Ten long beats passed before he nodded. "Where's Jack?"

Stinging tears swarmed the backs of her eyes, blurring her vision. *Damn it!* "Well, um, Jack is ... He died four years ago." She made an angry swipe at her cheek. "It'll be five years this July."

Gage snapped his head back to her, his mouth swinging open. "That's why you volunteer as a grief counselor."

Her answer came in a feeble nod.

"I'm sorry," he finally said.

Another brush at her cheek, with the heel of her hand this time. "Yeah, me too." She could practically hear her heart ripping in two. Again.

He bounced his thumb on the steering wheel for what seemed forever. "Can I ask you something?"

"Yes, of course," she sniffed.

"Is every female in your family named after a plant?"

She burst out with a laugh despite her tears. "What?"

"Lily, Ivy, Daisy, Violet. What's your mom's name?" One side of his mouth curled up, and his eyes held hers with kindness, understanding. Not the pity or disdain she'd expected. She found herself swamped with gratitude, warm and soothing, as though she'd immersed her body in a bubbling hot spring.

Half laughing, half crying, she said, "Her name's Rose."

He broke into a full grin. "Of course it is."

They sat quietly. He seemed to be giving her time to pull herself together.

"I'd better get inside before Derek comes back out," she finally said.

"I have another question."

"I probably have another answer." She smiled weakly, thinking she knew what the question was. Guilt, or obligation, prodded her to rush ahead. "Daisy was spending a week with my folks last summer when I met you at the wedding." She didn't want Gage thinking she was an irresponsible mom, sticking her daughter with some random sitter just so she could get herself good and fucked. Well, while she hadn't set out to do it, she *had* gotten herself good and fucked, but she hadn't foisted Daisy off just so she could.

"That wasn't the question." His voice was so low she barely heard him.

"Oh?"

He shocked the hell out of her—again—when he said, "Would it be all right if I met Daisy?"

Her jaw dropped, and a few pounds of worry weight came off. Was he for real?

"Not tonight," he quickly added, studying her expression. "But I would like to meet her. After all, you're working for me, and I make it a point to get to know my employees' families."

She wasn't sure what surprised her more: that he wanted to meet Daisy, or that he had other people working for him. "You ... you have other employees?"

"No, but I figure now's as good a time as any to put policies into place." He gave her a goofy grin that had her shoulders shedding even more weight.

What if she'd been wrong about Gage Nelson? What if he was an average, all-around nice guy? God, she wanted to throw her arms around his strong neck and hug him tight. Before she could let impulse take her, the curtain in her front window opened.

He lifted his chin toward it. "I think your brother-in-law's sending signals that he wants you inside and me gone."

She gathered up her purse. "Yeah, I should go. Daisy—"

"Will be anxious to see her mom." With that, he climbed out of the driver's seat and strode to the passenger door, opening it for her.

"I can see myself to the door."

One eyebrow arched. "I'm sure you can, but I'd feel better walking you there."

Suddenly shy, she squeaked out an "okay" and let him escort her up the walkway.

Her hand hovering on the doorknob, she looked up at him. "Thank you for tonight. I really enjoyed myself. It's been a long time."

He bowed his head. "My pleasure, Lily Everett. Sweet dreams." He pivoted and headed back to his car.

All of her wanted to run after him, to throw her arms around him and feel his solid warmth. But all of her opened the door and stepped inside instead. It was what good mothers did.

Gage pulled away from the curb. When he rounded the corner, he shot the car forward, his mind going at dragster speed but in a fractured line.

Slowing once more, he tugged his hand over his beard and puffed out a huge exhale. "Shit," he muttered.

Grandma must have hit him upside the head again because he immediately challenged himself. "So she's got a kid. So what? You're not even together."

"I don't know anything about kids anyway, Grandma," he said aloud, checking his rearview mirror, half expecting to see Grandma sitting in his backseat. Yeah, he was losing it.

"Back all the way up, doofus," he told himself, "this is a *business* arrangement. Which is a good thing because you don't have time to chase anything besides the Stanley Cup. No girlfriend, with *or* without kids. No touching, no ... Just no. You don't wanna go there. Not that she'd let you anyway," he huffed. Still, he'd felt that familiar electrical charge around her the entire day, and it had done funny things to him below the belt. Things he'd have to deal with on his own later.

He rolled to a stop at a traffic signal and darted his eyes to the rearview again. He threw out a "Fuck!" for good measure, then muttered, "You shouldn't have touched her hair, stupid." Yeah. Like *not* doing that could erase the kid and the dead husband. Or make her want *him*.

A horn sounded beside him. When he glanced over, two women were checking him out. One made a sad face, as if asking what the hell his problem was. Then she crooked her finger at him with a wicked smile. Yeah, he got that message loud and clear too. Drumming his fingers impatiently on the wheel, keeping his eyes focused straight ahead, he didn't realize the light had changed until the women pulled into the intersection and slowed, as if waiting for him to catch up. He turned on his signal and peeled off to the right.

What *was* the matter with him anyway?

"Take it Easy" sang through the speakers, and he paid attention, slowing the furious pace of his pounding heart. He got back on his route, got himself back on track, letting the thoughts come as he drove home, hoping to sort them out.

Clarity struck moments later, and he realized exactly what the matter was with him.

Today he'd loved arriving with Lily. Showing her off. Listening to the guys go on about how he'd scored. Even Mark's crude comments had brought his dormant caveman self to life. It was nice to have someone to introduce to his friends and teammates. To fetch a drink for. To share a conversation with inside a cluster of people. To stand close to. It didn't suck to be there because he wasn't holding up a wall by himself, dodging everyone's concerns, counting the minutes before he could make a polite escape. He'd *wanted* to be there, and it had all been because of her.

He'd believed—*scratch that*—he'd fooled himself, even if for only a short while, that they might be a couple. He'd gotten way ahead of himself, imagining bringing her to team events, having her wait for him after a game, just like Natalie waited for T.J. After all, Lily had fit in so well with Natalie and the other women. It had felt so natural. Hell, he'd even let the illusion grow legs and go a little crazy, picturing himself following her into her cute little house and getting his fingers tangled in those silky Goldilocks curls. About getting her naked again. Running his hands and lips over that soft skin. Spending the night and waking up with his body curled around hers.

Jackass!

The laugh that escaped his chest wasn't a funny one. More of a frustrated release at his own absurdity. What an idiot he'd been to let his mind wander down a primrose path. The shock of seeing Derek marching out of her house had done a thorough job of erasing Gage's mirage. Hell, it had blown it to smithereens.

After parking his car in the garage, he walked into the kitchen and flooded it with light. It was a gorgeous kitchen—dark wood, rich granite, lots of space for a cook to spread messes while whipping up something tasty to share. But it was an empty kitchen. A space he rarely used. Though the world beyond the huge window over the sink was dark, he pictured himself standing there, the backdrop of woods beyond, and someone's arms wrapped around his waist while he hurried through the dishes so he could pick her up and carry her to the bedroom upstairs. Her legs would be flailing, and they'd both be laughing.

Right now the kitchen was dead. Quiet. Soulless. Sound echoed through the room, and it wasn't kids giggling or a woman calling his name.

No, it was a meow.

He stepped into the family room just off the kitchen, flipped on an outside deck light, and peered through the sliding glass door at an orange tabby.

He opened the slider and let the stray waltz in, its tail held high. Hobbes meowed a greeting in response, looking for all the world like the king of the castle—until Gage walked toward the pantry and rustled a bag of cat food. The cat shot in like a dart, mewling and rubbing himself against his legs until Gage set a bowl down and filled it. He ruffled the cat's scruffy neck while the thing chowed down.

He had no idea where Hobbes had come from. He'd just shown up one day and become a frequent visitor. Though Gage had asked around and even posted a few flyers, no one had claimed the cat.

"Jesus, Hobbes," he said softly. "Maybe it's just you and me against the world." For the first time, Gage wondered if the cat had been checked by a vet lately. "You got a home, buddy? Or am I it for you? If so, that really sucks because I'm not around much, and my only family is a crazy, toothpaste-wielding Grandma, a mom whose sole mission in life is to marry me off to someone I'm not in love with, and a sister who lives too far away to have my back."

Huh. Maybe he and the cat could help each other out.

Gage turned on the gas fireplace, picked up his acoustic guitar, plopped down on his cushy leather couch, and started strumming "Take it Easy." He wasn't ready to head to his dark bedroom yet.

He had no idea how much time had passed when he startled awake to loud purring coming from a hot spot on his chest. He was stretched half-on and half-off the couch, Hobbes staring at his face as if it were something to eat.

His phone also seemed to be purring on the coffee table, and he put the cat aside to pick it up. A text from Lily glowed. *Make it home okay, Professor? I wanted to thank you again for today. It was a lot of fun.*

Apparently, the message had come in over an hour ago. He hesitated a moment—was she sleeping with her daughter? What if he woke them up by texting back? He'd take the chance.

Got home fine. Just hanging with Hobbes. I had a lot of fun too.

To his great delight, her reply came instantly.

Glad you have company.

He couldn't stop himself. *What about you? You have company too?*

Just me and D, who's sound asleep beside me. Did you know little girls snore?

"D" had to be Daisy and not Derek, right? Right. An image flitted through his brain of two sets of blond curls, one belonging to someone small and the other to someone smaller, snuggled together under a fluffy comforter. The image curved a corner of his mouth.

Gage: *Had no idea. Learn something new every day. You still up for coming to the game Tues?*

Lily: *I'd love to. OK to bring Ivy?*

What he wanted to say, but refrained from typing, was, *You can bring anyone as long as it isn't Derek.* He tried to block out Derek cozied up in Lily's house, waiting for Lily to get home. Instead, he typed, *Of course. Meet me tomorrow at the arena at 11? I'll hand over 2 tix and fan mail so you can start earning that paycheck and make me look good.*

Lily: *You already look good, Professor. See you tomorrow.*

"Whoa, do you see that, Hobbes?" He waved his phone in front the cat's face. Hobbes tracked it for a few seconds before striking a bored pose and licking his paw. "What do you think she means when she says I already look good? You think she wants to jump my bones? Or is she talking 'good' in a PR kinda way?" The cat looked up from his licking and blinked. "Yeah, you're probably right. Strictly PR, but hope shines eternal, or some bullshit like that."

Gage couldn't bring himself to put Hobbes back out in the cold and did something he'd never done before. He piled a few towels on the mudroom floor and closed the cat up with full bowls of food and water.

Tomorrow, he'd look into whatever the hell a cat needed—they used litter boxes, didn't they?—and he'd text Natalie about a vet. Gage didn't view his efforts as "adopting" Hobbes, though. He was simply providing temporary shelter from the cold and the coyotes. And why not? He had a big house, and the cat wasn't annoying or destructive.

A thought streaked in out of the blue. *What about a kid? Who's not mine? Would I want to take care of it ... her? That kind of shelter would be a helluva lot more permanent.*

Stepparents did it all the time, right? Gage had never been afforded a front-row seat to stepparenting. His mom hadn't remarried, and he had little experience with his stepmom since his dad had distanced himself. But still. Millions of people made it work every single day, so it couldn't be all *that* daunting. You only heard about the horror stories, not the boring ones where everybody acted like a family. A team.

He trudged upstairs, getting ready for bed while his mind continued winding along its merry, unlikely way. Did he want to be a dad someday? He'd always assumed he would be, though it wasn't exactly burning a hole in the bucket holding his topmost desires—in fact, it wasn't even *in* the bucket. Right now that bucket was filled to the rim with one thing: winning the Stanley Cup.

Lily, he realized suddenly, could worm her way into that bucket—which meant her kid, by default, would wind up in the bucket too. A child he didn't know, who wasn't his.

Tired of his whirlpooling thoughts, he stripped and slid between the sheets. Tonight the bed seemed bigger, colder. Sleeping by himself was getting old. He could change that if he wanted to; he didn't *have* to sleep alone.

His brain skimmed over women he'd dated and women he hadn't dated who'd shown interest when they'd slipped him cards or notes with inviting smiles on their faces—as recently as yesterday.

He sat up, clicked on the lamp, and riffled through the pile in his nightstand drawer. They wound up there simply because he emptied his pockets in his bedroom when he undressed, and he'd invariably come across one tucked away in his clothing. That card got tossed into the drawer with the others with the thought that *maybe* he'd follow up, only to be forgotten until he found one the next time and absentmindedly added it to the others.

As he shuffled through the impressive stack, he was struck by the fact that none of the names or faces stood out. Was he that obtuse, or were they that underwhelming? Maybe he was too picky. Maybe he should just take one of these women out and not wind up alone for a change. But the thought of digging for a spark, of searching for common ground over a meal, deflated him. It was exhausting. And having a body next to him for the sake of having a body next to him? Nah. Didn't appeal.

With a sigh, he tossed them all back in the drawer and slammed it shut. One of these days he needed to clean them out. But not tonight.

As he laced his hands across his chest, Lily's melodious laugh floated into his brain. Followed by her beautiful smile. Her bright blue eyes. Her glossy blond curls. Her skin that reminded him of cream. Her fragrance—like oranges and the star jasmine outside his mom's house. He'd inhaled it all through the party and on her doorstep when he'd walked her to her door.

Every detail about Lily Everett was branded in his brain. Nothing about her was fuzzy, unlike the women in the drawer. And if he dared try to blur her out, his body was having none of it, rousing to her electrifying effect on him. Despite the fact that she didn't want him.

With a sigh, he climbed out of bed and headed for the shower.

Chapter 10

Game Time

"Yes! Go, go! Yes!" Ivy shrieked behind Lily as they climbed over legs to reach their seats. Several heads turned their way.

"Ivy," Lily ground out, "they're just warming up. Save your voice for the actual game, okay?"

"Just getting my vocal chords ready."

Lily rolled her eyes. Maybe bringing Ivy hadn't been such a great idea after all. At least they weren't sitting among the players' families—those seats were gone, so Gage had gotten them club seats. Lily wasn't complaining. She didn't need the pressure, and on a swank factor, these rated just below box seats, and they were right at center ice. Perfect for watching the action at her first live NHL game.

She'd been scouring the ice since they'd entered and had a bead on the jersey with a huge six positioned below "Nelson." Her heart executed a few discreet flips at the sight of him speeding fluidly around the Blizzard's side of the rink, his dark blond hair ruffling as he went. Long, graceful strides made her breath stutter. A quick spin, and he was skating backward just as elegantly, stick dangling from his hand.

Hot!

Hands full of popcorn and beer, eyes glued on Alternate Captain Hotness, Lily goosed herself when she accidentally landed on the armrest. She recovered quickly and plopped into her seat, never taking her eyes from Gage. Beside her, Ivy began pointing out different players she found in her program, reciting their stats. Lily couldn't have cared less ... until Ivy started enthusing about "Star Center Gage Nelson."

"Oh yeah," the fan seated in front of them said as he turned in his seat, a difficult maneuver with his portly body, "Nelson is *awwwwesome*! Fast as lightning and slippery as an eel. Thank God he's ours. Other teams really have a hard time handling him."

Ivy gouged Lily's ribs with a sharp elbow. "Maybe *you* could handle him, Lil. He's a very fine specimen of hot hockey hunkiness! Hubba-hubba!"

"Ivy, hush!" Lily hissed.

"Why? Just because I'm married doesn't mean I can't feast my eyes on a mouthwatering piece of man-candy. Woo hoo! You go, Number Six!" She waved a foam finger above her head.

The fan's shoulders shuddered with laughter in front of them while Lily fought the urge to bury her face in her hands.

Meanwhile, the players lined up for drills. On the opposite side of the rink, Gage was casually bouncing a puck on his stick blade.

Whoa! How does he do that? Gotta be superior hand-to-eye coordination, and, uh, athletic prowess.

It should've been cold in the arena, but Lily suddenly felt warm. She fanned herself with Ivy's program. Gage dropped the puck, passed it to a teammate, and looked right at her, a huge grin plastered on his face. *Okay. He knew we were here the whole time. Showoff.* She returned the smile—couldn't stop herself—her blood effervescing like soda inside a shaken-up bottle.

The players finished their pregame warm-ups and began drifting off the ice until only two Blizzard players remained. One was Number Six. On one last loop, he skated by their section, slowing, balancing on a single skate with his other leg drawn up as he got closer. He thumped his heart with his fist and pointed at her before gunning for the exit chute. People in the stands turned toward her.

Her blazing face must have given her away because one enthusiastic fan hollered, "Nelson? Nice!"

"I just do his PR," she squawked to no one in particular.

From somewhere behind her came, "Sure that's *all* you do for him, Blondie?" followed by, "I'd be doing a lot more than his PR if I were you, honey. That man's a hottie!"

When Lily swiveled her head toward her sister, Ivy's eyes and mouth were round O's, her chin practically scraping her chest. "Is that ... Is he ...?"

Lily shushed her, but it didn't prevent Ivy leaning to her ear and whisper-shouting over the booming music, "He's your July guy, isn't he? Oh my fucking God, Lil! Way to go, Baby Sis!" She punched Lily's arm and gave her two thumbs-up before throwing her arms around her and squeezing tight. Lily doubted a red brighter than the color staining her face existed in the universe.

Gage was on fire tonight, playing stupid-out-of-his-mind. Everything he touched, everything he did *worked!* He was golden. Passing, skating, stealing the puck, protecting it. The damn thing seemed to find him and bend to his will. He flew up and down the ice, setting up plays, dekeing, putting on skating clinics. No one could touch him.

Late in the third period, with the score tied, he roofed the puck with a wicked wrist shot, popping the goalie's water bottle. He'd found the back of the net for his second goal of the game. *That one'll show up on the highlight reels!*

"Beauty goal, Admiral!" T.J shouted from across the ice.

Gage glided on one skate, pumping his arms, puffing his chest like a damn rooster before he threw himself at the glass and roared. On the other side, fans pounded their palms against the glass, making it bow and flex as they screamed their heads off. And he was right there with them.

God, what a rush! Nothing like it! Better than sex!

As his teammates skated over to mob him for the celly, his eyes lifted to Lily. Gorgeous smile on her gorgeous face, she clapped and jumped in place. For him. Her beautiful curls bounced on her slight shoulders. Other parts of her bounced too.

Okay. Not better than sex, but damn close.

He was engulfed by his teammates, hugging, slapping, telling him what a fucking awesome goal it was. He slapped them back. "Okay, boys. We got this. Let's finish these fuckers off. We're gonna win this one!"

And they did.

The locker room exploded when they came off the ice, guys celebrating, smacking each other with towels, clothes, gear. With playoffs right around the corner, every game counted, and they'd just gained two points on conference-leader Arizona in the standings. Soon he might be able to say, "Eat that, Beckett Miller!"

Gage snatched his phone from his locker and texted Lily before the press found him and held him up. *Natalie's on her way to find you. Go with her and wait for me?*

Stripping off his gear, he turned and faced the reporters and questions coming at him. He never believed the gushing crap they wrote about him—he knew only too well how imperfect he was—but tonight he might just buy in for a little while and enjoy himself.

"What happened on the ice tonight, Gage? You were unstoppable!"

He grinned. *Blond hair and blue eyes happened.* He couldn't wait to get out of there—he just hoped Lily would wait.

Another thirty minutes passed before he disentangled himself from the boisterous locker room crowd, showered, and made his way into the corridor alongside his captain, Dave "The Grim Reaper" Grimson. Grims heaped more praise on him as they walked.

"You were un-fucking-believable tonight, Admiral Nelson. I'm pretty sure you could've been out there all by yourself and still won the game for us."

"Hardly. Just one of those lucky nights."

"Lucky, my ass!"

Embarrassed, Gage dismissed the compliment, eager to steer the conversation in a different direction. "Hey, Grims, your girlfriend, Nicole. She's got a kid, right?"

Grims peered at him as if he'd sprouted a horn—or two. "Yeaaaaah. And?"

"And how does that work? I mean, when the kid's around? Can you tell her what to do? Does she think of you as a stepdad? How do you deal with it?"

Grims came to a dead stop. "First off, she's a he, and second, I just deal because Nicky's little boy is part of her. I knew they were a package deal. In fact, Nicky tried to talk me out of it," he chuckled. "But whatcha gonna do? You fall for the mom, you end up falling for the kid. The only part I'd change is her asshole ex—shit, would I love Nicky to be free of *that* fucktard. I've offered to get rid of him for her." Grims, who was a mountain of a man, smiled wide, showing off the gap where his front teeth should've been. If it were possible, dude was scarier *with* the smile than without.

Gage laughed.

Grims grasped his shoulder. "All I can say, Nelsy, is if you're gonna start something with a MILF, make it easy on yourself and pick a widow." He winked and walked toward a group of fans clamoring for autographs.

Gage stood in a stunned fog, chewing on Grims's words. *Who knew the Grim Reaper was a sage?*

Coming to, he headed toward a cluster of waiting friends and family. Lily hadn't texted him back, so when his eyes landed on her, he blew out a breath of relief, his spirits climbing like a helium-filled balloon making a break for the stratosphere. She smiled shyly, and he made a beeline for her, eyes fixed on only her, unaware at first that she stood between Natalie and a strawberry blond.

"Hey," she said softly.

"Hey, Goldilocks" was all he had.

"I'd like to introduce you to my sister, Ivy."

He broke his gaze and took in the strawberry blond staring at him with a glazed look. A little bigger than Lily, Ivy's coloring and blue eyes were darker than Lily's. She was pretty, but Lily outshone her in spades. Then again, he was beginning to think Lily outshone pretty damn near every woman on the planet.

"Happy to meet you, Ivy. You're gonna help me convince your sister to attend every one of my home games from now on, right?"

Shit. I'm in trouble.

Gage excused himself from the restaurant table and headed to the men's room. When he came out, Ivy was leaning against the wall by the ladies' room, and they had the hallway to themselves. She lifted her chin at him and, bold as you please, said, "So are you into my sister?"

While his mind processed the question and the reason behind it—*protective big sister? Nosy big sister?*—he deflected. "Why do you ask?"

"Call me curious." She tilted her head as if appraising him.

Gage arched an eyebrow. "Meaning?"

"Meaning my sister doesn't date."

Before he could stop himself, his posture straightened—probably because he felt his chest inflate. "We're not dating."

"Whatever." She flapped a hand at him. "The fact that she's here, and that she's actually introduced you to me, leads me to conclude you're different."

"Different from ...?"

"The idiots she typically meets."

Now he was off balance, and he wasn't sure what bothered him more: Lily meeting idiots or the possibility that Lily was introducing him to Ivy because she *wasn't* interested in him—the way he wanted her interested anyway.

"What kinds of idiots does she typically meet?" *And how do I keep her from meeting them in the first place?*

"They're irrelevant. As far as dating her, I suspect you'd like to change that, am I right?" Ivy gave him a sly smile.

He nearly blurted out a yes but stopped himself in time. Instead, he held an internal debate over how to respond. *Play it safe and stick to the "strictly business" scenario? Or admit I want to date her sister and run the risk of a) humiliating myself when big sister laughs in my face, or b) losing my balls when big sister's protective self rampages?*

Apparently, he was taking too long to formulate his answer because Ivy added, “You called her ‘Goldilocks,’ and I see how you look at her.”

This caught him by surprise. “How do I look at her?”

“Like a man who hasn’t eaten in a week.”

He coughed out a laugh. “Have you considered it’s because the appetizer plate was sitting in front of her?”

“Pfft. Nice try, ace, except the plate was empty when I caught you staring. And don’t worry. No one else picked up on it.”

He stuffed his hands in his front pockets. *Where the hell is this going?*

As if she’d read his mind, she said, “I love my little sister, and I want to see her happy. Something tells me you might be good for her.”

Ivy had just captured all of his attention. “I think you’re reading way too much into this.”

“Well, I don’t.” She cinched her arms over her chest. “Look, I’m pretty damn sure my sister’s last date was with her late husband, Jack.” She shot him a knowing look that had him giddy and squirming inside at the same time. Either that or what he’d eaten so far wasn’t settling right.

“You do know about Jack, right?” she said.

He nodded. “I know she was married to him, that he was Daisy’s father, and that he died. That’s about it.”

“Well, I’ll give you a few more insights.” She paused and raised her eyes to the ceiling, as if marshaling her thoughts, then leveled a penetrating gaze at him. “My sister was really young when she met Jack. He was eight or nine years older, and there’s been some debate as to whether she was even legal. In any case, she was dazzled and she fell hard. Now don’t get me wrong—we all loved Jack. He was an easy guy to love because he was charming as hell. He was also a magnetic, outgoing showman that people were drawn to—*especially* women. And boy, did he eat it up. I think flirting for him was as natural as breathing. I don’t think he was ever unfaithful, but I know he and Lily fought about the attention he used to get *and* give.”

Enthralled, Gage gave her a go-ahead nod.

“No one questioned that Jack loved Lily. He took good care of her, and they seemed happy.” Another pause, to pull in a breath this time. "But he wasn't perfect. No one is. She was young, head over heels, and overlooked his faults. The problem is that since his death, she's forgotten those faults ever existed and has built him up into this impossibly perfect paragon in her mind. Which he never was. Hell, if he came back today, *he* wouldn't live up to the image she's painted of him."

"So why are you telling me this?"

"I'd like to see someone make her forget Jack. Oh, not completely, of course, but enough so she can put those memories in a box, shelve it, and start living again."

He pointed his thumb at his chest. "And you think *I* can make her forget him?"

"I look at you, and you're a man who's used to the spotlight, yet you don't seem caught up in it. As a matter of fact, I think I owe you an apology."

His eyebrows crawled to his hairline. "Why?"

"Without having met you, I had you pegged for a cocky prick hot to fuck anything with a vagina."

"Whoa!" He put his hands up in surrender, trying not to laugh. "Are you always so direct?"

She shrugged. "I find it takes a lot less time and BS."

"Couldn't agree more." He glanced down the hallway, relieved no one was around to interrupt this very fascinating conversation. "So now that you've met me, am I still a cocky prick?"

She shot him a broad grin that made his insides uncoil a fraction. "I don't think so. I like to think I'm a pretty good judge of character, and you strike me as grounded. A surprisingly nice guy, but no pushover. Someone I would approve of for my little sister."

"Well, I'm glad to hear I pass the, uh, test. Maybe you'll put in a good word for me with your sis?"

A head dip was her answer. Curiosity had its talons hooked in him. "So what about the idiots she meets?"

She smirked. "Guys get starstruck. First of all—and I'm sure I'm not telling you something you don't already know—she's beautiful, and then they find out she sings. Or they see her perform—which doesn't happen as much as it used to—and they just want to get in her pants. They don't care who she really is, or that she has a daughter, or anything about this," she tapped two fingers against her temple, then her heart, "or this. I'm guessing you go through the same kind of thing, but on crack. Women only see the pro athlete, and they line up to suck your dick because they think you're this ... this god."

He tried to choke down his laughter, but he couldn't, and it escaped in a bark. "Could you please point me to this line of women?" he managed. "And tell them I am, in fact, a god?"

"You're funny," she scoffed good-naturedly.

"Yeah, I'm thinking of giving up hockey for stand-up. What do you think?"

She burst out with a laugh. "Don't quit your day job." In a gesture that warmed him, she placed her hand on his arm. "I hope I'm not making you *too* uncomfortable. I must say, though, you're taking it well."

He shrugged. "I'm flattered you think I'd be good for your sister, but it's really—"

She flung her hands in the air. "Yeah, yeah. She's feeding me the same bullshit. It's all business, yada, yada, yada." She added an eye-roll.

"No, I was going to say it's up to her." He gave her a pointed look, and her eyes gleamed with understanding at what he'd just confessed. The puck was in Lily's rink, so to speak, and all she had to do was pass it to him. He was ready to charge the net with it.

What Gage didn't reveal to Ivy was that despite Lily having a daughter he didn't know, despite the ghost of a husband hanging around, he couldn't deny the odd sensations in his chest when he was with her. His heart seemed to balloon and levitate and invert all at once. In fact, the damn thing tripped the same erratic way every time he thought about her, which was constantly.

Ivy brightened. "Okay, then. Consider me on your side. Anything I can do to further the cause of," she laced her fingers and brought them to her cheek while she fluttered her lashes, "*wuv, twue wuv*, you just let me know."

"*Princess Bride*?"

"None other." She scuffed her heel against the floor. "Why don't I give you my cell number?"

He chuckled and whipped out his phone. "Because?"

Her whole upper body seemed to shrug. “Oh, I don’t know. In case you want to take my sister out and you need someone to watch Daisy. In case you get stuck and need help interpreting her—Lily, not Daisy. Not that I’ll be able to shed light on her every word or move, but at least I’m closer than you are.”

I’m hoping that changes. “Thanks. I appreciate your, your ...”

“Butting in? It’s what big sisters are for.”

He’d been thinking more along the lines of her offer to help, but he chose to keep it to himself. He was still processing Lily’s big sister. Energy spun from Ivy like a dust devil spun dirt into Colorado’s shimmering July heat. Yeah, she was a firecracker on steroids, but she seemed genuine, and he liked her. She was probably a lot like his big sister: fierce and loyal and true.

“You know, you and *my* big sister would make quite the team. But seriously, thanks for coming with Lily tonight and for talking her into dinner afterward. I don’t normally do the dinners, and I’m really enjoying myself. I’m sure it’s because of the company.”

For an instant, Ivy seemed at a loss for words, but she recovered. “Yeah, I think you’d be good for her. Now all we have to do is convince *her* to let you in.”

Chapter 11

If Wishes Were Wings, I'd Crash

If Gage didn't believe he was in trouble the night before, he knew it for sure the next day when he called his sister for advice.

"Hey, Gage. Awesome game last night! I've been showing the video of your game-winning goal to everyone in the office. What the hell kind of explosives did they shove up your butt?"

He laughed. "No explosives. Just an extra dose of orneriness as we get closer to playoffs, I guess."

"Well, you should be *that* ornery more often, Baby Bro."

"Duly noted." He was seated at his kitchen counter, staring at the pines beyond the window, while Hobbes had a sniff-fest around the fireplace in the family room. The cat had been smelling his way around his new digs all morning. "Hey, Sar, have you, uh, ever dated anyone with kids?"

"No. Why?" Her voice had a decidedly suspicious ring to it. He'd expected as much.

"Just curious."

"Wait. Are you dating someone with kids? Wait. Are you *dating*?"

"Haha, very funny. And it's none of your business."

"Which means you *are* dating someone with kids." Her tone softened. "You must really like her. Do you think she's 'The One'?"

He pinched the bridge of his nose, double-guessing his wisdom in calling her. Three generations of women had hammered him with "The One." *Damn romance novels, setting ridiculously unbelievable standards.*

"Sarah, I haven't known her that long. How the hell would I know if she's the one, the two, or the nine-squared?"

"So back to this woman you're dating."

"We're not exactly *dating*, but the more I'm around her, the more I *want* to be dating her."

Whoa! Had he really said it out loud? To his sister? Shit, he was spewing confessions to sisters like a malfunctioning water dispenser.

His worry over the wisdom of sharing was erased a beat later when Sarah said, "And you're hesitant to date her because she has a kid?"

"No, I think I can work with that part."

"So what's holding you back?"

He let out a wry chuckle. "I'm not sure. *She* is. I think. It's weird because there's this ... this spark whenever we're together, and I'm pretty sure it goes both ways. But I also feel like she's got walls up, and I wonder if it's me reading her all wrong and she really *doesn't* want to date me, or if it has something to do with her daughter. I mean, that's gotta be tough, right? You want to protect your kid, and there are all these whack jobs running around. It'd probably make you think twice about getting involved with someone."

The other very real possibility, one he kept to himself, was that Lily was still in love with Jack. Had her loyalty made her run that night? Guilt was a powerful motivator, a fact Gage understood only too well.

"To tell the truth, Sar, I'm not sure what to do if I want to get close to this woman. I don't know a thing about kids. How am I supposed to act around them?"

His sister let out a strangled sigh. "Gage, I'm gonna tell you something—and don't you dare hold it over my head—but I've always thought you'd be a phenomenal dad. You have a shitload of patience.

You always take care of everyone without whining. I don't know what your family would do without you."

This touched him with warmth *and* guilt. He wasn't the Superman his family always made him out to be. Hell, if he weren't so self-centered, he'd be back in the Bay Area with them instead of chasing his pro hockey dreams. He "took care of them" by spending money, which was selfish in itself because it soothed his conscience.

"I think you're giving me way too much credit, Sar."

As if she hadn't heard him, she barreled on. "You're also wise beyond your years, Little Bro, though God knows where you get it from. Not Mom or Dad, that's for damn sure."

"I get it from Grandma," he said without thinking. He felt a familiar stab in his chest. God, he missed her. How long had it been since he'd talked to her? He needed to call her. Today. Would she know who he was? Would she know what a *phone* was?

"And another thing," his sister continued. "You *do* know how to act around kids. Don't you visit kids in the hospital and sponsor a kids' hockey team?"

"Yeah, but that's different."

"Is it? How old is the daughter?"

"Five." A thought flared in his brain. "Same age as my mites."

"There's your answer!" Triumph rang in Sarah's voice. "Take the little girl skating. Get to know her and let her get to know you. If she doesn't already skate, teach her. Hell, add her to your mites team!"

"Huh. Hadn't considered it."

"That's why you have me, the all-seeing, all-knowing—"

"Thanks, Yoda," he deadpanned. "What if I make her nervous, though?"

"You don't make anybody nervous. Well, except the goalies who want to drop their jockstraps when they see you streaking in," she laughed. "Look, just relax and be yourself. That's really all you need to do."

Though he wasn't convinced Sarah had it right, he texted Lily when he hung up. *About the fan mail ...*

His phone chirped immediately. *Well, hello to you too, Professor. I haven't had a chance to dig in yet.*

He could practically hear her musical laugh, and he found himself smiling at nothing in particular. Like a complete idiot.

Gage: *No problem. I was thinking we should go through it together here.*

Lily: *Where's here?*

Gage: *My place. That way you can see where and how I live. More background for social media. Or I could come to yours if it's easier.*

His breathing stalled during the long minutes it took her to reply.

Lily: *Probably better if I come to yours. When?*

Gage: *Two hours from now?*

That would give him enough time to spruce the place up and run out to buy drinks and snacks. What did kids eat anyway?

Lily: *I pick Daisy up from school in an hour so she'll be with me.*

What he'd hoped for. At least he thought so. He pulled in a breath to quell his spiking nerves. *Bring her. Perfect time for me to meet her. She can hang with Hobbes. Unless she's allergic. Is she allergic to cats? Or she can play video games. Do you let her play video games?*

Lily: *Are you sure you're not a serial killer luring us to our doom?*

Gage: *No, I'm not sure, but being a serial killer is bad for PR, right? Shit. Now I have to give it up before I even get started. You're taking all the fun out of this.*

Lily: *LOL. I do what I can.*

"And you do it very well," he chuckled aloud.

Hobbes gave him a look that seemed to say, "You're acting like a complete and utter doofus. You know this, right?"

"Yeah, I know," he answered the cat, as if to prove that yes, he *was* a total doofus by addressing the damn thing in the first place.

And if anyone was luring anyone to their doom, it was him luring himself.

Lily crept her Highlander up an inclined driveway to a wide wood-and-stone affair nestled among tall evergreens, with peaked roofs and massive decks. It screamed of masculinity yet was warm and inviting. Like its owner.

Said owner stepped out of the front door and pointed her farther up the drive toward a three-car garage.

She parked her SUV, and he opened her door before she could gather up the bin of mail, her coat, or anything else.

His eyes scanned the inside of her car, and his face seemed to fall. "You're alone?"

"Yeah, Derek called at the last minute and wanted Daisy to come with him and Vi to the Downtown Aquarium."

He took this news in, stepped back from the car, and nodded.

"Is that … is that okay?" Kinda late, but still, it hadn't occurred to her that Gage might actually be disappointed Daisy wasn't with her. No, she must have been reading him wrong. *What single twenty-six-year-old guy wants a five-year-old running around his place?*

He scratched his beard. "No, that's fine. I didn't know what she liked, so I stocked up on juice boxes and Goldfish and fruit leather and animal crackers and … But they'll hold."

Oh my God! He wanted her here? And oh my God! That's so sweet.

Lily stared at the gorgeous, adorably flummoxed man standing outside her car, dressed in soft, faded jeans, gray T-shirt under an open blue-and-gray flannel shirt cuffed midway up his strong forearms. And on his feet? Fuzzy sheepskin slippers.

She was speechless. And motionless until he held out his arms. "Load me up, Goldilocks."

Shaking herself from her daze, realizing he wasn't inviting *her* to jump into his arms, she fumbled and shoved the container at him, which he caught with an "Oof!"

Horrified, she leapt from the car. "Oh, I'm so sorry!"

"No, it's fine," he laughed as he bobbled it in his grasp. "I just wasn't expecting it to come at me quite so quickly. What else ya got?"

She snatched her purse and portfolio from the backseat, along with a few files. "Just these."

He thrust his full arms at her. "Throw them in here."

She did as he asked, noticing the way his bare forearms flexed as he adjusted the load. He canted his head toward the front door, and she headed inside with him trailing behind. The place was open, spacious, with lots of angles and windows, yet it somehow maintained a coziness that reminded her of him. The foyer where they stood opened onto a sunken family room with a stone fireplace that soared to a vaulted wooden ceiling. To one side was a dining room with a rustic table and too many chairs to count. Did he entertain a lot? Behind it, open to the family room, was a cook's dream kitchen that featured a wide window running the length of a granite counter. The view beyond was of manicured pines on a sloping hill hugged by natural ground cover.

Gage veered off in the opposite direction. "This way."

She followed him into a manly office with lots of dark wood and an enormous desk that spanned a width of floor-to-ceiling windows, offering the same evergreen scene.

"Wow! What a view!"

He deposited the container on one end of the desk. "Like it? Me too. It's one of the reasons I bought the place. C'mon. I'll show you around."

Um ... "That'd be great?" When was the last time she'd been alone with a man—who wasn't Derek—in his house? A *hot* man at that.

Gage arched an eyebrow at her. "If you're going to do my PR, you need to get a feel for how I live and what I do in my downtime at home, right?"

"Makes sense." She pulled out her chain, sliding the ring smoothly along its length, suddenly in need of its weighty comfort as she followed him out of the office.

"And if you're a good girl and work really hard, I'll even cook you something. I make killer wings. T.J. once asked me to marry him, he liked them so much." Pride made an appearance on his chiseled features.

Another surprising side to this man she had so much more to learn about.

Okay. Onward. But no deets about bedroom downtime, please. Why did that make her uncomfortable? Give her a twinge of jealousy?

A little scowl creased the space between his brows. "Don't like wings?"

Her nerves all seemed to fire at once. "No. I mean, yes! I mean, um, how long will you need me here today?"

My inner idiot's brilliant attempt at redirection.

His scowl twisted into a question mark. "I don't know. How long have you got?" They entered the kitchen, and he paused to point out the pantry and laundry room before coming to a stop and perching his fists on his hips. And there was that lethal smile in its full, brilliant wattage. It made her knees feel all gooey, and that was bad. Really bad. The familiar flutters from last summer were wreaking havoc in her body, and she told herself to keep her distance.

Gage's eyes caught on the ring she jerked over her necklace. "Is that ...? Never mind."

She heaved out a breath just as an orange tabby cat sauntered in, the tip of its tail dancing in the air as though on an invisible string. "This must be Hobbes?" She dropped to a knee and offered her hand for the cat to smell.

"Yep, that's Hobbes. I sort of adopted him, but I didn't think it through very well."

The cat took a sniff, then rubbed its head against the back of her hand. "What do you mean?"

He leaned against the counter and crossed his arms. A slight flex did wonders for both his forearms *and* the chest filling the T-shirt, and she quickly diverted her gaze back to Hobbes.

"Well," he said, "I set up an appointment with Natalie's vet but totally spaced that I'm out of town for an away game. I can probably reschedule that, but now that I've let him move in, I'll need to find a pet-sitter to take care of him when I'm gone for long stretches. And Natalie only does dogs. Like I said, I didn't think it through."

"I might be able to take the cat to the vet, if it would help you out. I could also stop by to check on food and water and make sure the litter box stays clean. Cats don't need much."

Um, exactly why am I volunteering for cat duty?

Gage's blue eyes brightened. "You'd do that?"

And his sweet reaction is exactly why. "Sure. You don't live that far away."

He smoothed the back of his neck. "Wow. That's ... Are you a cat person?"

"Not really, but I grew up with them. Oh, and I know enough to tell that Hobbes is definitely not a boy." Her mouth quirked as she tried to corral a grin.

"What?" Gage appeared genuinely shocked.

The cat nuzzled her chin as if to say, "We chicas gotta stick together." Lily stood and let the grin break out. "You might need a lesson in anatomy, Professor."

Bright pink slashes decorated his sculpted cheekbones. "Kinda thought I had a good grasp on anatomy," he muttered. "At least the human kind."

An unexpected jolt traveled from her chest to her lady parts. "Um, while that may be true, cats are a different breed. Literally." Now *her* cheekbones heated.

He flashed her a playful smile. "Well, thanks for that anyway. I think."

An awkward pause hung heavy between them. "So," he said, "any suggestions for what to call the cat?"

"If she's used to Hobbes, I'd just stick with that. She doesn't need to know you gave her a boy name." Lily winked at him before she could stop herself, and if it were possible, his cheekbones flushed a darker shade of pink.

She checked a giggle and squared her shoulders. "About that tour ..."

"Ah. Right this way." He seemed glad for the distraction.

The tour lasted all of ten minutes and ended in a second family room repurposed as a TV-slash-gaming-slash music room featuring an impressive collection of basses and guitars adorning the walls. Lily took her time running her eyes over a variety of vintage Fenders and Gibsons.

"My collection's only a fraction of say, Joe Bonamassa's," he said behind her, "but I'm hoping to add to it over time."

She hovered her fingers over a lustrous Fender Stratocaster Sunburst. "What a beauty," she whispered reverently.

"You know that one?" His voice was full of surprise. "Of course you do. What was I thinking? Do you play?"

She shook her head, refraining from adding that Jack had always coveted this particular guitar. Funny how thinking about him wasn't causing her eyes to burn with unshed tears—for which she was blissfully grateful.

Pivoting on her heel, she nearly ran into Gage standing behind her. He took a step back, looking a little lost, as though he searched for words to steer them out of another awkward moment. "Did Jack play in the band too?"

Not what she expected. "Yes. He and Derek started it in high school." Gage gave her an encouraging nod, and she went on. "Jack could play just about anything, but he especially loved the guitar," she explained. "Derek was the more accomplished guitarist of the two, so Jack became the bass player." Until now, she'd forgotten that Jack hadn't been as good as Derek and that he'd fought Derek over the change.

Gage's deep, mellow voice soothed her back to the present. "Does it help to talk about him?"

His expression, so heartfelt, so genuine, plucked her heartstrings. "I'm not sure," she answered truthfully, searching his eyes. For what, she couldn't say. Something else caught her attention. "Did you know your eyes are two different colors of blue?"

He shrugged. "Depends on the day. Usually, they're the same."

"I hadn't noticed it before. They're beautiful," she blurted.

He didn't move, but his eyes dug a little deeper into hers. "So are yours," he said softly. "I thought so the first time I saw you."

A meow came from the floor, startling them both.

Gage rolled his eyes. "Jesus, cat! Scared the shit out of me!" Hobbes rubbed herself against his leg as if to make amends.

Lily burst out with a pent-up laugh that was more laced with emotion than it was with humor.

"Probably time we got to work on the fan mail anyway," Gage said,

Right. Fan mail. Focus, Lil. Somehow she knew it wasn't going to be that easy.

Chapter 12

Crush, Crush

Cockblocked by a cat. Not that Gage had planned to do anything about the burgeoning problem in his pants—the one that had been bothering him since Lily had first arrived. Too many pictures had been streaming through his head, and they'd taken a detour to his groin: tracing his thumbs over her silky skin, pulling that bottom lip between his and running the tip of his tongue along it, drawing her close and feeling all that pillowy softness against him. Exploring the mouthwatering roundness of her hips and breasts between the curvy guitar bodies that always reminded him of curvy female bodies. Taking her against the wall right here in the music room.

Stop. This. Shit. Now.

"Professor, why don't you date?"

The question shocked him right out of his racy reverie, doing a better job shutting down his lust than any rebuke he could inflict on himself. "Excuse me?"

"You don't date. There are dozens of women dying to get their hands on you—maybe even all at the same time—yet you seem ... nonplussed by it. Uninterested. Why?"

The last bit she said nonchalantly, as if *not* referring to their previous sexcapade, which left him contemplating the same question. Did she have any interest in dating him at all? Did she think about it like *he* did, which was pretty much all the time? "Why, exactly, are you asking?" Hope floated.

"Judging by your mail, women make up a huge percentage of your fan base. Understanding more about you will help me craft the best approach when I respond to them on your behalf."

Hope sank. *Damn*. "Ah. I see. Well, the women I meet are ... For the most part, they're interested in the hockey player, not me."

"Don't you meet women you're attracted to outside that world?"

At the moment, he could only think of one. "If I do, they're usually unavailable."

"Unavailable as in married?"

He stared at the bookshelves beyond her. "Not married. Just ... unobtainable."

"Can you give me an example?"

Yeah, the one I'm looking at right now. But if she knows, she'll bolt quicker than a bronc out of his pen.

He searched his brain for a name, any name, and unfortunately blurted out, "Kathryn Tappen."

Lily's expression transformed from curious to downright bewildered. And who could blame her? He was giving himself another Grandma head slap, trying to shake sense into his addled brain because, really, could he sound any stupider? The thought he *could* was disconcerting.

Lily now sported a triumphant look. "Oho!" she sang. "Don't tell me. Supermodel?"

He hid his mouth behind his fist, biting back a laugh, and shook his head.

"Actress? Victoria's Secret Angel? Playboy Playmate?" she prodded, her face eager like Hobbes when he—she—got a Meow Mix treat. Lily was too damn irresistible when she thought she was about to solve a mystery.

"Let's go back to the office," he deflected. *Less chance of getting distracted by curvy guitars and everything I want to do to you here.* He needed clean, hard angles to get himself back on track, to remain rooted in reality. To settle the fuck down until he could properly address his aching need.

Her head did an odd nod-and-shake motion, as if she couldn't decide yes or no. Then it dipped, exposing the smooth line of her neck. He pictured his tongue and teeth on that neck, and his dick perked up. Again.

"Okay," she agreed.

Office, asshole! She means going to the office, not sinking your teeth in her neck.

Back in said office, he pointed her to his executive chair and stood as far from her as he could while still staying inside the room. No need getting a noseful of sweet flowers and fresh something. His mind was messed up enough, thank you very much, being controlled as it was by his clamoring cock.

"So who's Kathryn Tapping?" was Lily's next logical question.

"Kathryn *Tappen,*" he corrected, pausing to clear his shockingly Mickey Mouse-like voice, "is a sports announcer."

Confusion clouded Lily's features once more. She slid her phone from the pocket of her ass-clinging jeans and began scrolling. "Ohhhh, I see. And wow! She's stunning."

"Yeah, but she's smart, and she knows her hockey, probably better than the personalities she's paired with," he added helpfully. Yeah, that didn't make him sound like he had a schoolboy crush in the least—which he didn't. He just liked watching her on TV, like lots of fans did.

Lily blinked. "Do you know her?"

"Nope. Never met the lady."

Pixie-ish nose pointed back at her phone, she said, "Looks like she's single. So if she's the reason you're not dating, are you, you know, saving yourself for her?"

He burst out with a laugh. "Saving myself?"

"Yes. Like you don't want to get involved with someone else because you might miss a chance with her."

Was she serious? He scanned her face but didn't find the answer. "Lily, I was only joking. I'm not worried about missing a chance because I'm not looking for a chance. While I may *be* stupid, I'm not stupid enough to believe I ever stood a chance." *Shit. That didn't come out right. Makes it sound as though no one can live up to Kathryn T, including Lily.*

"It's fantasy, like looking at an actor on the screen and daydreaming. That's all," he tried to explain but only seemed to deepen the hole he was digging. "I ... It's nothing. She's nothing." *And frankly, Lily Everett, after setting eyes on you, I'd forgotten who Kathryn Tappen is.*

Lily gave him a calculating look without a hint that she thought he was a babbling moron. She slid her phone back into her pocket and tapped a finger against that plump lower lip of hers. "I have an idea, Professor."

If that idea involves me showing you how comfortable my mattress is, I'm all in.

His semi stiffened to full mast. *Shit.* Why had he thought having Lily work at his home was a good idea?

Because he was, in fact, stupid.

While Gage shifted from one foot to the other, Lily fought the smile that tugged her lips. Oh Lord, this man was going to kill her with cuteness. And if it was an act to cover up a smooth playboy persona, he was doing a damn fine job, though she had a hard time believing it was an act.

He reached down to scratch Hobbes's ears. "You have an idea?" he prompted.

"Would you like to meet her?" Lily ventured.

Gage looked as though he'd just been shaken out of a dozy nap. "Meet her who?"

Lily waved her hand grandly in the air. "This Kathryn person. I mean, you're certainly ... uh ..." Her brain locked on to the words "hotness personified" for some unfathomable reason, and she gave herself an inner shake and recovered. "What I meant to say was that lots of hockey players date A-list celebrities. Look at Mike Fisher and Carrie Underwood."

One dark eyebrow dipped. "If I'm the player picked for an interview between periods, and if Kathryn Tappen's the one with the mic, then I'd be happy to meet her."

"Would you ask her out?"

Wide blue eyes and the rest of his expression broadcast that he thought she was nuts. "Would I *what*?"

She crammed on her social media consultant hat. "Hear me out. What if I set something up through Twitter for you? Like when Anthony Beauvillier tweeted Anna Kendrick? That flirtation went viral! Did you see how many other NHL players jumped on the bandwagon to get those two together? And they only made up a fraction of the likes."

Shock—no, horror—overtook his features. "What? Why would I do that?"

"So you can meet her. Kathryn, not Anna."

His head began shaking before Lily had finished the sentence. "No way. Absolutely not."

Oddly buoyed by his reactions, she let genuine curiosity spur her on. "You don't want to meet her?"

"First of all, I prefer to keep my private life private." He gave her a pointed look. "If I'm going to embarrass myself, I'm not doing it in public. Second of all, how and why did we get on this subject, and can we just move on?"

"I don't get it. You just want to, what, admire her from afar?"

He shot upright from the edge of the desk. "I don't want anything! She's just someone I admire. I admire Mario Lemieux and Mother Teresa, but it doesn't mean I want to date them."

"Well, Mother Teresa *is* dead."

His mouth curled into a smirk. "You're being a total pain in the ass, you know that?"

Yeah, she knew it, but she was having too much fun trying to push buttons and see if she could get a rise out of him. Undaunted, she raced on. "What if I could get an interview set up with Kathryn?"

His mouth opened, but nothing came out. A look of—was that disappointment?—flashed across his face and morphed into a frown. "While I have no doubt you could pull off anything you set your mind to, I don't want you playing my social director. Let's just stick to the script we agreed to—social *media*—when you first twisted my arm into hiring you."

A laugh squeezed from her lungs. "I didn't twist your arm."

"Yeah, you did." He gave her a sly wink. "You should never underestimate your power of persuasion, Goldilocks. I sure don't." His chiseled cheekbones flushed fuchsia.

Where they still talking about the same thing? Or had they segued to last summer's intimate encounter? *Her* cheeks flared with heat.

"Um, okay. So no setups, Professor?"

A chuckle rumbled from his chest. "No setups."

In that moment, it struck Lily that Kathryn—*any* woman—would be lucky to have Gage Nelson pursue her. She tried to shake off her mind's meanderings with a sharp inhale. Fortunately for her, her phone vibrated in her back pocket and gave her something else to do besides standing there looking into Gage's uneven—and thoroughly amused—blue eyes.

Seeing Derek's face on her screen sent her heart into worry overdrive.

"Hey, Der. Is everything okay?" She glanced at Gage, whose playful expression had shifted, reflecting the uneasiness she felt.

"Everything's fine, Lil. Just wanted you to know we got to your place a little early. What time were you planning on being home?"

Her shoulders dropped with relief. Still holding Gage's gaze, she said, "I can leave now and be there in fifteen."

"That's fine. Don't rush. I'm good to hang out for a little bit."

"Okay, thanks. If you're hungry, there's some roast beef in the fridge. Feel free to make yourself a sandwich."

He laughed. "I like the way you make them better."

She suppressed an eye-roll but smiled in spite of herself. "Is this your way of telling me you want me to make you one when I get home?"

"Bingo! That's exactly what I'm telling you."

"All right. I'll be there soon." She ended the call.

Gage's eyes bored into hers. She glimpsed ... hurt? Disappointment? "So Daisy's okay?" he said.

"She's fine. Derek was just giving me a heads-up that they got home early."

"To your place. I guess he has a key?"

"Well, yes." Something in his demeanor made her rush to explain. "I have a key to his place too. It makes it easier with the kids."

He folded his arms across his chest. "Ah. Is it just Derek, then?"

Gage's question teetered her off balance. "Who has a key, you mean?" Why was he asking?

"No, I meant does Derek have other family? Siblings? Parents?"

"No. Their parents died in a helicopter crash years ago, which left the two brothers. Now it's just Derek." The finality brought a rush of tears, building pressure behind her eyes and clawing her throat. With a hard swallow and a series of rapid blinks, she squeezed them off.

Gage nodded. "You make him dinner often?" His expression was neutral, bland even, giving away none of the thoughts streaming behind those blue eyes.

"No. And I only said I'd make him a sandwich when I got home. It's just a snack. Which is the least I can do, considering how much he helps me out. Not just with Daisy, but he does little things around the house for me all the time. He takes good care of us." *Because Jack can't.* She dropped her voice, fighting a telltale quaver. "Where are you going with this?"

He shrugged. "Just curious. Wondering if there's a chance you and he might ..."

Now she folded her arms across her chest and cocked a brow. Why did she feel like a lover being put on the spot for ... what, exactly? "Might what?"

"If you've ever gotten together. If you think you might ever *get* together."

She suspected what he'd been aiming at, but suspecting and hearing were completely different, and his words about Derek made her recoil. And why was Gage asking anyway? Did she detect a hint of jealousy? Possessiveness? Funny. She warmed slightly to the feeling it evoked—of being wanted.

But Derek and her? "Absolutely not."

"It just seems like a natural—"

"He tried. Once. When he was really drunk." Admitting it aloud shocked her. She'd never told anyone, not even Ivy.

Gage's expression hardened, and though he didn't say a word, his posture reflected a steeliness that made her rush to explain. She wanted the episode off her chest anyway.

She pulled in a deep breath. "I have no idea why I'm telling you this, but it was on the anniversary of Jack's death a few years ago. Derek and Violet's mom had just split up. We'd both been drinking, talking, grieving. And then we were crying, and Derek put his arms around me to ... to comfort me. He was emotional. We both were. He got a little carried away. I don't know who was more mortified." A shoulder shrug eased some of her tension. "It was ... awkward, to say the least. He apologized, and that was it. Nothing else ever happened, so I'd call it a blip of weirdness that came and went. End of story."

Gage's expression hadn't wavered. "Do you worry he'll try again?"

"What? No! He ... he feels protective of Daisy and me, like it's his job now that Jack's gone. Derek's the only Everett male left. He's taking care of his tribe. It's the same way you are with your family. Does it make sense in that context?"

Seeming to ease, Gage glanced at the ceiling before landing his gaze back on her. "Yeah, it makes sense."

She felt a flush of unexpected relief.

"C'mon. I'll walk you to your car so you can get home and make Derek a sandwich." He smiled, and whatever had been tilted inside her was suddenly upright again.

Chapter 13

Game On

A thought struck Gage as Lily drove away. He'd been so thrown off by trying to grasp the nature of her relationship with Derek that he'd totally forgotten to ask about another chance to meet Daisy. Didn't help that Derek had interrupted. Just like it didn't help to learn he'd made a move on Lily once. The thought twisted Gage's insides with surprising primal fierceness.

Fucking Derek.

Pushing a few cleansing breaths through his lungs, he put the thorny thought aside and swiped his phone.

"Hello?" his grandma said after two rings.

"Hi, Grandma. It's Gage."

"Hello?"

"Grandma? Can you hear me?"

"Hello?"

"Grandma!" he shouted.

Some fumbling on the other end, and he repeated her name once, twice with no answer. Then the line went dead. He dialed again, but it rang and rang and eventually went to voicemail she would never check. Had no comprehension *how* to check.

After reaching Evelyn, Skyview's receptionist, to be sure his grandmother was, in fact, all right, he dialed his mom.

"Gage," she bubbled. "Honey, it's so nice to finally hear your voice."

Yeah, heap on a helping of guilt. He should have called sooner.

They chatted about benign subjects like the weather, hockey, and Grandma.

During a lull in the conversation, his mother took an unfortunate detour. "Have you spoken to Jessica lately?"

Caught off guard, he sputtered, "No. Why?"

"Oh, Gage," his mother tsked, disappointment dripping from her voice. "She says she's left you messages. Haven't you returned *any* of her calls yet? I thought I raised you with better manners than that."

The rebuke made him bristle, but he let it go. Not wanting to let his mom down—again—he opted for a different strategy besides the out-and-out direct approach. "With playoffs coming and everything on my plate right now, I've just been too busy."

"Maybe she could come stay with you and take your mind off things for a few days. She has some time off coming up, you know."

Astonishment rocked him. *Jesus, pushy much?* He opted not to ask how his mom knew Jessica's vacation schedule and went for casual instead. "Not a good idea, Mom. I wouldn't be able to keep her company. She'd just be sitting around staring at four walls."

"She could come to your games, cook you some nice meals, do your laundry."

"You mean be my maid? Maybe she could trim the trees while she's at it or refinish my deck," he joked, hoping she'd get the hint.

Either she didn't get it or she refused to. "Jessica's a master in the kitchen, Gage. Remember? And she thinks you're so perfect, you know, like we all do. You can't be upset with her for wanting to be part of your life again."

Oh man, she is not going to give up! And there was that word again—perfect. Ha! If he were so damn perfect, he wouldn't have gotten all bent out of shape over Derek *or* Jack Everett when he had no right to.

Squelching his frustration, he used a familiar dodge. "Look, Mom, I've gotta go. I, uh, have a team meeting I need to get to."

This was met by a long-suffering sigh. "Please just think about it, Gage."

"Think about what?"

"About inviting Jessica out. Your house must be so empty and quiet. Wouldn't it be lovely to hear a woman's voice?"

It *had* been nice to hear a woman's voice in his house today—because of who that woman was. Someone entirely different from the one his mom had in mind. "Mom, I've really got to go."

Another fluttering sigh. "All right. Honestly, Gage, I wouldn't carry on if I weren't worried about you."

Fingers massaging his forehead, patience on a fine thread, Gage cut off the call. "I love you, Mom. Don't worry, okay? I'm fine. I'll call you next week."

An exasperated breath whooshed from him after he disconnected. He plopped on his couch, picked up his guitar, and cranked up the amplifier. *Time for some blues.* He played classics like "Mustang Sally" and "Shelter Me," but the songs didn't keep his mom's words from ringing in his ears, so he switched his mind's grinding gears.

His conversation with Grims had been on a loop in his head, and he tuned in a little more closely. *Fall for the mom, fall for the kid.* What about the reverse? What if the kid fell for you? Would the mom follow?

Back all the way up, dude. You are so far ahead of yourself that you're gonna get whistled for offsides.

But then his conversation with Sarah floated to the forefront. Locating his phone, he tapped out a message to Lily: *Does Daisy skate?*

Lily: *Sort of?*

Gage: *Would she like to learn?*

He thought better of the text and replaced it with: *Would you like her to learn? I know a professor who can teach her. LOL.*

Lily: *She'd love it.*

Gage: *How about her mama?*

Lily: *She's pretty iffy. LOL.*

Gage: *I have mini mites Saturday morning. Come by and I'll get her set up.*

Lily: *To play mites???*

Gage: *Probably best if she has the basics first, but whatever she wants.*

Lily: *Are you serious?*

Gage: *As a game misconduct.*

Lily: *She'll be so excited. See you then, Professor.*

He sent her details, slid the phone on the coffee table, and leaned back, hands laced behind his head. For the first time in hours, satisfaction thrummed in his chest.

Saturday morning couldn't come fast enough. He was on the ice setting up practice cones with the assistant coaches when his gaze caught on a froth of blond hair on the other side of the glass, close by the open door where the mini mites would soon stream onto the ice.

He squinted. Either he was seeing double or there were *two* heads with springy blond curls, one taller than the other. He made for the door, and the sight through the Plexiglas sharpened. Lily, a tentative smile on her face, stood behind a little girl no taller than his mites. The girl's wide eyes were fixed on the rink, and she sported a smile that seemed to take over her whole face. Pointing at the ice, she tilted her head upward at Lily and began bouncing in place. He nearly laughed out loud.

Lily kept her eyes pinned to his as he reached the door and stepped onto the rubberized floor. No lie, that step was more of a spring. He found himself buoyed, excited to meet this pint-sized replica of her mom.

"Hey." He flashed Lily the first smile.

"Hey," she replied, her smile growing a little surer, a little wider.

His eyes traveled to the little girl, who was unabashedly gawking at him. He dropped into a crouch in front of her, leveling his gaze with hers. She had clear silvery-gray orbs and was missing a tooth.

"Hi." He held out his hand. "I'm Gage."

With a shy giggle, she pressed her back into Lily's legs. Lily rested her hands on the girl's shoulders and gave her a light squeeze.

"Daisy, use your manners. Say hello to ... to Mr. Gage."

He dropped his hand, dangling it from his knee. "Did you know your mom helps me with my work? She and I are friends, so I think that makes you and me friends too." He cocked a questioning eyebrow at Lily, silently asking for guidance. *How do I play this? What do I do next?*

Lily seemed to haul in a breath. "Gage, this is—"

"I'm Daisy," the girl declared. "And this is my mom." Another giggle, and she threw her head against Lily and gazed up at her.

Lily ran her fingers through Daisy's whorls. "You've told him your name, but you still haven't said hello. Can you say hello now?"

Those luminous gray eyes locked on to his. "Hello, Mr. Cage." She squirmed in her mother's arms.

Lily leaned down to Daisy's ear. "Mr. Gage, sweetie."

"Mr. Cage."

"Mr. Cage is fine," he offered. "Your mom tells me you're ready to skate."

She nodded solemnly before roaming her eyes back to the ice, where something seemed to capture all her attention. She left the shelter of her mother's legs and pressed her forehead to the glass, her conversation with Gage utterly abandoned.

He stood, taking note of the tender look in Lily's eyes as she watched her daughter. The inexplicable urge to circle his arms around them both seized him until he mentally shook it off. He steadied his breath and schooled his features before leaning down to Lily. "Ready to go to the pro shop and get her fitted for some skates?"

"Yes." *Thank you*, she mouthed, making him feel about twelve feet tall. She extended her hand to Daisy. "Come on, sweet pea. Let's get you some skates."

Daisy spun, bypassed her mom's hand, and slipped her tiny one into Gage's, surprising him. With her head thrown back to look up at him, she said, "My mom says you're gonna teach me to play hockey, Mr. Cage."

If all it took was looks to fall under someone's spell, he was a goner for this little cutie.

He gave her doll-like hand a squeeze of his fingers. “I am. And I bet you’ll be flying around the rink in no time.” He winked at Lily. “And maybe we can get your mom out there too. What do you think, Daisy?”

Blond curls bobbed. “I like that. I like you, Mr. Cage.”

His heart might have cracked open and oozed. Or maybe it had been turned to putty. He wasn’t sure. But he was sure of what he said next.

“I like you too, Daisy.”

Though Lily had only brought Daisy to skate with Gage—well, Gage’s mites team—a few times now, she was growing accustomed to the unpleasant smells that assaulted her whenever she set foot inside the rink complex: a combination of chemicals, an odd variant on mustiness, and the tang of reeking gear bags. She was making other adjustments too, like weaving Gage’s crazy schedule into hers and feeding Hobbes when the Blizzard hit the road. The routine—if one could call it that—had become comfortable, like a cozy wool wrap.

Skating, playing on mini mites, was all Daisy could talk about—and “Mr. Cage.” Mr. Cage was making his first appearance today in over two weeks, having flown in early this morning after an extended road trip. Lily felt a lift of excitement as her eyes searched him out on the ice. They caught on Derek at the bottom of the bleachers, laughing with one of the hockey moms.

He gave a start when he spotted Lily. “Hey, didn’t see you come in.” The mom withdrew with an eyelash-fluttering, “See you soon, Derek.”

Lily bit back a smirk. “Thanks for bringing Daisy. I really appreciate it.” She stared into his eyes for a beat, trying to recall if Jack’s had been the same shade of gray.

“Yeah, no problem. I’m always there for you, Lil. You know that.”

A figure clad in black warm-ups, sporting a backward Blizzard ball cap, skated at them and loomed on the other side of the glass.

She'd recognize that dazzling smile anywhere, and her heart knocked a little harder against her ribcage. She beamed back at "Mr. Cage." His eyes strafed Derek, who gave him a frosty chin jerk before turning and leaving.

Gage yelled through the glass, his muffled voice asking if she wanted to lace up and join them. His grin broadened. She shook her head adamantly. Yeah, she hadn't done that yet, self-conscious as she was by her wobbly ankles next to Gage's smooth, even strides. The man was silk on ice.

Once more alone, Lily began a slow walk around the perimeter of the rink, taking pictures from different angles with her phone. Careful not to record the kids' features or jersey numbers, she threw herself into capturing candid shots for social media. *Number Six doing his part for the kids and the community.*

Lingering a moment, pondering a different vantage point, she watched Daisy skirt a series of orange cones. She laughed inwardly at the huge helmet that seemed three times too big for her little body. All the mites wore them, reminding Lily of a gang of Dark Helmet clones from *Spaceballs.*

Daisy toppled to the ice and slid into oncoming skaters like a bowling ball heading for quaking pins. Lily sucked in a breath. Before she could let it out, Gage was there, easily scooping Daisy up and out of harm's way. He set her upright on her skates, his big hand splayed across the width of her tummy. Bending over her, almost cradling her, he was telling Daisy something because her huge helmet bobbed vigorously. He released her, and she flew toward her teammates lining up for the next drill.

Lily's heart stuttered for a beat before liquefying into a warm puddle of glop. Tears rushed up her throat and throbbed behind her eyes. She blinked furiously to keep them in check. Gage chose just that moment to look up at her, wave, and send her another smile that was probably meant to reassure her but about cut her off at the knees. What was wrong with her? Crap. She was so damn emotional lately.

Shaking it off, she told herself it was nothing more than a monthly surge of hormones. Except her monthlies never affected her. Not like this.

The session ended, and the kids corralled pucks before filing off the ice. Gage and two other men stacked the cones, skated the nets to the side, and gathered assorted debris. Lily made her way to the waiting area outside the locker rooms, glancing at the chattering mothers too absorbed to notice her.

"Goldilocks!" a rich, deep voice called playfully behind her. She wheeled, oddly gratified that Gage's eyes were fastened on her. Only her. "Glad to see you could make it," he breathed as he drew up beside her. He sent the moms a smile and a quick head bob.

"Derek was watching her, and he offered to bring her so I could finish up some errands."

"Ah. That explains—"

"Would you like to grab some coffee somewhere?" she interrupted.

One side of his mouth hitched up in another smile. "Absolutely."

They stopped at Caribou Coffee, where Gage let Lily treat him to a latte. Seated at a small round table by a fireplace, Daisy took turns drinking her hot chocolate and talking animatedly about the fluky goal she'd squeaked in during the scrimmage.

"That was a beauty five-hole, Daisy. You slid that sucker in right between his pads before he could close it down. Way to show the other kids how it's done." He held out his fist for a bump, then high-fived, middle-fived, and low-fived her.

Daisy beamed. "That's Mr. Cage's and my special handshake, Mommy."

"It's the goal-scorer's handshake." Gage winked at Lily before turning his eyes back to Daisy. "You can call me Coach, Daisy. All the other kids do."

A very solemn nod. "I will, Mr. Cage." She slurped her drink.

He reached out, hovering his hand by her cup. "You're running low on whipped cream, kiddo. If your mom says it's okay, why don't I ask them to add more? Goal-scorers should get extra whipped cream."

His heart-melting sweetness shot straight to Lily's heart.

Daisy flashed her a gap-toothed hockey smile. "Can I, Mom? Pleeeeeeease?"

Lily wasn't sure what touched her more: Daisy's plea, Gage's waggling eyebrows, or the fact the two seemed to be conspiring against her in good fun ... like a family would.

She put up a mock protest and gave in quickly. Unable to stop herself, she tracked Gage as he headed to the counter, his powerful thighs visible in gym shorts, a long-sleeved, body-hugging T-shirt showing off his fine chiseled torso. The man had muscles on top of muscles; muscles in places Lily hadn't known existed on the human body. Maybe she needed a refresher course in anatomy herself.

He still sported the backward ball cap, and his hair poked through the hole in front, tempting Lily to tug on it when he returned with a full cup of whipped cream. He sat and braced sculpted forearms on his impossibly thick thighs.

Is it hot in here, or is it him?

He passed his hand in front of her face, snapping her to attention. He was giving her his blinding, high-wattage smile—the one she wished she could capture and bottle. "Where'd you go, Goldilocks?"

Crap! He'd busted her.

"I was just ... thinking about the loads of laundry I still have to do," she stammered. Thank God he had no clue she'd been caught up in lusty daydreams about *him*.

"Ah," he grinned. "No shortage of exciting thoughts in that busy brain of yours."

She barked out a completely over-the-top laugh, which did nothing to blow off her rising nervousness.

Every minute spent with him shifted her image of Gage Nelson, even as it nudged her into a world of mixed-up emotions that confounded her. She felt as though she chased fireflies circling just above her head. Dazzling, alluring. If only she could snatch them, but the farther she stretched, the more elusive they became. One wrong move, an overreach, and she would stumble and face-plant.

Chapter 14

Careless Whispers

Days later, Lily sat in her counseling session, her gaze roving around the room to the inky world beyond the window panes. The group's attention was currently commandeered by Eva, but Lily's focus was like that kid walking with one sneakered foot on the sidewalk and the other barefoot in the grass. Partly on its proper concrete course, and partly sinking into cool lushness.

Her thoughts meandered to the Sapphire Club next door and how her plodding course had quickened and changed since Gage strode back into her life—like a stagnant stream that transforms into boiling rapids.

His world seemed to be steadily, effortlessly entwining with Daisy's and hers. He was crispness and color, and his presence lifted the veil that had cast Lily in shades of blue-grays. She found herself wanting to breathe in more and more of him.

Eva's hiss jarred her back to the present. "He asked me out!"

"Your *dentist* asked you out?" one of the others said, and Lily exhaled a little sigh of relief. At least she wouldn't have to guess who *he* was. Admonishing herself, she made an inner promise to tune in to the conversation and stay engaged.

Eva nodded, looking utterly appalled. "Yes! Can you believe it?"

"Eva," Lily began, "you're a lovely woman, and he obviously finds you attractive. Take it for the compliment it is. It doesn't mean you have to accept his invitation. I understand it's a bit awkward because of his professional—"

"It's not that, Lily." Eva shook her head. "I don't mind that part. What I *mind* is the audacity of the man. He's only been widowed a few years! Has he gotten over his wife so quickly? What does that say about *him*? Why would I want to get involved with someone who gets over someone else so quickly?"

Expectant eyes fastened on Lily, and she straightened, her back as rigid as her seat. She squelched an eye-roll. "Everyone, let's talk about the grieving process again. As we've discussed, there isn't a set timetable. Some of us move on quickly, while some of us never move on. It doesn't mean we didn't love just as much as the next person. Think of those who have lost their husband or wife who never marry again because they were in an abusive relationship and don't want a repeat. If you judged based on the length of time they remained single, you'd say that person loved their spouse more, which just isn't true. On the other hand, you might see someone who marries within six months. Maybe that person had such a wonderful marriage that they want to do it again. So you see, everyone has a journey unique to *them*, and we shouldn't judge based on how long the grieving process takes within *us*. Does that make sense?"

The thought niggled that Lily was a harsh judge of her own grieving process, that she should listen to her own counsel, but she quickly dismissed it, instead watching the bobbing heads surrounding her.

"It's not at all unusual for a widower to seek companionship at this stage," she continued. "On average, they remarry sooner than widows."

"Well," Eva huffed, "I still can't see myself becoming romantically involved so soon."

"Which is perfectly fine," Lily said, "because you're on the timetable that works for *you*, Eva."

Though Lily's lips were tipped in a smile, she let shame claw its way up from her gut. Eva had been widowed longer than she, yet Lily had let herself fall into bed with a hot hockey player mere hours after meeting him! And here she was, getting all warm and fuzzy about enmeshing her life with his, and all the while her undeniable physical attraction to him was mounting.

"I hope you let him down easy, Eva," Brett laughed. "If you reacted to him the way you're reacting with us, you probably just shattered a fragile ego. It'll take him another few years to ask out someone else."

Eva struck a prim pose. "I was extremely polite."

The mood lightened, allowing Lily to shove down her self-flagellation while recovering herself. As the discussion came to a close, a last thought flared before she doused it: Was it so wrong for her mind to sometimes take a flight back to how good it had felt lying in Gage's arms? To feel the solid strength of a man's embrace?

Though it wasn't late, Eva waited while she locked up. Since Gage's appearance in the parking lot, Brett no longer tried to corner Lily, for which she was grateful. She was pretty sure he'd been shocked *and* intimidated by Gage's presence. And if he believed Gage was a love interest, she wasn't about to set him straight—the illusion kept things simpler.

"I really admire you, Lily," Eva said as they walked to their cars.

Lily didn't hide her delight. "Thank you, Eva. That means a lot. I hope these sessions are helping."

"They are, but that's not what I meant."

Lily paused and frowned. Eva dropped her voice, as if an unwelcome audience listened in. "What I meant was, I admire you because you're remaining true to your husband's memory. Oh, I know the others say you're young and you should get on with your life, but I say good for you! By not rushing out there, you're showing the world how much you loved him. I can relate to that."

Did she hear nothing I said?

Eva gave her a quick hug. "The world needs more loyal people like us, Lily."

Is waiting four years rushing it?

Lily climbed into her car in a muddled daze, trying to muster Jack's face as she drove. Without looking at a picture, his image in her mind's eye grew blurrier every day. As she'd done with Derek the week before, she concentrated hard to recall the exact shade of Jack's eyes. Two mismatched blue orbs popped into her head instead, and her guilt consumed her once more.

What was wrong with her?

When she got home, she marched straight to the rogues' gallery in the hallway and stared at the pictures hanging there. In some, Jack's eyes looked blue. In others, gray. In a few, they even appeared hazel. She grew frustrated trying to remember their color and flipped off the light.

She turned on an eighties station, poured herself a healthy glass of wine, and settled into her couch. Despite the music playing in the background, the house enveloped Lily in suffocating silence. Daisy was at Derek's tonight, and every wailing creak and lonely cry echoed around her.

God, she needed a distraction, or she'd spend another sleepless night thrashing in bed, trying to sharpen her dimming memories of Jack, keeping them alive for Daisy as much as herself—except Daisy hadn't asked about him in ages. What had he smelled like? She shuffled to her closet and stuck her nose in one of his shirts. The scent was faint, elusive. She slid it from the hanger, shrugged it on, and wrapped it around herself, inhaling the collar. She'd lost the smell.

Gage's fresh, masculine scent drifted in her mind, firing an inappropriate tickle inside her. She pressed her fists into her belly.

How had her body fit Jack's? What had it felt like to wind her arms around him? Splintered memories, like tattered dreams, streaked through her mind. She couldn't recall, but she knew exactly where her head nestled on Gage's warm chest.

"This is ridiculous!" She stomped to the kitchen and filled her wineglass. "I'll call Ivy." But Ivy was at work and wouldn't be able to talk Lily off of her present path. It was too late for Lily to call their parents, and she'd just traded news with them the day before anyway.

Loneliness was getting the best of her, and her mind leapt to calling Gage. But no, that might be weird. Plus, he was playing out of town.

Call Derek? Besides the girls, what would they talk about?

She palmed her forehead. God, she was pathetic.

Fisting the stem of her wineglass, she pulled in a few cleansing breaths. A familiar, haunting tune started up. George Michael's "Careless Whisper" seemed to climb in volume and surround her. As soon as his voice reached the part about guilty feet, tears welled, coming hot and fast, overwhelming the hollow space inside her. She folded over. Sobs racked her body as anguish swamped her.

When would it ever stop?

Time passed—she had no idea how long—and her phone chirped. Brushing the wetness from her chin and cheeks, she glanced at it, and a warm flood of relief washed through her when she realized it was from Gage.

About to take off and just wanted to see how your group went tonight.

A laugh escaped through her tears. Suddenly, she didn't feel so alone.

Gage took a seat beside T.J. on the team plane, feeling as haggard as T.J. looked, before thumbing Lily a quick text.

He pointed at T.J.'s smartphone screen. "More Roman history?"

T.J. grunted in response.

"I know just how you feel," Gage replied.

"Jesus, it's been a long trip. I can't wait to get home and sleep in my own bed tonight ... with my own wife."

Gage arched an eyebrow. "As opposed to someone else's wife?"

"Shut up, Nelson. You know what I mean."

From behind them, Hunter groused, "Losing tonight's game was *not* the ending I'd been hoping for. Shit, all we do is trade the number one spot with Arizona. We can't seem to hold on to it for more than a few hours."

One row ahead sat Grims. The Grim Reaper twisted in his seat and gave them all the stink-eye. "It's one game, boys. One game. Let it go."

"It's a tight race," Gage nodded, "but look at it this way: Arizona's pushing us, reminding us we need to bring our A-game. Every. Single. Night."

"You saying I don't bring my best game every night, Nelson?" Hunter challenged.

Grims's hand had been resting on the back of the seat, and he flicked it at Gage while he fixed his gaze on Hunter. "Listen to the man, moron. That's not what he said."

"I *did* listen, asshole! And that's what's pissing me off!"

Grims unbuckled and rose quickly. So did Hunter.

T.J. and Gage both moved, standing at the same time. T.J.'s hand splayed across Hunter's chest in the blink of an eye while Gage's shot to Grims's arm.

T.J. stared daggers at Hunter. "What the fuck's wrong with you? You *don't* talk to your captain that way. Now sit the fuck down."

Other than the humming engines, the interior of the plane had gone dead quiet. No one moved.

"Not much of a captain," Hunter grumbled.

Gage turned his body, blocking Grims behind him, as T.J. shoved Hunter backward into his seat. "*What* did you say?"

Hunter muttered, "Nothing."

"Keep it that way," T.J. snapped.

Grims had been pressing into Gage and now snarled, "Next time, McMurphy, keep your fucking mouth shut so everyone won't know what a dumb fuck you really are."

Gage swiveled his head to Grims. His eyes were wild. Gage had never seen him like that, and for a split second he wondered if he'd need to defend himself against his captain. He lowered his voice. "Maybe you should take a seat, Cap, so we can all get home?"

Grims's eyes blazed for another beat before they seemed to flicker. He gave Gage a jerky nod and dropped into his seat.

Gage let out a breath and exchanged a what-the-fuck-was-that glance with T.J. as they retook their seats. T.J. shrugged, shoved in his earbuds, and closed his eyes.

A few minutes passed, and Quinn, who sat across the aisle from Gage, craned his neck in Hunter's direction and grinned. "Hunts, when we get home, let's get you laid, bud. That's what I plan to do. I'm pretty sure I'll come to practice on Saturday with a song in my heart"—he sang out the last four words—"and a whole new attitude." Then he broke into a really bad rendition of Patti LaBelle's "New Attitude," making everyone chuckle.

Just like that, the ice was broken.

"Jesuuus, Hadley. Didn't you get enough in Detroit?" one player called out.

Quinn picked up a trio of bean bags he always had with him and started juggling. "Is there such a thing as 'enough'? Besides, that was two nights ago."

Hunter guffawed. "Which bunny did you tap?"

"Which time?" Quinn shot back.

Gage tracked the bean bags, fascinated by how Quinn kept them in the air. Gage had tried, multiple times, and had never gotten the hang of it.

Grims, the only guy who wasn't amused by the banter, growled something indecipherable. Gage tapped him on the shoulder. "You okay?"

"Why wouldn't I be?" he barked.

Whoa! Gage sat back. "Easy, dude."

"He was just being *nice*," Quinn joked. "It's what Nelsy does." He sent Gage a wink.

Grims turned in his seat. "Just shut the fuck up, Hadley."

Quinn was still smiling when he said, "What's gotten into you, Grims?"

"Shit, I don't know, Hadley. Could it be your face?"

Quinn dropped the bean bags and opened his mouth, but Gage prodded his shoulder and shook his head. In a booming voice, he said, "We'll all get some rest, blow off some steam. We'll have a good practice Saturday and take it to Arizona Sunday."

Hunter piped up. "So Hadley's gonna spend a few days in the sack. What're your plans, Nelsy?"

Gage's phone vibrated, and he broke out in a smile despite the leftover tension crackling in the air. "Working on 'em now."

Lily: *Group went well. Thanks for asking. Sorry about the loss.*

Gage: *It's just a game. You and Daisy are still coming to mites, right?*

Lily: *Wouldn't miss it, Professor.*

The charged atmosphere seemed to dissipate while the weariness that had been weighing his limbs down seemed to disappear.

Gage: *They're about to make us shut off our phones. How about I take you girls out to dinner tomorrow night?*

Lily: *Sounds nice. What time?*

He suppressed the urge to pump his arm. *Pick you up at 5:30?*

Lily: *See you then.*

The last three words took away his lingering agitation, giving him a lift. Locking out the unsettling exchange between his teammates, he turned his thoughts in a much more pleasant direction and drifted off.

The next day, he parked in front of her house a few minutes early. Before he could pull his bundles out of the car, Daisy opened the front door and yelled, "Hello, Mr. Cage!" Her big eyes widened as he strode up the walkway. "Are those for my mom?"

Lily appeared behind her daughter, and when her eyes landed on the bouquets he held, they widened too.

"One's for your mom, but the other one's for you." He climbed the few steps and handed Daisy an arrangement bursting with yellow daisies and tulips. It was so big she needed both arms to wrap around it. On her face, pure delight made his chest swell.

"Mom! Mommy! We got flowers!"

Laughing, Lily accepted his gift—an even bigger arrangement of spring flowers that included different kinds of lilies—and beckoned him inside. "Yes, we did. Wasn't that nice of Mr. Cage? What do you say, sweetie?"

"Thank you." Daisy beamed. "I'm gonna put these in water." She scampered away.

Gage resisted the urge to lean down and kiss Lily, even though doing so seemed so right. Maybe she felt it too because her cheeks pinked, and she let out a nervous laugh. He also laughed, for no reason, feeling like a total idiot.

"Do we have a few minutes to get these in vases?" she asked shyly.

"Yeah, of course."

"Kitchen's this way. Thank you for the flowers—for both of us. It was very thoughtful, and they're lovely. It's been a long time since anyone's brought me flowers."

"Really?" he blurted. "You should get flowers every day."

Her blush deepened, turning his heart into a jackhammer. As he followed her, his eyes swept the living room, dining room, and kitchen beyond. Though it was an older home, it had been brought into the twenty-first century and had an open, airy, comfortable feel. It was exactly like its owner. It even smelled like her—clean, fresh, and flowery. In a spotless white-and-gray kitchen splashed in yellow and turquoise, Daisy was chattering excitedly about the flowers as she struggled with the top-heavy bouquet.

While the ladies busied themselves, his eyes explored the space. A long hallway to one side beckoned with an array of pictures. Curiosity piqued—were there photos among them of Lily as a girl?—he pointed toward it. "Do you mind if I ..."

Lily's eyes darted that way. "Um ..."

Holding up his hands in surrender, he laughed. "It's okay. If you don't want me to see any messes ..."

"I don't have a messy house." She gave him an impish grin. "Go ahead. Help yourself."

He ambled that direction, stopped, and studied. Bands constricted his chest. Where he thought he'd see at least a few pictures of Lily and many of Daisy, he was stunned to find instead a wall of what could only be Jack from the time he was a baby until he was a grown man. And it wasn't just pictures. It was a collection of mementos, like backstage passes, awards, a guitar strap. The hallway was a veritable two-walled shrine.

One of the rare pictures that featured Lily depicted her with a mic in her hand and that soulful expression he'd been inexorably drawn to. Onstage with her were Derek and Jack, whose coloring and build mimicked one another's. Jack was playing bass, his eyes riveted on Lily and a smile splitting his face. The scene about knocked the wind from Gage's lungs. He felt like a voyeur peeking behind the privacy curtain belonging to a husband and wife.

When Lily called to him from the kitchen, he didn't register it at first. He was fixated on Jack. The ghost. His rival.

Lily called to him again, and he turned to find her watching him with curious eyes.

"I guess I've finally met Jack," he said evenly.

Her eyebrows shot to her forehead. "Oh?"

"And now I understand," he said simply.

I understand you worshipped him. That you still worship him.

He also understood she was a beautiful, vibrant woman stuck in the past. A woman who deserved a living man to take care of her, to worship her.

And looking at her made him want to be that man.

It would be an uphill battle, and it would take determination. Persistence. Patience. Traits that were ingrained in him. Did he want to go to battle to win a place in Lily's heart? Even if it meant sharing space with Jack?

Hell yeah.

Chapter 15

Stuck in the Discovery Channel

Lily was pulling into Gage's driveway when Ivy's number lit her phone screen.

"Hey, Ive. I'm at Gage's. What's up?" She parked and turned off the engine.

"Isn't he still out of town?"

"Well, he got back last week, but he left again, so I'm checking on his cat."

Ivy chuckled. "Oh, I love it. The more weeks go by, the cozier you two get."

The tease prodded at Lily's nerves. "It's not like that."

"Of course not. You just keep convincing yourself, Little Sis."

Lily tucked the phone between her shoulder and ear, slung her purse over her shoulder, and climbed out of her Highlander. "Is there a purpose for your call besides giving me crap?"

"A little sensitive, aren't we?" Another sisterly chuckle rocketed Lily's irritation. "Actually, I was calling to see if you wanted to meet up for lunch after my shift ends? That's in two hours."

Lily crossed the driveway and paused at Gage's front door, eyeing the keypad built into the lock. "That should work if we keep it short."

They settled on a meeting place and Lily punched in Gage's code and let herself in, warily studying the alarm system he claimed he didn't use, in case it decided to spring to life and bring on a squad of police cars to haul her butt to jail.

Hobbes sauntered toward her. Lily dropped into a crouch to scratch the cat's ears. "Hi, Hobbes. I bet you miss your dad. I think I miss him too, but don't tell him I said so. He might try to act cuter than he already is."

Gage and she texted multiple times a day, and while she had fun doing it, it wasn't the same as seeing his face light up or feeling his rich, deep baritone roll into her every nook and cranny whenever he spoke.

After refilling Hobbes's bowls and cleaning her litter box, Lily stood in the family room and pulled in the gorgeous view outside the windows. From there, she drifted into his office and looked over the piles of mail she'd been answering. Before long, she was sticking her head into other rooms to be sure nothing was out of order.

Poised at the foot of his wooden-tread, metal-railed staircase, she debated heading upstairs to check the rooms on the second level. Hobbes bounded up the steps, making up Lily's mind for her. She followed the cat, who wandered into Gage's master bedroom, a space Lily had only seen briefly once before.

Understated and oh so masculine, the scene twined a seductive, invisible lasso around her and tugged her inside. She scanned clean, angular lines splashed with blacks, whites, and warm grays as she breathed in a musk-and-cedar man smell permeating the room. Soothing yet strong. Like him.

Hobbes leapt onto the bed.

"Oh, I see how it is. And just how do you rate?" Lily plopped on the edge of the mattress and stretched her hand toward Hobbes. "I'm betting *you* sneak off in the middle of the night and he doesn't get bent out of shape."

What the hell am I saying?

Lily straightened, ready to leave the room when Hobbes started hacking. She recognized the sound immediately. "Oh no, Hobbes! Don't throw up on the bed!"

Little good the command did. As Hobbes continued retching, Lily scrambled for something, anything to catch the hairball that was about to erupt. First she yanked open the nightstand drawer—so hard, stuff came flying out of it. *Whoops!* No tissues.

Hobbes's yaks grew more urgent. Lily wrenched open a cabinet door below the drawer and rummaged around for a box of tissues. Her hand landed on different shapes, none resembling a tissue box, and as she withdrew, she inadvertently hauled out more stuff that hit the floor with a dull thud.

She vaulted upright and sprinted to the bathroom. Not a single tissue. *Toilet paper!* She snatched a wad and ran back to the bedroom, just as Hobbes coughed up her treasure. The cat then sprang off the bed and scurried from the scene of the crime.

"That's it! Run away, you ... you cat!"

Lily gathered the offending hairball in the toilet paper, disposed of it, and returned to the bedroom to survey the mess *she'd* created. Cards of various sizes and shapes were scattered over the rug like an explosion of giant confetti. With a sigh, she knelt and began gathering them into a pile before she realized what she was looking at. As she gave them a closer look, her stomach twisted into knots.

A number were regular business cards—many with thumbnail-sized headshots of women—while others were postcards from bars, restaurants, sports venues. Even music stores. Others were girlie note cards. Greeting cards.

Though they came in all shapes and sizes, they all appeared to be from women, their hand-scrawled messages some variant of "Let's get together" or urging him to "Call me."

Was this some weird trophy collection? *How many women has he been through?* The Gage she *thought* she knew collided with the Gage these women knew. *Maybe* knew.

A headache began blooming behind her eyes from the confusing emotions detonating inside her. She turned her attention to the items she'd accidentally yanked from the cabinet's interior. One proved to be a box of Trojan Magnum condoms.

Large size. Yeah, that fits—literally. On closer inspection, she noted it was an unopened three-pack. Judging by the expiration date, it was also not a new purchase. She peered inside the cabinet but found no other telltale packages. The possibility popped into her head that he'd worked his way through a few Costco economy-sized boxes as he'd worked his way through the stack in his drawer.

Lily shook off the thought, thinking back to the night she'd spent with Gage. He'd had two condoms with him, and those, he'd claimed with endearing awkwardness, had been in his wallet a long time because he hadn't been close enough to anyone to put them to use.

The memory of being under him, on top of him, beside him replayed in her head. Their tongues twining. The melting pleasure of him inside her. The lust that had pulsed through her body. All that hardness and heat. Had the B&B had a condom-dispensing machine, they'd have put those in play too. She refrained from fanning herself.

That night she hadn't thought of him as a pro athlete who charmed his way in and out of women's panties. Nothing she'd learned about him since had shot down that opinion either, but she'd be wise to remain wary, wouldn't she? Eyeballing the drawer teeming with women reinforced her caution.

She handled the box, putting it back in its proper place, and a giggle bubbled up inside. The giggle died in the next instant when she picked up the other item that lay on the floor. As her eyes scanned it, her chest compressed. Staring at her from an eight-by-ten gold frame was the picture of Gage cuddled up with the beautiful blue-eyed brunette. The same picture Lily had seen on the Internet. Across the bottom, inscribed in loopy black letters, were the words: "Had such a wonderful time at the all-star weekend! Looking forward to many more nights together. With all my love, Jess XO."

Lily's hands trembled as they returned the picture to its hiding place inside the nightstand. Her heart felt leaden, achy. Here, surrounded by his scent, she told herself what she'd discovered didn't matter because she wasn't about to fall in love with him.

Lily kept her discoveries to herself at lunch with Ivy, who vented on and on about work. Thank God because all Lily had to do was offer understanding nods and uh-huhs without tuning in. Unfortunately, the picture of beautiful "Jess" and her gushing words about spending more nights with Gage took center stage instead.

That evening, as Daisy and Violet helped Lily clear the dinner dishes, Daisy took her by surprise. "Momma, when can I see Mr. Cage play hockey?"

"You mean on TV?" Gage was on an East Coast road swing, and tonight the Blizzard were playing Tampa.

"No, I wanna watch him play for real. He said I could."

"Oh, he did, did he?" When had he told Daisy that? Lily bristled with the thought he'd extended the offer without consulting her first. Then she immediately softened, recalling the seemingly bottomless patience he showed Daisy and the other kids on the ice. For a man with no children, he had a way about him that warmed her through and through.

Lily gave herself a mental shake and bottled up the feels. "How about we ask him when he comes back to Denver? In the meantime, you can watch him on TV tonight."

Both girls clapped and bounced, squealing, "Yes!"

Lily wrangled the remote. "Okay. Let's see what Mr. Cage is up to tonight."

She refused to let her mind wander to what he'd be doing *after* the game or how many "cards" he was collecting on the trip. No doubt he had plenty of options throwing themselves at him. Just like Jack had. The thought jarred her. She'd long ago buried her insecurities over Jack's sex appeal and the way he'd drawn women like flies to honey. He'd downplayed the part he'd played in the pheromone-fest, just as he'd dismissed the reasons behind Lily's uneasiness. "You're making a big deal out of nothing, babe," he'd say. "It's because you're still so young." Translation: she was acting immaturely.

Locking away the old hurts, Lily cleaned up the kitchen while in the background the girls' excited chatter blended with sounds of the game. When their attention spans stretched beyond their natural limits, they wandered off to play in Daisy's bedroom.

Lily perched on the edge of the couch as a seemingly endless loop of commercials aired on TV. She startled when her phone rang.

"Our boy's really tearing it up on the road," Ivy gushed. "Did you watch tonight's game?"

Lily smiled at Ivy's use of "our boy." "Is it over? I think I missed it. What did he do?"

"What *didn't* he do? He had a Gordie Howe hat trick!"

Alarm bells clanged in Lily's head. "You mean he got in a *fight*? But Gage doesn't fight!"

"Well, he did tonight, and he won! Plus, it was *after* the fight that he scored his goal and picked up an apple. That's hockey talk for assist."

Lily would have rolled her eyes, but her heart was racing like a greyhound around a track. "So he's okay?"

"He's fine. You really need to watch the highlights, Lil."

The TV switched to Gage standing in front of a locker, surrounded by iPads, phones, and mics. Gear stripped off, he was down to a black Under Armour shirt. His head was tilted as he listened to a question, and sweat beaded his forehead and cheeks. He shoved his wet hair back and raised his head, his eyes shifting side to side as though he were contemplating. Lily's breath caught in her throat when she saw his entire face.

"Mr. Cage has an owie, Mom." Daisy stood in the doorway pointing at the TV, Violet peeking over her shoulder.

Ivy piped up. "Oh. I forgot to mention he took a punch during the fight."

Over his left eyebrow spanned two butterfly bandages. A purplish-red bruise ringed his under eye.

He broke out in a smile, and relief flooded Lily. He still had all his teeth! Not that it mattered to her ... except from a social media standpoint, of course.

When he began talking, Lily upped the volume.

"Yeah, I can't remember the last time I got in a fight. Juniors, probably." There was that self-deprecating grin, so typical for him. His default grin. Then came a shrug. "But it all worked out for us. The boys were going tonight, and they battled hard. Every game's important, and we needed those two points."

A voice said, "Tell us about your goal, Gage."

He swiped moisture from his forehead. *God, those hands!* Lily nearly swiped her own forehead.

His eyes were animated, his eyebrows dancing above them as he spoke. "Well, it was a really lucky break. They had that turnover in our zone, and I wound up with the puck on my stick. Shanny was right there, and it turned into a two-on-one. My shooting lane was blocked, so I passed it to Shanny. Their D-man committed, Shanny made an unbelievable pass back to me, and I was able to lift it over their goalie."

"Have you seen the standings?" another voice asked.

"No, I've been too busy talking to you guys," he laughed. Then his blue eyes went wide. "Did Arizona lose? Are we in first place?" A mumbled answer, then he said, "This was a good win for us, but it's only one game. We have to get ready for the next one. And we have to keep the momentum going, stay sharp, and head into the playoffs on a hot streak. There aren't any easy games, and we can't afford to take any nights off."

"Speaking of hot," came Ivy's voice. Lily had almost forgotten she was still on the phone. "Don't get me wrong, Lil, because that man cleans up really well, but all hot and sweaty like that? Hubba, hubba! And don't even get me started on him fighting."

Lily barked out a laugh.

"Mom, is Mr. Cage okay?" Daisy's lower lip wobbled.

"He's fine, honey. Come see for yourself. He's talking to all those people. If he weren't okay, he wouldn't be able to talk to them."

Daisy tiptoed to her, eyes glued to the TV, and nodded. "He's okay," she whispered to Violet. Her concern made a puddle of Lily's heart.

Ivy again. "Guy interviews well, not like a dumb jock at all."

Lily did roll her eyes this time. "Because he's *not* a dumb jock." She couldn't hold back the pride swelling in her chest or the tingle in her toes as she watched him handle the reporters with grace, poise, and humor.

Is Kathryn Tappen in the locker room with him? Would he want to ask her out? Would she want to ask *him* out? Did he have fresh condoms with him on the trip?

"Mommy, what's a dumb jock?"

"Lil! You gotta jump that man. At least one more time. And take pics to share with your sister."

"Ivy, stop! I am *not—*" She bit back the "jumping him" on the tip of her tongue.

Daisy's wide gray eyes were on her. "What's a dumb jock?"

"Well, he just might want you to," Ivy cackled.

Lily ran her fingers through Daisy's hair. "Hang on a minute, sweetie. Let me finish talking to Aunt Ivy. Aunt Ivy," she sang, "what are you talking about?"

"Oh nothing," she sang back innocently.

"Ivy—"

"Gotta go, Lil. Don't forget to watch those highlights!"

"Mad World" queued up in Lily's head.

After explaining what a jock was—*he's a sporty guy and Mommy shouldn't have used the word "dumb"*—and settling the girls, Lily returned to watch the highlights on TV. But her pinging phone interrupted her. She picked it up, and a smile twitched her lips.

Gage: *Did you see the game, GL?*

Lily: *GL?*

Gage: *Goldilocks.*

Lily: *LOL. Only part. Are you OK?*

Gage: *So you saw the fight? What about the goal?*

She laughed out loud. Though texted words didn't convey tone, his excitement was easy to pick up. God, he was adorable. *No, he's a grown man. Grown men aren't adorable. They're masculine and sexy and they can do things ... God, I want him to do things. No, no, no, I don't! Once every five years is good. I'm a sex camel.*

If only she could get the man out of her fantasies.

Lily: *Didn't see either. Was hoping to catch your Gordie Howe on the highlights.*

Gage: *That's my first Gordie!*

Lily: *Congrats, Professor. Is your eye OK?*

Gage: *All good. Just another cut.*

Lily: *I'm glad, but you're looking a little heavy on the purple eyeshadow. Got a big date tonight?*

Yeah, she couldn't help but slide that in.

Gage: *You know it. A double date with room service and an ice pack. If you were here, though, I'd lose both and take you out, purple eyeshadow and all. If you could stand looking at my face, that is.*

A fluttering sensation tickled Lily's tummy. She held it in check and typed, *Ivy says the fighting makes you look hot.*

Gage: *LOL. You should listen to your big sister.*

Wait. Were they text-flirting now? How had that happened? No idea, but she was enjoying it. Too much. She conjured an image of the sea of cards—*next to his bed*—and the pretty brunette.

Lily: *I should go tuck the girls in.*

Gage: *Tell them hi for me.*

Lily: *D was really worried about you BTW.*

A selfie of Gage—sans shirt—reclining against his hotel headboard popped up on her screen. He had his infectious grin plastered on his face.

Gage: *Show her this. Then call me when you're done putting them to bed.*

Lily: *Call you why?*

Gage: *So you can sing me to sleep? It's turning into a long week.* He added a praying hands emoji.

Lily's heart was thumping in her chest when she put the girls to bed, poured herself a glass of white wine, and returned to her phone. She tapped a quick text. *It's kinda late. Still want me to call?* Her phone rang almost immediately.

"It's never too late." Gage's voice was low and gravelly.

"So you want me to sing you to sleep?" she squeaked. Part of her brain registered that he wasn't out with one of his many admirers if he was on the phone with her, right?

He rumbled a chuckle. "Yeah, but first I wanted to find out how my girls are doing."

My girls? Oh, that sounded nice. "You mean Daisy and Hobbes?"

"Hobbes. Right," he snorted. "I worry about *you* way more than I worry about that cat."

Lily lowered her drawbridge a few inches. "You worry about me?" A warm, sticky feeling enveloped her from her toes to her neck.

"Yeah. Not that you can't take care of yourself, but I worry when I'm not around. So what've you been up to?"

Words caught in her throat. She cleared them out. "Getting Paige's social media campaign up and running."

Another warm chuckle. "I guess this means I'm second fiddle to Paige now, despite how much I value twittering out to the world."

Lily let out a laugh. "It's tweeting, not twittering. Speaking of which, have you checked Twitter in the last half hour, Professor?"

"No, why?"

"I might've posted your selfie."

"*What?* Shit! That was strictly for you and Daisy." Laughter lingered in his voice. "That's the last time I send you a racy picture."

"That's racy?" She sipped her wine. "Don't worry. I cropped it so your bare chest isn't showing." *Although* I'm *enjoying the uncropped version.*

He dropped his voice. "Well, maybe you should reciprocate."

"Meaning?"

"I sent you a picture of *my* bare chest, so ..."

If she hadn't swallowed her wine, she would've sprayed it everywhere. "Have you been drinking?"

"I take it that's a no? Damn." His laugh rolled through the phone, long and low and sexed-up. A delicious flutter waved its way through her body before she could rein it in.

Okay. Now I'm talking to Sexy Gage. Yet another side of the same man. Did he flirt with other women this way? Maybe this was the Gage who got all the cards. The thought unsettled her. "Do you do this a lot?"

"What?"

"Ask women to send you pictures?"

A loud, decidedly unsexy sputtering noise was her answer. "No! Shit! I was only kidding." He raced on. "Lily, it was a joke. A bad joke, obviously. I mean, if you *wanted* to send me a picture, any kind of picture, I'd totally be on board." A noisy exhale. "Damn it. You're not going to sing me to sleep now, are you? I could've used it too."

The playfulness disappeared from his voice, and worry grabbed hold of her. "Why? What's going on?"

Her heart squeezed when he sighed on the other end. "Grandma fell today."

"Oh no! How?"

"Shit, I didn't mean to bring this up and kill our fun conversation."

"Gage, what happened? Please tell me."

He told her how he'd gotten a call from his mother right before his pre-game nap. His grandmother had either lost her balance or tripped over something in her apartment and landed on her face. Nothing broken, but she looked as though she'd been hit by a car.

"Mom says they spent nearly eight hours in emergency," he continued, his voice quiet. "My little scratch pales in comparison to what she looks like."

Oh, how Lily wished she could bring his teasing tone back. Help him get his mind off a situation he was powerless to change. How well she understood that helpless feeling.

"Grandma was freaking out because she didn't know where she was and she wanted to go home—her *old* home, where she lived when she was a girl. God, Lily, I should have *been* there."

"There's nothing you could've done, Gage."

"I could've kept Grandma calm! I could've helped my mom. It all fell on her." He followed this up quickly with, "I'm sorry. I shouldn't be taking it out on you."

The regret and blame in his voice chiseled a little chink out of her heart.

"You're not. You're taking it out on *you*. Gage, you're the best son I know, and you're doing all you can, but you can't control everything that happens. Your grandma could've fallen from a simple twist as she was sitting down or getting out of bed."

When he didn't respond, she went on. "Don't be so hard on yourself. Some things are just inescapable. I should know. I've spent the last five years telling myself the same thing." The words slid out so easily it took a moment for her surprise she'd uttered them to catch up.

"You're talking about Jack," he said softly.

She tugged out her necklace. "Yes."

"Lily, can you ... Will you tell me what happened?"

God, this man was making her feel things she wasn't ready to feel ... like the urge to climb into the warmth and safety of his strong arms and cling to him for dear life.

Chapter 16

Spectral Visions

Gage settled more deeply into the mattress and folded an arm behind his head, trying to get as comfortable as possible. Though he'd grown up around women's tears, they still flustered him. Hearing Lily cry would shake him up even more, so he braced himself for the potential storm. But beneath his concern, unease bristled. Though he was curious about Jack, he was also jealous. Hearing about Jack would only remind him Jack was first in Lily's life. The anticipation inside him, prickly like sea urchin spikes, was akin to meeting someone you disliked face-to-face.

As Lily began to talk, he sucked in a breath.

"Daisy was six months old when she came down with her first cold. Nothing unusual, though the symptoms always seem amplified in a baby. Jack got sick about a week later. We'd been on an exhausting tour through Colorado, Kansas, and Oklahoma, so it didn't seem strange that one of us came down with something, especially with a sick baby in the mix."

"Daisy went on tour with you?" Why this surprised him, he had little idea.

"Yes. She was a good little baby and could sleep anywhere. If it had come down to it, I'd have given up the band and stayed home. But we were one big family, and someone was always there to take care of her when I was onstage. Not your typical nine-to-five, but it worked for us.

"Jack and I decided to keep it going as long as we could. We knew one day she'd have to go to school, and that those were precious times, so we took full advantage." She paused on a shaky breath. "Anyway, Jack got sick. We thought he'd caught Daisy's cold, and maybe he had at first, but he wasn't getting better. In fact, he got worse, so I took him to a doctor when we reached Missouri. They gave him flu medicine and sent him on his way. He felt a little better and made it through the rest of the trip. But when we got back to Colorado, it seemed to come back and bite him hard." Her voice hitched.

"Lily," Gage made his voice as gentle as he could, "you don't need to keep going." He plucked a water bottle from the nightstand and downed a big gulp.

"No, I do. I haven't really talked to anyone besides Ivy like this, and not for a long time. I need to get it out. If you're still willing to listen to me ramble, that is."

Knowing she wanted him as her sounding board was a score that lifted him more than netting a game-winning goal. "Always. And you're not rambling."

"Thank you." Her voice was small, and it tugged at him. After a thorough throat clearing, she continued. "I took him in when we got home, and they ran a battery of tests. They couldn't find anything and said he hadn't gotten enough rest and was still fighting the flu. He wound up in the hospital for a night, and the doctor there ran a few more tests. He called us in when he got the results."

She paused. A long, eerily silent pause.

"I'm here," he offered, "whenever you're ready to talk. And if you want to stop, that's okay too. Whatever you need, Lily."

"I'll never forget sitting in the doctor's office that day." Her voice shuddered with tears that ripped into him. "He, um, he told us Jack had stage four lung cancer. It had already spread to his vital organs and was in his bones. It was everywhere."

Gage was stunned speechless.

"The strange thing was," she continued, "he didn't smoke. Never had. The doctor said it didn't matter, that not all lung cancer comes from smoking. Anyway, he told us Jack could undergo chemo, but it wouldn't do much good because the cancer was too far along. We stumbled out of there that day in a fog. Funny, though. I can still recall a blue Dodge parked next to us; I remember what the clouds looked like that day and that a small flight of geese lifted off from a pond. It's all crystal clear, almost frozen in time." Another pause and a sniffle. "We went to a Village Inn, of all places, and talked like we were having a business discussion. What we'd do in the next few weeks, what kind of funeral he wanted, what Daisy and I would do after ... after ... um ..."

"Lily," Gage whispered. God, this was killing him. He couldn't fathom what it was doing to *her*. Frustrated that he couldn't *do* anything to chase her pain away, he took another long pull of his water. The cool liquid flowed around the lump in his throat.

She rallied. "No, I'm okay." He could practically hear her shaking off her sorrow. "At first, he seemed okay. He coughed a lot, but his color was good. He still ate like a horse, cracked jokes, and he was, you know, the Jack I knew. He worked on songs with Derek, practiced with the band, spent time with us. For a short while, I kidded myself that he'd beat this thing. That they'd been looking at the wrong test results, that Jack's were switched with someone else's. Or that a miracle had happened. But that didn't last long.

"It's devastating to watch someone deteriorate—you've seen it firsthand, watching your grandma. Jack's decline seemed to pick up, like someone flipped a switch or sped up the film, and we couldn't stop it."

Her sniffles were coming hard and fast, her voice breaking. "I'm sorry," she whimpered.

"There's nothing to apologize for." His whole body vibrated with wanting to reach through the damn phone and wrap her up. He realized he was seated upright on the bed, his knees bent, his elbows resting on them. His core was tight, his muscles taut, as though he prepared to take a stick check to the gut.

On the other end, she seemed to recover. "I stayed with him. In the hospital. I'd get up and take walks through the hallway or get coffee, and by the time I'd get back his complexion would have turned grayer and his body seemed more shriveled. It was as though he was wasting away right in front of me. And oh my God, then the pain took over." Now her voice took on an angry, gritty quality, as though her teeth were clenching. "It got worse and worse. It was excruciating, no matter how much they upped his meds. And there was absolutely. Nothing. I. Could. Do. Just curl up beside him and watch."

Gage dug the heel of his hand into his eyes, wiping moisture from them as Lily pulled in a long breath on the other end and released it. And again.

Her voice quavered. "Finally, they had him so doped up that he ... I don't know how much he was aware of at the end, whether he knew we were there with him—I hope he knew."

"He knew, Lily. He did," was all he could muster.

A little soul-tearing sob escaped her. "I'll never forget when he stopped breathing. The lines on the monitor went flat, there was no pulse blipping. It was 10:44 in the morning, six weeks from the day he was diagnosed. But I swear—and no one will ever talk me out of this—even though the machines had gone quiet, his fingers squeezed mine. Then he was gone."

They sat for a long time without talking, the only sound her soft sobs and her sniffles mingling with his. When Gage had enough presence of mind to look around for his empty water bottle, he discovered he'd crushed it.

"Are you still with me?" she said with a humorless laugh. "Or did I scare you off?"

He steadied his voice. "Never. I don't scare that easily, Goldilocks, and I'm not going anywhere."

She pulled in a breath. "No, I don't believe you would. You're a good man, Gage Nelson. Your family's lucky to have you."

"Would you please tell my mom that?"

"I'm sure she thinks you're perfect." She laughed, and it uncoiled his bunched muscles. He laughed too, and, God, it felt good.

"Something I've been wondering about, and if I'm overstepping, tell me to shut up," he said.

"What is it?"

“Does social media consulting bring in enough to support you and Daisy?” Crap, the question didn’t come out the way he intended. “I’m sorry,” he backpedaled. “None of my business.”

“No, it’s fine. Jack took out a hefty life insurance policy when we got married. Neither of us ever imagined I’d have to use it.” Her voice seemed to catch. A beat later, she’d recovered. “I live off the interest from the policy. As for the social media, it brings in extra money for little splurges. Mostly, I do it because it keeps me sharp, it’s flexible, and I enjoy it. It gives me something to do now that Daisy’s in school.”

A silent sigh of relief whooshed out of him. At least he could rid himself of the worry she was struggling to make ends meet. “Well, you’re damn good at it.” He sounded clumsy, even to his own ears.

“Thank you.” A few beats later, she said, “So I don’t think I’ve ever known a fighting professor before, and I’m curious. What started it?”

Gage was grateful for the distraction. “I’m not sure I remember. Some gutterance.”

“Gutterance?” She sounded highly amused.

“Guttural utterance. He disparaged my family. And I think my manhood. Doesn’t matter.” Truth was, he really couldn’t remember the exact remark, only that it had been about his sister and had come from a douchebag he didn’t like, and he’d exploded. Nothing to be proud of, but sometimes shit happened on the ice.

“Were you on edge about your grandmother at the time?”

Yes. “No. Maybe. I don’t know, but it didn’t take much to set me off.”

“You don’t strike me as someone who loses his cool, so you must have been really upset to let whatever it was get to you.” Another pause, then her voice took on a lilting, soothing tone that seemed to stroke his overstretched nerves into submission. “I’m so sorry about your grandmother’s accident. Is there anything I can do?”

This woman’s comforting me*? After the story* she *just told? You gotta be shitting me.*

“No,” he croaked. “But I appreciate the offer.”

In that moment, it struck him he *was* capable of falling in love. Because he was pretty sure he was already there. And by some strange magic, he couldn’t care less if he had the time or not or if she had a child or not. None of that mattered. He'd met the woman he needed to meet, and she was a sweet, sultry songbird named Lily Everett.

His world had been tipped completely upside down. And it scared the shit out of him. Because unless he could convince her he should own a place in her heart—despite the dead husband already living there—he'd never be able to set it right side up again.

Chapter 17

Shall He Do Her?

Days after Gage's return from his road trip, Lily was working in his office, surrounded by boxes holding fan mail she'd been opening, reading, and sorting. Hobbes lounged in a late-morning, sun-splashed corner of the desk, flicking her tail in time with soft jazz playing in the background. A tall shadow slid down the hall.

"How's your grandmother?" Lily called out.

"Much better, thanks," Gage called back. "Everything seems to be back to normal at good ol' Skyview Acres."

Lily slit open a letter and pulled out a folded piece of pink paper. Her eyes quickly scanned the contents. "Oh my God," she shrieked. "This ... this ..."

Gage stuck his damp head around the door frame. "What's going on?"

Apparently, she'd gotten somewhat comfortable padding around his place without him there because moments like this—when his sexy self appeared out of nowhere—jarred her while simultaneously igniting her. Even with the telltale yellow-green hue of his fading bruise and the angry gash above his eye, he was all delectable hotness. And he seemed to be getting better and better looking every time she laid eyes on him, if that were even possible.

There was that urge to fan herself again, which she deftly ignored. "She describes—in graphic detail—what she wants to do to you," she spluttered instead. "And my God, her name!"

His interest obviously piqued, he stepped fully into the office and cocked his head. "What's her name?"

She rolled her eyes. "Shally Dewar."

He blinked. "Shall he do her? As in—" A light bulb seemed to wink on, and a grin spread over his face.

"I swear, the crazies box is overflowing with letters just like this one. Is this normal?"

"Normal for what?" He came closer, leaning in over her shoulder, his eyes traveling to where her finger pointed. Fresh from morning skate, he'd just showered, and a heavenly man smell wrapped her up and clouded her brain.

Apparently, *his* brain was functioning at its usual above-average speed. "If you're talking about the licking part and riding me all night long, yeah, that's pretty normal," he said matter-of-factly. "As for the handcuffs and blindfolding me with my tie? Those are an interesting twist I haven't seen in a while. Could be fun." He shrugged. "Most women propose sucking and licking—so do the guys—that's standard fare. I guess the other stuff is too." He shifted his gaze back to her, the hint of a smirk hiding in his beard. "Are you offended, Goldilocks?"

"Me?" she squeaked. "No, but *you* should be." She reminded herself of the prim librarian stereotype: so tightly laced she'd need a button hook to get herself unwound. Which she wasn't. Even if she was performing an awesome imitation of one.

Her mind took a wander to his drawer full of women, just waiting to be plucked out of their hiding place. Did they elbow each other when he opened that drawer? *"Pick me, Gage, pick me!"* Had any of *them* come from letters like these?

"By 'other stuff,'" she repeated, "you mean ..."

He casually planted a hand on the back of her chair and the other on the desk, his rigid arm so close its warmth teased her shoulder. She tried to round up her gallivanting thoughts, tried not to picture Gage's broad back underneath his tight T-shirt. She was a back-and-shoulders girl, and Gage's were an outstanding example, all defined muscle under smooth skin. The sight had been on a loop inside her head since last July and hadn't gotten old. But she was also a strong-rough-hands kinda girl, and the recollection of *his* on her body played on a separate loop. She averted her gaze from the hand currently gripping the edge of the desk.

His dark eyebrows peaked over very amused, crystal-clear eyes tinged in different shades of the Caribbean Sea. "Sexual intercourse. Yes. That's what I meant. Like what you and I—"

She craned her neck to put some distance between them. "What *she's* describing, Professor, isn't straightforward, missionary-style, vanilla sex."

Now his eyebrows kissed his hairline. "As I recall, neither was what *we* engaged in. Well, at least not one time. And there was plenty of"—he bent over, peering at the letter as though reading—"licking and sucking that night too. On both our parts. You were pretty enthusiastic and plainly weren't offended since you yourself suggested a few of those other-flavored positions."

A hot flush surged over every square inch of her skin. "I didn't suggest *anything*!"

Still bracketing her in the office chair, he darted his eyes to the ceiling. "Well, maybe not verbally. Nonverbally, you were very clear. And it was"—his voice took on that gravelly quality—"incredibly. Insanely. Hot."

Heat engulfed her face. She'd need a fire extinguisher any minute now. He was obviously getting a big kick out of this. "I don't remember being ... assertive," she muttered.

"Trust me, you were. I have excellent recall." He leaned down closer, his mouth inches from her ear, his warm, moist breath a soft caress. "In fact, I *recall* it all the time. And I haven't forgotten a *single* detail," he whispered, sending shivers up her spine. Her body betrayed her with a telltale shudder.

Upright again, he shot her a devilish grin. This was a different side of his personality, and, God, it was turning her body into an incendiary device. Forget the fire extinguisher. She needed to dunk herself in one of the team's ice baths.

What did it say about her that Cocky Gage, combined with Sexy Gage, got all her pistons firing at top-fuel-dragster speed? Did top-fuel dragsters *have* pistons? *Who cares?*

With a tap of his finger on the letter, he grew more serious. "These we ignore. File them away, but don't acknowledge."

Her brain came back on board. So did her snark. "In other words, I *don't* send them the autographed eight-by-ten glossy of you posing naked with a strategically placed helmet that says, 'Eat me' on it?" *Don't picture it, Lil, just don't!*

With a laugh that seemed to rumble through his chest, he pivoted and headed for the door, where he stopped, turned, and smirked. "It's nice to hear you say it takes something as big as a helmet to cover my junk. Apple?"

Her head on spin cycle, she repeated his question. "Apple?"

"Okay. I'll bring you one too. Be right back." With a wink and a waggle, he was gone.

Oh my God!

Lily dropped her head on her arms and broke into an unstoppable giggle fest. *This man is going to be the death of me!* The thought occurred to her that there were worse ways to go.

When Lily had first screeched, Gage had expected to find a mouse or a spider or something sinister crawling on her. Instead, she'd shaken another pervy letter at him. The letters were ridiculous and normally got tossed as soon as they were opened, but Lily's shock was turning it into a game that had him in stitches. Her reaction was adorable. *She* was adorable. And sexy all at the same time, which, he was discovering, was a lethal combination.

He took a moment, or five, to rearrange himself before grabbing two apples from a bowl on his kitchen counter. Sauntering back to the office, he tossed one at her, which she caught and promptly placed on the desk.

"Let's read another one," he goaded. *Game on, Lily Everett.*

She gaped at him.

God, this was fun. He shuffled through a box designated the so-called crazies stack and plucked out a letter with a picture of a half-naked woman attached. He pretended to inspect the picture. "Not bad." For effect, he then lifted the letter to his nose. "Mmm. Interesting, like 'Perfume de Panties.'" He handed Lily the letter without looking at her—he'd bust a gut if he did—and tossed his apple in the air and pointed. "Read that one, Goldilocks."

Pinching the letter by its corners, she scanned the contents, her pretty blue eyes getting rounder by the second. He held back a slew of snickers.

"This woman not only describes what she'd like to do to you but wonders if you'd like to meet her. She's given you her home address and will even tell you where she's hidden a key, for God's sake!"

He burst out with the laugh he could no longer hold back. "Oh, is that all?"

"Is that *all*? You mean this is *also* normal?"

"God yeah. Some even mail me the key *with* the letter." An exaggeration, but it was too fun to resist. He took a satisfying chomp of the crispy apple. "So what does this one want to do to me? I might be interested," he teased.

Lily shot him daggers. "Ew. Just ew." After a beat, she said, "You should steer clear of *fans* like this." She shook the letter under his nose.

"You really think so?" He rubbed his chin thoughtfully. "I dunno. She *is* making it easy for me—"

"Because *she's* easy," she snapped. "And probably diseased."

He coughed to mask a laugh. "Yeah, but this one's leaving a trail of big, fat crumbs that a blind man could follow, and it *has* been a while." He caught her eyes with his. "Since T.J.'s wedding, to be exact."

Surprise and disbelief played in her sparkly blues. "No way," she tossed back, her voice sounding a bit wobbly, as if she wasn't sure.

"No? You been spying on me?"

A bright blush washed over her cheeks, and he was pretty sure her cute ass was squirming in the chair. He loved it. As his mind leapt to how he might get his hands between said cute ass and the seat, she stammered out, "N-no, but you *are* a hockey player—"

The good feels evaporated. "And you're a singer, and we all know about rock stars, don't we?" He bounced his eyebrows on his forehead. "How long's it been for you?" *Shit. I don't want to know.*

She barked out a laugh. "Why, an hour ago, of course! With my reverse harem of firefighters."

"What's a reverse harem? Oh! Didn't know that was a thing. You're kidding, right, about a reverse harem? And why firefighters?" He exaggerated a scoff.

She gave him a dramatic eye-roll. "Yes, Professor, I'm kidding. Why firefighters? Because they do it with heat."

"Ha! Cute."

"As for your comment, I'm not sure if I should be flattered or completely insulted. On the one hand, I think you're calling me a rock star. On the other hand, I also think you're calling me a slut."

"You're kinda dodging my question." *The question I don't really want answered unless it's a good answer. So why the hell do I keep asking?*

"Which question?"

He rolled his hand in a hurry-along motion. "How long?"

"Is that any of your business?"

"No, it's not."

Her eyes slid to the side, and she blew out an exasperated-sounding breath. Yeah, he was a complete idiot. "The wedding," she conceded quietly, and a small riot broke out in his stomach. He almost punched his fist in the air and shouted out a "Yes!"

"Speaking of dodging, Professor, I'd like an explanation for your slut comment."

"Ah. I didn't actually *call* you a slut, nor do I think you resemble anything remotely slut-like. I was just making a point about presumptions. Being a hockey player doesn't make me a *player*. And just because I get lots of stupid letters *and* I slept with you that night doesn't mean I fall into bed with every woman who asks. Actually, come to think of it," he took another bite, "you didn't really ask. You just kind of, you know, seduced me."

"Seduced you?" she squawked.

"I seem to recall someone asking someone else not to leave."

The look on her face was unreadable. Part-sheepishness, but she also seemed to be holding something back. Her eyes traveled to the ceiling, then landed back on him. "And being the gentleman you are, you had no choice but to *let* me seduce you, am I right?"

He gave her a wicked grin and shook his head. "I don't recall being a gentleman that night."

She paused mid-protest, her mouth hanging open. Her face and throat were covered with bright pink blotches that reminded him of what her skin had looked like right after sex. Yeah, he should stop, but it was so much fun to rile her up. And she was hotter than hell when she was riled up. Which was riling him up. Shit. He stuffed what was left of the apple in his mouth, grabbed a box of letters, and sat with it in his lap.

"These are letters from the kids?" He was going for casual, but his voice betrayed him when it cracked an octave higher. He eyed his half-eaten apple before returning his gaze to her. "So. How are you going to respond on my behalf to this vixen who wants to assault me with her tongue?"

Lily's eyes widened, if that were possible, and an unintelligible croaking noise rolled from her throat. She straightened her shoulders, striking a dignified pose. "You didn't read the letter, so how do you know what she wrote?"

"Because they all write the same thing," he sighed. "Does this one describe what kind of outfit she'll wear?" He gave her another eyebrow waggle and took a bite of his apple.

Lily barked out a laugh, then proceeded to hiccup. "Okay. I see what you're doing here. I'll just answer for you and tell her, 'Meet me at Bar Louie Friday at five o'clock.' Better yet, in the parking lot? No point in spending money on cocktails if you don't have to."

He shook his head and laughed. "Put that one in a file in case she decides to stalk my ass, which she probably won't, but otherwise forget it."

"Sorry you can't indulge your fantasies, Professor?" Sporting a smug look, she folded her arms across her chest, the little minx.

"Oh, don't you worry about me. I indulge my fantasies just fine. Usually, I'm in the shower, and I'm picturing this beautiful blond, and she's got these gorgeous blue eyes, and this nice—"

Lily put up a hand. "I don't want to hear about your Kathryn Tappen fantasies."

"They're not about her. Didn't I mention this particular blond has long, curly hair?"

She blinked. "Stop. Right. There. Just stop."

"Okay," he chuckled. "Sorry." *Not.* Especially after getting an eyeful of that tantalizing telltale blush.

She dropped her forehead into her hand. "I was just thinking the other day how nice it was that you weren't one of those *cocky* athletes, but I stand corrected."

"Don't you mean confident?" he tossed out and nearly gave himself a Grandma head slap.

She groaned in response. Not a good kind of groan.

"Damn. And here I thought I was playful and endearing."

"*And* I didn't know you were a smartass."

"And *I* didn't know how many shades of pink your face turns. Like right now it's *flaming* pink. See all this great stuff we're learning about each other now that you're here?"

With a headshake, she returned to her letters. "Just go away." She was fighting a losing battle with the giggles, which shot him through with warmth. Making her laugh might have just become his new all-time favorite thing to do.

Unfortunately, her giggle battle did other things to him, like cause his growing problem to transform into a full-masted problem. He waited until her back was turned and stood, box in front of him, mumbling about going through the kids' letters himself because they were his favorites. As he lurched out of the office, his mind grasped at inventorying the mites' gear, filling out insurance forms, deciphering musical notes—anything to keep him from lingering on the curve of Lily's neck or the flare of her hips or the pink pout of her lips.

In the family room, he sat down with the box and stared at its contents without seeing them. Mentally, he meandered in and around the game tonight, the playoffs, the chase for the Cup. Despite his mind's wanderings, though, it was never far from Lily. He could practically feel the strings growing, attaching him more solidly to her, to her world.

Fifteen minutes later, she tiptoed out from the office. "Finished for today. I have to hit the grocery store before the bus drops Daisy off."

He stood and came toward her until a mere foot separated them. "Ah."

"And if I'm not mistaken, it's about nap time for you, right?" Her lips curved in a way that wasn't exactly suggestive, though it nudged his mind toward the suggestive side.

Right. Nap. He had a game tonight. He needed to focus. But damn if his head didn't succumb to his dick and leap to a different sort of nap—one that involved no sleep with a sexy blond. "You sure you can't be there tonight?"

She shook her head, and her curls bounced around her. He pictured the silk twisted around his fingers. "I wish I could, but there's no one to watch Daisy." She gave him a cute pout.

"I'll get a ticket for her too."

"It's a school night."

Tongue-tied, his synapses firing haphazardly, he was incapable of lobbing a retort because desire lit him like a damn torch. He needed to wrestle the beast back where it belonged.

He blew out an exasperated breath. "Nothing says you have to stay for the entire game. Just leave before the end."

Blue eyes stared into his, and for a moment the space between them seemed to shrink, their bodies leaning closer together. It was becoming difficult to breathe.

Please want me as much as I want you, right here, right now.

She straightened and began brushing at her shoulder, looking far too interested for the invisible something it was. "Daisy would like to attend one of your games."

His heart did a little flip. "I'd love it. Just say when. There's a matinee coming up if that would work better with her school schedule."

"That would be great. Well, um, I really should ..."

"What?"

"Go."

He stepped back and let out a nervous laugh. "So tomorrow?"

She tilted her head. "Tomorrow?"

"Carla's yoga class?"

"Oh right!" she barked, sounding as nervous as he felt.

"Why don't you bring Daisy, and I'll take us out for hot chocolate afterward?"

"I won't have Daisy with me. There's no school the next day, so she's spending the night at—"

"Derek's?" *Fucking Derek!* The sudden flare of jealousy had him reeling. *Whoa! Get a grip.*

"No, Ivy's actually. They're going to have a girls' day together."

He masked a ridiculous surge of relief. "Ah. Sounds fun. Tea parties and tutus and such?"

"You're funny." She gave him a sweet grin.

"Looks aren't everything."

"Yeah, well, it's not your looks I'm talking about, Professor. Those aren't funny."

"Worse than funny?"

"Hardly."

"Uh, thank you?"

She winked. "Just go with it."

Right. Been doing a lot of that lately. "So about yoga tomorrow."

"Yes?"

"Can I take *you* out for hot chocolate afterward?"

"Yes, Professor. I'd like that."

Chapter 18

Is It Hot in Here, or Is It You?

Carla's yoga class more closely resembled a reunion of the Super Bowl party guests than a body-twisting meditation session. With yoga togs the only clothing holding her in, Lily's self-consciousness had her positioning her mat between Natalie and Katie. She faced Gage's back, and by the end of the session she was more hot and bothered than relaxed because oh, mama, watching all those wonderful muscles flex was almost more than she could take. And with him in shorts and a sleeveless tank, there were plenty of muscles for her to keep track of. It was a wonder she hadn't jumped his back like a monkey.

At one point, she'd been so busy watching him that she'd humiliated herself by falling over with all the grace of a waterlogged elephant. Natalie had shot her a face-torching wink before jerking her head toward Gage and mouthing, "Nice tush. Just friends? Why?"

Not helping in the least, the object of Lily's hot-and-botheredness peered over his shoulder at her. "What's going on back there?"

Sipping wine afterward—because nearly everyone from the class joined them, and the majority opted for a pub rather than a coffee bar—Lily stole peeks at Gage, tracking how he joined in his teammates' good-natured abuse with self-deprecation. When talk turned to praise, he was vocal if that praise was aimed at the others but fell silent or dodged the spotlight when they bandied his name about for, say, league MVP.

"You keep tearing it up like you are, Admiral," his teammate Quinn said, "and they'll have no choice but to toss your name in the Hart Trophy ring."

"He's already *in* the running, *and* he's the favorite to win," T.J. scoffed. He slapped Gage on the back. "Our boy's got this. No question."

Gage raised his hands, palms out. "Whoa, whoa, whoa. There's *plenty* of question. There are guys playing way better who are way more deserving than me."

"Like who?" T.J. challenged.

"Like Mikelev! Guy's been carrying his team on his shoulders all season."

T.J. smirked. "So have you."

Gage gave a headshake, his expression one of pure embarrassment. He looked around at his teammates' faces. "No, everybody on this team's contributing. Hell, Shanny, if I didn't have you and Quinn for wingers, my numbers would look a whole lot different." He pointed at Wyatt. "And look at him! What's your goals-against average right now? One-nine-eight?"

"Two-oh-one," Wyatt chuckled.

"That's un-fucking-believable! You're the stingiest netminder in the NHL. How can we lose with a goalie who stands on his head, game in, game out? Talk about an MVP." Gage sipped his beer and steered the conversation toward recent sick—as he called them—plays by his teammates.

Was he really that humble? Shy? Or was he the quiet, still-waters type? *Maybe all three.* His eyes found hers with a look that flashed and sizzled like a long-tail comet. Her pulse zoomed. Quickly, he cut his gaze to his pint glass, but the effect lingered, leaving Lily a little breathless.

Oh, to know what had passed through that man's mind. There was probably nothing shy about it. Lily raised her wineglass and hovered it in front of her mouth to hide her fluster.

"So," he began as he walked her to her car afterward, "what's on Goldilocks's agenda the rest of today?"

She glanced up at a low-hanging, snow-heavy gray sky. "Scheduling a few posts for her demanding client, the Professor."

"Ah. I hear the guy's a real slave driver. Were you planning to do this work at his place?"

Her eyes darted from left to right and back again.

"Because if you are," he continued, "I hear he'd like to take you to dinner or, if you prefer, he could be talked into whipping you up something to eat."

"Really? Something other than a healthy green smoothie?"

He grinned. "Definitely something other than a healthy green smoothie."

"What sorts of things does he cook? I could post his favorite recipes on Facebook."

"Well, why don't you come over and find out?" He playfully touched the tip of her nose with his finger. "His place is on your way home."

"True." Before she had a chance to say more, he turned and headed for his Porsche.

"See you there, Goldilocks," he called over his shoulder.

Planting a fist on her hip, she watched him walk away with a sort of lazy swagger. *Pretty sure of yourself, Mr. Cage.* Oh, what the hell? Only an empty house waited for her. She'd follow him home and pick up more fan mail. A little voice popped up, warning her it would be dangerous to stick around. She told it to be quiet; skedaddling was her only agenda item once she got the letters.

Gage was waiting for her when she pulled into his driveway, and he motioned her into his wide-open, empty middle garage bay. On one side sat his Panamera. On the other, a white Range Rover.

"Why here, Professor?"

With a shrug, he depressed the garage remote, and the door began humming. "It might snow. This way your car stays dry and toasty."

Right. Dry and toasty.

They entered his kitchen through the mudroom, where he dropped his gear. Keys and wallet landed on the kitchen desk. Something beeped.

"Be right back." He hustled off toward the entryway.

He returned a few moments later. "Had to turn off the security cameras. Water?"

Cameras? Her mind rocketed to rifling his nightstand while her heart plunged to her stomach. *Oh shit!* "Water sounds good," she choked out.

He grabbed two glasses, filled them, and passed one to her. Leaning his back against the kitchen island, he took a long drink that had his neck muscles on full display and the knot of his Adam's apple bobbing.

She gulped a lungful of air. "How long have you had security cameras?"

He straightened, looking utterly dumbfounded. "Uh, since the system was installed?"

"I thought you didn't use your system." She ducked her face so her flush didn't give her away.

"I fire it up on occasion to test everything out and because my insurance agent yells at me if I don't keep it on," he chuckled.

"I've never noticed the cameras. Where are they?"

He shrugged. "Here and there. That's good you can't see them. Means I can spy on you when you're here and I'm out of town."

Just kill me now! She ducked her face so her flush didn't give her away and momentarily recovered her wits. "I should pick up your mail and get going."

His blue eyes widened. "Whoa. Did I say something wrong?"

"What? No, nothing." She flapped a hand at him and started toward his office. God, did her face have to broadcast *every* emotion?

His hand encircled her arm, like a cuff of heat. "That's not nothing that went through your eyes just now." He dipped his head and peered deep. "And your face is bright pink."

He was all up in her personal bubble now, and she tried to break free of his grasp *and* his gaze.

"Lily," he said softly. "What's. Going. On?"

She pulled away and cinched her arms over her chest. "I ... You're not going to like me very much."

He frowned. "I doubt that, but why?"

She puffed out a hair-lifting breath. *Here goes nothing.* "When you were gone a few weeks ago, Hobbes jumped on your bed and started coughing up a hairball. I was looking for something to catch it with before she got it all over your comforter, and I ..." The words jammed in her throat.

His frown deepened, but one corner of his mouth twitched. "You what? Filled my bed with crackers? Used all my bubble bath? Ruined my prized, nonexistent cactus collection?"

It wasn't funny, but damn if her catapulting nerves and his ridiculously random scenarios didn't make her want to explode with laughter. "No, worse." Fighting the smile tipping her lips, she raised sheepish eyes to his.

"Worse than ruining my cactus collection?"

"I rifled your nightstand looking for tissues."

His expression didn't waver. "Okaaaaay? Did you fill *that* with crackers?"

A little laugh did escape her despite her best efforts to bottle it up. "No, but I didn't find any tissues. I found other stuff."

He grabbed her hand and tugged her up the stairs. "Show me."

"*Show* you?" she yelped to his back, horrified.

"Yeah, show me what you found that's bothering you."

"Nothing's *bother—*" She entered the bedroom just as he opened the drawer.

He slapped his palm against his forehead. "Aw, shit! I've been meaning to get rid of these forever, but I keep forgetting until I add the next one, and by then I'm in bed and too tired to deal."

Into the bathroom he marched, and when he reappeared, he held a trash can that he placed on the floor. He slid the drawer out, dumped the contents into the can, and reset the now-empty drawer back in its slot.

His fists went to his hips. "Damning, but only circumstantial. I swear. Any other mysteries we need to clear up?"

A ration of relief, along with a pinch of guilt, lifted her. "Not today, Professor." The brunette was none of her business, and Lily was content to let her stay hidden from the light.

It's not like we're, well, anything to each other anyway.

"Okay," Gage puffed. "Glad to hear that's all that's hanging out there."

Damn it! That's what he got for slacking on the decluttering, but it hadn't been an issue because he'd never had any dates over. Hadn't wanted any here before the one who now stood in front of him—not that Lily was exactly a *date*. Or was she? *Irrelevant*. Whether she was or wasn't, he hadn't planned on her being here, although he'd certainly fantasized about it enough. And now that she was here? He wasn't sure what to do about it. She wasn't giving clear cues. The way her leggings and sweater clung to her curves, however, gave him a few awesome ideas, cues or not. But he didn't want to scare her away.

She chewed her thumbnail. "Are you mad I went through your drawer?"

"Hell no." And surprisingly, he wasn't. Maybe he was in the grip of lunacy, but the notion that she might have been jealous gave him a warm, fuzzy feeling. He also liked the intimacy, the familiarity of having her look through his drawer. Maybe someday she'd have some of *her* stuff in there.

The final thought had come out of nowhere, though he couldn't say it was unwelcome. In fact, it sounded nice.

"I don't have anything to hide from you," he tossed out.

When her only response was a nod, he continued. "I hate that you've got the wrong idea about me."

She stepped close to him. So close he could smell her shampoo, the scent of flowers rising from her skin. His body tensed, on high alert. He thought she might rise up on tiptoe and kiss him, and fuck, did he want her to. More than anything in the world.

In a voice soft and husky, she said, "I don't know that I've got the wrong idea."

He dove into her deep blue pools. "Do you ever think we went about everything the wrong way, Lily? That we got things backward?"

Her brows furrowed in question, and her eyes flicked over him. The space between them seemed to shrink. So did his lung capacity.

"I'm not sure I understand. There's no ... We're not a *we* to get things backward," she replied.

True, but we could be a we. Something told him this wasn't the time.

Acutely aware they stood a mere five feet from his bed, he tugged on her chain to distract himself. "Is this what I think it is?"

She glanced down. "It was my wedding band. It seemed weird to wear it, but weird to take it off, so this was the compromise I came up with."

Ah. Late husband's hanging around her neck. That was distraction enough. With an inner sigh, he gave her a shoulder nudge to guide her out of the bedroom. She grasped his bicep, and electrical current surged through his bloodstream.

Before he knew what happened, before he knew who started it, their lips were touching, and his hands were on her back, running over her dips and flares while his tongue pushed into her sweet, soft mouth. Whether it was her or her lip stuff, she tasted like cherries. Her small hands slid around his waist, under his shirt, sweeping over his skin, shooting chills to every part of his body. One part in particular woke right the hell up.

She pulled back abruptly, seeming to steady herself by hanging onto his arms. He was a little unsteady himself.

"Lily?"

"I'm sweaty. The yoga was intense ... um ..."

"I don't care." He held her gaze. "To me, you smell like a field full of flowers."

She stepped back, out of his reach, and waved her hand between their bodies. "Okay. Wow. Apparently, there's still some crazy chemistry happening here."

He didn't need a glimpse at himself to know he looked as if he hid Pinocchio's nose in his gym shorts. But he didn't care about that either. "Is crazy chemistry between us such a bad thing?"

Her hand flew to her forehead. "Yes. No. I don't know. I'm working for you now, and there's Daisy and ... I shouldn't be ... There's so much at stake!"

Despite all the blood rushing below his waistband, the switches in his brain miraculously began flipping on. And damn if the dizzying endorphin rush that had been coursing through his veins didn't fizzle under the weight of her statement.

He stepped toward her and ran his hands up and down her arms. "Lily, what if we don't fight the crazy chemistry and see where it takes us?" he coaxed. With a shrug, he added, "And if I have to, I'll just fire you."

Her blue eyes darkened, reflecting amusement. She reached up and traced the healing cut above his eye. Her touch sent tingles dancing along his spine.

"You said no hanky-panky, Professor," she whispered.

He slipped one arm around her, reeling her in tight. Her scent swirled up his nose and invaded his senses. Her hands landed on his chest. With his other hand, he caressed her cheek, pushing her riotous curls from her face while he studied her. "I never said that. *You* said that. I simply acknowledged you."

She spluttered. "But you—"

He placed a finger against her lips. "I."

Slid the finger away, lowered his mouth to the base of her throat, and hovered. "Never."

Placed a kiss there. "Promised."

Another kiss, and he inched up. "To."

Planted a lingering kiss and moved again. "Keep."

Softly sucked below her ear. "My."

With a sigh, she tilted her head to the side, elongating her neck. Fingers tangled in her hair, he tugged her head back, giving him better access to her sweetly salty skin. "Hands."

His lips on her ear, he whispered, "Off."

With the tip of his tongue, he traced the shell of her ear. "You."

She shuddered in his arms, and a sound like a musical, drawn-out "oh" escaped her, pushing his heartbeat into anaerobic territory. He leaned back and gazed at her half-lidded eyes and parted mouth. She looked drunk, mirroring the thought-paralysis taking place inside his own intoxicated brain.

Her plump, cherry-stained lips were too tempting to resist, and he took them gently, ready to stop if she said no. She didn't resist, instead gliding her hands to his shoulders, so he kept going, continuing the onslaught he'd begun on her neck. Raising up on tiptoe, she hooked an arm around his neck and dropped the other around his waist, cinching herself closer still. He tightened his hold, nearly engulfing her small frame in his arms. Her tongue found his, sparred with it, and softly sucked it into her mouth. His conscious mind cut out entirely, and he angled her head to deepen the kiss.

She met him stroke for stroke, riding the intense wave of the kiss with him, but she pulled away the moment it ended. Her ragged breathing matched his, and her pink cheeks looked as though they were smudged with strawberry juice. "I must smell awful after the workout."

Somewhere downstairs, a phone was ringing.

Drumming his palm against his chest, he watched her as though he watched a darting chipmunk. He tried to mask his amusement. "You smell perfect. Now if this is your way of telling me *I* smell awful, then just say it."

Her eyes flew wide. "No! That's not ... You ... You're not ... You smell ... really good."

He backed up, sat on the edge of the bed, crossed his ankle over his leg, and pulled off a sock, wearing an expression he hoped was a grin and not a leer. "If you're that self-conscious, I've got a shower that accommodates two."

Jabbing her thumb over her shoulder, she turned. "I should ... That call could be about Daisy."

"That was *my* phone, and I don't give a shit who's calling." He held out his hand and curled a finger at her. "Come here, beautiful."

Chapter 19

I'M NOT SHY

Guilt nibbled at Lily over what she'd been doing with the sexy, mussed-up man sitting on the edge of his bed. Over the *more* her girlie parts had her contemplating doing. There'd be no turning back if she followed their lead. Her body was so ready to jump him, but her mind was putting up a fight. Sort of.

Even before the kiss, her stomach had been gyrating. Hell, her whole body! Now she could swear squirrels were scrabbling inside it, making it hard to think.

He didn't need a shower. He smelled like leather in the pines, and her babbling hormones told her she wanted that intoxicating scent all over her.

Let's see where the crazy chemistry takes us. Straight to a laboratory explosion of epic proportions! Keeping her hands off him lately had been tougher than doing all of her Christmas shopping on Black Friday. At the mall.

As he eyed her, her rational mind threw up one last gasp, warning her not to give in to her burgeoning desire. But the urge to touch him, to feel his smooth, solid warmth beneath her fingertips nudged away reason, and she leaned against the door frame, arms folded over her chest as if barricading herself. Ankle resting casually on his knee, he pulled off his other sock. The sight of him, in gym shorts and sleeveless T-shirt that exposed his sculpted biceps and powerful shoulders, shot tingles throughout her body, seeming to congregate in her core. Even his feet were beautiful.

Gage regarded her and smiled. Not his usual dazzling smile, but a hesitant one, as though he wasn't confident what to do next. He straightened. "Are we okay here?"

Little alarm bells clanged. "Why wouldn't we be?" She waved her hand between them before tucking it back in place. "Nothing's changed. We're friends." The words sounded all wrong for what she wanted to convey. But what exactly did she want to convey? She drew a blank and shut her mouth before it could run away from her. One big barrel of confused, roiling emotions heading for a plunge from the cliffs—that's what she was.

He arched an eyebrow at her, then neatly placed his socks next to him before swinging his gaze back to her. "Lily, I need to set a few things straight." Resting his elbows on his thighs, he leaned forward and sighed. Her heart jumped into her throat.

Where's he going with this?

"I've been thinking about this a lot," he said. "I'm not interested in being friends or business acquaintances or whatever hell label you want to put on it. Not with you. Not anymore."

Excited, terrified, she stood frozen and blinked.

"What I want you to understand ..." He swallowed. "I intend to take this to the next level because being in the friend zone isn't enough for me. And I hope you're okay with that. If not, we need to stop this before it goes any further."

She stared at him, his words scoring their message on her heart. In the dim corners of her mind, that little voice told her what she was planning to do was wrong. Her stomach tightened, one coil at a time. "Um ..."

Smoldering blue eyes held hers as he leaned back on fisted hands. "People think I don't date because I'm shy or something like that." He shook his head. "I'm not. The reason I don't date is because I'm particular, which means I don't chase indiscriminately. But make no mistake. It might take me a while, but I'm not easily deterred when I make up my mind I want something."

Processing, processing, processing!

Her pulse rate ratcheted up, and blood pounded between her ears. Was the thudding preventing her from hearing him correctly? From thinking coherently? Her head nodded without asking her permission.

She masked her inner reeling self, the one whose engines were revving at peak RPMs, primed to burn rubber. As though her body were tethered to an unseen line, she toed off her shoes and moved toward him.

A sparkle in his eyes hypnotized, drawing her in. Like Svengali. Dracula. Without the bloodshot whites. She had no choice but to obey; she couldn't summon any will but his. If he ordered her into the shower, that's where she'd go—pasty skin, lumps, and bumps on full display.

With her thighs nearly bumping his knees, he wrapped an arm around her waist and tugged her between his legs, eyes still locked on hers as he looked up at her. His other hand, big and warm, glided over her hip.

"So are you on board?" he murmured.

God, yes! The only answer she gave him was another nod. Apparently, she'd been stupefied speechless.

Breaking the connection, he lifted the hem of her thin sweater and focused on her exposed stomach. "Hold that," he commanded softly. Wholly under his spell, she gripped the knit fabric in one hand. His hands slid slowly to her ass. Cupping her cheeks, he pulled her to within an inch of his lips. Her skin burned with anticipation, and when his open, moist mouth landed on it, she could've sworn it sizzled.

His kisses were warm, languid affairs that coaxed her skin into a goose-bumped landscape. Taking his time, he worked his way across her belly, first one way and then the other, pausing to lightly suck, lick. She dropped her free hand on his shoulder, out of his way, not wanting to interfere with his determined track. Behind her, long, strong fingers began kneading her flesh through her leggings. Her head dropped back, and a moan bubbled up in her chest.

He brought a hand back to her stomach, eliciting a gasp from her when his fingertips brushed her sensitive skin. Mouth adhered to her abdomen, still performing its magic, he pushed her bra up, exposing the swell below her breasts. Instinctively, she cinched her sweater tighter, lifting it higher, giving him access, inwardly begging him to work his way up. Wetness was pooling in her panties, and she vaguely wondered if he could smell her surging arousal.

Kissing the undersides of her breasts, he took care to touch his lips to every inch. As he passed over the tender flesh, he flicked his tongue out, licking a warm trail back and forth. Legs quivering, she fought to stay upright. She released the sweater, and it fell on his head. She scrabbled to regather the hem. He pushed it away and mumbled, “Off,” before withdrawing his lips and all that heat. Disappointment swelled inside her until he raised his head, his perusal skipping over her stomach and chest and landing on her eyes. A heady combination of affection and awe swam in a sea of blatant, blue-eyed lust, flipping her stomach upside down.

With a gentle tug on her sweater, he repeated his demand. “Off. Now.”

She complied, jerking the top over her head. His gaze fixed on her breasts. She felt her taut nipples poking the sheer lace of her bra cups. Whatever had possessed her to wear her best underwear today didn’t matter at the moment, but she was grateful she had. With his finger pads, he traced the bare contours of her breasts below the bra’s underwire. A flurry of shivers shimmied up her spine, shooting along her arms, down her legs. His thumbs strummed her nipples while he watched, seemingly entranced. Then his mouth latched on, his tongue and lips assaulting her nipple through the lace while his thumb circled the other one. Unable to stop herself, she wrapped her hands around his head, tunneling her fingers in his strands. The smell of his hair, him, teased her nose, and she pulled in his scent, looking on in a daze while his mouth and hands moved from one breast to the other. Her breathing ragged and shallow, her mind spun out into the Kuiper Belt, where it tumbled end over end.

Her hips began writhing, trying to find purchase against him. Without breaking contact, he slung an arm between her legs, splaying his fingers across her ass and the small of her back. She ground herself with shameless abandon against the makeshift saddle formed by his rock-hard forearm and bicep. The gauzy fabric of her bra became saturated as he moved back and forth, back and forth.

Either nipple his mouth abandoned chilled, and she moaned an incoherent plea for its return.

When he stopped and withdrew his arm, she pulled back and met his smoky gaze. His hands snaked up her back, and he released her bra clasp, peeling the straps slowly down her arms, his fingers grazing her as they went. The promise of what was to come ignited her like a backdrafting fire. She ached to feel his skin against hers. To have him buried deep inside her.

In a surprising move, he pulled her into his body and twisted, flipping her on her back on the bed. Fingers lacing with hers, he stretched her arms wide and scanned her bared chest beneath him.

“Beautiful,” he murmured, his voice thick and reverent. “Absolutely beautiful.”

He dipped his head and drew a breast into his mouth, circling her nipple with his tongue. Rolling it between his teeth, he bit down, sending shards of pleasure along her nerve endings, making her body throb all the more for him. Straddling her hips, he rose up, reached behind his back, and tugged off his T-shirt with one hand. She glimpsed a wall of glistening muscle before he bent his head and devoted equal attention to the other breast. Squirming, bucking against him, her inner pleas that he take her came out in moans and gasps. But he seemed to be on his own tortuous timetable.

Minutes or hours later—she wasn’t sure which—while his mouth continued to demonstrate his adoration for her breasts, his fingers hooked the sides of her leggings and dragged them down her legs, bringing her panties with them. She helped him along, kicking her clothing off her ankles.

Now she was totally naked to him. In broad daylight. He sat up once more, sliding beside her on the bed, sitting back on his heels, one leg nestled against her, creating a stripe of heat where it touched. Suffocating self-doubt rose to the fore as he roamed his hand over her body, his eyes following with primal intensity. And again. And again.

As she watched him taking her in, something unexpected happened. Her modesty scattered. The way he looked at her, with so much hunger and heat, and the way he touched her, as though worshipping every square inch of her, made her soar inside. She’d never felt more beautiful, alluring, bewitching. The bulge in his shorts told her he was affected too.

He ran a warm, calloused hand up her inner thigh, and she reflexively parted her legs, inviting him in, wanting more. After ghosting a teasing touch over her apex that made her clench with desire, he trailed his fingers down the other thigh. "So soft," he whispered with awe.

Re-positioning himself between her ankles, he draped his heavy arms on her thighs and planted his hands in place. Once he had her pinned, he began leisurely licking and kissing the trail his hand had just blazed up her thigh. The closer his mouth came to her juncture, the more her lungs stuttered and her hips struggled to rise off the mattress to meet his mouth, but his grip kept her grounded. Her moans grew louder, her panting more uneven, and she bit down on her bottom lip. Just as he reached her entrance, he switched direction to the other leg, working his way slowly back down to her foot. His soft hair brushed her sensitive skin. She wanted to yell in frustration and yank him back up.

He kissed her toes and the tops of her feet and fondled the insides of her ankles with his tongue before moving to the outsides, leaving her gasping for breath. Oh so slowly, he tormented her with exquisite, erotic, nearly unbearable sensations as he moved up her calves to the backs of her knees.

Muscles alternately bunching and stretching with ripples of pleasure, her body became a live wire, buzzing, sizzling, primed and ready for him. And then he stopped.

He crawled up her body, swept the hair off her forehead, and kissed a corner of her mouth. "Good so far?"

A cacophony of unformed thoughts bounced around her brain; they seemed to swarm around demands she both wanted and didn't want to make of him. Push, pull.

While she fought for a coherent answer, his hand swept down her chest to her breast, caressing, stroking, teasing. A mewl escaped her before she could swallow it. He let out a soft chuckle. "I take that as a 'yes.'"

"Yes," she finally managed, "but you're driving me crazy."

He nuzzled her neck and feathered kisses over her shoulder and collar bone while his hands explored her breasts. His touch was sometimes gentle, other times insistent. “Driving you crazy is the whole idea,” he breathed against her throat.

“I know, but—”

He took her mouth hard, cutting off the rest of what she’d meant to say. His tongue plundered at will, fragmenting her feeble train of thought. Her arms wrapped around his neck and shoulders, holding him in place.

The kiss ended with a few soft pecks, and he lifted his head, his eyes mining hers. “But?”

They were both breathing heavily.

“I want you inside me,” she whispered, running the back of her hand along his jaw, over his sculpted arm, down to the hard shaft in his shorts, gratified when a groan rumbled in his chest.

He captured her hand and trapped it above her head. “Not yet.”

While his mouth kept hers busy with another feverish kiss, his hand slid farther down her body. He slipped a finger inside her, then another, stroking, curling, manipulating with a perfect touch, and her body arched off the bed.

Oh. My. God!

She turned her lips away from the kiss so she could breathe, her eyes rolling back in her head. An orgasm crashed over her before she even realized it was building. No warning, catching her by surprise as she shattered and clenched around his fingers.

Wind knocked from her lungs, she lay in his arms breathing hard, coming down. His unmoving fingers were still inside her. Warm lips caressed the shell of her ear. “Better?” he breathed.

She nodded against his solid chest. “Better.”

He dusted tender kisses across her eyelids and forehead before rolling to his side and propping himself up on an elbow. Her eyes fluttered open and were immediately caught in his gaze. His fingers started their rhythmic stroking once more, and her body responded as if acting on its own, her hips rocking to the tempo his hand set. All of her wanted to press herself against him, but he braced his arm, keeping her on her back.

“I want to watch you.” His eyes swept from her face down her body, pausing where his fingers slid slowly in and out, in and out.

His heated gaze settled back on hers, and she lost herself in their depths. The cadence picked up, his strokes intensifying, hitting that mind-bending chord. Her breath caught in her throat as she watched his shifting expression through half-lidded eyes, watched the pleasure build on his face as the pleasure he unleashed mounted inside her body.

"God, you are so beautiful," he said.

Closing her eyes, locking out everything but the crescendo being orchestrated inside her, she spiraled upward to a carnal height, where she let herself go, falling to pieces in front of him, all over him, hissing God's name in an endless loop.

He slipped his fingers out and kissed her deeply, then turned her on her stomach before her conscious mind landed back on Planet Earth. Kneeling between her legs, he caressed her with his hands and mouth from the backs of her knees to her shoulder blades, taking his sweet time with her ass. Then she was on her back again, and he opened her legs, nestling his broad shoulders between them, his soft beard and hot breath tickling the delicate skin between her thighs. His mouth zeroed in on her with a single-minded purpose. He lapped in long, unbroken sweeps, top to bottom.

She sucked in a breath, and he traced her again with the tip of that lethal tongue, licking and lashing, his fingertips trailing after, feathering over her.

Nearly out of her body and mind, she hovered on a knife's edge where he continually took her only to haul her back in when she got close to another climax. Sensations filling her, rocking her, she yelped when his taut tongue ran over her unbearably sensitive flesh and plunged inside her. His big hands kept her in place while she grinded against him. Groans of pleasure vibrated through his mouth as his tongue fucked her.

Her body shuddered, and she went over the cliff, lost in ecstasy, her cries echoing somewhere outside herself as if in a distant, cottony cloud. Like a rag doll, her limbs hung useless and boneless. She vaguely registered the rustling of fabric, then his heat and weight sank on top of her, his bare skin brushing hers, slick and smooth. Hands in her hair, he covered her mouth with his. She tasted herself on his tongue as it swept deep inside, probing, exploring, claiming her mouth. Rolling her tongue over his, she pushed back and sucked his bottom lip between her teeth. His cock, thick and heavy, was trapped between them, and she reached down and ran her fingertips along its length. He shifted his weight to give her full access, then rewarded her with a chest-rumbling growl when she took him in her hand.

He broke the kiss and rubbed his nose against hers. "I need to get my wallet."

Confused, she asked, "What's in your wallet?"

He kissed a corner of her mouth and gave her a lopsided grin. "It's not a credit card."

A giggle bubbled up. "A condom?"

He nodded as he kissed the other corner of her mouth. She continued stroking him, and he hissed, "Oh Jesuuuus!"

"Don't you have some up here?" she asked.

He raised his head and peered at her. "I don't think so. Do I?"

Her eyes slid to the side. "I'm pretty sure there are some in your nightstand."

Surprise flickered in his eyes. Had he forgotten them? She'd deal with that later because right now, she had more important things on her mind. "I have an IUD."

His eyebrows inched up his forehead.

"Since neither of us has been with anyone since the last time we slept together ..."

"I'm clean," he said instantly. "So are you, right?"

Nodding slowly, she raked her fingers through his hair and teased his stiff cock with the other hand.

He sucked in a breath, and his eyes rolled back. "Are you sure about this?" he gritted out.

"I'm sure." She kissed a trail along his strong jaw to his ear.

"Christ almighty, you make me fucking crazy, Lily. I want you so bad." Unadulterated desperation and longing reverberated in his voice, and Lily's spirit surged. Boldness bloomed.

"Tell me how I make you crazy, Gage," she whispered back, nibbling his earlobe while her hand worked his silky shaft.

He wrapped his long fingers around her throat and nuzzled her cheek, panting against her skin. "You're all I think about. Being buried so deep inside you I don't know where I end and you begin."

She opened her legs to accommodate him, and he repositioned himself until he nudged her entrance. Her hands moved to his back. "Vanilla sex, Professor?"

A strangled sound came from him. She thought it was a laugh. “Vanilla, strawberry, pecan praline. You name the flavor. I aim to please.” His hands back in her hair, eyes locked on hers, he inched inside her. His breath stuttered. “You feel incredible.”

While her body adjusted to his girth, taking him in bit by bit, a series of moans rolled from him. He feathered kisses over her cheek, her jaw, and laid his mouth alongside her ear. “Watching you get off was the hottest fucking thing I’ve ever seen in my entire life. Jesus, I want to make you come all over me again and again.”

Now it was her turn to pull in a sharp breath. She didn’t have much experience with dirty talk, but between that and the sensation of him sinking deeper inside her, without latex between them, she stood on the brink of another climax. He flexed his hips and thrust deeper, gaining headway within her walls, ripping a throaty moan from her chest.

“That’s it, beautiful girl. Moan for me. Fuck, I love the sexy sounds you make.”

He withdrew partway and drove in harder, burying himself to the hilt. A sound that was part-moan, part-wail escaped her. He began to move, his rhythm deep and slow. She stroked his back and dug her fingers into his ass, urging him to go faster.

Another chuckle. “Not yet. I plan to make this last a while.” He paused. “In fact, I think it’s time to change flavors.”

Before she could react, he withdrew and flipped her on her stomach. He wedged a pillow under her hips, and he was back inside her. His hand slid to her front, and his fingers expertly circled and teased while his hips began moving in time, making her groan and writhe and see stars exploding in her head.

The slow, steady tempo brought him deeper inside her. Pleasure so intense it was almost painful coursed through her bloodstream like a river of fire, drenching her in sensations she’d never felt before.

He kept up the unhurried, steady strokes, driving her out of her mind. But it was his words that pushed her higher into the stratosphere.

“I want to fuck you into next week, Lily. I want to fuck you till you can’t walk without thinking of me buried inside you.”

The power was all his. She’d relinquished it, a spellbound captive of his words, his lips, his fingers, his glorious cock. This quiet, unassuming man strummed her body like a damn guitar, plucking and coaxing at will. She longed to explode, implode, disintegrate around him.

He shifted behind her, flattening his palm against her belly to hold her in place while his hips picked up speed. His free hand cupped her breast, pinching her nipple. He dropped his head to the base of her neck, sank his teeth into her flesh, and sucked her skin hard.

Shy he was not.

Mind splintering into a million fragments, she babbled incoherently as she was lifted into soul-bending euphoria. Her unstoppable moans transformed into hoarse shouts that seemed to spur him on, and he slammed into her over and over.

As he rode her harder and harder, the pillow flattened, and her knees slid out. He collapsed on top of her and stopped mid-stroke. Chest heaving, he pulled out. An icy ache rushed into the hollow he no longer filled.

She glanced at him over her shoulder. “What are you doing?” she gasped.

Grabbing her ankles, he turned her over. Cold air raced over her, puckering her skin, turning her nipples to hard peaks. He stretched out above her, bracing his weight on his forearms, bracketing her. Panting hard, he peered down at her, his burnished eyes on the wild side. Wet and steely, his cock prodded her. “What do you *want* me to do, Lily?”

She tugged on his shoulders to pull him to her, but he didn’t budge.

His eyes remained fixed on hers. “Tell me what you want, Lily.”

She exhaled a frustrated growl.

He dropped his head to her breast, drawing it into his mouth, rolling her nipple between his teeth before he bit down lightly.

“Don’t be shy. Tell me what you want me to do to you,” he murmured.

Licking, sucking, devouring, there was nothing gentle about his mouth’s assault, and it made her want to climb him, to impale herself on him. God, so much!

He blew on her wet nipple, stiffening it until it throbbed. "Talk to me, Lily." He moved to her other breast, subjecting it to the same treatment.

Her voice came out strained, small, and reedy. "I want you to fuck me."

"Tell me again. Louder this time. Make me believe you. Use that beautiful voice of yours." His body still a hard plank suspended above her, his head bobbed as he clamped down and gave her nipple a hard flick of his tongue. His rigid cock prodded her stomach.

"Gage," she gasped, "I want to feel you inside me, filling me. I want you to fuck me hard."

Raising his head, he looked deep into her eyes with blazing heat. He grabbed her hips and tossed her legs over his shoulders, his cock poised at her entrance.

He drove into her slowly at first, stroking deeper, deeper, over and over, his breathing growing labored, his guttural grunts pitching louder as he picked up speed. He squeezed his eyes shut as pleasure played over his chiseled features and built in intensity, as though he were ready to detonate inside. Captured in his grip, helpless to match his rocketing thrusts, she held on while he pounded relentlessly.

And, God help her, she loved it!

This time when she crashed into the abyss, he followed, hissing her name and praising God, Christ, and all the saints as he went.

Chapter 20

WHAT'S PASSED ISN'T PAST

Gage came to, realizing he had not, in fact, died. Lily lay beside him, her wild hair strewn over the comforter, her eyes on the ceiling, her creamy breasts rising and falling as she caught her breath. Her face, throat, and chest were flushed a beautiful shade of deep pink. A wave of satisfaction washed over him knowing he was the reason she looked that way.

Apparently, he'd rolled off of her, though he couldn't remember doing it. Couldn't remember a whole lot of anything except the bombs bursting in air and the in-fucking-credible feeling of being inside her.

Shit. Had he gone too far? What the hell had gotten into him?

Lily. Getting into her had gotten into him.

He glanced over at her, a little worried about the expression he'd find. Her bright blue eyes were on him. Breaking into a soft smile, she ran the back of her hand along his beard. *Okay. She's smiling. That's a good thing*. He covered her hand with his, pulled it to his mouth, and kissed it. Unbidden, *I love you* popped into his head. *Whoa! A little soon*. Oh yeah. He'd need to keep that to himself.

"Hi, beautiful," he rasped instead.

"Hi, yourself." She raised up on an elbow, facing him, giving him a full view of her forever curves—a view he could get used to seeing every day.

He wrapped one of her curls around his finger. "That was ... that was ..."

She arched an eyebrow.

"Not vanilla," he laughed.

"And not July," she countered.

He wasn't sure if that was a good or bad thing, but when she draped her arm and leg over him and snuggled against his chest, he took it as a good sign. He wrapped his arms around her and pulled her close, nuzzling her hair.

"What kind of shampoo do you use?" His voice came out thick and fuzzy.

"It's something with almonds. I just started using it. Why?"

He brushed her hair back, dropped a kiss on it, and inhaled. "It smells really good."

She wiggled in a little closer, and a smile curved his lips. He could get used to this too. "Cold?" he asked.

"Just the parts of me that are exposed," she murmured.

He grasped the comforter and dragged it over her, then settled into the mattress with a deep, contented sigh as he held her.

A little while later, he startled, only to find the comforter completely covering him and Lily gone. His heart bottomed out. How long had he been asleep? It was still daytime, though the light was thinning. Hobbes stared at him with curiosity from a foot away. Not the female he wanted to wake up to.

Water was running in the bathroom, and he sank back in relief. A moment later, Lily emerged, panties on, tugging her sweater around her hips. Her eyes widened. "Did I wake you up?"

He rolled to his side and faced her. "No. How long was I out?"

She sat on the edge of the bed, the mattress barely dipping, and began pulling on her leggings. "Maybe fifteen minutes? You looked so peaceful, and I didn't want to disturb you."

An alarm went off inside him. "Are you leaving?

Planting one hand behind him, she leaned over and kissed him, long and sweet. "No, I was planning on raiding your fridge to see what I could find for us to eat, and I didn't think I should be traipsing around your house half-naked with all those open windows."

He wound an arm around her, his cheeks stretched into a stupid grin. "I can't see my closest neighbor from here. Feel free to take off your clothes and traipse at will."

Lips quirking, she smoothed his hair off his forehead, making it impossible for him to wipe the smile from his face.

"It's a little chilly in the kitchen," she said, "so I'll just leave them on for now. Besides, it might be fun having you take them off me later." She wiggled her eyebrows, and his cock danced to life.

He slipped his hand under her sweater and pulled her down to him. "How about right now?" As his fingers traveled up her back, he realized she wore nothing under the sweater, and his dancing cock became a full-on boner. His hand slid down her back, around her ribcage, until he palmed her breast. It filled his hand perfectly. Her nipple beaded as soon as his fingers brushed it, and he found himself lifting the sweater, angling his mouth closer to her skin.

A giggle bubbled out of her. "I could use a little food before the *next* workout, Professor. I'm guessing you could too?"

Eyes on her, he flicked his tongue out and licked. She pulled in a quick breath, then faked a stern look. "Are you going to help me in your kitchen or not?"

"I will as long as you keep giving me a reason to keep up my strength."

"Keeping up your strength is good—among other things you should keep up."

"Goldilocks, you have a one-track mind." *And I love it.*

With a wink, she pulled away, rearranged her sweater, and stood. "Right now that one-track is all about food."

"I'll be right down," he said. *As soon as I get something else down.* He watched as her ass swayed out the door, then rolled onto his back with a happy groan and a plan to keep her there formulating in his head.

Minutes later, he got up, threw on a pair of sweatpants, and jogged downstairs to the kitchen. The sight of Lily on tiptoe, peering into one of his cabinets, brought him to a halt. Yeah, another sight he could get used to. She glanced over her shoulder at him and smiled.

"Going through my stuff again?" he teased.

Her cheeks instantly pinked. "I was looking for measuring cups."

"Ah." He walked toward a different cabinet, opened it, and slid out a rolling shelf. "They should all be there." Crossing his arms, he leaned back against the counter and watched her sort through varying glass and plastic bowls and cups. "So, speaking of going through my stuff ..."

She froze and fastened wide eyes on him.

He fought a smile. "You were right about the, ah, condoms in the nightstand." An old three-pack he'd totally spaced, but what interested him more was what he found beside it.

"Well," she paused and cleared her throat, "when I didn't find any tissues in the drawer, I ..."

"You naturally checked the cabinet."

A slow nod.

"Did you find anything else in there?" he asked.

She reared back, placed her hand on her hip, and struck a sassy pose that had him wanting to carry her cute ass right back to bed. "You must know I did if you're asking."

With a low chuckle, he reached for her and drew her between his legs, lacing his hands at the small of her back. "You saw the picture."

Her index finger traced a lazy circle on his bare chest, and her gaze followed it. "I saw the picture. But I don't need to know about it."

"You don't need to know, but I want to tell you anyway." He lifted her chin with a knuckle. "You okay with that?"

"I'm okay with that," she whispered. The look in her eyes told him differently.

"Jessica is a girl Sarah and I grew up with. Our moms were best friends, and they took care of each other's kids. Consequently, we kids all had a second mom. Well, I actually had *three*, considering Grandma, and sometimes four, if you count Sarah."

Lily rewarded him with a half-smile. "Poor guy."

"Oh, you have *no* idea! It was like living in a foreign country, not to mention all the lady things *everywhere*. Every night they seemed to reproduce. Not that I mind lady things. Well, I don't mind *your* lady things. But then, they're smaller and lacier and a hell of a lot sexier." He felt himself tighten again. "Sorry. Where were we?"

She quirked an eyebrow. “You and Jessica?”

And now things quieted down below his waistband. “Right. Jess and I were childhood friends, and about five years ago, we, uh, decided to try dating. That picture was taken during my first all-star weekend—I was picked as a rookie sub. Jess and I were seeing each other at the time, so I brought her with me. That’s it.” He held on to Lily, and she continued tracing outlines on his skin.

A furrow appeared on her forehead. “I assume things fell apart.”

“Shortly after that weekend, as a matter of fact. I think we lasted a whopping six weeks.”

“What happened?”

He pulled in a cleansing breath. “It just wasn’t … It didn’t work. Turns out we were better friends than lovers.”

Staring into Lily’s eyes, he noticed for the first time they held gold flecks and were ringed in a deep, dark blue. *Wonder if T.J. would paint them?*

“Who broke it off?”

He lifted her hand from his chest and kissed her fingers before putting it back. “I did.” The small spark that had existed between him and Jess had died a quick death. At least for him, and guilt still haunted him. He’d done a piss-poor job ending it.

“But you kept the picture.”

“No, I left it in the Bay Area, and when my mom and sister came out to help me decorate this place, Mom brought it with her. She thought I wanted it, and I didn’t have the heart to tell her I didn’t after she went to the trouble. It’s been in the nightstand ever since. I never look in there, which is why I have condoms and a picture I forgot existed.”

Lily’s expression turned thoughtful. “What’s the longest relationship you’ve been in?”

Suppressing a flinch, he barked out, “Me?” *Oh yeah, that didn’t give away anything.*

She flashed him an impish smile. “I wasn’t asking Hobbes. Yes, Professor. *You.*”

“Well, that would be … a few months?”

Three rapid-fire blinks. “So Jessica’s among the longest relationships you’ve had?”

He nodded. “It’s not that I don’t want one, it’s just that—”

"You don't chase indiscriminately."

He craned his head and stole a kiss. "Relationships take time and energy, and hockey's been priority one. But it's more than that. I guess I've just been disappointed. I start seeing someone, but then I find out they're way more interested in what I do than who I am. I got tired of it, got tired of meeting the same clones over and over, so I took a break from dating. I was still on that break when I met you at the wedding."

She nodded as if this explained everything, then rose in his arms, cradled his face, and laid a long, slow, spine-tingling kiss on him.

His heart rate was skyrocketing when she pulled away, and little breath was left in his lungs. "What was that for? I'm not complaining. I just want to know so I can keep doing whatever made you kiss me like that."

Head canted, a dreamy smile on her face, she seemed to study him. "Checking to see if I'm a clone. Or was it a clown?"

"Neither!" *You're different from anyone I've ever known.*

She giggled. "Well, that's a relief." Her expression shifted, and she suddenly looked embarrassed.

He gave her a squeeze. "What is it?"

Her eyes slid to the side, and her lashes fluttered against her smooth skin. Then she riveted her beautiful blues on him. "You're, um ..." She gave her head a little shake, and her silky coils bounced.

He traced her jaw with his fingertips. "What are you trying to say?"

A huge inhale, and then she rushed out with, "You're the second man I've ever slept with."

To say he was stunned was an understatement, and he froze in place. "Seriously?"

Cheeks pink and polished, she gave him a head bob. "Seriously. Does that make me lame?"

A "Wha—" escaped him in a half laugh, half choke. He shook his head until he could get his tongue working again. "Of course that doesn't make you lame."

It makes me one lucky son of a bitch.

Though she was smiling, her eyes were shiny with tears. *Oh no! No, no, no! No tears.* Hand cupping her head, fingers threading into her curls, he pulled her to his chest and wrapped his arm around her protectively.

Something had been triggered inside him, and he couldn't make heads or tails out of it, but it was raw, and it was visceral. On one hand, his blood effervesced with joy—he wanted to pound his chest and let loose with a Tarzan howl—yet on the other, it troubled him that she could think being with only two men made her lame. His overarching emotion, though, and the one thundering through him as he held her, was the need to make her his.

Chapter 21

Making Beautiful Music

While Lily worked in his kitchen, her back to him, Gage watched her with something like star mist clouding his brain—maybe he was still floating in a post-sex haze. Pretty certain he had a fuck-me grin permanently frozen on his face, he basked in the domestic scene and let his mind wander. *This is what it could be like every day*. Everything about this felt *right*, though he couldn't form it into precise words. No, the feels were flowing over him, but like quicksilver, he couldn't grasp them. He just knew that when he was with her, he didn't want to stop being with her. Didn't want to miss a minute. Not tonight, not any night.

She turned and slid a full platter of colorful food onto the island. "I found all kinds of great stuff. You eat really healthy."

"Because I pay someone to cook my meals and stock the healthy stuff. Otherwise, it'd be burgers and fries all the way."

"Oh! I'm surprised we haven't crossed paths when I've stopped by to feed Hobbes."

"That's because I only get the service when I'm in town for long stretches."

"Well, she does a good job. Here are some veggies and dip, and hummus and whole grain toast points," she said. "I've also got a quiche baking, and I'll make us a fruit salad. These are all things you can eat, right?"

"Wow! Yeah, this is perfect." When was the last time someone besides his mom—or someone he paid—had gone all out like this? "God, I'm suddenly ravenous. She's a guy, by the way." He dipped a red pepper strip in hummus and chomped.

Lily was back at the counter, chopping fruit; she glanced at him over her shoulder. "Who's a guy?"

He sidled up behind her and snaked his arms around her waist. "The chef's a guy."

She tipped her head to the side, and he kissed a line to her ear, where he nibbled her earlobe.

"Do you cook?" she asked.

"A little, when I have the time." He ran the tip of his nose along her neck. "Hey, Lily?"

She stopped chopping and sagged against him. "Mmm?"

"Stay with me tonight?"

Was that a flinch? *Time for the sales pitch.* "Daisy's at Ivy's," he began, "and I don't have to be at the rink until late tomorrow. If you need to finish anything for Paige, you can do it from here on my computer."

He'd discovered a few extra-sensitive spots on her neck, and he zeroed in on them. "So what do you say? Don't go home. It'll be quiet and lonely there," he mumbled, skimming his lips and tongue over her skin.

Her hair tickled his nose. God, she smelled good.

"I still need a shower, and I don't have a change of clothes." Her sultry voice vibrated like it did when she sang her soulful tunes.

Warmth pooled in his gut and spread downward, firing up his dick. "I have something better than a shower—a soaking tub I've never used. Help me break it in. As far as a change of clothes, Sarah has a few things in one of the guest rooms. Or you can wear something of mine or ... the outfit you were born in."

She wiggled her ass against his crotch. "I'm guessing you're in favor of option three."

Fuck, she was doing an awesome job of torturing him. Fantasies roared to life, and pictures of everything he imagined doing to her scrolled through his head.

"Got that right." His voice came out thick, husky. "Can you tell the effect thinking about option three has on me?" Grinding against her, he ran his hands across her thighs, her stomach, her chest before wrapping her middle in a boa-constrictor hold.

A breathy moan escaped her, and she hugged his arms to her. "I'm all yours tonight."

Excitement surged. He barely got his thoughts corralled before they skipped back to fantasyland.

"And you'll still be here in the morning when I wake up?"

"Yes, Professor. I'll still be here."

Oh, he liked the sound of that.

Night had fallen, cloaking the outside in wintry darkness. Sitting beside Lily at his kitchen counter in his sweatpants and a T-shirt, Gage wolfed down half the quiche. She'd fried up a pound of thick-cut bacon, and he'd polished off most of that too.

He was debating about going for more quiche when he caught her mischievous blue eyes watching him over the rim of her wineglass.

"What?" He grinned. "You're probably saying to yourself, who is this animal scarfing down everything in sight?"

Shaking her head, she set the wineglass down. "Not at all. Don't forget, I've seen you eat a pile of chicken waffles, or whatever that crap was at IHOP. I'm just enjoying watching *you* enjoy the food I made for you. There's something satisfying in that. And for the record, I'm fond of the animal." Blond eyebrows bounced on her forehead.

Between what she said about feeding him, *and* the fact she hadn't minded the dirtier side he'd revealed, his *animal* dick sprang up, ready for action.

She took the last tiny bite of her quiche and pointed her fork at his plate. "Are you a sequential eater?"

He swiped his napkin across his mouth. "Am I a what?"

"You eat your food sequentially. First the quiche, then the bacon, then the fruit."

"Because that's the order I piled them on the plate." He shrugged. "Simple. Neat. Everything fits in its place."

"Black-and-white?"

"Pretty much."

"Is that your philosophy for life, Professor?"

"Pretty much. That and following your moral compass."

Her brows drew together. "Meaning?"

"If you always follow your moral compass—in other words, if you always do the right thing—the answer to a problem should be a no-brainer."

"You mean it's easy?"

"No, not easy, but clear. Straightforward." He knifed his hand.

"I'm not sure it's so simple. What about the gray areas?"

"The gray areas become crisper when you do the right thing."

"What if there's more than one right answer?"

"You get extra credit." He grinned.

She tossed her hair back with a musical laugh. God, he loved the sound of her laughter. Rich and full, like her voice.

He slid her plate onto his, deposited the dishes in the sink, and topped off their wineglasses before tilting his chin at her glass. "Grab your wine." Taking her free hand in his, he led her to the couch and flipped on the fireplace. The gas flames added a cheerful glow to the room.

She eyed his acoustic guitar propped beside the couch. "Play something for me?"

He was suddenly self-conscious. "I'm not good. I just dick around to help me relax."

"How long have you been playing?"

"Since middle school, I guess, so maybe thirteen, fourteen years?"

She pushed her hair off her face. "Then I doubt you sound like you're just 'dicking around.' C'mon, Professor. Let's make some music together."

Something tickled in his chest as he reached over and hoisted his guitar. "I play and you sing?"

Her blue eyes sparkled like diamonds floating on ocean waves. "Let's do it."

A flush of excitement raced through him even as doubts churned away in his mind's crank sifter, and it showed in the nervous rhythm he beat out on the guitar body with his thumb. "Being a blues girl, you should know this one."

He began playing "Why Don't You Do Right," and to his delight, she started right in. Entranced, he watched her expressions as he played, took in the vibrations of her beautiful voice. While she sang, she kept her eyes shut, seeming to feel every note.

The song ended, and her eyes fluttered open. "You play very well, Professor." She gave him a smile that lit her eyes. "What do you think? We're not too bad, huh?"

He swallowed, trying to coat his dry throat. It was all he could do to keep from throwing the guitar aside and pulling her against him. "Not bad," he rasped. "You have such a pretty voice."

An hour later, they were still making music together. Lily stood in front of the fireplace, her voice sending chills dancing up and down his spine as she belted out a final chorus. Hobbes lounged on an armchair, her tail flicking in time to the song that poured from Lily's soul.

When it ended, Gage clapped and whistled with all he had. Lily took bows in all directions and even gave him a goofy curtsy, erupting in laughter. She looked as though she belonged there. Maybe because she did.

Without doubt, she was the most perfect woman he'd ever known.

When he'd first spotted her at the wedding, he'd been struck by her music. That had morphed into like at first sight. Lust at first sight. But love at first sight? He hadn't believed the phenomenon existed, but now he was reconsidering. How else could he explain feeling so much so intensely so fast?

The notion threw him, and he masked his discomfort by strumming a random tune. She closed her eyes and waved her arms gracefully above her head like sea grass swaying in a current. Her top crept up, and a stripe of creamy skin flashed him. He pictured what was concealed beneath the sweater, and his cock stirred. Again.

He was resigned to the fact that he'd be in a permanent state of semi or full wood around her. She opened her eyes again and glided her hands down her sides with a sultry smile.

Fuck yeah! Semi became steel in a nanosecond. He put the guitar aside. "I like."

She cocked an eyebrow. "Maybe we should clean up the kitchen? I'll help."

"Kitchen. Right." *Cockblocked by dirty dishes.*

When he finished loading the dishwasher, she came up behind him and wrapped her arms around his waist. "Almost done, Professor?"

He turned in her hold. She raised up on tiptoe and gave him a kiss that zapped all conscious thought.

"Hey," he breathed when they uncoupled their lips. "I'm feeling a little dirty. Bath?"

She smirked. "Dirty as in dirty, or dirty as in filthy?"

"Yes." He waggled his eyebrows.

The look she gave him could've scorched his pants off. He picked her up in his arms, and she began giggling and kicking her legs.

"Settle down now," he laughed. "Don't make me play harem fireman and throw you over my shoulder."

She stopped kicking, dropped her arms around his shoulders, and he wasted no time carrying her upstairs.

Chapter 22

Phantom Shadows

Lily lay between Gage's legs, her back to his front, steamy water lapping around her torso. Singing with him had been ... magical. Like nothing she'd felt since Jack's death. And like Jack had always done, Gage complimented her singing, though she picked up an awe in Gage's tone she'd never heard in Jack's.

The comparison caused a tear inside her where guilt rushed in. Suddenly, Jack's presence clouded her mind, and she once again questioned her loyalty. She shouldn't be here with Gage. But she was. And being here, with him, was where she wanted to be. At least for tonight. Was that so wrong?

"Where'd you go, Goldilocks?"

Gage's voice stirred her back to his tub. How had he sensed her mind floating off to a distant time and place? "I guess I just drifted for a moment. How did you know?"

"You seemed to tense up."

Willing her muscles to relax against Gage, she pushed Jack's ghost from her mind and focused on her surroundings: the luxurious stone-and-tile bathroom, the pines swaying outside the window, Gage's bent knees that she used like armrests.

Armrests of a throne. Queen Lily. Queen Lily and her sex stud.

Oh yeah.

His chin resting on her head, her sex stud scooped water over her bare shoulders and breasts. She closed her eyes and let her senses fill with the smell of burning vanilla-scented candles, the sound of blues playing softly in the background, and the feel of Gage's hard planes against her. One especially hard plane—well, rod, to be more precise—had been lodged along the channel of her spine since they'd climbed into his tub-for-two. He seemed to be in no hurry to do anything with it.

"How do you like the tub so far?" he asked.

"Your tub is awesome."

His fingertips feathered across a spot on her shoulder. "Looks like I got a little carried away earlier and left a mark. Does this hurt?"

She craned her neck but couldn't see. "No, I don't feel anything. What kind of mark?"

"A big hickey."

She let out a laugh. "I don't think I've had a hickey since high school."

"I don't think I've *given* one since high school." He drizzled water over the spot he'd been inspecting. "Lean forward."

When she did, he turned on a hand-held sprayer and worked it over her head and neck. Then he dispensed shampoo into his palm and began rubbing it into her hair, building up a thick lather.

She dropped her head back. "That feels soooooo good," she moaned.

Wordlessly, he kneaded her scalp. She pushed into his touch like a lazy cat. He rinsed her hair and pulled her back against him. As she drifted in bliss, she was vaguely aware he was soaping his big hands. Those hands began massaging her shoulders, her arms, her fingers, and glided to her breasts where they lingered, no doubt to give them a thorough cleaning.

God, yes! Please be my sex stud.

His mouth lay alongside her ear. "I'll gladly be your sex stud."

Her eyes popped open. "I said that out loud?"

"You sure did." His magic hands didn't skip a beat. "How's that?" he whispered. "Pressure okay?"

"Perrrrrrfect." Her hips might have bucked in response.

"You know," he rumbled in that deep, panty-melting voice of his as he re-lathered and moved his hands over the rest of her body, "I looked for you after the wedding."

This brought her out of her lust-filled daze. "Really?"

"Yep." A low chuckle vibrated his chest. "Turns out it's hard to find the right Lily when you don't have a last name." His hands slid between her legs.

Really, he was making it hard for her to keep a string of coherent thoughts together.

"I'm sorry," she whispered.

"Don't be. I just wanted you to know I looked for you, that's all."

Back then, it had never occurred to her he would look for her because she'd assumed her one hot night was only one hot night for him too. She hadn't counted on anything different—she hadn't counted on Gage Nelson.

"And by the way?" he added.

She wriggled from his hold, rolled over, and parked her chin on his chest.

He tapped the end of her nose with his finger. "The wait was totally worth it."

As expertly as his hands turned her body into putty, this man was doing the same to her heart, and a wave of something warm washed over her, igniting other parts of her.

Using his shoulders for leverage, she pulled herself up and straddled him. His eyes swept over her languidly, darkening with desire, while his hands stroked her sides. "Have I told you how beautiful you are?"

Oh my God, so are you. She ran her fingers over his ridged abdomen and carved chest, drinking in the sight of him while he drank her in.

"Maybe once or twice." She pressed her soft curves against his hard angles and covered his stubbled neck and jaw with unhurried, open-mouthed kisses.

"Well, you are," he sighed.

You sure make me feel that way. "Thank you. Now I'd be remiss if I didn't give you as thorough a cleaning as you just gave me. Ready?"

Heat flashed in his eyes right before his lips crashed onto hers. Their tongues dueled, their hands roamed all over each other, and water splashed onto the floor as they grappled together, trying to gain purchase on slick porcelain.

He grasped her head and pulled her mouth away. "I'm not sure the tub's so great right now," he panted.

Still astride him, she pushed him back. "Well, maybe if you'd be a good stud and lie still, we could make this work to everyone's satisfaction."

A sly grin played on his face. "Yes, ma'am. Whatever her ladyship commands. Do your worst."

She wiggled her eyebrows. "How about my best?"

His hands gripped her hips. "Oh God, yeah. That too."

She removed his hands from her hips and wagged a finger at him. "No touching."

A skeptical eyebrow lifted to his hairline. "How's that gonna wo—"

"And no talking." She leaned down, pinning his arms, her breasts brushing his chest, and sucked his bottom lip into her mouth before he could protest. She ran the tip of her tongue just inside his mouth, over his teeth and lips, then nibbled and nipped before kissing him greedily.

His chest heaved against hers, and she swayed over him so only her nipples brushed his skin, back and forth. His arms flexed, and she put more weight on them to hold them down. A growl rose in his throat. She teased him with her body and worshipped his mouth, sinking into its soft depths, and he let out a series of groans.

With light flicks of her tongue, she traced a path to his ear and whispered, "Behave." This was met with a chuckle until she dragged her mouth down his neck, over his chest, and grazed each of his nipples with her teeth. He lifted himself higher out of the water, sending more splashing over the edge.

Now fully pressed against him, she worked her way down his body. His breathing grew more ragged, and she paused at his stomach, taking her sweet time tracing each of his blocky muscles with her tongue. Lingering to nibble his skin, she let out a few moans of her own. He squirmed, and his muscles twitched. But when she finally took him in her hand, in her mouth, his entire body shuddered to a stop. His eyes locked on hers. She cupped his balls, then licked every inch of him like an ice pop, swirling and sucking his length while he watched. He muttered something unintelligible and finally dropped his head back with a lung-emptying, "Fuuuuuuuuck!"

His balls tightened, but before she could finish him off, he sat up and hauled her upright. Somehow, the water level had dropped to about a foot.

"I want to be inside you," he gritted out.

Hands planted on the tub walls on either side of his head, she positioned herself above him. He stroked himself once, twice, then held himself in place.

He was breathing hard, and a jaw muscle jumped. "Ride me, beautiful Lily."

She lowered herself gradually, fascinated by his contorted expressions as she took him in inch by sweet inch. His features cycled between concentration, frustration, and pure pleasure. Eyes half-lidded, hands clamped on her hips, he repeated her name in one long, continuous exhale as she started to move. It was the most beautiful sound she'd ever heard.

She willed herself to keep a slow rhythm, to prolong the exquisite torment, but her knees dug into the porcelain. His hands and powerful thrusts took over the pace, speeding up. Her moans turned to cries, and his groans became shouts. Her orgasm blasted through her body, shattering her into fragments. He followed right after, clutching her to him, and buried his face in the crook of her neck.

Her heart beat double-time in sync with his, and her breathing was labored and uneven. She remained pressed to him until the world finally stopped spinning, and she pulled back and smiled at him. "You make an excellent sex stud."

A smile lifted one corner of his mouth as he caught his breath. "It's all about the woman who rules me." He pushed his hands into her damp hair and gathered it up. His eyes softened and mined hers, his expression unbearably tender. "And you do rule me, Lily."

His words made part of her leap with joy, but they struck terror into another, darker part deep down inside her—the part where her specters roamed.

Warning bells clanged dimly in the background, but she ignored them.

The bathtub inauguration was followed by a shower—to clean up after the bath, of course. A shower filled with scorching kisses and more soapy explorations of one another's bodies. They were squeaky clean when the hot water finally ran out.

Lily's proverbial Pandora's box had been blown wide open, and though she was as sore as a trail rider after ten days in the saddle—totally worth it—she couldn't get enough of Gage's body. Her stud muffin took his job seriously and was up to the task, so to speak, of satisfying her suddenly insatiable appetite.

When they finally fell into bed, utterly wrung out, she drifted off instantly, cradled in his arms.

She awoke sometime during the night, sweating beside his blasting furnace self. He was wrapped around her like a tortilla wrapped around the contents of a burrito, his body generating enough heat to warm a yurt. She inched away to cool down, propping herself against a pillow. He let out a low moan but remained on his side, facing her.

Dim light touched the angles of his face, softened by sleep. Long eyelashes fanned across high cheekbones, and his full mouth was parted oh so enticingly. She fought the urge to nibble those lips she was growing so fond of.

A sheet covered the lower half of his body, leaving his shoulders, chest and arms exposed. Her eyes surveyed it all, drinking him in, memorizing every detail. Even though his muscles were slack, their definition was no less impressive, and she wanted to run her tongue over them again. She licked her lips and instantly admonished herself for it.

Lily Everett, nymphomaniac.

But it wasn't just the sex, which was so far out of this world it existed in its own galaxy. No, the sex wouldn't have been so amazing had it not been for the man himself. A man she enjoyed doing little things for, who spurred her to want to feed him, love him, take care of him.

Her heart suddenly flooded with tenderness over the small, ever-present things—the way he pushed her hair off her face, the way his eyes gleamed when she sang, the way he let the cat he'd rescued own him. The way he spoke of his grandmother.

In less than twelve hours, she would go back to her world. And then what? Was tonight just an extension of July? She didn't want it to be, yet how could it be otherwise? Her daughter had already lost a father. If Lily let herself fall in love and it didn't work out, it wouldn't be only her heart that would be broken—Daisy's would become part of the wreckage. What right did she have to drag her daughter through a minefield of *her* love affairs?

And then there was Jack. Though she tried to lock out the crushing guilt over being with another man, it was always there, lurking in the back corners of her mind, taunting her with the word "betrayal."

During his last weeks, Jack had teased her about not finding another man too soon. To make her laugh, he'd said, to see her smile through the rivers of tears they'd shed together. But had he been teasing?

What if he were looking down on her now? Would he be hurt? Was this how she served his memory? By lying in another man's bed?

But she was alive, damn it, and he wasn't.

Gage sighed in his sleep, startling Lily from her memories. She swiped at a tear that slid down her cheek and went back to studying him.

Though there was much she didn't know about Gage Nelson, she did know he was a good man. With a big heart. He put others first, in quiet, humble ways, like giving of himself to his family, his team, his community from his seemingly bottomless well.

But he was also a professional athlete in his prime. Barring injury, his career stretched far into the future and would dictate his life for years to come. What would it be like to be bound to someone who could be bounced from city to city? To another country? How would those moves affect Daisy? Gage had described being traded from San Jose, how he'd had to leave the very day he'd been traded and play for his new team that night. How difficult it had been. What if she and Daisy were at the mercy of that sort of upheaval?

A chill settled in, and Lily pulled the covers to her chest and slid beneath them. Beside her, Gage mumbled, and his hand stirred over the sheets until it brushed her arm. He closed around it and hauled her against him, moaning soft and long. As he spooned her, his hands glided over her bare skin, coming to rest on her shoulder and stomach. She tugged his hands to her chest and covered them with hers.

"Lily," he mumbled as he settled against her.

Too many questions ran through her head. For now, she would enjoy the simple contentment of feeling safe in his arms—safer than she'd felt in a long, long time.

Chapter 23

Red Light, Green Light

Gage stood behind the wheel of a speedboat. As it smoothly skimmed the water, its engine purred with a powerful rumble. Wind whipped his hair. The freedom was awesome!

"Meow."

He lifted one eyelid. The speedboat dissolved into an orange tabby cat who reverberated with a loud purr.

"Meow." Hobbes batted at his nose.

"Are you serious right now?" Gage grumbled. Beside him something soft, warm, and naked stirred, and he glanced over his shoulder and smiled.

A dull dawn washed the room in varying shades of monochrome, offering weak light that illuminated golden curls on the pillow beside his. Lily was snuggled against his back, her arm draped over his middle, her weighty breasts squashed against him. Cute little mewling noises came from her. Cool as the speedboat dream was, coming out of it was so much nicer. He'd awakened in heaven.

"Meow."

A heaven the damn cat was dragging him away from.

"Bad timing, cat." He gingerly slid out of bed, gathering Hobbes in his arms, and trudged downstairs. "Remind me again why I thought letting you live here was a good idea because right now I can't come up with a single reason."

A series of body-shaking yawns later, he'd filled the cat's bowls, taken a leak, and was back upstairs. When he walked into his bedroom, he was squarely back in heaven because Lily was seated upright, naked to her waist, stretching her arms above her head, her eyes closed. Her curls were a silky blond froth surrounding her angelic face. She took his breath away. He gawked like a horny teenager—or a horny twenty-six-year-old man. The sight jolted him awake quicker than downing a pot of coffee.

He closed the door behind him. Her arms dropped, and her eyes popped open. A shy smile curved her lips, and she began pulling the covers up.

"Morning, Goldilocks." He climbed on the bed, walking on his knees, and pulled the covers from her. "I hate to see this perfect view covered up." A pretty blush rose up her cheeks, and he leaned down and kissed her.

When he pulled away and sat back on his knees, her eyes roamed over him, settling unabashedly on his engorged cock. "Is this how you walk around every morning, Professor?"

"You mean without clothes, or with a raging hard-on?"

"Both," she giggled.

"Only when you're here." Still on his knees, he sat up and stroked himself. "See something you want?" Yeah, he was playing a cocky SOB, but he was having hella fun. She didn't seem to mind.

She pulled her bottom lip between her teeth. "For a professor, you sure don't act very professor-y." Her smile turned wicked, and her eyes traveled back to his hand on his shaft—and widened.

That was all the encouragement he needed. He slid his hand up and down, flashing her a grin. "I thought you changed my job description last night from professor to sex stud." He paused and struck a beefcake pose, adding a Michael Jackson pelvic thrust because he thought he could.

Turns out he *couldn't* because she fell to one side and began laughing hysterically.

He choked back his own laughter. “Killing me here.” Hips gyrating, his movements becoming more ridiculous, he was fairly certain he looked like a cross between a mechanical bull and Gumby. He really didn’t want to know.

She was whooping now and slapping her palm against the mattress.

“Hey!” he barked. “Putting on my best stud moves, and you’re *laughing*?” He could barely get the words out without falling over in a fit of laughter. He walked on his knees toward her until he was inches away. “And as you can see, I am one hundred percent primed, although if you keep laughing ...”

She pulled herself upright and wiped silly tears from her face, no longer aware that she was fully exposed herself. And he wasn’t stupid enough to remind her of this fact.

With a chuckle, he stroked himself again. “All yours if you care to take over.”

Body still shuddering with giggles, she sat up on her knees and faced him. Then she wrapped her hand around him. He pulled in a sharp breath, going from hilarity to gotta-have-you-now in a heartbeat.

Her fingers played along his length, sending his heart rate into outer space. She nipped his neck, then soothed it with her tongue. “Bossy sex stud,” she purred, “It’s past time you performed your duties.”

“On it. I will not let it be said that I am a sex stud who shirks his duties.”

Covers drawn to her necklace, Lily snuggled against Gage’s chest as he reclined against the headboard, his arm draped around her slender shoulders. He dropped a kiss on her head. “If we were smokers ...”

She chuckled, and the motion tickled him. “What do you call what we just did? I’m surprised we didn’t incinerate the room.”

He didn't disagree, which was probably obvious from his stupid grin. "What would Goldilocks like for breakfast this morning? I can cook something, or we can go out."

"What time is it?"

"A little after six, I think."

"Oh! So early. What time did you wake up?"

"Five? Four thirty? Technically, Hobbes woke me up. It couldn't have been too early because it was getting light out." He brushed her hair back, more because he loved touching it than because it needed to be brushed back. She canted her head and looked up at him.

"What?" he asked.

"Just thinking how quickly things can change in twenty-four hours. Yesterday morning, I wouldn't have dreamed we'd be doing this." She waved a hand between them.

"You mean having sex, eating, having more sex, sleeping fifteen minutes, fucking, and fucking again?" A laugh rumbled through his chest. "Gotta say I'm a big fan of how I woke up *this* morning. You?" *I could so get used to this.*

Her laughter joined his. "Don't forget the bath and shower."

"I rolled those into the general fucking category."

"Seriously, how does that work when you have to be in tip-top shape for your games?"

"You think what we're doing isn't keeping me in tip-top shape?"

She slapped his chest. "You know what I mean. You have to eat healthy, sleep healthy, work out healthy. How does sex fit in? Especially if you're awake all night doing it?" A mischievous gleam danced in her eyes.

"Well, there's a little room for less-than-perfect behavior. But Coach likes us to ... well, abstain for at least forty-eight hours before a game. He thinks the extra testosterone makes us more aggressive. But my last coach said sex was fine the night before. *He* thought it helped take the edge off and made it easier to focus."

She sat up, an alarmed expression on her face. "You have a game tonight."

"And you and Daisy are coming." The thought warmed him—he was stoked to have Daisy there. Showing off was a definite possibility tonight.

"That's not what I meant. Did I just mess you up for tonight? And don't you have to go skate this morning?"

"No morning skate. Coach suspends it this late in the season. As for 'messing me up,'" he shrugged, "I doubt it makes a difference. But in any case, it's too late now. Which means we can keep doing this all day and it won't change how I play tonight." He playfully tugged at her covers, but she kept them firmly in place.

"Uh-uh, Professor. You need to save your strength. I'm not going to be the reason you have a bad game."

"I won't have a bad game." He leaned in for a kiss, which she gave him. "But you're right about one thing. I need to start fueling up."

A half-hour later, he slid poached eggs on their plates and added whole-grain toast. They were back at the kitchen counter, and Lily's eyes were fixed on the gray palette beyond the windows as she nibbled at her food. She was dressed in Sarah's pajama pants and a light blue sweatshirt that highlighted her eyes. The clothes were a little baggy on her, but it didn't matter. Lily would look beautiful in a sack.

He couldn't remember feeling this comfortable with anyone before. They laughed at the same jokes, enjoyed the same music, and shared a similar, even demeanor. They could be talking or not, and it felt right.

And in bed? He'd never experienced anything like it. Ever. Their lovemaking went to a whole new level he'd never known existed. She brought out a boldness in him and matched it with her own. They fed off each other's energy, practically combusting when they got going. It left him hungry for more.

He sipped his orange juice, studying her over the rim of the glass. Flawless skin, golden hair like twining silk, and eyes with the depths of the blue Pacific. As he took her in, an arrow buried itself in his chest. It was almost painful, but at the same time something warm seeped out and encased his heart. He could feel himself tumbling, falling deeper under her spell.

Emotions bubbled over and rushed out of him at once.

"Come with me to the Bay Area and meet my family," he blurted.

Shit. Judging by her wide-eyed expression and the fork clattering from her hand, he should have kept that idea bottled up.

At least it was better than yelling the second half of the thought: "Come live with me!"

"What?" she part-laughed, part-yelped.

He reached over and took her hands in his. "Listen, I'm serious. We get a couple of days off in a few weeks before the big playoff push. I want to bring you and Daisy with me."

She blinked, and her mouth went slack.

Too much too soon. Shit! Back the hell up, doofus.

With a headshake, she seemed to recover. "That's really sweet, but it feels a bit, um, sudden. Besides, Daisy's in school."

But he liked the idea of going on vacation with them. Maybe someplace else? Where his family *didn't* live? "Okay. Here's a different idea. Ever seen the ice castles in Dillon?"

She shook her head.

"Neither have I, but they look really cool, and we could drive there in under two hours."

Lily's mouth opened and closed a few times. He barreled ahead. "Can Daisy miss a few days of kindergarten? That's about all the time I'll have anyway."

"Where would we stay?"

His heart rate did a two-step—she hadn't said no. "I can rent us a house or a condo with plenty of room." He grabbed his phone, swiped, tapped, and scrolled. "Here's an Airbnb three-bedroom house with a hot tub and views." He held it up to her. "You could even have your own room. Of course, if you decide to visit your sex stud in the middle of the night and put him to work, he'd be totally down with it."

She glanced up at him, and he winked. Her eyes landed back on his phone. "It's almost six hundred dollars a night!"

"Your point being ...?"

"That's a lot of money!" Her gaze shot back to his. So much seemed to stream through her eyes, as though she were calculating a series of equations.

"I can afford it."

"I don't know what to say," she murmured.

"I do. Say yes."

"Can I think about it?"

"Of course." He lifted her hands to his lips and placed a kiss in each palm.

A wave of pink colored her face. He liked his chances. He'd figure out later how to break it to his mom that he was canceling his plans to come home.

They spent the rest of the morning lounging—playing music, laughing, talking, and abandoning a board game midway through to roll around in the sheets one more time. Lily couldn't remember when she'd been so relaxed, and it wasn't only the sex marathon that had chilled her out. It was simply being with him.

But while she wanted to linger in that carefree state, real life was buzzing an annoying wake-up call, so she left Gage to his pre-game nap and returned to her quiet house.

With time on her hands before Ivy brought Daisy home, Lily stretched out on the couch, even though a mound of laundry cried for attention. She plucked out her wedding ring and slid it along her chain, staring at the distorted reflection in its gold surface as thoughts of Gage infiltrated her mind and crowded out most everything else. And no surprise. Even now, gone from him a mere hour, she craved the easy smile that lit her up, the deep voice that shot tingles through her, and the laugh that filled her hollow spaces like warm honey.

Having his body close to hers in the dark hours had made her feel safe and ... whole.

But what really transported her was the tenderness in his mismatched blue eyes when he looked at her—as though she was the sun to his orbiting planet. No one had ever looked at her that way.

Suddenly, inexplicable fear rose up and grabbed her by the throat. For every moment spent with him, she was relinquishing another piece of her heart. A dangerous trade.

He was addictive. A potent drug that clouded her brain.

"No," her rational mind argued. "You're tired. Not thinking straight."

Thinking straight or not, it wasn't just about her. While Gage seemed genuine in his desire to weave Daisy and her into his life, Lily had to consider possible consequences. What if Daisy got attached and it didn't last? What if *she* got attached, only to lose another man? Could her heart take being shattered again?

Too late. I'm already attached.

Chapter 24

I'M GOING TO ... DILLON?

"Go, Mr. Cage, gooooooooo!" Daisy shrieked as she bounced up and down in her chair. Gage was streaking down the ice toward the opposing net—he was breathtaking, and Lily couldn't get enough of watching him. Entering the other team's zone, he made a drop pass, but no one was there to pick it up. A defender corralled it and blazed in the other direction.

"What the hell was *that*, Nelson?" a fan bellowed behind them.

Gage was hot on the other team's heels, playing chase. He'd been in that position a half-dozen times tonight. Fortunately, his linemate Quinn stole the puck back and lobbed it down the ice before they skated to the bench for a line change.

The fan continued his loud remarks, offering Gage helpful tips such as, "Get your head out of your ass, Nelson, and stop with the drop passes to nowhere!"

Ivy and she both craned their heads, but she couldn't figure out which asshole was mouthing off. She turned back around, rolling her lips between her teeth and clamping down, feeling heat rising in her cheeks. *You try skating while you're holding on to the puck and dodging guys trying to knock you into next week, jerk-off!*

Apparently, Jerk-off had more to say. “Jesus Christ, Nelson! Stop turning over the goddamn puck!”

How did Natalie and the other wives keep their cool? Now Lily understood why Gisele Bündchen had mouthed off about Tom Brady’s crap receivers.

Ivy squeezed her arm. “I got this.” Before Lily could stop her, Ivy stood, faced the seats behind them, and hollered, “He’s one of the best damn centers in the league. He’s in the running for MVP, for Christ’s sake! What more do you want? Give the guy a break.”

“Momma, why’s Aunt Ivy yelling bad words at that man?”

“Um ...”

“You’re just saying that ’cause you’re wearing his damn jersey!” the man retorted. Gage had sweetly left jerseys for Daisy, Ivy, Parker, and her. “All of you just have a hard-on for six!” Jerk-off added as if just noticing they were a Wall of Gage.

“There are kids here, asshole,” another fan admonished.

“Mom?”

Lily pulled Daisy in close. “It’s okay, sweetheart. Aunt Ivy was just—”

“Lady, sit down already! Some of us came here to watch the game.”

Ivy turned and lowered herself into her seat. The hubbub seemed to level off. She winked at Lily and dropped a kiss on Daisy’s head. “Aunt Ivy was sticking up for her team, Daisy-do.”

Jerk-off couldn’t let it go. “Try learning some hockey, red.”

Ivy shot up, faced backward again, and pointed at her head. “Try getting some glasses, jackass! It’s strawberry blond!”

A collective groan rose from behind them. The heat in Lily’s face spread to her neck and chest, prickling her skin. Her stomach churned like a concrete mixer turning over sludge.

Parker, who was seated on Daisy’s other side, reached a long arm across their laps to tug Ivy’s jersey. With a satisfied head bob, she sat as if it had been her idea all along.

“Hey, strawberry blondie,” Jerk-off sang.

Parker stood to his full six-three, EMT-buff height, casually tucking his shirt into the back of his pants. “Buddy, let it go. You don’t want to get in an argument with my wife. Trust me. I speak from experience.”

His good-natured approach garnered a few chuckles, along with another fan's "shut it" aimed at Jerk-off. Parker re-took his seat slowly, giving Ivy an eye-roll and a headshake. His lips quirked as he obviously fought a grin.

"Mom, I'm thirsty," Daisy said.

Parker patted her arm. "Why don't you and I find some lemonade during intermission, Daisy-do?"

Bless him. Lily's emotions were wound tighter than bobbin thread. She couldn't untangle which bothered her more: the idiots behind her talking about Gage like he was a no-talent duster or the worry she was the cause for his less-than-Gagely play. A little gush dampened her panties as her mind detoured once again to last night, ratcheting up the guilt factor a notch.

"No doubt Uncle Parker needs another beer while he's at it," Ivy chided.

He grinned at her. "You know it. Especially if you're going to get us into a fight. Is it safe to leave you two alone for a few minutes?" He reached for Daisy, who admonished him.

"We hafta wait, Uncle Parker. They're not done playing yet."

Despite her flaring emotions, Lily smiled inside. Gage was teaching her little rule-follower well.

"Wow," Ivy whisper-shouted. "You-know-who's really off his game tonight."

Lily jabbed a finger toward Daisy and mouthed, "Shut up."

Ivy mimed a lip-zip.

A horn sounded, signaling the end of the first period. Parker guided Daisy through legs and laps to the aisle while Lily craned to watch the ritual of Gage leaving the ice. She couldn't remember being so interested in it before. He and T.J. stood on either side of the chute, fist- or elbow-bumping their teammates as they filed past into the corridor that led to the locker room. Gage was the last to leave, falling in behind T.J. He tapped hands dangling over the chute the entire way, and her heart ballooned. She could practically feel heat glowing in it.

Lily turned to her sister. "You-know-who asked if he could take Daisy and me to see the Dillon ice castles."

Ivy's face lit with a big-ass smile. "Nice!"

"I said I'd think about it."

Ivy rapped her on the head. "Hello, earth to Lily! What's to think about? Hot, rich guy—who also happens to be nice—wants to whisk you away. How can there be any answer but yes?"

Lily rubbed her head. "I don't know. I mean ... you see how Daisy idolizes him. What if we get close and it all ends up in the toilet?"

Fans excused themselves to get past, and Ivy and she stood to make way.

Ivy spoke out of the side of her mouth, her tone soft. "What if? If you're ever going to take a chance again, he's a great candidate. You said he's really good with Daisy. And if she idolizes him, doesn't that make things easier?"

Lily chewed her lip. "Maybe. Maybe not."

"Hey, I get that it's scary. But even if you pass on him, that's not gonna change. The next one will be scarier, and the one after that until you've scared yourself into a lonely corner you can't get out of." She tugged a strand of Lily's hair. "And speaking of idolizing, I've seen the way that man looks at you."

"What does that mean?"

"It means I think he's in love with you. You have feelings for him too, right?"

Without a doubt. But Gage in love with her? Was she in love with him? "Yes."

"So go with it. See where it takes you. Live a little." Ivy wrapped an arm around her shoulders and squeezed.

Lily realized she'd needed validation, and Ivy had given it to her. Something akin to champagne bubbles rushed up from her belly and popped in her head, leaving her a little dizzy. "I guess I'm going to Dillon."

Chapter 25

PARENTING 101

Gage sat in his running car in the arena parking lot, shaking his head. He'd just played the shittiest game of his life. They'd lost seven-to-four, and he'd barely registered a shot, much less a point. His legs had felt like lead, and his precision had been so off it was in a different time zone. His brain had been stuck on an endless lazy river ride.

The only bright spot had been seeing Lily and Daisy in the stands wearing his jersey. It had done funny things to his insides and dosed him with a huge measure of pride.

His attention caught on someone walking purposefully toward his car. *Hunter. Shit.* Gage lowered his window, and Hunter leaned down when he reached him.

"Me and the boys are going clubbing. There's a good chance we'll wind up at the Sapphire. I figured after the shitty game you just had, you could stand some adult entertainment to take your minds off things." Hunter gave him a smirk.

"While I appreciate your concern and the kind offer," Gage's voice dripped with sarcasm, "going to a strip joint is *not* going to help my mood."

"Suit yourself." With a shrug, Hunter loped away.

Gage dragged his hands over his face and through his hair, expelling a lungful of air. Going home to a cold, quiet house wasn't going to do anything to lift his dark mood either. He thumbed Lily a text.

Gage: *You still awake?*

Lily: *Barely. Someone kept me up all night.*

That brought his first chuckle tonight.

Gage: *And he loved every minute of it.* He added a winkie emoji and kept going. *Wish you guys could have stuck around till the end. Did Daisy enjoy the game? Other than me stinking up the ice like a boatload of fish?*

He wasn't sure why, but the question of whether Daisy enjoyed herself was important to him.

Lily: *LOL. She was over the moon to be there watching her "Mr. Cage." You're her hero. And the jersey? A big hit. Thank you again.*

Shoulders he hadn't realized were tight eased, and his chest expanded an inch or two.

Gage: *Looked a little big on her. Guess I got the wrong size.*

Lily: *She'll grow into it. Literally. She won't take it off. She wore it to bed tonight.*

He laughed aloud. *Seriously?*

Lily: *Seriously. You made one little girl very happy.*

This pulled his spirits out of the dumpster.

Gage: *Glad to do it. Did I make one big girl happy too?*

Lily: *Without a doubt.*

Suddenly, he felt as if he was running on empty, and it wasn't because he was tired. He missed Lily, and he wasn't even home yet.

Gage: *Can I come see you?*

Lily: *Now?*

He cringed a little but fired off his reply. *Yes, now.*

Long minutes passed.

Lily: *Hoping to get lucky, Professor?*

Gage: *Hoping you'll sing to me and cheer me up. Just want to see your pretty face.*

Lily: *That bad?*

Seeing her and holding her while he pulled in the sunshine scent of her hair were what he needed right now. They were the cure-all to his blues.

Gage: *I'm only 10 mins away. Promise I won't stay long.*

So much time passed—at least it felt that way—that he started to back out of his parking space. The text he'd been waiting for finally chimed.

Lily: *Then I'll see you in 10.*

His heart grew wings and started to fly. By the time he parked in front of her tidy little house, the recall of the awful game was fading. When she opened the door—still wearing his jersey—raised up on tiptoe, and threw her arms around him, the memory vanished from his consciousness altogether.

"Hey," she murmured when she'd finally pulled away and closed the door behind them. Her curls were piled on top of her head.

"Hey. Thanks for letting me stop by." *I needed this.*

The lights were low, lending the place a warm ambiance.

"Something to drink?" she offered.

"Bourbon, if you've got it."

She crooked a finger. "Right this way."

She reached into an upper cabinet, and that's when he noticed her legs were bare. He took in the sight as the jersey hiked up, revealing her curvy ass hidden by short shorts. Mostly hidden. His hands itched to touch the parts that peeked out and teased him, causing him to rethink his promise not to stay long.

After pouring him a measure of amber liquid and topping off her white wine, she led him back to the living room and curled up on one end of a wide, deep, cream-colored couch in front of a cozy fire. He averted his eyes from the hallway shrine, locking it out of his mind as he lowered himself beside her. They clinked glasses. One sip, and the liquor burned its way down to his stomach. "I met Parker after the game. Nice guy."

"You did? How?"

"He and Ivy were waiting to say thanks when I left the arena." Another heat-filled sip. "Have you given the Dillon ice castles any more thought?"

She let out a little laugh. "I thought you said 'take your time'?"

He dropped his arm on her leg, his thumb caressing circles on her smooth skin. “I did, but I figured it doesn’t hurt to ask. Plus, I’d like to have it squared away before I head out on the road.”

“Oh right. That makes sense.” Her eyes darted around the room. She seemed fidgety all of a sudden, and he expected her to haul out her necklace at any second.

He splayed his fingers over her thigh and canted his head to get a better look at her. “Hey, are we okay here? Did my asking about Dillon make you uncomfortable?”

A few twitches of her head told him no.

“Then what’s going on?” Inner alarms were rising, and he found himself hoping she wasn’t about to tell him she regretted last night.

She took a tiny sip of her wine. “I didn’t want to bring up the game, but do you think … I mean, it wasn’t your best game, and I wonder—”

“That’s putting it mildly,” he huffed. He scooted a little closer, pulling her legs across his lap. “I think I know where you’re going, and no, I don’t think last night had anything to do with my lousy game.” Her curls caught the light, and he had a hankering to tangle his fingers in them. “I have off games, and that’s what tonight was. An off game.” He reached out and pulled some of her strands loose.

“What are you doing?” she laughed.

“I guess I’m taking your hair down.”

“And you’re doing this why?”

He freed a few more curls and set his drink aside so he could devote both hands to the job. “Because I’ve never seen such soft, curly hair, and I love touching it.” It all came tumbling down, and he played with it as he arranged it on her shoulders.

“Better?” She gave him a knowing smile.

“Yeah. It makes it easier to do this.” He took her wineglass from her and placed it next to his half-full drink. Then he ran his hands in her hair and held her head, stroking his thumbs over her smooth cheeks while he drew her mouth to his. She parted her lips for him, and their tongues met for one long, lingering kiss. She pulled away, her half-lidded eyes on him. A lazy smile tipped her plump lips. He kissed her again, harder this time, and her hands wound around his shoulders to press him closer. He snaked one hand under the hem of her jersey while he continued holding her head in place. The kiss deepened, becoming more urgent, and a mewl rose in her throat. Suddenly, his body was on fire. He broke away and trailed kisses to her ear. "Jesuuuus, Lil. The more I'm with you, the more I want you."

She dropped her shoulder, giving him better access to her throat. "So I didn't wear you out last night, Professor?" she breathed.

Between open-mouthed kisses up and down her neck, he murmured, "Not even close. You're my superhero drug." He nudged her collar, nibbling the skin at the base of her neck, while under her jersey his fingers dipped into her bra cup and fondled her soft flesh.

A wail rose from somewhere behind him. He was still turning to see what it was when Lily disentangled herself and sprang from the couch with lightning speed. Daisy stood between the living room and hallway, her face red, tears staining her cheeks, her eyes trained on him.

"Mommy," she whimpered.

His heart nearly imploded. Had seeing him kiss her mom—and feeling her up—freaked the poor kid out? He rearranged his pants and stood.

Lily was on her knees, her hands on Daisy's arms. "What is it, sweetheart?"

"I threw up." She began to cry, her little body shuddering. All of him wanted to do something, but he had no idea what, so he shoved his hands in his pockets and stood there like a dumbass.

Lily rose, scooping Daisy into her arms, and shot him a backward glance. "If you need to get going, I understand."

Shit! What's the translation? "I want you to leave" or "If you want to run the hell away, I won't hold it against you"?

"Is there anything I can do to help?" he called after her, feeling lamer by the second.

"No." As she carried Daisy down the hall, he could hear the little girl's voice. "Why is Mr. Cage here, Momma?" He should have left right then, but something wouldn't let him.

The evening turned out far different than he'd ever imagined. Though it took time, he eventually wore down some serious Lily walls. Whether they were mama bear walls or stubbornly independent ones, he couldn't say. When Lily finally caved, she let him help remake Daisy's bed. At one point, he even read Daisy a few pages from *Is Your Mama a Llama?*—one he recognized from his own childhood—while Lily steam cleaned the rug in Daisy's bedroom. He tried to infuse a lilt in his voice as he read, which seemed to work because Daisy burrowed into him. *Probably needs the body heat.* She said little but occasionally gave him a big-eyed stare, which he took to mean, "Why the hell is my hockey coach here?"

As he moved about the house, he tried not only to ignore the imposing Jack shrine but surprising mini ones that seemed to be scattered everywhere.

Hours after Daisy's stomach bug had first started wreaking havoc inside her, Lily had him run a load of laundry while she helped Daisy through another puking jag. How so much could come out of one small girl was beyond him, but eventually the hurling and heaving stopped, and she fell asleep in her bed, exhausted, cradled in her mother's arms.

It must have been four in the morning—he didn't dare check—and he sat facing them in a too-small rocking chair. Surveying the room, he found nothing else that needed to be done. "Can I get you anything?" he whispered to Lily, who looked as exhausted as Daisy. She shook her head and closed her eyes, mouthing, "Thank you," a ghost of a smile playing on her lips.

Leaning his forearms on his thighs, he watched the pair, searching for a sign they needed him to do something, anything. The peaceful picture touched him deep inside, turning his gut as gooey as glucose gel.

When they didn't stir after several minutes, he stood and pulled the comforter around Lily's shoulders and sat back down, wedging himself in the uncomfortable chair.

Next thing he knew, Lily was whispering in his ear, her hand on his shoulder, her hair tickling his ear. "Gage? Gage?"

"Mmmph?" As he came to, he tried to shift, but the chair was hugging his hips, and his neck was on fire from being bent over.

"You fell asleep, Gage. I didn't mean to make you stay."

He blinked at the vision standing beside him. It occurred to him she hadn't called him Professor, and he liked the sound of his name on her lips. "You didn't make me do anything. I wanted to stay. How's Daisy?"

Lily nodded toward the bed. "I think she's through the worst of it."

"Good," he mumbled.

"You can probably guess I won't be bringing her to hockey this morning."

Shit. Mites. That's right.

He pressed the heels of his hands into eyes that felt like they'd been sandpapered. "Good," he mumbled again. Wrestling the chair off himself, he stood and steered Lily out of the room. "Now her mom needs to get some sleep."

Lily went quietly, letting him lead her to her bedroom, where she climbed under the covers and sighed into the pillows. He didn't allow himself to linger. Just tucked her in, leaned down to kiss her forehead, and crept out the front door, pulling the locked doorknob behind him.

Late that afternoon, after a nap and a shower, he returned to Lily's—no warning, taking a chance—armed with three different soups he'd picked up at a favorite restaurant. It paid off because, Jesus Christ, the smile she gave him when she opened the door made him feel like he was a damn superhero.

Sudden nerves made him shuffle with awkwardness, and he thrust the bags at her. "I thought Daisy might like some chicken noodle ... or turkey and wild rice. The guy said this other one's good for the stomach flu too—it's something like miso."

Lily took the packages from him, beckoning him inside with a head tilt, and he followed her into the kitchen.

"What she'd really like, Mr. Cage, is for you to read to her again. It's all she can talk about." She gave him a backward glance as she unloaded the soup containers.

His eyes popped wide. "Seriously?" Lily nodded. "So she didn't freak out over me being here?" he whisper-shouted. Lily's head shook. "Or playing tonsil hockey with her mom?"

A laugh burst from her as she pivoted and faced him. "Tonsil hockey? That's a new one on me. But no, catching her mom and Mr. Cage *playing tonsil hockey* didn't seem to faze her. In fact, she asked if you could come over for dinner."

"Tonight?"

"Tonight."

"So she's not sick anymore?" How was that possible? Christ, he'd seen the volumes that had erupted from that little girl's body.

"Nope. Just napping. I'm pretty sure it was the arena food that didn't sit well. She bounced right back once it was out of her system. Children are resilient like that." Lily gave him that sassy pose that made his inner caveman want to drag her off to his lair. "So, Mr. Cage, are you staying for dinner? Looks like we're having soup." She winked at him.

Oh, this made him all kinds of happy, and he was sure he wore a shit-eating grin that broadcast it. He pulled her into his arms. "I might need some convincing."

She looped her arms around his neck and wiggled her eyebrows. "I can do that."

Chapter 26

You Know What They Say About Assuming

Weeks went by in a blissful blur. When he wasn't training, playing on the road, or playing at home, Gage spent every spare minute with Lily and Daisy. Trips to the zoo and the aquarium, sitting through *Disney on Ice*, and outings to all kinds of kid-oriented places he never knew existed. The Butterfly Pavilion. Santa's Village. Who knew? He even spent a few entertaining hours in Daisy's kindergarten class for Career Day, where she put him on display and declared that she too would be a "hockey player like Mr. Cage" someday.

Life was sweet. In-fucking-credible. He devoured it whole.

Idle time that wasn't consumed by hanging with "his girls" was expended in one of Gage's favorite pastimes: lingering in bed with Lily. Morning and afternoon delight when Daisy was in school, with a rare whole night of delight whenever Daisy stayed with family. Gage paid little attention to the timing of these interludes, simply taking advantage of every chance to make love to Lily. The day before a game, the night before, an hour before. Didn't matter. He was like a dry camel, drinking his fill, and life was damn good.

Lily seemed to be warming to the idea of a “we.” Even so, Gage held himself in check. He teetered on the edge of a skate blade, wanting to tell her how he felt but wary she’d dash off like a scared rabbit if he acted too soon. *Let her get more comfortable.* Dillon would be a good measure of where their relationship stood and how far he could push.

If anything could poke Gage’s idyllic bubble, it was the thorn he labeled his “slumping play.” Coach had demoted him to the third line, where he couldn’t get enough ice time to bring his play back up to its usual first-line level. A vicious cycle that frustrated the hell out of him, especially as he watched Hunter replace him and tear it up. Guy was unstoppable, and Gage couldn’t keep a lid on his mushrooming dislike. Didn’t help that the few times Gage brought Lily around, Hunter looked her over like she was a juicy piece of prime rib.

While Gage managed to ignore criticism about his play in the press, he couldn’t ignore the guilt whenever he faced his team. Not that anyone said anything. They didn’t have to. His speeches about bringing their A-game replayed in his head constantly, ringing hollow. Playing better started at *his* doorstep. His club was counting on him, for fuck’s sake. But the harder he worked, the more his A-game plummeted into D-territory.

As he was turning over his crappy play on his way to practice, his phone rang, and a different kind of guilt clobbered him over the head.

“Hey, Mom. What’s going on?” he answered breezily.

“I’m calling to ask you the same thing, Gage. Where have you been? Why haven’t you called?”

Ah, shit. He folded inside. “Been busy, Mom. Playoffs are almost here and—”

“That’s never stopped you before.” Her voice carried a hint of hurt.

True, but he hadn’t had Lily before. Not that his mom knew she existed. Not that he was about to tell her. “I’m sorry, Mom. I just—things got away from me. So how are you? How’s Grandma?”

A typical long-suffering sigh came through the phone. “About the same, except there was an incident—”

“What kind of incident?” Alarm bells clanged in his head.

"Grandma tried to jailbreak in nothing but a pajama top." His mom actually laughed.

"What? I take it she's okay?"

"She's fine. I swear, if I didn't laugh about this, I'd be crying instead."

He puffed out a breath. "Yeah, I hear ya. I should call her."

"May be better to wait until you see her next week."

His attention had been wandering to his grandma but came slamming back. "Uh ..."

"You're still coming out, right? I'm getting everything ready."

Shit! He'd put off telling her for so long that he'd completely forgotten.

"I, ah, I've got some bad news, Mom. There won't be time this year. I have to stick around and put in extra time. My play's been off lately, and, uh, the coaching staff wants me to work it out." Another white lie.

Not giving up the ice castles with my girls.

"*What?* They can't do that!" Indignation rattled the phone. "You work so hard, and you never get a break. That's not right." Guilt pinched him when he heard the disappointment in her voice.

"I do get breaks, but this time of year a guy's gotta do what a guy's gotta do." Hearing her sigh again made him wince. "I miss you guys, but I'll have to wait until the season's over. It's only a few more months."

Maybe less if we keep playing like shit.

Gage soon put the conversation—and his guilt—behind him and lost himself on the ice. A charged practice where Hunter and Grims nearly got into it after Grims fired a puck at Hunter's chest. Hunter deserved every bit of crap coming his way, but even that move seemed over the top. Though Gage resented the hell out of Hunter's surging play, the team needed the guy's scoring streak to continue.

T.J. caught his eye and jerked his head toward the pair, and he and Gage exchanged a look. Yeah, chemistry on the team had taken a nosedive. When a club was playing well, winning games, things worked a lot more smoothly. Instead of a well-oiled machine, they were a boiling pot of chunky stew.

Gage carried the blame on his shoulders.

But if Gage was spiraling downward in his play, his captain was doing the same in the locker room. Keyed-up and half-cocked, Grims's messages to his teammates had devolved into barking and snapping. Gage had heard rumors Grims and Nicole were having problems. Figuring it was none of his damn business, he kept his mouth shut and shouldered more of the leadership role, diffusing the growing unrest in the locker room, but it wasn't enough. The wheels were coming off the team's bus, and it showed in their slide in the standings with a three-game winless streak. Only Hunter and Quinn seemed to be racking up points.

"We need to talk to Grims," T.J. said after practice. They sat in the locker room, where only a few guys milled around out of earshot.

Gage yanked at his skate laces hard, breaking one. "Yeah." He blew out a breath. "Let me do it."

T.J.'s eyebrows flew to his forehead. "Alone?"

"Don't look so surprised," Gage chuffed. "You two going at it is a volatile mix this locker room doesn't need."

"Who says we'll go at it?"

"He's become a hothead, and you're already a hothead. 'Nuff said."

T.J. regarded him a moment and nodded. "Yeah, that makes sense. Let me know if you need my help."

"Don't worry," Gage chuckled. "You'll be the first person I call for backup."

"Want me to stick around?"

"Nope. I got this."

Gage showered, dressed, and was loading up his bag, waiting on Grims to finish up in Coach's office. The locker room was practically deserted.

As he was practicing what to say and how to say it in his head, the main door opened. Gage looked up. One of the trainers, a young guy named Bobby, was scanning the room with wide eyes.

Gage gave him a chin jerk. "'Sup, Bobby?"

"Uh, Hunter here?"

The guy was fidgety, and Gage narrowed his eyes on something he seemed to be holding out of sight in his hand. The object almost looked as if it was tucked up his sleeve. "Hunts is getting cleaned up."

Bobby wiped his nose with his free hand. "I'll come back."

"Want me to tell him you're looking for him?"

"No, no!" Bobby let out a shrill laugh. "It's a surprise. I'll find him later."

Gage frowned. "Yeah, okay."

Bobby scampered out the door, and Gage left to take a leak. When he returned, he thought he caught sight of Bobby leaving as the main door was snicking shut. He glanced around, his gaze snagging on Hunter's backpack gaping open. *Huh.* He sidestepped over to it and glanced inside.

What the actual fuck?

Shock electrified Gage's body, and his blood surged to a boil. Lying on top of the backpack's contents was a capped, full syringe. He reached down to touch it and stopped himself.

"What are you doing?" Hunter stood in the doorway between the locker room and showers, his eyes traveling from the backpack to Gage's face.

Gage clenched his fists while anger vibrated up his arms. "You son of a bitch! Now I know why you've been playing out of your mind, you fucker!"

Hunter was beside him in a heartbeat, staring down into his backpack. He let out a gasp. "That's not mine," he said hoarsely.

"Of course it's yours! Bobby left it here for you."

"Bobby?" Hunter's eyes widened, and his mouth dropped open. "Bobby was in my backpack? When?"

"Just now. As if you didn't know he was leaving you PEDs. Fucking lowlife."

Hunter's mouth flattened into a grim line. "This isn't what you think, Nelson."

"No? A trainer leaves you a fucking syringe, and I'm supposed to believe you're *not* doping? You make me sick!" It all made sense now. Hunter's stellar play was one big lie built on juicing.

Gage's mind traveled back to the confrontation on the airplane. "Grims knows, doesn't he?" he gritted out.

Hunter's eyes hardened. "Yeah, he knows." He paused and pulled in a breath. "Because *he's* the one doping. Bobby's his source."

The frustration and resentment that had been building detonated inside Gage, and he slammed Hunter against the open locker.

"Motherfucker!" Hunter shouted. "What the fuck's wrong with you?"

"Oh. Did that hurt?" Sneering, Gage pushed off him, giving his shoulder an extra shove. "Take your HGH, or whatever the fuck that is, asshole. You'll recover in no time."

"What the fuck's going on?" Quinn yelled behind them.

"Ask him," Gage jabbed his thumb over his shoulder, snatched his bag, and stormed out of the room. He marched to Coach LeBrun's office, but the door was closed. He dropped his bag, dragged his hands over his face, and began pacing the corridor.

One of the assistant coaches popped his head out of a different office. "Waiting for Coach LeBrun?"

"Yeah, I need to talk to him."

"He's in there with the GM. Might be a while."

This both surprised and confused Gage. "He's not meeting with Grimson?"

The assistant shook his head. "No, he left a while ago."

Gage threw his back against the wall and expelled a huge breath. "Well, fuck."

"Something I can help you with?" The assistant was frowning at him now.

Straightening, Gage opened his mouth to ask the guy for a sit-down when Hunter appeared in the hallway, eyebrows a dark slash above his eyes. "We need to talk, Nelson."

The assistant looked between them before pointing at Gage. "You two going at it again? Look, you're the alternate captain. Fix this." He pivoted and retreated into his office.

Gage turned to face Hunter, his insides on simmer. For an absurd instant, the scene reminded him of two gunmen in a western showdown. "All right," he growled and trailed Hunter to the parking lot.

"Let's go someplace less conspicuous." Hunter gave the arena a sidelong glance. "Follow me."

They climbed into their respective cars and wound up in some dive bar Gage had never been to. Hunter ordered a beer; Gage passed.

"What's with the cloak-and-dagger?" he grumbled.

"Did you say anything about what you saw to anyone?" was Hunter's reply.

"Didn't get the chance," Gage scoffed.

"Look, I know you don't like me, Nelson. I don't much like you either. But this isn't what it looks like."

"You already said that. So tell me what *it* is." Gage laid his hands on the table, only to pick them up when his fingers brushed something sticky.

Hunter ran a hand through his hair, and his expression shifted from a scowl to something unreadable. "I caught Grims," he said on a long exhale. "On our last road trip. I saw him using. He begged me not to say anything."

Now Gage wished he *had* ordered something to drink. Although he might just hurl it back up again for choking on Hunter's bullshit.

"At first, I didn't say anything," Hunter continued. "He told me he'd only used the one time and wouldn't do it again, and I wanted to believe him—so fucking bad." He shook his head. "I found out he lied, so I rode him about it. What you saw on the plane? He was pissed because we'd just had it out."

Gage held back a skeptical smirk. "Why didn't you tell anyone?"

"And what? Shit all over the team?" Hunter hissed. He looked around and dropped his voice, leaning in a little closer. "We're about to start the playoffs, for fuck's sake. So I rat Grims out, and the team suffers along with him? I couldn't do that to my teammates. Besides, plenty of guys dope."

"No, they don't!" Gage whisper-shouted.

"Believe what you want, Nelson. Look, I feel like our team's on the verge of finding its groove again. It's this close." He pinched his finger and thumb together. "If this gets out, it'll set us way back."

Something barb-like stuck in Gage's throat, and he tried to cough it out. Couldn't. "If you're not doping, why's Bobby putting that shit in your bag?"

Hunter took his first sip of beer. “I didn’t know what to do. I couldn’t make Grims stop, and I wasn’t going to turn him in. I figured out Bobby was his source, so I confronted him.”

“Doesn’t look like it worked.”

“No,” Hunter growled. “Instead, that little prick’s trying to set me up.”

“This doesn’t fly. Why would he do that? He’d be slitting his own throat.”

Hunter gave him a look that communicated his dislike for Gage. “Would he? How could I prove it was him? He’s not stupid enough to give Grims the shit at the arena, so there’s no way to catch him there. By putting that shit in *my* bag, Bobby was firing a warning shot.”

Gage wiped his palms over his thighs. “You’re saying that’s the first time Bobby’s slipped one into your bag?”

“First time.” Hunter nodded.

“What does he gain? Even if someone turned you in, they’d test you and find out you’re clean. Unless you are, in fact, doping.”

Hunter glared at him. “I have TOS, asshole.”

Gage’s confusion must’ve shown because Hunter went on after an exasperated sigh. “Blood clots. It’s under control now. I’m not about to put shit in my body that could jack with it.”

Gage’s head involuntarily snapped backward, his mind racing, processing.

“Only management and the medical staff know,” Hunter explained. “And now you. I don’t want my teammates thinking I can’t skate, so I’d appreciate you keeping it to yourself.”

A few beats of silence passed.

“Why not get Bobby’s ass fired?” Gage said.

Hunter gave him a mirthless chuckle. “He and Travis have a bromance. He’s not going anywhere.”

“The owner’s son? *That* Travis?”

“Yep. Travis likes to party. Maybe Bobby hooks him up with different stuff and that’s why they’re tight. Whatever. Bobby’s shit doesn’t stink, according to Travis.”

Gage glanced around the dim bar, letting the truth sink in. Sunlight outlined a crack around an exit door. He returned his gaze to Hunter. “Why’re you telling me all this?”

Another mirthless laugh. "Believe it or not, Nelson, I trust you. You're a Boy Scout. I haven't told another soul about Grims." A breath whooshed from him. "And fuck, it's a relief to tell someone else."

Gage sat in dazed, heartsick silence while a huge weight climbed onto his shoulders and pressed down. Hard.

Chapter 27

Wisdom Is an Elusive Pearl

Gage was reeling when he emerged from the depths of the bar. Dread swelled inside him as fragments of exchanges during the last few weeks sifted through his mind, clicking into place the more he dug through his memory banks. Grims doping explained so much. But, Jesus, he didn't want to believe it. The thought made his chest compress like a ton of bricks was stacked on it.

Dave Grimson was his captain. His teammate. His friend. A guy he looked up to. Respected. Admired. Would follow into battle. He was also a cheater.

What the hell was Gage supposed to do?

If he turned Grimson in, the whole club would go down. He'd end up hurting countless others who'd had no part in it. Never mind the unspoken code that you never ratted out your teammates—especially your *captain*. But turning a blind eye was wrong too. And what about Grims himself? If Hunter's story was true—and Gage was clinging by a frayed skate lace to the possibility it wasn't—Dave Grimson was on a dangerous path. Turning a blind eye also meant helping Grims along that path to ruin.

They were about to leave on a big road trip. Should Gage take action now? After they got back? Not take action?

His moral compass was cast overboard, lost in the Bermuda Triangle.

His buzzing head hurt as he walked into his house. He sent Lily a text, grateful for a distraction. *Ready for me to come get you and Daisy?*

He'd been looking forward to tonight, though his conversation with Hunter had thrown a moldy blanket over his excitement. Time to get his head right. Daisy was staying at Ivy and Parker's, and tomorrow would be one of those rare, precious mornings when he would wake up with Lily in his bed. His slice of sanctuary. And, God, did he need it! Not the sex—sex was the extra helping of whipped cream. What he needed was Lily singing to him, wrapping her arms around him, keeping him grounded while he fought to haul his compass from its mucky depths.

His knee bounced as he leaned against the counter. Then came her reply: *Can you give me 60 or 90 mins? Derek's here talking about a possible gig.*

Gage felt as though he'd been slapped with a mackerel. Derek was there? Derek wasn't supposed to be *there*. He didn't even have Vi this week!

"Fucking Derek!" Hobbes trained a wary gold eye on him.

She can sing if she wants to.

Unbidden, the words replayed to the tune of "Safety Dance" in his head. "Yeah, she can sing. Even if dozens of guys are eye-fucking her," he groused.

His mind ran through what she might wear onstage. She'd bowled him over in her red dress when he'd first laid eyes on her, but she'd since shown him some of her other stage outfits, so he *knew* racier stuff lived in her closet, though she claimed she'd retired those getups. She only kept them as a remembrance of her days in the band. With Jack.

Shit! This day was just getting better and better.

He pulled in a few cleansing breaths, determined to calm down the thoughts jostling in his head like kids waiting for a turn at the water slide on a hot summer day.

With time to cool his heels, he dialed Grandma—and struck gold.

"Oh my goodness, Gage! I've missed you so much! I want to see your face. Do you do FaceTime?"

Shocked she even knew the term, he let out a laugh. "I've missed you too, Grandma. More than you know. Yeah, I do FaceTime. Do you?"

"Oscar knows these things. He says he'll set it up for me. You just hang on, son."

Thanks to awesome Oscar, Gage was soon FaceTiming with his grandmother. His *real* grandmother. Not the shell, not the impostor, but her living, breathing essence. Her eyes were bright, and she seemed eager to hear it all, as if she knew she had this one window of lucidity and she wanted to drink it all in before the window slammed shut.

So they talked, her face at times hovering so close she looked as though she were a contorted reflection in a house of mirrors, making him laugh the way only she could.

She knocked Gage for a loop when she said, "So you're in a slump lately, but these things have their ups and downs. What I really want to hear about is your new girl."

"My new girl?" Who'd told her about Lily? *He* hadn't told anyone except the first conversation he'd had with Sarah. Ah. Grandma was fishing, the sly fox. "You mean Jessica?"

She flapped her hand in front of the screen. "No, I'm not talking about the Phelan girl! She's not for you, Gage."

Funny. Grandma was the only one of his family who thought so.

"I really don't have a girl, Grandma."

"What!" she exclaimed loudly. "A handsome boy like you? Where have you been living? Under a rock?"

"No, Grandma. Under a puck."

She guffawed, then gave him a smug look. "Your sister tells me you really like this one, and that she has a little girl of her own."

Shit, Sarah! What happened to the bro code? "Well, it's not ... We're not ... I like her, but it's not serious ..." Why did he feel like a heel saying so?

"What a boatload of crap! She has you stammering, Gage Nelson, so it's obviously more than you're letting on. And good for you! Oh, your mother will be fit to be tied if you pick someone besides Jessica, but you listen to me, young man."

"Yes, Grandma." He smirked, loving her uppity tone. He'd missed it.

"Go grab yourself another gear on the stick shift of life."

His puzzlement, and amusement, might have shown all over his face, but nothing slowed her roll. "You make a decision in the moment based on what you know or think you know, but you live with the outcome forever. And life is too short. Don't let Nola bully you or pick for you. *You* pick your best life, and pick someone who loves you for who you are inside, not for what you do or for what your friends and family think. You have to build your life with her, no one else. So listen to your heart and find that girl you're crazy about, and make sure she takes good care of you because you deserve nothing less."

She laughed a heartfelt, belly-rumbling laugh that sent warmth spiraling through him, that took him back to being a boy being scolded and loved by her at the same time.

"Are you giving me another pearl, Grandma?" *A precious Grandma pearl of wisdom.* "I think I have enough to string a whole necklace now."

It struck him that she could help him with his Grims dilemma, and he grew hopeful. But suddenly, she seemed confused and began looking around as if she had no idea where she was.

"Grandma?" His voice broke as he tried to haul her back to him.

Now Oscar's face was on the screen. "I think your grandma's tired from all the excitement, Gage, so you might want to say good-bye for now."

Oscar moved away, and Grandma was back. Hands he assumed were Oscar's rested on her shoulders, seeming to steady her, and once again Gage was grateful the man was there.

"Oscar says I should go now. Gage?" Her voice sounded panicky, and it twisted his heart into knots. If only he could reach her and hold on to her!

He took a calming breath. "I'm here, Grandma."

"There you are. Before I go, I want you to know you are so very special. Have I told you lately? No, I don't think I have." Her voice was laced with sadness. "Anyway, you stay on that right path. Don't deviate."

"It isn't always so easy."

"You'll make it out. And if you veer from it, I'll leave my grave, hunt you down, and haunt you!" Her chuckle didn't resonate; she was fading from him fast.

He kissed his hand and pressed it to the screen. "Grandma, I love you."

She kissed her hand and pressed back. "I know, sweetheart, and I love you. You've always been a good boy. You make me so proud. Don't ever stop. Don't hold back. Live full-out."

"Grab the next gear on the stick shift of life?"

"That's it." She shook her fist. "Living isn't for wussies. No chickenshit crap now, you hear?"

"Never," he choked out.

Chapter 28

Claiming a Stake

Derek stood in Lily's open doorway, his hand poised on the doorknob as they exchanged good-byes. Daisy was reaching up to hug her uncle when Gage's car glided curbside. Lily glanced at her phone. No message from him. Why was he early?

When he strode up the walkway and paused at the bottom of the stoop, she knew why.

With his hands in the front pockets of his jeans, sunglasses on, he projected California casual, but she didn't have to look very hard to know it was an act. There was nothing casual about the testosterone pouring off of him in heady waves. She could practically smell it, hear it crackle in the air.

He wore a tight brown button-down that displayed every ripped muscle. And every ripped muscle was taut. His sleeves were cuffed at his elbows, and his flexing forearms showed off the corded veins along their surface. A neck muscle jumped. He looked as though he'd just bench-pressed a bus.

Saying Derek's name in a rumble that reminded her of thunder, Gage gave him the curtest of man nods. Derek's fist clenched at his side, and he wordlessly returned the same short nod. And didn't move—except to turn his body so it blocked Gage's way to the landing where he and Lily stood.

A glare-down ensued.

Oh my God! How soon before they ram horns? Pee all over my steps?

Lily placed herself between the two men, who both seemed to snap out of their male hormone-induced standoff and act surprised to see her there. Derek stepped back, and Lily leaned down from where she stood on the top step and gave Gage a quick peck before he could haul her in, thump his chest, and bellow, "Mine!"

"You're early." Her voice held a little ice, and she detected a slight flinch. *Yeah, you should be sorry, you bullheaded caveman!* He had no right to stake a claim. Even so, a tendril of feminine satisfaction wound itself up from her core. It was nice to be an object of desire sometimes, and Gage was good at letting her know how desirable she was. All. The. Time.

God, what was wrong with her?

Derek didn't stick around, and once he was gone, Daisy happily chattered at Gage, who nodded patiently and acted as though he hung on her every word.

"Sweetheart," Lily said to her daughter, "we're leaving for Aunt Ivy's soon. Go find your babies and your new books, okay?"

"Yay!" Daisy cried. "Will you come help me, Mr. Cage?" She grabbed his hand.

"Sure, kiddo. Let's go."

After dropping Daisy at Ivy's, Gage barely spoke.

Lily threw him a sidelong glance. "Everything okay over there in the driver's seat?"

Sunglasses firmly in place, thumb tapping a rhythm on the steering wheel, he lobbed a gruff reply. "Yep. Just have a few things on my mind before I leave."

"You're gone a long time."

"Ten days. Five critical games. Our spot in the standings will be pretty well solidified at the end of it."

"Do you think the coaches will move you up from the third line?"

He kept his focus straight ahead. "I'm trying my damnedest to convince them."

"Being on the third line's really bothering you, huh?"

He slid his sunglasses down his nose and side-eyed her. "Yeah." Icicles in his voice, so foreign, sent a warning chill through her.

Whoops, wrong question!

She straightened in her seat, fortifying herself for what, she had little idea. Paranoia was probably setting in, but she detected that it wasn't just his game eating at him. "Going to Dillon after you get back will be a nice break for you." Her words sounded lame even to her own ears, and he must have agreed because he let those words hang with barely a nod to acknowledge them. She abandoned the conversation, and they rode in silence the rest of the way to his house. Tonight would be their last just-them time for a while, and she wasn't going to ruin it by prodding for answers.

As she walked inside Gage's house, Hobbes ran to her and rubbed against her legs. Lily looked around, letting the space envelop her in a warm blanket of comfort. The guitars, the sprawling leather couch, the framed hockey memorabilia. It was all a reflection of him that she loved.

He stuck his head in the refrigerator and began pulling out ingredients.

"What are you making?" she asked.

"The Nelson specialty of the house." He glanced up and beamed; the icicles from before had completely melted, and relief rippled through her. "I hope you like cheesecake."

"I *love* cheesecake. You know how to make it?" Her voice broadcast her surprise. The man had all kinds of hidden talents.

They stood at opposite ends of the kitchen, a space of about ten feet dividing them.

"Yep. And Italian meatballs. Those are also on tonight's menu." He pointed a brick of cream cheese at her. "You're in charge of the green stuff."

A laugh bubbled in her chest. "What's the 'green stuff'?"

Easing, she folded her arms across her chest. Under an open fleece jacket, she wore a white tank top. She didn't miss how his eyes traveled down to the swell along the tank's neckline. Like a kid caught with his hand in the cookie jar, he snapped his gaze back to hers. "Uh, the usual stuff. Salad. Green beans. No kale smoothies."

The air between them grew electrified. Her mind was already jumping to getting him out of his clothes. She took a few steps toward him.

"Did you know," he said in his best professor voice, "too much kale might be bad for you? And spinach."

"Too much of anything is bad."

"Not true." He waggled his eyebrows.

"Is that so, Professor?" A few more steps and she'd closed the distance.

With his back against the counter, he reached out and ran his big, warm hands up and down her arms, sending tingles skittering up her shoulders and neck. Her eyes wandered to his chest and the brown shirt molding itself to him. Chocolate-covered muscles. She pictured running her tongue over those muscles, nipping, sucking, driving him out of his mind. Watching his usually composed expression dissolve and contort with agonizing pleasure when he was in the throes was one of her favorite things about their sexy times. She loved watching him fall apart.

As if he could read each of her filthy thoughts, he kissed her forehead and set her apart from him. "Time to cook food. We'll cook up other things later."

"Promise?" she teased.

He swatted her butt. "Behave."

"Or what, Professor?"

"I'll bend you over my knee and spank your bare ass with my ruler."

She fluttered her eyes. "Oh, Professor. You've given me more reason than ever to misbehave."

He shook his head and chuckled. Soon they were cooking together while music played in the background. She was in a happy, uncomplicated place. Tab Benoit sang about southern ladies sashaying by, and she swung her hips in time.

"Yoga tomorrow afternoon, Professor?" She was prepping green beans, and he was checking the baking cheesecake.

He topped off her wine and leaned in for a kiss. "Yes, but you absolutely cannot stand in front of me."

"Why not?"

Sliding behind her, he placed his hands on her hips and glided them slowly, sensually, over her ass. She bit back a gasp. He dropped his head and sucked her neck softly, making her break out in goose bumps in spite of the kitchen's warmth.

"Because," he whispered huskily, "you'll be wearing something kinda stretchy and clingy, and I'll think you're trying to seduce me again." He paused a beat. "Unless, of course, that's what you're going for, and then by all means, seduce away. But I don't think Carla will appreciate me taking you on her studio floor in front of her students. It might not be the vibe she's going for."

"No, I don't imagine she's going for an X-rated vibe." A little laugh burst from her. "You're ridiculous, you know that? Does your grandmother know how naughty you are?"

"Oh, Grandma would be cheering me on."

Lily craned her neck and kissed him. "I hope I get to meet her someday."

Sadness flashed in his eyes. "Yeah, me too."

After dinner, Gage put on Marvin Gaye, took her in his arms, and began to sway in a tight circle in the middle of the family room. He pulled back and gave her a goofy grin. "Like my dance move?"

She laughed—she'd been doing that a lot tonight. Whether it was the wine, him, or a combination, she couldn't say. She didn't care. "Yeah, I like your dance move."

He laced their fingers together and trapped their coupled hands against his chest. "Makes it easier to do this." Dropping his head, he started working on her neck. He had a very talented mouth he used on her generously—she couldn't get enough, and she let him know it with a series of soft moans.

By the time he took her upstairs, she was putty in his hands. Making love was languid and sweet, and when they were done, she snuggled into his arms and drifted off in a contented fog.

Later she awakened to moaning—her own, as it turned out—and wet pleasure radiating from her core. As she came to on her back, she realized Gage was between her legs, which were draped over his shoulders, and his mouth was on her with ravenous intensity. Suspended between excruciating pleasure and explosive torment, she bucked against him, rising to meet his mouth while trying to escape it at the same time. But he held her in place, his strong hands gripping her thighs. His tongue stroked her, lashed her, while his lips nibbled and sucked her swollen flesh. Orgasms crashed over her like tidal waves until her body trembled uncontrollably.

He released her and climbed up her body, pulling her wrists above her head. As he hovered above her, fuzzy light from somewhere illuminated his chiseled cheekbones, glistening lips, and eyes that gleamed like dark pearls. His chest rose and fell with heavy breaths. "You awake now, Goldilocks?"

She gasped out an "uh-huh."

"Good," he murmured. His rock-hard shaft grazed her entrance. "I *want* you awake so you know everything I do to you. First I want you to taste what I taste because you're better than any fucking dessert I've ever eaten."

God, she soared inside when he talked like that.

He took her mouth hard, his tongue invading, sweeping, devouring. Breaking the kiss, he brushed her lips with his as he spoke. "Do you taste yourself on my tongue? Do you taste what I taste?"

"Yes," she panted.

"God, you're so fucking gorgeous. You make me fucking nuts because I don't know where to start."

He dipped his head and pulled a nipple into his mouth, biting down softly as his tongue swirled around her taut bead over and over. He released her. "Do I start there? Or here?" Now he dropped lower, his tongue flicking her navel, softly sucking the tender skin on her stomach. "Or here?" He rose back up and latched on to her other nipple. She couldn't stop squirming beneath him.

His wet mouth and tongue seemed to be everywhere, spurring her to the brink of ignition. "Do you like it when I suck you there?"

"God, yes."

"You're gonna tell me everything you like, Lily."

"Mmm."

"You ready?"

She inhaled a stuttering breath. "For what?"

He didn't answer. Not with words. Instead, he hooked his hands under her arms, towed her to her knees as though she weighed nothing, and turned her so she faced the headboard. His heat radiated behind her, the tip of his shaft grazing her. He ran his hands over her back and spread her thighs, every touch a caress. One hand slid between her legs and cupped her, and the other slid up her back and wound itself in her hair.

He bent her over. “Hands on the headboard, beautiful.”

She grabbed on, anticipation tingling her every nerve, her body blazing.

A sharp inhale, then he muttered, “For fuck’s sake. You are so perfect.” She could practically feel his greedy gaze running over her. While one hand held her hair, he slid two fingers inside her. She let out a strangled moan.

He tugged her head back, his warm breath brushing her ear as his fingers worked their magic. “You’re gonna come for me again, Lily, but first you’re going to let me know what turns you on.” He slid his fingers in and out, stroking them over her, in her, the whole time asking, “Is this good? And this?”

She couldn’t talk. His touch was splintering her consciousness. Only pants, groans, and her bucking body told him what he wanted to know, and once he had his answers, he honed in and took her from one shattering climax to another.

“Fuck yeah,” he grunted behind her. “Love making you come.”

The interval between her peaks grew shorter and shorter until she seemed to orgasm with each stroke of his fingers.

He stopped, and she sagged, her lungs dragging in air as she clung to the headboard like it was a piece of wood keeping her afloat in a boiling sea. Hauling her upright against him, her back mated to his front, he wrapped his arms around her, holding her while she came down. He dusted her neck, her ears, her shoulders with sweet kisses.

“Good?” he whispered, and she nodded weakly. He chuckled lustily. Cupping her breasts, he nudged her so she bent over once more, her ass snugged against his groin, trapping his steely cock between their bodies. He draped himself over her back, dropping his mouth beside her ear again, and flexed his hips, grinding against her.

“You still with me, beautiful?”

“Mmm.”

His fingers kneaded her breasts, circled her nipples, squeezing them. “Can’t get enough of you, Lil. You’re a fucking dream come true. I don’t ever want to let go.”

She shimmied in his grasp and hooked an arm behind his neck, pulling his head down.

His lips landed in the crook of her neck. “Don’t think I can hang on much longer. Gonna explode.”

“Then what are you waiting for, Professor?”

“Hands back on the headboard, Goldilocks.” She complied, and his fingers feathered over the small of her back, her hips, her ass.

Goose bumps peppered her flesh. She’d never been more aroused. A drawn-out sigh escaped her lungs as she readied to take him inside. It might have been a whimper.

One of his hands still palmed her breast while the other glided between her legs. His fingers slipped back inside, and he let out a hiss. “Jesus, you’re so fucking tight.”

Fingers glided out, replaced with his cock. Teasing her entrance, dipping in her wetness, he pushed inside, tunneling in on one long stroke. A groan ripped from his lungs as he filled her, stretched her.

Buried to the root, he stopped and wrapped his hand in her hair once more, tugging her head back. His other hand dropped between them and began stroking her. She clenched around him. He pulled out and drove into her. A pitched moan flew from her. He did it again. And again. His breathing grew labored.

He yanked her head back a little harder. “I’m going to fuck you over and over,” he growled, “so every man smells me on you and knows you’re mine.”

Slam.

“Oh God,” she yelped with pleasure.

Slam.

“What am I going to do to you, beautiful?”

Slam.

She gasped. “You’re going to ... to ...” Her words dissolved into moans.

Slam.

“Fuck you until what, Lily? Say it.”

Slam. Slam. Slam.

The hand that had been toying with her splayed across her abdomen, holding her tight, and his thrusts came harder, faster, deeper.

“Every man ... smells you ... on me,” she panted.

He released her hair and grabbed on to her hips, digging his fingers in. “Yesssss,” he gritted out.

Spiraling ever upward in a state of rapture, she gripped the headboard while he pounded her over and over and over, his grunts growing louder, more primal. Powerful, fast, frantic. A groan tore from her throat, and her body shuddered and seized around him.

He pitched a second later, following her over the edge. “Fuuuuuuuuuck!”

She collapsed, and he landed on her back, his heavy breaths falling on her neck, his hand trapped beneath them. Her chest heaved erratically and not at all in time with his.

When their pumping hearts finally slowed, he slid off her back and pulled her into his arms, covering her face and neck with tender kisses. “Love waking you up that way.” His voice was a low, breathless rasp. “Wanna do that again and again. Forever.”

She nestled her head against his chest before floating away in a sex-inebriated cloud, faintly aware she'd never been more content.

Chapter 29

Deep Into That Darkness Peering

Lily roused to the sound of desperate cries, but she couldn't move. Her feet were concrete blocks. Someone grabbed her shoulder. Panic swelling, she tried to scream, but no sound came out. Her body quaked as she fought her attacker.

"Lily? Lily!" a strong voice pierced the fog.

That strong voice belonged to Gage, and he was shaking her. "Lily! Sweetheart, wake up!"

She bolted upright, her heart slamming against her ribcage, whimpers still keening in her chest. With a series of gasps, she ran her hands over her body. *It was a nightmare. It wasn't real.*

A warm hand grasped her chin and turned her head. Her eyes met Gage's. A bedside lamp was on. "You were having a nightmare." He pulled her into his arms, his voice soothing. "It's okay, Goldilocks. You're safe with me in our bed."

Panic rose inside her again. *Our bed? No!* Wisps of thoughts chased each other in her head. She shouldn't be here! She began struggling, pushing at his chest.

He tightened his hold, apparently not understanding. "Shh. I've got you."

His embrace felt so good that she finally melted into it. He kissed the top of her head and laid his cheek on it.

Fragments streaked through her mind: shadowed people judging her, Derek accusing her of being a bad mother, carrying off a screaming Daisy. Jack had been there too, his face ashen against a white pillow, begging, "Don't leave me!"

Burning bile rose in her throat; it tasted like guilt.

Chest heaving, tears wetting her cheeks, she forced words out of her mouth. "I need to ... to go."

A warm chuckle rumbled through Gage. "No, you don't. It's three o'clock in the morning. I'll get you some water, then you can tell me about the dream?"

"Bathroom." The word came out strangled.

He relaxed his hold, and she untangled herself from the covers, from him.

Concern etched his face. "Do you need help?"

Her voice shook. "N-no."

Dragging in ragged breaths, she staggered into the bathroom and flipped a switch. Light glared down at her, putting her on full display in an endless mirror. She swallowed hard at her reflection. Naked, hair disheveled, eyes wild, her body trembled. Only hours ago, she'd been in the throes of carnal euphoria, but now shame crept inside her, leaving her chilled.

Her hand went to her neck, and she slumped in relief when her fingers closed around her ring. She ran it along the length of the chain.

A robe hung from a hook on the back of Gage's bathroom door, and she yanked it down. Wrapped it around herself. Cinched the belt tight.

A light knock made her jump.

"Everything all right, beautiful?"

I'm not beautiful! She gulped air. "I-I'm fine."

Squaring herself up in the mirror, she ran her quivering hands over her body, telling herself she'd had a bad dream, that this was solid, this was real. Her heartbeat decelerated.

But a storm continued raging in her soul.

Later that morning, Lily awoke in an empty bed, still covered with Gage's robe. Shivers raced along her spine as shards of the same vivid images came roaring back. With them, they brought crushing guilt.

Smells of breakfast wafted up her nose as she made her way downstairs. Her stomach turned. She padded into the kitchen. Gage's back was to her, and he wielded a spatula at the stove. Dressed in a T-shirt and plaid lounge pants, he moved fluidly, and she watched him for a moment. He must have sensed her because he wheeled and offered her a tentative smile.

"Better this morning?"

She gave him an overzealous head bob. "All good, thanks."

His eyebrows knotted. "That must've been one hell of a dream. What was it about?"

"Um, nothing." She let out a nervous laugh. "I mean, I don't remember. You know how dreams are."

"Yeah." He gave her a skeptical look before turning back to his cooking. "You hungry?"

Her eyes caught on his square shoulders. She loved looking at them. Loved running her hands over them. She shook herself from her wandering thoughts. "I could eat a little."

Soft music played in the background while he plated omelet, potatoes, and fruit. They sat silently at the counter. His plate half-finished, he straightened on his stool, a playful smile dancing on his lips. "*I* didn't give you that nightmare, did I? I mean, with how I woke you up ..."

Her hand flew to her neck and grasped her chain. His gaze dipped to the movement. "What? Of course not!" Her volume was set to high.

The ghost of a frown touched his brows before he turned back to his meal. "So something we didn't talk about yesterday," he paused for a swallow of juice, "is what's up with the gig?"

She nibbled at her potatoes. "The gig?"

"Derek's gig?" He used air quotes on the last word, and though his expression was guileless, her temper flared white. She couldn't say why.

She arched an eyebrow at him. "What about the *gig*?" She tossed the air quotes right back.

Surprise flitted across his face, and he threw up his hands in surrender. "Sorry. I only wondered if you were going to do it."

"Why does it bother you?" Her voice sliced through the air between them.

Leaning his elbows on the countertop, he blew out a breath. "I guess it's the idea of guys—lots of guys—eye-fucking you, lining you up in their sights."

"I can handle it."

"I know you can. Doesn't mean I like it."

Her temper spiked again, and she felt like a train about to derail, still with little idea why. "You're talking as if you have a say."

Something hard passed through his eyes—something she'd never seen before—vanishing as quickly as it appeared.

She cleared her throat. "So what is it with you and Derek anyway?"

"You want honest?"

Did she? She was trying to balance on a teeter-totter of emotions. One false move and she'd be on her ass.

She nodded.

"I'm not fond of the guy, and I'm pretty sure he isn't fond of me."

She laughed bitterly. "This would be obvious to a blind person. Still doesn't answer what you have against him."

Gage's blue eyes, different shades today, pierced hers. "Look, I'm glad he's in your life. It's obvious he cares about you and Daisy. He's a stand-up guy."

"But?"

"But ... besides being a constant reminder of his brother, I think he'd like to put the moves on you."

"You're crazy!" she yelped. Gage was only saying it because his inner caveman saw *everyone* as a rival.

"I'm going to fuck you until every man smells me on you and knows you're mine."

Last night, she'd reveled in his possessiveness. This morning, it rubbed her like gravel on a raw spot.

He regarded her intently.

She rolled her eyes and threw down her napkin. "I never should've told you! You're just acting jealous."

"Can you blame me?" he sighed. "Lily, it can't come as a surprise how I feel about you. Maybe I'm jealous of Derek because *I* want to be that guy for you—the one you depend on."

Before yesterday, Gage's confession would have let loose a squadron of fluttery things in her belly. Today? Today everything was off kilter, and his words had her stomach clenching and her defenses flailing to hoist boundaries. Too little, too late. She'd let it go too far. They were straying into territory she hadn't paid attention to, and she was suddenly terrified, frantically backpedaling. Confusing emotions roiled inside her, and she fought an urge to run.

She pulled in a lungful of air. "Gage, there's no denying the physical attraction between us is off the charts. It's intoxicating. In fact, I might need to check into rehab to get over my addiction to you," she laughed. He didn't.

He sat quietly. When he finally spoke, he softly asked, "Where do you see things going between us, Lily?"

Where *did* she see things going? Not forward, but she didn't want to go backward either. There was no escaping the bubbling lake of molten fire at her core whenever he was around. She loved how he smelled and tasted and the feel of his heavy body on top of her. Loved running her hands over him, loved the hardness of his muscles, loved how quickly and how big he grew when she touched him. Loved how he held her at night as though she were a treasure. He made her feel things she'd never felt before.

Was it all about sex?

No. Because she loved talking to him, loved how easy it was to be with him. She trusted him. Felt safe with him. Loved how he treated Daisy. How he treated everyone.

But she couldn't escape the sinking notion she felt *too* much, that it was too soon.

"Why do things have to go anywhere?" she said in a near-whisper to keep it from coming out in a squawk. "Can't they just stay the way they are?"

He twirled his now-empty juice glass. "I spoke to Grandma yesterday. She was having a lucid day, and we talked a long time. Before she zoned out, she said something that's had me thinking ever since." He caught her eyes with his. "Life's short. You grab and go, and you hang on. Full-out. You probably know this better than anyone with what you've been through."

"I don't follow." And she didn't.

Sadness was mirrored in his eyes. He shook his head. "Never mind."

A need to touch him had her running her foot up his leg. She yearned to pull him in tight and know they hadn't lost their connection.

"So ... we have an hour before we have to pick up Daisy. You wanna," she lifted her chin toward the stairs and gave him what she thought was an alluring smile, "you know?"

What the hell am I doing? She was swinging from one extreme to another with dizzying speed. One minute she wanted to flee, and the next she wanted to fuck. Her mental hopscotching was running roughshod over her. She wanted him because he made her feel alive like no one else ever had. She didn't want him because that same intimacy was crushing her.

In a very un-Gage-like move, he pulled his leg away, gathered up their dishes, and made for the sink. "Maybe later, beautiful."

"So ... no bath either?"

He began rinsing the dishes, a half-smile on his face. "A bath with you will take much longer than an hour."

Right. At the sink, she nudged him with her hip. "You cooked. I'll do the dishes."

Without protest, he sat back at the counter, picked up his phone, and began scrolling.

"What time does your plane leave tomorrow?" she asked.

"Hmm?" He didn't look up.

She turned and perched her hands on her hips. "Your road trip? When do you leave?"

Blue eyes rose to hers, then darted back to his phone. "Early afternoon. You're still okay checking on Hobbes?"

"Yes. And you're back a week from Wednesday?"

"Yep."

She crossed her arms over her chest. "Wednesday's when Derek's band is performing."

"You've decided to do it, I take it?"

"I told him I'm in. Will you come watch us?"

He raised his head and blinked. She was almost hoping for a little Derek-directed animosity, a glimpse of the caveman, but nothing like that showed in his expression. "Uh, yeah. Of course. Just send me the details. Shouldn't be a problem to head your way after I land."

Head back down, both thumbs now worked his phone.

Miffed, she couldn't stop herself. "What's so interesting?"

He turned off the screen and set the phone down. "Nothing." Bringing his full six-foot-one frame upright, he stood and stretched. "I'm gonna skip Carla's class and get in a workout today instead. With playoffs right around the corner, I need to concentrate on my training." He trotted toward the stairs. "I'll grab a quick shower, and then we'll go."

Wow! And, Lily, you're not invited.

She nodded at his back, wondering what the hell kind of wall had just slammed between them. In the background, a familiar melody piqued her ears. "Have I Told You Lately?"—Jack's and her song—played.

An arrow embedded itself in her heart, and she folded over, desperate for breath as tears rushed into her throat.

Chapter 30

Grabbing a Gear on the Stick Shift of Life

Gage let the water sluice over his body, hoping it would wash away the anger, confusion, and hurt pulsing inside him.

He'd believed there was more between Lily and him, but he'd made the same mistake the first time too. *Never should have admitted how I feel.* Instead of grabbing the damn stick shift of life, he'd stripped the gears and ground everything to a halt.

Apparently, he was the only one who'd fallen.

Add to it the Grims gorilla sitting on his chest, and Gage felt as though he'd been gut-checked.

He took his time in the shower, trimmed his beard, clipped his nails—to avoid facing Lily. Looking at her hurt too much, which was why he'd buried his nose in his phone, checking crap like weather and NHL standings. Also why he was skipping yoga.

What did Lily want from him?

Yeah, sex was off the charts, but was that it for her? He *should* be thankful. Go with the flow, right? The hottest sex of his life, and all he had to do was show up.

Wham, bam, thank you, ma'am.

Thing was, he could have that now, with lots of women. But he didn't want lots of women. He wanted Lily. All of Lily. Her body, her mind, and most of all, her heart. He wanted her to feel for him what she felt for Jack. Anything less was too hard. So was holding himself back.

He *did* want to claim her as his so the dickheads of the world knew they didn't have a shot, damn it!

And there was Daisy. Somewhere along the way, he'd fallen for that little girl too. He wanted to be more than "Mr. Cage." He wanted to protect her, step in if kids bullied her, threaten to mangle any boys who came sniffing around. He *wanted* to be that guy. And right now Derek had a solid grasp on that position. Fucking Derek.

These thoughts and what the fuck he was going to do about Grims went through the meat grinder in his mind on the ride to Ivy and Parker's house. Lily busily worked over her thumbnail beside him in the passenger seat, giving it all her interest.

He wandered back to her nightmare and how her demeanor had flipped a switch afterward. What the hell had it been about? He'd probably never find out because she wouldn't share that either.

Maybe this break was for the best, he told himself. Get some distance, take some time. Cool things off for a week. Solve his Grims conundrum. Get his head screwed on right and get his mojo back. Mentally prepare for playoffs.

The team needed him at a hundred percent now more than ever.

He had to make this all work.

Daisy kept him entertained on the way to Lily's with a recap of her mites' "season." It had ended the Saturday before, and she was jabbering about ways to "up her game" next year and what did Mr. Cage think about this and that. He continually slid his gaze to the rearview just to watch her as she ran on, her silver eyes sparkling and her smile brightening her face like a high-beam light shone on it. How her curls bounced. She sprinkled her narrative with little girl giggles that nearly undid him.

He parked and walked the girls inside. Lily gave him sad eyes, so he followed her into the kitchen while Daisy skipped to her room to put her "babies to bed." Her babies, as far as Gage could tell, consisted of a once-pink bunny, a well-loved doll, and something that resembled an armadillo.

In Lily's kitchen, he stood transfixed by the way she attacked her counters. Without glancing up, she said, "Will I see you tonight?"

"I don't know," he answered honestly. "Depends on you."

She stopped buffing to face him, a little scowl forming on her face. "What does *that* mean?"

Daisy startled them when she bounced in. "Mr. Cage, wanna see my new books?"

He crossed the room, and leaned down to her. "Help me out here, kiddo. How do I get you to call me something besides Mr. Cage?"

"I don't know," she giggled. An idea seemed to flash, and she grabbed his hand with her tiny one. "What's your middle name?"

He dropped into a one-kneed crouch so they were eye to eye. "Mitchell."

Her body began rocking, and her eyes took a tour around the room. "I can call you Mitchell," Daisy proclaimed.

"No, you really can't. Not even my mom calls me Mitchell." He squeezed her hand in his. "Besides, if you can say 'Mitchell,' you can say 'Gage,' princess." He quirked an eyebrow at her and gave her shirt a tug.

Lily's head snapped up from the counter, and she trained a strange look on him. *Is it not okay to tell her to call me Gage?*

"Gaaage," Daisy finally said, drawing out the *a*. "Gage," she added with a head bob, as if putting the final dot on an *i*.

He popped his eyes dramatically. "Wow! I like how you say it." Cocked an ear. "Say it again?"

"Gage!"

"Nice!" He held up his palm. "Five up high."

She smacked his hand hard.

He lowered his palm. "Five in the middle." She obliged him with another smack and a giggle.

"Five down low."

A final smack. "Too slow!" she cried triumphantly.

A laugh rolled through his chest. "That's not how it works, princess."

"You didn't move your hand fast enough."

Without warning, she launched herself at him, nearly knocking him off balance, and wrapped her skinny little arms around his neck. Stunned, he enveloped her and lifted his gaze to Lily, who stood frozen, her eyes wide like a proverbial deer caught in the headlights. Daisy burrowed her head into his chest, her tiny hand patting his back as she whispered, "I love you, Gage."

Thunk! Shot straight through the heart. He recovered and did the first thing that occurred to him. He dropped a kiss on Daisy's curls and whispered back, "I love you too, princess."

The moment was broken the instant she wiggled out of his arms and scampered away. Gage rose to his feet. Lily's eyes were still locked on him, her lower lip wobbling. She wiped moistness from her cheeks. Two strides and he was beside her.

"Hey. What's all this?" His fingers brushed her tears. "I don't know what's going on here, and it's scaring me. Let me in. Please."

In his second surprise in that kitchen, Lily threw her arms around him and clung tightly. Helpless to figure out what the hell was happening, he held her close, stroking her back until she pulled away.

"Jack," she rasped, then cleared her throat, "Jack used to call her his princess."

Why did everything circle back to Jack? Gage pushed her curls away from her face and grasped her chin between his thumb and forefinger. "Should I not call her that? Tell me what to do here."

Tears still rimming and spilling, she shoved at his shoulder playfully. "No, you big lug. I mean, yes. You can call her princess."

Bewildered, he smiled tentatively. *Big lug is good, I think.*

With a shuddering sigh, she looked up at him. God, he wished he could read what was going through her head. Her eyes were like windows in a car that was speeding so fast the scenes flew by in a blur and you couldn't pick out a damn thing. To say she was sending mixed signals was the understatement of the century. He grasped at the ones he most wanted to latch on to.

Resting his forehead against hers, he held her. "I don't know what's going on with you, or what I've done wrong, but there's something I need to say."

"Okay," she sniffed.

Heart thudding in his chest, Grandma whispering that he should grab that next gear, he drew in a calming breath. "I love Daisy's mama too."

Lily stiffened. He'd blown it.

She wriggled away, putting a huge gap between them. Her lashes were clumped in tears, like star points surrounding her eyes. "You're so good with her, and I just ... I wish I could ... I'm so mixed up."

His heart physically hurt, as though someone had pounded nails into it. He told himself to give her space. But he wasn't sure he could keep convincing himself it would change anything.

"Lily," his voice broke, "you may as well put the ring back on your finger because you're still wearing it. Will you ever let go?"

Tearful turned to angry. "That's not fair."

From the living room came a question as innocent as it was devastating. "Are you gonna marry my mom, Gage?"

Two sets of eyes were on him. Hopeful gray ones and frightened blue ones. He drummed his fingers against his heart, searching for an answer. *If the daughter falls for you, she'll bring the mom along.*

"I'd like to someday, princess." He swung his gaze to Lily. "But only if your mom wants to." There. He'd said it.

Daisy covered her mouth and giggled behind her hands. Then she hopped in place as though she were on a mini trampoline. "I'm gonna go tell my babies!" She ran through her father's shrine toward her room.

When Gage looked back at Lily, her wide eyes sparked. "What?" He braced himself for the buffeting coming his way.

"How could you say that in front of her? Don't you think you should have at least talked to me before you put it out there in front of *her*?"

Once again, he'd blown it, and his heart caved. "I was just saying it like it is."

Lily's voice rose. "She's just a little girl! I don't want her getting her hopes up and having them crushed."

He frowned. "What makes you think her hopes will be crushed?"

"She's already lost her father."

Confusion and frustration ramped up inside him. *It's always about Jack.* He felt as though he were fighting his way out of a choke hold that constricted the harder he pushed against it. "Losing her father has nothing to do with me."

Lily blew out a long breath. "You don't get it."

"Call me obtuse, but no, I don't. Can you spell it out for me?" He tried to keep the grit from his tone.

She rubbed her forehead. "Maybe we should save this discussion for another time."

"Like when, Lily?"

"I don't know."

"You're dodging me."

"And you're pushing me."

He put his hands up. "I gotta get to the rink." With a resigned sigh, he headed for her door.

Another storm awaited him.

Grims was squirting water in his mouth beside the bench. He gave Gage a toothless grin. "Good workout, Admiral."

Gage had been in the training room when Grims walked in, and he'd invited his captain to join him on the ice. Gage had taken out his frustrations on each and every puck, and now he was cooling down, catching his breath beside Grims. No one else was around.

"Hey, did you ever get things worked out with your MILF?"

Suddenly, Gage was seeing red. Lily wasn't a MILF. She was ... a sweet, mixed-up mom of a little girl he adored as much as he adored her. He knew he hadn't handled things well, but shit, he just couldn't understand why she wouldn't let go.

He wiped sweat from his forehead with the hem of his jersey. "She's not my MILF."

"Oh. Sorry, man."

"Yeah, me too," Gage grumbled. Maybe the red he was seeing was because of the guy standing next to him. He looked at Grims dead-on. "How long have you been juicing?"

Grims's eyes widened, then narrowed. "Who says I'm juicing?"

"I know you get your shit from Bobby, and I know Bobby's jacking with Hunter because Hunter found out."

Grims pulled at some tape on his blade. "Hunter's a fucktard, and you believe him?"

Gage hadn't wanted to believe Hunter, but after he'd run what he knew through an objective filter, he'd come to the gut-wrenching conclusion the guy had been telling the truth. Which sucked. It would have been so much easier to blame Hunter and keep his image of Grims intact.

Gage puffed out a breath. "I won't argue that he's a fucktard, but I believe him, Grims."

Grims stared at him for several long beats, and Gage could've sworn anger, chased by regret, flashed in his eyes. "So, Boy Scout, what do you plan on doing with his story?"

Gage leaned on his stick. "You admit it?"

"I'm admitting nothing."

Gage nodded. "I'm not sure, Grims." And that was the truth. Though he'd wrestled mightily with the dilemma, Gage had yet to pick the lesser of two evils—but he needed to decide soon. He was hosed if he did, hosed if he didn't, and he resented the hell out of being dead center in this cluster-fuck. His choices were to keep his mouth shut and let the team roll into the playoffs with its captain or tell Coach and watch his club implode. Either option made him sick to his stomach. "I just want what's best for the team."

Grims's eyes flicked to Gage's. "So do I. Where you and I differ, though, is that I understand how one false move could tear this club apart. But hey, don't let that get in the way of what your conscience tells you, Boy Scout."

And there, in so many words, was the heart of Gage's conundrum.

What his conscience told him to do was follow the rules, which included seeing that others did too. A level playing field. No cheaters.

But the *right* way sure as shit didn't feel right. If he outed Grimson, shit would hit the fan and cause a ripple the team wouldn't recover from before the start of playoffs. *Everyone* would get hurt. Gage would be labeled a snitch, and no one would want to play with him again. On the other hand, letting it go was the same as covering it up. He'd be aiding and abetting, becoming part of the doping problem, making him as dirty as Grimson. And where would it end?

What he really wanted was to un-see everything, but that wasn't an option. Too bad it wasn't that simple.

Grims was watching him, his expression sad, weary. Where Gage had been pissed, he suddenly felt a pang of sympathy, even though Grims had brought it on himself. *Brought it on* all *of us*. His anger climbed back up.

Quinn walked up the chute, seemingly unaware of the tension. "Hey, you guys wanna grab a beer?"

Gage considered his empty house. He also considered compartmentalizing his anger—for now—for the sake of the team. His club was gonna need all it could get to survive whatever fallout was headed its way. Eyes on Grimson, he said, "Why not?"

"Grims?" Quinn said.

Grims gave Gage another long look. "Yeah, Hads. I'm in."

Forty-five minutes later, they were halfway through their second round when Grims's girlfriend, Nicole, walked into the bar, another woman on her heels.

Grims stood to kiss Nicky, who shot him a flinty look—*things rocky at home?*—before leaning in to kiss the other woman's cheek. "Hey, Kendra," he said quietly.

Nicole turned a brilliant smile on Gage. "Hi, Gage. You remember my sister, Kendra?"

He remembered Kendra all right, and despite wanting to run the hell away, he stood and shook her hand. "Good to see you again, Kendra."

The hot little blond gave him the same man-eater smile she'd given him the last time he'd seen her—the night she'd set her sights on T.J. Except T.J. had chosen a bottle of Jameson instead. Gage had wound up taking her to her front door, and she'd tried her damnedest to pull him inside. *No good deed goes unpunished.*

While Grims and his girlfriend put their heads together in private but obviously strained conversation, Kendra slid into the chair beside Gage. "I owe you an apology."

He sipped his beer. "Why's that?"

She looked at her nails intently, then at him. "Last time I saw you, I'd just gone through a breakup and was after some 'sexual healing,' like the old song says. I came on a little strong. I cringe whenever I think back."

He chuckled. "It's all good. And anyone who likes Marvin Gaye can't be all bad."

She smiled broadly. "Thank you. You were a gentleman that night too."

Soon they were talking, and Gage was able to ship his troubles to the back of his mind. When Grims ordered another round, Gage didn't protest. The crowd at their table grew bigger and noisier as more teammates ambled in.

Quinn gave him a shit-eating grin. "Nelson, I can't believe you're actually hanging out. I must have landed in an alternate universe."

Gage laughed. "Eh. Gotta keep you guys on your toes."

A couple of fans sidled up to their table and asked if they could take a few photos. So many Blizzard players and their SOs surrounded the table now that they had to crowd in. Girls ended up on guys' laps, which is how Kendra wound up on his. One hand on her waist to steady her, his other waved his beer bottle while he wore a cheesy grin for the phones capturing the scene.

Kendra slid back into her own seat just as his phone vibrated in his pocket. He pulled it out.

Lily: *Coming over tonight? Daisy will be going to bed soon.*

Full-throttle annoyance slammed him. They'd exchanged a few text messages since he'd left, and everything had been civil, though she'd made it clear she didn't want to carry on the "discussion" tonight. Would she ever be ready? "No," his cynical, dejected self said. In the meantime, her message was clear: *Come over and fuck me, stud man.* Yeah, playing sex stud had been a fun fantasy, but he hadn't expected it to become a job assignment.

Gage: *Hanging with some buddies tonight. Then it's early to bed.*

Lily: *I won't see you before you go?*

Gage: *You did see me.*

And truthfully, the only Everett he wanted to see in that moment was the five-year-old.

Lily: *Brutal, Professor.*

He huffed at his phone.

Kendra nudged his shoulder. "You're looking grumpy all of a sudden. Bad news?"

"No," he sighed. "Just trying to wrap up a few things."

Lily texted him again before he could come up with a sign-off. *Are we still on for our getaway?*

Gage: *Why wouldn't we be?*

Lily: *Trying to "gage" where this is going.*

Fuck! She had balls of steel, this one. "Where this was going" was nowhere, and she was the one driving the bus.

Gage: *Thought we already had THAT discussion.* He needed to end this exchange before his temper had him saying things he might regret. *'Night, Lily. I'll see you when I get home.*

He stowed the phone. Kendra went eyebrows-up on him. It was none of her damn business, but he went ahead and told her anyway because, apparently, the beer was making it easier to give in to the urge to get it off his chest.

"A woman I've been seeing is in love with someone else."

She frowned. "I'm sorry. That's what happened to me too."

"Was yours a ghost?" he snorted.

"What do you mean?"

"She's in love with her dead husband, even though the guy's been gone four fucking years. How do I fight that? He doesn't even have to show up and prove himself, yet he's this perfect guy. I can't call him out, arm-wrestle him, or challenge him to a shoot-out. He's on a pedestal so high I can't even climb up and knock him off. How does a mortal man stand a fucking chance?"

Kendra placed a hand on his arm, staring at him with sympathy—or maybe it was a "this guy's out of his freaking mind" look. Not only was he acting like a jackass, but he was also a blithering idiot. Time to cut his losses and call it a night.

"Kendra, it's been nice seeing you again. Sorry I dumped on you."

She gave him a kind smile. "No worries. Good luck."

Quinn caught his eye. "You leaving?"

"Yep. I've got a cat waiting for me."

Chapter 31

Reveals and Reasons

Lily sat riveted to the TV. Daisy was wrapped up in her arms, her little body trembling with excitement. Beside them, Violet bounced up and down on the couch.

"Is it almost time for Gage, Momma?" Daisy whisper-shouted.

"Yes, honey. Just a few more min—oh! Here we go!"

Kathryn Tappen's smile was the first thing Lily noticed when the programming returned to the second intermission player interview. She was talking into the microphone, and as the camera panned back, Gage came fully into view.

"There he is!" the girls shrieked.

Lily shushed them, as much to quiet her inner groan as their squeals. The woman beside Gage was gorgeous. "Let's hear what he has to say, okay?"

Something spiky stabbed at Lily's gut. Gage was looking at Ms. Tappen, a smile on his face, while she asked him about a goal he'd scored in the second period. He'd been tearing it up on his road trip. Tonight he'd been involved in every goal and registered a whopping four points—a goal and three assists—and the Blizzard were leading the Rangers four-to-three.

With a swipe of his hand across his sweaty forehead, he laughed. "I'm not sure. I rang the first one off the iron, but then it came to Shanny, and he made an unbelievable pass. The puck seemed to be coming at me in slow-mo, and I had time to wind up and take the shot. Next thing I knew, it dropped behind the goalie into the net."

As he nodded beside her, she asked about his stellar play over the past week. He shrugged, the smile still on his face. "It's not just me. The guys are working hard, bringing it every night. Everybody's chipping in. We're peaking at the right time. Playoffs are a week away. This is the best time of year, and we're pumped, our fans are pumped. We can't wait."

She thanked him, and Lily could have sworn they exchanged a smile. And though the interview was over, she could still see his jersey in the background. Was he hanging around so he could finally ask her out?

Stop it, Lil. It didn't help that he'd communicated little and only in texts. Usually, he asked about Daisy. If Lily pushed for more, he'd tell her he had to go do something for "the club."

Her thoughts were interrupted by two little girls buzzing about having seen their favorite player on TV. A text chimed, and her heart leapt, only to sink when she saw it was a text from Ivy.

Ivy: *Did you see our boy?*

Lily: *Sure did.*

Ivy: *I think you're blowing it.*

Lily: *You're a bitch, Ivy.*

Ivy: *Whatever you need to believe.*

Lily puffed out a breath and opened her laptop, ready to lose herself in some work for Paige. She should post something about Gage's interview too. When she opened his Facebook page, she scanned the notifications and stopped on one where he'd been mentioned by someone who appeared to be an everyday fan.

Dave Grimson, Gage Nelson, Quinn Hadley and the boys at Rhein Haus. They were so gracious, autographing stuff and letting us take these pics. Love these guys! Go Blizzard!

Lily clicked on the photo. Her heart dropped to her knees when she saw Gage with a beer in one hand and a pretty blond in the other, a huge smile splitting his face. The blond looked comfortable sitting in his lap, her arms draped around his shoulders. Lily's eyes darted to the posted date, which only wrecked her further. It had been the night before he left, the night he said he was "hanging with some buddies." Obviously, he'd lied.

Bands tightened around her chest, and tears stung the backs of her eyes. Her mind spun out of control. *Who is she? You never said you were exclusive. Did we have to actually say it? It's why he's been so abrupt. But this isn't like him. There's an explanation. There has to be. He was mad at me. I pushed him away. A one-night stand. A revenge fuck. Ugh!*

The thought of him doing to that woman what he'd been doing to her nearly gutted her, and she doubled over, wrapping her arms around her middle. *This is why it's no good to let someone get close.*

Her phone chirped again.

Natalie: *The boys are home tomorrow. Woot woot! Wanna join us to greet them?*

Lily pulled in a few cleansing breaths and pressed her thumb against her eyelid to stave off gathering tears.

Lily: *Thx but can't. Singing tomorrow. Gage is catching the performance.*

Tomorrow. She'd see him tomorrow at the concert. The three of them would be leaving the next day for their getaway. It would be all right. They'd clear the air and work everything out. But as she thought back to the pretty blond, she felt a pang dig deep in her heart.

Lily drove up Gage's driveway, surprised to find another car parked there. He wasn't due home yet. Her heart skittered in her chest until she remembered he had a housekeeper and a chef. *Must be one of them.* She stepped out of the car and wriggled her short skirt into place—again. Stage garb was fine for the stage, but not so much for real life tasks like driving. Oh well. She'd be done soon enough. Besides, she knew how much Gage liked this particular outfit, and she wanted to wow him when he arrived.

"Ready to feed Hobbes?" she said over her shoulder to Daisy.

Daisy threw her hands in the air. "Hobbes!" The few times Daisy had been to Gage's, she'd been enamored with the cat. And the cat, it seemed, had been enamored with Daisy.

Lily unfastened Daisy's booster seat as her daughter patted her face, seeming to stare at her makeup job. It was a bit overdone, but it was going to be a long night under the lights. "Pretty Momma."

"Thank you, sweetheart." She gave Daisy a kiss. "Just a few minutes with Hobbes. We need to get you to Aunt Ivy's."

Lily's high heels clicked over the concrete as she and Daisy walked to the front door. She'd been on pins and needles all day, anticipating Gage's return. She'd missed him—so much—and couldn't wait to breathe him in. But she was nervous too. How would he react to her after ten days of silence punctuated with his scant messages? He'd confirmed he'd be at the show in a short text this morning, even adding he was looking forward to it. Her heart had lifted when she'd read his message.

Lily punched in the code, opened the front door, and stepped inside. Voices drifted down from upstairs. Maybe the housekeeper had a helper?

Beside her, Daisy bounced in place. "Wanna see Hobbes, Mom."

"Let's find out who's here first. Hello?" she called.

Daisy dashed off toward the mudroom.

"Hello?" came an answer.

Standing in the entryway, Lily swiveled her head between where Daisy had gone and the top of the stairs where two women appeared. Before she could open her mouth to introduce herself, the older of the two snapped, "Just what are *you*?"

Wow! Rude maid.

The woman ran swiftly down the stairs, facing Lily in short order. The other one had followed behind at a less frantic pace, and when Lily's eyes landed on her, she let out a gasp. Only to have her attention yanked back to the older one who was looking her up and down, hands on her hips and disgust etched in her features.

"You're not the maid," the woman spat. "Are you a hooker?"

"Excuse me?" Offense and shock shot through Lily's tone. She glanced around, relieved Daisy wasn't in sight.

The woman inched her chin in the air.

"I'm ... the cat ..." Lily spluttered, frustrated by her helpless, mute self. *I'm the cat? Seriously, Lil?* She shook her head. "Here for the cat."

The woman's eyes narrowed. "What cat? There's no cat." She snapped her fingers under Lily's nose. "Unless it's the one that's got your tongue. Better tell me who you are before I call the cops."

Jessica, who looked every bit as beautiful as her picture, moved from behind the she-devil and rested an elegant hand on the woman's shoulder. To Lily, she said, "I'm Jessica Phelan, an old friend of Gage's, and this is Nola Nelson, his mother."

Lily's stupor must have been written all over her face as her eyes bounced between the two, her thoughts zooming between *What the hell are you doing here* to *Why didn't Gage warn me?* "I'm," she squeaked before clearing her throat, "Lily Everett. I'm here to feed Gage's cat."

"I didn't know hookers fed cats." Nasty Nola smirked.

"I'm *not* a hooker! I'm a performer."

"Oh! A stripper, then! Same difference."

Jessica stepped between them. With her four-inch heels, Lily was just about even with her. And as much as she wanted to hate her, she was grateful for the woman's calming presence in that moment. It allowed coherent thoughts to form in her head and connect to her mouth. Daisy's wail brought the exchange to a halt just as Hobbes tore from out of nowhere toward Lily, stopped, took in the strangers, and streaked the other way.

Surprise flitted over the woman's face as she looked at Daisy and back to Lily. Lily picked her daughter up, balancing her on her hip, soothing her.

"That was Hobbes. She's Gage's cat. I'm Lily Everett, and this is my daughter, Daisy. I'm a singer on my way to perform in a concert, which is why I'm dressed this way. Gage asked me to take care of Hobbes while he was away. I haven't checked on her in a few days, and he's coming home today, so I thought I'd get the cat squared away for him. Does he know you're here?"

Nola stepped beside Jessica. "Why else would we be here?"

"Doesn't answer my question."

Jessica smiled sweetly. "He has a few days off before his playoff season starts, and he usually comes home for a visit, but he said he couldn't make it this time. Apparently, something," Jessica's eyes swept Lily and Daisy, "came up. We thought we'd, um, bring California to him."

Scratch being grateful for Jessica's presence. Lily wanted to blurt out that she and Daisy were the "something," but she stifled the inclination, more muddled by the minute. "Well, then, I guess I'll feed the cat and be on my way."

"Don't bother," Nola huffed. "Now that we know there's a cat, we'll feed him."

"Her." Lily stole a glance at Hobbes before heading for the door. *Good luck, girl.*

"How do you know my son?" Nola's voice was laced with suspicion.

Lily pivoted on her high heels. "We met at a wedding last summer and became friends. He hired me to take care of his social media."

"Social something, at any rate," Nola muttered. "I can see why he's never mentioned you."

Lily felt the burn creeping up her cheeks. "Look, you don't know anything about me, yet you've been nothing but rude since I walked in. As for why your son's never mentioned me, you'll have to ask him. Now if you'll excuse us, we have other places to be."

Nola unfolded her arms long enough to give Lily a shooing motion. "Don't want you to be late."

Lily's shaking hands made it hard to buckle Daisy in.

"Why was that lady mad at us, Mom?" Daisy sniffed.

"Oh, baby, she wasn't mad at *you*. She was just surprised to see me, and it upset her. That's all. You didn't do anything wrong."

On the verge of hyperventilating, Lily gulped air as she situated herself behind the wheel. *Don't cry, don't cry, don't cry.*

She pushed out a breath and drove, her mind rapid-firing through questions. How long had Gage known they were coming? Why hadn't he told her? The getaway had to be off, right? Would he go with Jessica and his rabid wolverine of a mother instead? Jessica was more beautiful than Lily had imagined. Would Gage want his old flame when he saw her again? The fact he hadn't mentioned her and Daisy to his mother stung like the lash of a whip. But he had to have some reasonable explanation. She'd find out when she talked to him after the show.

When Lily took the stage, she was still trembling and holding tears at bay. But then magic happened. The dregs of her day dissolved into the lights, the sea of people, and the sounds of laughter and music. Their joy enveloped her, lifting her up. And even that faded into the background, leaving a river of music that carried her along. It rushed through her, filled her, pushing everything else from her mind, and she let herself dissolve in its soothing current.

Every emotion that had been coursing through her came out in melodies. She nailed every note, her voice resonating with power from her core. She was strong, alive, her soul a bright beam.

It wasn't until the last song was over and deafening applause drowned out every other sound that she re-entered her body. The crowd pulsed with energy, and she pulled it in, radiating it back out again. This was different than the emotion that had overcome her last July when she'd been pulled toward Gage.

Gage.

Scanning a sea of shadowed faces through bright lights made it impossible to spot him, so she waited for him to find her as the band packed up.

He didn't come.

When she finally checked her phone, two texts from him flashed. *Running late*, followed hours later by *Sorry, can't make it. Sure you understand. Text me when you're done.*

Yeah, she understood all right.

Her soaring spirit suddenly folded over, crumpling in on itself like a dying star.

Chapter 32

Nice to Meet You, Rod Serling

A shit-show. No other way to describe what Gage had walked into. Stunned to find his mother and Jessica at his house, he'd been even more astonished to learn they'd met Lily and Daisy. *Now* he wished he'd told his mom about them, but he hadn't wanted to subject himself to the third degree. Besides, the cow was out of the barn now, or whatever the hell the expression was, and he was in damage-control mode.

According to his mom, the meeting had been brief but cordial, though she couldn't understand why "the woman dressed so suggestively in front of her daughter."

"Obviously things are a little different in Denver," she'd said. He ignored the jab, his mind instead distracted by how many starstruck "idiots" were ogling Lily. He needed to get to the venue pronto.

Being away from her had been tough, and ghosting her even tougher. But he'd thrown everything into playing for his team while trying to come to terms with his Grimson quandary. He'd been thoroughly occupied and exhausted. Through it all, he'd rediscovered his mojo. He was keeping it simple, focused on only hockey, and he was playing out of his mind back on the first line. And honestly, he'd been a little hesitant to reach out to Lily and possibly jinx his turnaround.

But, God, he missed her!

And right now all of him wanted to get to her and convince her to forgive him for going dark, but he didn't know how soon he'd get the chance because his mom wouldn't stop talking.

"Oh, and I also changed your front door combination. This way, the *wrong* people can't get into your home because you *never* know ..."

Yeah, Nola was right. He should have changed it before *she* showed up. It was the same combo he'd had when she'd been here with Sarah helping him set up his place. *Won't make that mistake again.*

"So," his mother beamed, "where are you taking us for dinner? Or we could stay in and cook for you, if that's better. Whatever you want, son."

What the actual fuck? The "whatever I want" is not what I'm dealing with at the moment.

Jessica hadn't said two words. Just smiled a lot. Yeah, he wasn't going to get backup from her. She was as much a part of this hostile takeover as Nola.

"I'm sorry, Mom, but you two are on your own tonight. I promised Lily I'd—"

"*What?* We fly all the way out here, *for you,* because we were worried, and you're just walking out for that ... that—"

"Mom, I had other plans. I wasn't expecting—"

"Well, that's *obvious,*" she huffed. "And here I thought we could all get your grandmother on the phone to make her feel better."

"Why? I just called this morning and—"

"Did you actually speak to her?" His mother's eyes narrowed.

"No." Grandma had had absolutely no idea who he was. Mistook him for a damn telemarketer. Even though Oscar had gently coaxed, Grandma would have none of it. That had sucked. Big-time.

"Well, she's not doing so hot."

"Then why are you *here*? Shouldn't you be *there*?"

"Oh, you mean like how *you're* here and not there?" his mom countered.

Behind Nola, Jessica was shaking her head and giving him a disapproving frown. "Gage," she said, her voice laced with a grating motherly tone, "maybe you could tell your, ah, singer friend you'll meet her later? Surely she'll understand. This has been a rough week for your mother, but she didn't want to bother you. I know you weren't expecting us, but now that we're here, it would be nice if we could all sit down for a quiet meal so Nola can fill you in."

There was something they weren't telling him. The clangor of a five-alarm fire was rising inside him.

"Please," Jessica added with saccharin sweetness.

"Yes, please, Gage." Were those tears in his mother's eyes?

Jesus Fucking Christ!

"All right," he sighed dejectedly. "Let me text Lily."

Dinner was a trip to the twilight zone. Both women chatted and laughed as though absolutely nothing was wrong. He was regaled with stories of Jessica's countless accomplishments as a financial analyst, volunteer, and blah, blah, blah. Gage smiled politely at first, but his composure began cracking. He had to find out about Grandma, and he still had a decision to make about Grims—something he'd put off long enough already.

After stealing into his office, Gage called Oscar, who had no idea what Nola was talking about. With Oscar's help, he established a FaceTime connection and invited the two women in so they could all see for themselves what was up with Grandma. His mother's eye-darting between him and the screen reminded him of a panicky rabbit, and he soon understood why. The little patience remaining in his reserves completely imploded. *Nothing* out of the ordinary was wrong with Grandma. She was still in and out of reality. Still doing outrageous, though benign, crap. And despite his graciousness, poor Oscar suffered Nola's disdain.

"It's not good for her to be squinting into a computer! We can see her when we get home," Nola groused.

“Mom, you’re not making any sense.” Gage kept his voice low. “Let’s just talk to her now while we’re together.”

“Together” became his mother and him because Jessica soon drifted out of the office. What should have been a pleasant virtual visit turned strained, and his mother also left the conversation. Gage was oddly relieved and closed the door to take advantage of the privacy.

“Oscar, I really appreciate your help, and I apologize for my mom.”

Wise eyes crinkled with a smile. “No need to apologize, son. At my age, pretty much everything rolls off me like water off a duck’s back.”

In her most lucid moment of the evening, Grandma interjected, “Gage, I love your mother, but she is a bossy thing. Don’t let her push you around. You’re a good boy, and you work hard to put everybody on your strong shoulders, but you need to take care of you too. You’re wise enough to make the right decisions. Go live your life *your* way. Find your own bongo player to follow and forget how the rest of the band is marching. They’re all out of tune anyway.”

He couldn’t help but bust out with a laugh—it was the best he’d felt since walking into his own house. “You mean march to the beat of my own drum, Grandma?”

“No, son.” Her eyes twinkled mischievously. “Unlike sometimes, I know what I’m saying right now. Bongo player. They’re much more fun than drummers.”

A chuckle rumbled in his chest, and he rolled his eyes. “I don’t want to know how you know this. Let me live in ignorant bliss.”

She kissed her fingers and placed them against the screen. Tears sprang in her eyes, causing a chain reaction in him. “I love you so much,” she said.

He met her hand with his own and blinked back tears. “I love you too, Grandma. So much.”

She pulled away with a nod. “And don’t you forget it. You’re not too big to put over my knee.”

“I’d like to see you try,” he laughed.

“Don’t test me, young man.” She shook a crooked finger at him, but the smile on her face told him all he needed to know. She loved him unconditionally.

The call ended, and Gage checked his phone expectantly, disappointed to find no messages from Lily. The performance had finished an hour ago. Where the hell was she? He texted her. Fifteen minutes later, he texted her again. Then he called. To his astonishment, she actually picked up. In the background, he heard the clinking and murmur of a restaurant.

"Where are you?" he blurted.

"Well, how nice of you to call, Professor. I'd almost forgotten what you sounded like." Her tone dripped with frost.

He barreled on, idiot that he was. "Seriously, Lily, I was worried. Where are you?"

"Funny how that worry thing works when you haven't heard from someone."

"I've been busy on the ice." He fought to keep sheepishness from his voice.

"And off, if Facebook and your Kathryn Tappen interview are any indication."

What the actual fuck? Something told him he was blindly stepping into it and needed to backpedal quick. Before he could form an answer, she continued. "I'm grabbing a bite with Derek and some friends. We had an awesome performance. Brought the house down. Too bad you missed it. Anyway, we're celebrating."

He put the sarcasm—and pretty much everything else spinning in his head—aside. "Where's Daisy?"

"You're kidding, right?"

"No, I'm not."

"Look, I'm not having this discussion with you right now. I'm enjoying myself, and I don't want to ruin it," she hissed. "You've managed to stay out of our lives nicely these past ten days, so just keep on. Daisy's fine. She's at Ivy's tonight." She hung up.

A veil of red descended. He dragged cleansing breaths into his lungs. *Damn it!*

She's out of joint because of an interview? And what the hell's with Facebook?

Phone in hand, he headed for the stairs. "Mom," he called, "I'm tired. I'm going to bed. You guys have everything you need, right?" *Shit. I still gotta figure out what we're doing about going to Dillon.*

His mother's surprised voice called back, "We're set. Anything we can do for you?"

"I've got everything I need, thanks." Except he didn't.

"Jessica's staying in the room next to yours."

Of course she is.

After closing his bedroom door, he sprawled on the bed and texted Ivy. Her curt answer told him Daisy was fine. When he asked about Lily, Ivy's response startled him. *She was fine when I saw her, especially considering she'd just been destroyed by your freight train of a mother.*

What?

He texted Ivy again, but she told him to talk to Lily. When he pulled up Facebook and scrolled through the posts, he got an eyeful of what Lily must've been talking about. There he was, moronic grin and all, with Kendra looking cozy on his lap. Some idiot had the nerve to leave a comment about a lap dance. Shit, this looked bad.

As far as Lily being pissed about an interview, he had no fucking clue—he'd given lots of interviews on the trip, including a very brief, very chaotic one to Kathryn Tappen where the mic kept bleeping out. They'd delayed him, made him hang around. It'd been nothing but a pain in his ass.

The urge to see Lily and explain the post seized him. He texted her about coming over and got an immediate answer telling him she was tired and didn't want company.

A soft knock on his door had him absently inviting whomever in. Add one more mistake onto the ever growing pile. Jessica slipped in, closing the door behind her. She looked stunning in sheer silk and lace.

He swallowed hard, ransacking his brain for the right way to word his question. He went with the polite version of "What do you want?" which came out, "What can I do for you?"

"So many things," she purred as she floated toward him.

Should've stuck with blunt.

"Jessica, you've got the wrong idea here."

She gave him a sly smile and sat on the edge of the mattress. "Do I? I saw you looking me over just now."

Yeah, well, I'm a guy.

He jumped up. "Look, I need to be somewhere."

She pouted. "You just said you were going to bed."

"I forgot I need to talk to someone about something." Lame, but he didn't care. His brain was ordering him to escape, and he was inclined to obey.

He practically ran to the garage, passing a hiding Hobbes in the mudroom. "Sorry, sweetheart. You're on your own."

In the car, he dialed Sarah. "Pick up, pick up, pick up!" Relief flooded him when she did.

"Waffle-butt! How's it hangin'?"

"Sar, I need your help. Can you come stay for a few days?"

"When?"

"Now."

Chapter 33

And This Is Why

Twenty minutes later, Gage was a few houses from Lily's when he spotted the familiar Ford pickup in her driveway. He drove past, U-turned, and parked a block away on the other side of the street. Jealousy and fury coiled inside him, ready to be unleashed, as he walked toward her place. It was nearly midnight, for God's sake. What the hell was fucking Derek doing there? He decided not to ponder the question.

When he had a line of sight to Lily's front door, Gage paused in the shelter of a tree. Yeah, he was becoming *that* guy—the stalker. He'd never done a thing like this in his whole damn life, but this was how crazy Lily made him.

Her front door opened, Derek blocking the doorway. Her blond curls were visible just above his shoulder. Derek leaned down, gave her a quick hug, and left. Gage walked across the street at a pace just short of a run. Knocked. Lily opened the door, her eyes widening when they landed on him. "What are you doing here?" She stuck her head out and looked up and down the street.

"He's gone. You shouldn't open your door when you don't know who's on the other side," he offered, his voice calmer than he would've expected.

A scowl greeted him in return. "Are you stalking me now?"

Yes. "No. I need to talk to you about going to Dillon, and I didn't want to do it over the phone."

"At midnight?"

"It turned out to be the only time we were both free." He bit back the snark about *Derek* being here at midnight. It wouldn't help him get inside.

She seemed to consider for a moment, then opened the door and invited him in. He slowed his breathing, slowed the whirring blender of emotions inside him, like downshifting his mind when a puck came blistering at him across the ice. *Don't overthink.*

His eyes locked on Lily. Evidence of her stage getup was completely gone, and she was casual in bare feet, leggings, and a baggy sweater that revealed a black strap over pearly skin. He loved this look on her. He fought the longing to pull her against him. Judging by her body language, she wouldn't have allowed it anyway.

Folding her arms across her chest, she leaned against the couch, where she was out of reach. "So. What about Dillon? I assume it's off since you have *guests*." She practically hissed the last word.

He smoothed his beard. "I was thinking I could rent a bigger place, and we could all go. Sarah's coming too."

Lily looked at him like he was out of his mind. She wouldn't have been wrong. Recognition seemed to dawn in her bright blues. "You're serious."

"It's the only way I can think of to make this all work."

"I have a much better idea. You go. Daisy and I will stay here," she huffed.

"Look, I'm sorry Mom and Jess hijacked our trip. I had *no* clue they were coming. I asked Sarah just now because I wanted ... balance."

"Balance for who?"

"Me? You? But let's back up a sec. I'd like to hear your version of meeting my mom."

Her eyes narrowed. "Why?"

"Because she told me *her* version, and I suspect she left out a few details."

Lily rolled her eyes. "My version isn't pretty." She filled him in, and he nearly choked. Was Lily exaggerating? Had to be.

"My mom wouldn't do that," he declared before he could stop himself.

Lily shot him daggers.

"Did Daisy hear?" he asked.

"No, but she got a full dose of your mom's scintillating personality. And I've got to say, it was a slap in the face to find out you've never told her about us. I felt like your dirty little secret. Of course, seeing the way you jump in and defend her, it all makes perfect sense."

The hair on his neck lifted. A normal reaction when someone, no matter the source, disparaged his mom or anyone in his family.

"Oh, for Christ's—" He blew out an exasperated breath. "I'm not jumping in to defend her. I didn't tell her because I knew it would stress her out, and I didn't want to add on to the pile. Plus, she would've hounded the shit out of me."

Lily gave him an eye-roll. "Right. Sure. Got it."

Emotions began unraveling inside him, and his control slipped. His mind veered to the dick side. "Mom said you were dressed in a sexy outfit and had on a lot of makeup. You can understand where she might've reached the wrong conclusion."

Though bright pink was working its way up Lily's neck, he kept going. "What's up with dressing like that anyway? And why did you go out with Derek and *friends* in that getup?"

Her mouth swung open. "Are you for real right now? You don't even ask if I *was* dressed that way for dinner. You just assume. And since when do you have *any* right to throw your caveman weight around? You act as if you have some ownership claim, so let me remind you: you *don't*. And let's not forget, if you'd been there tonight like you said you would, if you hadn't chosen to stay home with your old girlfriend—oh, who also knew nothing about Daisy and me—I wouldn't have gone out with Derek and *friends*."

"I wasn't *with* my old girlfriend," he gritted out.

"As long as we're on the subject of who's doing what with whom," she continued, "at least *I* didn't lie. I didn't tell you I couldn't see you because I was hanging with buddies while what I was *really* doing was having some chick give me a lap dance." The pink splotches on Lily's neck spread upward, blazing brighter.

He laced his hands on top of his head. "Fuuuuuck! It's not how it looks. I wasn't lying." He careened onward and told her about Kendra and how she wound up on his lap. "I *was* hanging with buddies, and I *did* go home early. Alone."

A "who cares" shrug was her answer.

"You're sending mixed signals, Lily. On one hand, you act like a jealous girlfriend. On the other hand, you're telling me I have no right. Which is it?"

She flapped a "whatever" hand at him. "Doesn't matter."

He felt as if he rode on a runaway roller coaster ride. "What you're really saying is you refuse to accept my explanation. If you don't believe me, just ask anyone who was there. Hell, ask Wyatt. *He* ended up with Kendra that night." He pulled in a breath. "But I want to circle back to something you said. How do *you* define us?"

It took her a beat to answer. "We're friends."

"And?"

"And what?"

Fuck no! "That's it? Just friends?" His rising anger heated his cheeks, colliding with hurt and disappointment. "*That's* what you think this is? Friends? With benefits? How does Daisy fit in?"

"She doesn't. You're her coach. *Were* her coach. Beyond that, you're a nice guy she likes."

"Loves," he snapped.

"And that's why whatever's between us won't go further."

What. The. Actual. Hell? He was getting whiplash, growing more confused by the minute. "What does *that* mean?"

Her blue eyes flared. "It means I can't get close to anyone and risk hurting her. Look at the mistake I've already made by spending time with you. If I get in deep and get my heart broken, that's one thing. I won't have her getting attached and getting hers broken too."

Another punch to the gut. "Well, fuck. That's just great. Now I'm a mistake, and you're *assuming* I'm going to break not only *your* heart but hers too. Based on what exactly?"

Her answer was to bite her thumbnail.

He could feel his connection to her slipping away, and it made his chest ache. “Lily, I want you. I want Daisy. Can’t you see that?”

Still no answer.

His head reeled. “So what’s your plan? You’re gonna fuck random men for the next fifteen years and *maybe* start a real relationship after she’s left home?”

“I’m not going to *fuck random men.*” She leaned toward him, on the attack, her expression matching her tone—dark and tight. “Nor am I going to expose my daughter to people like *your* mother, if I can help it. I don’t need to bring more drama into Daisy’s life. I *will* do whatever I have to, to protect my daughter.”

“What if someone else is interested in protecting her too? You’re just going to go it alone?”

“She has Derek.”

Slap! “Right. How stupid of me to forget my place. I’m just the guy you fuck when the mood strikes. Only Everett men are worthy of more.”

Her scowl deepened. “Derek is part of Jack, and he always will be, whether you like it or not.”

“Because you’ll never let Jack go.”

“What’s that supposed to mean?”

He scanned the room a moment, not seeing any details, while he marshaled his thoughts and kept himself in check. His gaze returned to hers. She stood with her arms locked over her chest like an armored breastplate.

“It means, Lily, you’re not fooling anyone except yourself. Up here,” he tapped his temple, “you’re still married, even though it’s to a ghost. It also means I’m tired of being nothing more to you than your stable stud. You’ve confused a fantasy with real life. I’m not your 2:00 a.m. booty call. I’m not your fuckboy. There are plenty of guys out there who’ll jump at the chance, but I won’t be confused with them anymore.”

Her chin lifted in defiance. “That’s not fair.”

“No? Last summer, you used me. Was *that* fair?”

“You didn’t complain.”

“At the time, I didn’t. But I didn’t expect to wake up and find myself alone, and I didn’t expect to spend the next six months wondering where the hell you’d gone. That’s jacked up, Lily.”

None of this makes sense anymore.

He let out a mirthless laugh. "Shit, you're *still* using me, and I'm the dumbass letting it happen. I fooled myself into believing that maybe, just maybe, you'd fallen for me as hard as I fell for you. That what we had was more than an extended one-night stand." He paused to exhale. "Go pick on someone else. Leave me the hell out of it." The instant the statement left his mouth, he knew he didn't mean it—which hurt even more.

Shaking his head, he placed his hands on his hips. Anger and hurt and longing whirlpooled inside him like a sinking ship, but he kept his voice calm. "For months now, I've been competing with a ghost. But I never stood a chance and was too blind to see it." He stabbed a finger at her hallway. "You live in a shrine, Lily. Every day you come home and worship a man who's dead. When are you going to move on and live?"

Though her eyes pooled and her lips quivered, her face was locked in a fierce glare. He spun and walked out the door, wrenching it closed behind him without a backward glance.

And this, ladies and gentlemen, is why Gage Nelson doesn't date.

Lily Everett had been after one thing from him, and he'd been idiotic enough to give it to her—along with his heart—without demanding more in return.

Anger and hurt razored into him as he drove back home. When he dropped into bed, he was surprised his heart was still beating. Because damn! It was in shreds.

Chapter 34

Big Sister Knows Best

Lily stomped into the kitchen.

Who the hell does he think he is?

Yanked out the cleaning supplies.

Jerk!

Attacked the sink.

Asshole!

She threw the sponge down and looked around her spotless kitchen. She'd get no satisfaction from cleaning because it already sparkled. *Damn it!*

Next she picked up her phone and texted Ivy. *You awake?*

Ivy: *No. Go away.*

Lily: *I need to talk.*

Lily's phone lit up. "You'd better just have lost a limb." Ivy yawned.

"You weren't sleeping," Lily scoffed.

"I *could* have been if I hadn't downed an espresso an hour ago. What's going on?"

"Argh! Gage! If I kill him, will you visit me in prison?"

"No. I don't hang with convicts. What did that awful, horrible man do?"

Lily dismissed the sarcasm. "He had the balls to say I'm still in love with Jack. Then he got all bent out of shape, accusing me of using him for sex."

Silence on the other end confounded her. "Ivy? Are you listening?"

"I'm listening. I'm a little surprised he's bent out of shape over being your fuck puppy. Most guys—"

"He's not *most guys*."

"Which is why he gets under your skin."

"He does *not* get under my skin."

"Right, Lil. Whatever you say." Ivy yawned again.

The thought of throttling Ivy crossed Lily's mind. "Well, to add insult to injury, he stuck up for his mom. He scoffed when I told him what she said! Dismissed it, like I was lying!"

"Well, she's his mom, so I get him sticking up for her. He was probably having a hard time processing." Ivy's tone was way too casual, and it grated on Lily's exposed nerves.

"What about me processing what his mother said? That hurt, Ivy," Lily gritted out. "Plus, he never told her about us."

"Probably because she'd give him a ration of shit. Forget her, Sis. She's a raving bitch with her own mysterious agenda. 'Nuff said."

Lily let out an indignant huff.

Ivy sighed. "Okay. So he stuck up for his mom. Bad on him. But honestly, the other stuff? I don't disagree."

Lily's free hand yanked her hair in frustration. "Whose side are you on?"

"I'm on your side. Yours and Daisy's."

Lily's mama-bear antenna shot up. "Why are you bringing Daisy into this?"

Ivy let out a sisterly you-don't-know-anything sigh. "Because Daisy *is* in this. Do you think her seeing you lonely, unhappy, and bitter is setting a good example? The only time I've really seen you come alive since Jack died is when you're with Gage."

"I'm *not* bitter."

"Not yet. Look, you're not gonna like this, but I'll say it anyway. You remind me of one of those wives—I forget which culture it is—

but when the husband died, they'd burn his body and she'd throw herself on the pyre with him. You're *that* wife. Only you're still walking around, going through the motions. Your heart's beating, but it's empty."

Lily's face was catching fire. "You're ... That's ... Ugh! You're wrong."

Ivy's voice rose a decibel level. "If I'm so wrong, then why the hell are you having a meltdown? Huh? Listen to yourself. First you don't want to betray Jack. That's noble, Lil. Good for you. But Jack's *dead*! And somehow you've become the torch-bearer for a man who's so perfect, he resembles the *real* Jack less every day. If the situation were reversed, would you have gone to your grave expecting Jack to fill his lonely nights reliving your time together? God, I hope not because that's just fucking selfish, which is basically what you're saying about him. Add to that you pretending *not* to be in love with Gage, who is a living, breathing man who's actually pretty damn close to perfect. Your head must hurt with all the circles you're running around yourself."

Lily wanted to tell Ivy to shut up, so badly, but she wasn't confident she could muster a strong counterargument. Gage's maddening words blared in her brain. *"Are you just going to fuck random guys for the next fifteen years?"*

"Let's look at your other reasons, shall we?" Ivy went on, damn her. "You don't want to get hurt—no one does. You don't want Daisy to get hurt—yay! You're a good mom. But you're already hurting, Lil. And Daisy will too. By the way, you're doing a bang-up job teaching your daughter about commitment when you run from a good guy who loves you both. What about showing her a loving relationship between two people who adore and respect each other? Actions, Lil. What do they speak louder than?"

"Gah! Stop patronizing me!"

"Then grow the hell up!"

The rebuke stung worse than a swarm of fire ants, and Lily couldn't hold back the flow of tears. She wrapped her arms around herself. A fissure began opening in her heart, radiating tiny cracks. In that moment, she imagined her arms to be Gage's, and an undeniable ache bloomed and settled heavily in her soul.

"So let me see if I have this straight." Sarah perched her fists on her hips and eyed Gage with a frown as he dropped her bag in the spare guest room. At five foot five—with their father's brown hair and hazel eyes—she wasn't big, but she packed a wallop. Add the whole "Big Sister" mystique, and she could be intimidating as hell, but Gage would never tell her that.

Especially with the chewing-out he knew was coming. He could see it looming on his horizon like dark funnel clouds.

Sarah's eyes drilled into him. "Mom tells your girlfriend, to her face, that she looks like a hooker, and *you* tell your girlfriend she's blowing it out of proportion? In other words, you sided with Mom over your girlfriend. And then you *told* your girlfriend this?"

He'd only filled Sarah in briefly during the few minutes they'd had alone since they'd all piled out of the car. Mom and Jessica had insisted on coming with him to the airport to pick her up.

He let out an exasperated sigh. "First of all, her name is Lily. Secondly, she's not my girlfriend. At least that's what she says."

"Ha! Then she's not. And who can blame her? Jesus, Gage, how can you be so smart and so clueless?"

"Who says I'm smart? I'm seriously wondering why the hell I flew you out here."

She arched an eyebrow at him. "Because you needed backup. I'm happy to fly home and let you fend for yourself, Baby Bro."

"Nah. I don't feel like driving back to the airport." Despite her scolding, he was relieved to have her here.

"Any communication with Lily since your blowup?"

"Nope. I haven't tried to contact her, and she's dead silent." Truth be told, he was still licking his wounds and wasn't sure when he'd be ready to stop. He rubbed the back of his neck. "So you're suggesting I might have screwed up?"

During his argument with Lily, it hadn't occurred to him how defending his mom might have come across. He'd just said what was on his mind. That wasn't so bad, was it? Of course, now that he'd had a chance to sleep on it—or not, as the case was—he wasn't sure of everything he'd said or how he'd said it, and he was racking his brain trying to recall anything but Lily's sharp barbs that had cut him to ribbons.

Sarah pulled a colorful, girlie-looking version of a dopp kit out of her bag and tossed it on the bed.

"*Might* have?" Her guffaw wasn't encouraging.

Deflect, deflect. The ache was still too raw to deal with. "Let's leave it for now. There's a team dinner day after tomorrow. Wanna go with?"

"What about Jess?"

Gage's stomach cinched. No way was Jess going to stay behind. He shrugged off his annoyance. "She's invited, if she wants to come."

"Oh, I'm sure she will." Sarah pasted on a fake smile. "Gee, these next few days are gonna be so much fun. What do you have planned next? Bamboo shoots under our eyelids?"

"Bamboo shoots are food. You mean bamboo slivers."

"Whatever." She flapped her hand.

"I have no frickin' clue. You guys shop and leave me alone?" Gage had canceled the Dillon trip. Seeing the ice castles didn't hold the same appeal without Lily and Daisy.

Jessica stuck her head in. "Hey, you two. There's a fresh pot of coffee. Ready to come downstairs?"

Gage sent Sarah a look that conveyed how much he didn't want to. She acknowledged it with a subtle head wag. "Sure, Jess. Just give us a few more minutes, huh?"

When she'd left, Sarah turned to Gage. "So what are you gonna do?"

"Try to survive the next few days, then throw myself into the playoffs."

While trying to figure out how to swallow my decision about Dave Grimson without choking to death.

Late last night, in the midst of all the other crap, he'd opted not to throw his captain under the bus—because it meant the least amount of fallout for everyone connected to Dave Grimson. What they didn't know and all that, or so Gage told himself. But he couldn't escape the truth: saving his captain's ass meant saving his own ass. And it wasn't sitting well. Grimson had broken the rules, and Gage was helping him do it.

Lord Stanley beckoned, and he'd chosen not to lose sight of the puck above black, white, and following his moral compass. That decision left a hole in his chest and an ache in his gut.

The morning of the team dinner, Gage leaned back against the couch, hands laced behind his head, enjoying the first quiet he'd had in days. Sarah and Jess were out, and his mom was in her room, packing for her trip home tomorrow. Hobbes sat beside him, scrutinizing him with that smug humans-are-so-stupid look.

Not disagreeing with you, fuzzball.

Since the breakup with Lily, he'd been practicing his ass off, blowing off pent-up steam. But it didn't keep him from missing her and Daisy, like a beaver missed its front teeth. *If Lily weren't so damn stubborn ...*

He could feel anger heating up his neck again, so he picked up his guitar and began strumming, the same questions looping through his head. Could he go back to being Lily's fuckboy—assuming she'd let him—and be content? Or be her fuckboy while covertly chipping away at her walls? *Didn't work the first time.*

The circle of questions continually led back to the same answers. No, he didn't want to be friends with benefits. Either Lily was his or she wasn't. Black or white. As for whether she'd decided to let him in, her deafening silence was his answer.

A new doubt wormed its way into his consciousness. Had expecting her to give Jack up been right? He mentally added it to the list of other unanswered questions labeled right and wrong. Questions he didn't want to wrestle with right now.

His phone chirped, and he picked it up. As soon as he realized it was Lily, his blood began percolating.

Lily: *Just wanted to wish you luck in the playoffs.*

Gage: *Thanks. How have you and Daisy been?*

Lily: *Good. She says hi BTW.*

Gage: *Tell her hello for me. I miss her.*

Minutes ticked by. Hobbes blinked her eyes slowly, as if to say, "Why not just call her?"

"Sometimes you're a smart cat." He swiped Lily's number, his heart lurching into machine-gun mode, and his stomach twisted itself into tight coils.

"Hey." Her voice sounded weary.

"Hey, uh ... I thought it'd be easier to call."

"Okay."

After several squirm-worthy beats, he said, "So you guys are okay?"

"We're good."

"That's good." An incredibly long pause had bands constricting his chest. Maybe calling hadn't been such a good idea. "I'm fine too, in case you were wondering."

Silence. *Apparently, she isn't. Why the hell did I call?*

"I was on my way out the door. Was there a reason you called?" Her tone was flinty.

He steeled himself. "What's the status of the social media stuff?"

"You have a great following now. You can take some time off, and it'll run itself for a while. I'll send you my final invoice."

His pounding heart was sinking faster than a waterlogged gear bag. He hardened it. His anger thick, tar-like, was heating low in his belly. "I think we have more to say to each other."

"I think we said it all."

"No, we didn't. At least I didn't."

"What is it you needed to say, Gage?" she sighed. "And can you make it short? I really do need to go."

His slow boil bubbled over, releasing everything he'd been bottling up. "Our falling out wasn't about my mother, and it wasn't about the Facebook picture. If it had been about my mother, you'd have come to me. As for the picture, I *hope* you would've given me the benefit of the doubt before you jumped off the conclusions bridge. I think you use Daisy and Jack like shields to protect you from getting too invested."

"I—"

"I'm not done. It's obvious Daisy comes first. I get it. I was brought up by a single mom, and I know the struggles you go through raising Daisy. But you use her as an excuse, just like my mom did.

And now Mom's an unhappy busybody who can't stop running her kids' lives because that's all she's left for herself. You say you don't want Daisy getting close, but *you're* the one holding her back, just like you're holding yourself back. You can't have it both ways, Lily, and someday Daisy will resent you for it.

"As for Jack, I have no doubt he was a good man. I wish I could've known him. And your loyalty is unshakable—it's one of the things I love about you. But it's time you give yourself permission to join the land of the living instead of hanging out in virtual graveyards where you don't belong. From what I know about Jack, he'd want a different life for you. I've been trying to put myself in his shoes, and I'd want someone taking care of those I love if I couldn't take care of them myself. And I would never have asked you to forget him, Lily, but I could never play second fiddle."

He rubbed his forehead. Her sniffles told him she was still on the other end. Suddenly exhausted, a long, low exhale escaped his lungs. "That, Lily, is what I had to say to you."

"Okay. You got it off your chest," she said so quietly he barely heard her. "Good-bye."

"Yeah." He refrained from wishing her a wonderful life.

After disconnecting, he hung his head, elbows on his knees, his heart crumbling.

His mother cleared her throat.

He jerked his head up. "How long have been standing there?"

"Long enough." She wiped her cheek. "You really think I try to run you and your sister's lives?"

Ah, shit. This just gets better and better.

He stood, walked over to her, and placed his hands on her shoulders. "Mom, you worked your ass off, and you raised two good people. You should be proud."

She chuckled through her tears. "Which means 'yes, Mom, you try to run our lives.' But Gage, I can't sit quietly by while someone like that woman ... It's clear she's all wrong for you."

In that moment, it dawned on him that nothing was clear. Straightforward was a direction on a map, and black and white were colors. For all his talk about protecting Lily, he hadn't defended her against his mom, no matter how much he'd convinced himself he'd done the right thing. When had he gotten so confused about what the right thing was?

He squared his shoulders and dug deep, clearing his mind. "What's wrong is how you treated Lily, whether she meant anything to me or not. You've always drummed common courtesy into Sarah and me. You never would've tolerated the kind of behavior you showed Lily, nor should you have." He tilted his head and peered at her. Her tears were spilling freely now. "Mom, I'm a grown man who can think for himself. I *like* being there for others, and I learned that from you. So trust me to make my own decisions. I'm living proof your sacrifice paid off. But I'm not four years old anymore, and I'll live my life my way. That means I pick my own friends. And if the day comes, my own wife."

"But I don't want to lose you," she whimpered.

"You're not going to lose me, Mom. I'll still take care of you and Grandma. That won't change. I'll try to never disappoint either of you, but you're gonna have to let go and accept my choices, whether you agree with them or not."

She looked up at him and nodded. "I'm sorry."

He pulled her into a hug. "Yeah, I know."

His mind leapt back to Lily, and he suddenly felt sorry too.

Half the team was at the restaurant when they arrived. Noticeably absent was Grims, and while Gage was puzzled, he was also relieved. Not seeing Grims might help him put aside, at least for a little while, the fact he had chosen the coward's way out.

He grabbed three seats by Quinn and sat between Sarah and Jessica.

Jesus, he didn't want to be here.

Sarah and Quinn immediately struck up a conversation, and he sent Quinn a few warning daggers. *Not on my watch, fucker.* Quinn's eyes widened before he gave him a subtle nod.

On Gage's other side, Hunter's new girl had Jessica's attention. Gage took the time to study Jess's profile. She really was a knockout.

Why couldn't he just lose himself with her? It should have been easy enough. If he let her, she'd wrap her whole life around him, place him at the center of her universe. And stick to him like aphids on a rosebush.

A tap to his shoulder surprised him. Even more surprising was realizing who'd delivered the tap.

"Nelson? I'd like to talk to you in private," Coach LeBrun said.

"Sure, Coach." Gage stood and followed him, his mind racing through what Coach wanted.

He found out in a small, empty dining room tucked out of the way when Coach turned on him, hands fisted on his hips. "You knew." His voice was low and tight, his brow knotted.

"Knew—"

"You knew about Grimson doping, but you said nothing. Did it occur to you what would happen if he'd been picked for testing?"

Oh shit. Gage blew out a long breath. "Yeah. It did. Just like it occurred to me what would happen if I told management. I had no way to prove it. All I had was rumor and speculation. It didn't seem like enough to warrant throwing the entire club into chaos. Right or wrong, I made a judgment call. I figured my teammates needed their captain more than they needed me mouthing off with my suspicions."

"Well, the team's not going to have its captain."

Gage's eyebrows shot to his hairline.

"Dave Grimson has been placed on the IR, and Bobby no longer works for this organization." Coach's voice was part-anger, part-disappointment, and all distaste. "Grimson will sit out the playoffs. I'm assigning a third *A* to Hunter McMurphy. I know you and McMurphy don't like each other, but that's tough shit because you two, along with Shanstrom, will lead this team *together*, and you'll rally your club around their 'injured' captain."

How had Coach found out anyway? Gage considered asking, but Coach's fiery expression shredded that idea all to hell. Gage gave him a head bob instead.

"I'm sure I don't need to ask you to keep your mouth shut," Coach continued.

Shame, dosed with self-recrimination, rose up Gage's neck and flamed his cheeks. He'd made a personal decision he wasn't proud of and had never planned to share—let alone have his coach discover. And now he was part of a dirty little secret he'd wanted no part of.

But faced with the horrible choice all over again? The sad truth was he'd come to the same conclusion.

Coach gave him a pointed look. "Have I made myself clear?"

Gage returned a curt nod. "Crystal."

"Good. Now let's get back to the dinner and act like we're having a hell of a great time."

Chapter 35

The Long Good-bye

Two weeks into the playoffs, Lily got a call from Natalie, who squealed, "Baby Miller arrived last night!"

"Oh my God! How is everyone? Was Beckett there?"

"Mom and baby are doing great. Beckett *just* made it, but he's heading back to Arizona shortly."

As Natalie ran through the details, Lily's spirits lifted from the dumpster where they'd been these past weeks. She'd had no contact with Gage since the day he gave her his dissertation on her life. Oh, she'd been as mad as a hornet, but her temper had since cooled, and a murmur had stirred inside her. What if he'd been right?

As for her fury over how he'd handled his mom, Lily had begun examining his actions through a different lens. After seeing his piece-of-work mom in action, she understood why he hadn't told Nola about her and Daisy. That he defended his mom still stung, but his behavior brought to light something Lily had previously overlooked. In spite of his frustrations with his mom, Gage didn't waver. He didn't turn on those he loved; he knocked himself out to take care of them. He showed steadfastness and loyalty. Traits she liked. Loved.

"You'd better not sit on your ass too long, Little Sis," Ivy had lectured. "Guys like him are rare. Sometimes you have to seize the opportunity while it's in front of you. Kinda like the three-for-one fleece top sale."

Lily had shaken her head. "What are you talking about?"

"You don't need them yet, you really don't want to spend the money, but you'll never see that kinda deal again. It's the same with Gage. He's gonna get snapped up by some shopper who's way smarter than you."

Now that the angry wind in Lily's sails had dropped to a light breeze, she had to allow Ivy might be right. What if someday—when Lily had *finally* "moved on"—Gage was gone? What if he never came back through her door?

Lily hadn't told Daisy the truth—*I pushed him away*—instead making excuses about him being too busy with playoffs to see them.

So they watched him on TV, like they were doing today with Ivy and Parker, who had just walked into Lily's house. Natalie's voice yanked her back to the present conversation. "Gage has been looking *great* in the playoffs, don't you think?"

"Yeah, he's the points leader in the whole Western Conference right now, not that I'm watching that closely." Ivy shot her a skeptical smirk. *Yeah, liar.*

Natalie must have agreed Lily was a liar because she snorted. "Glad to see you're *not* watching closely."

When Lily hung up, Daisy's big eyes fastened on her. "Miss Paige had her baby?"

"Yep. Baby Audrey."

Daisy clapped on the couch. She paused a moment, looking thoughtful. "Is Mr. Miller the baby's daddy?"

Lily stifled a laugh. "Yes, sweetheart. He's the daddy."

"I want Gage to be my daddy." A plea shone in her eyes.

Lily about choked on her spit. Her eyes locked with Ivy's over Daisy's head. Parker was in man mode, glued to the pre-game show on TV, oblivious to the shock wave that had just passed through Lily's living room.

Lily finally untangled her tongue. "Why?"

"Because then he'll be *my* very own dad."

"What about Uncle Derek?" Ivy suggested with a smirk meant only for Lily.

Daisy wrinkled her nose. "He's Violet's dad. Besides, Gage looks at Momma the same way Uncle Parker looks at you, Aunt Ivy."

Ivy winked at Lily. "Ah, from the mouths of babes."

As Lily watched Gage play that night, she drank him in. Power and agility rolled into one beautiful body in motion. A sliver of realization wormed its way into her consciousness: she *was* alive with Gage. One hundred percent present. More than she'd been in a long, long while.

Two weeks later, the Blizzard were battling Arizona in the Western Conference Final, which had Paige talking a lot of smack. Lily had had no idea the woman had it in her, and she was still laughing at a text exchange when she arrived at her grief counseling meeting.

Brett held the door for her. "Something funny?"

"Just trash-talking with the girls."

He blinked, looking confused. A moment later, he said, "Before the others get here, I wanted to let you know this will be my last session."

Her surprise must have shown all over her face because he rushed on. "It's nothing to do with you."

Uncensored, she blurted, "Oh! You found someone?"

He shook his head. "No, and I'm going stop looking for a while. You've always shared good advice, Lily, but something you said finally got through to me—about the process being different for everyone, and that there's no right or wrong way." He adjusted his glasses. "I married and lost my soul mate, and I realized I've been searching for a placeholder. Someone to sit across from me at the dinner table. To hold hands with. But if I'm going to find a second soul mate—and I truly believe we have more than one—I need to get my life unstuck and back on track. So that's what I'm going to do."

Lily couldn't help herself. She opened her arms wide and gave him a fierce hug. "I'm so proud of you, Brett."

"What's all this?" Eva said behind them as she walked in.

Lily wiped a tear from her cheek. "This is Brett's last session."

Eva's mouth swung open. "Really?" She reached out to hug him. "It's mine too."

"What?" Brett and Lily exclaimed.

Lily tried not to choke. "Is there something in the water?"

"No," Eva laughed. "I went out with my dentist." She flushed red. "And I really enjoyed myself. So I thought I'd fly without my safety net for a while," she squeezed Lily's arm, "and see how it goes."

For the rest of the session, Lily fought a smile. She was like a mama bird whose fledglings were leaving the nest, and she was damn proud.

Driving home later, her mind drifted along with sixties songs on the radio. She thought of her group. Getting to the next phase took courage. Did *she* lack that courage? While she was proud of *herself*—her independence, her resilience, the life she'd made for Daisy and herself—she realized how much she'd loved having Gage in their lives and *doing* for him too. He made it easy to feel that way, yet she'd thrown up barricades.

A blue-eyed soul tune she hadn't heard in a long while came on, and she cranked up the volume. "Unchained Melody" was a song she knew well. The irony that it had been featured in the movie *Ghost* wasn't lost on her.

As she belted it out, every word, every sad note, every strain of longing resonated within her. But it wasn't Jack—*her* ghost—she fixed on. It was Gage. And by the time she reached her house, tears were spilling freely. She let them come, let them release heartbreak and regret and yearning.

Inside, she flipped on the hallway light, and her eyes roamed over the pictures. Gage had called the walls a shrine. Were they? A new focus, through *his* lens, sharpened. Fragments of words and images came at her, locking together like lost pieces of one giant puzzle.

"He was right," she whispered.

But she hadn't just put up a shrine to Jack; she'd made the house a mausoleum.

A jolt of electricity traveled along her spine. On went the radio, in came empty boxes from the garage, and soon she sat in the hallway with a generous portion of wine. She raised her glass with a trembling hand. In a quavering voice, she said, "Time for me to move on, love."

The first picture she plucked from the wall was their wedding picture. *Tear the Band-Aid off.* She stared at it, ran her fingers over it, and let the memories play on her mind's movie screen. Finally, she let go and laid it to rest in a box. The process sped up after that, though she allowed herself to linger on every object, laughing or crying as she recalled her other life. Her *past* life.

The walls emptied and the boxes filled. Next came her closet, Daisy's bedroom, and every niche and nook that held a visual reminder. She spared only a few. An odd lightness took hold as she went, as if she could pull more fresh, sweet air into her lungs and float.

When she finished, the hallway was a mess, and she attacked it, scouring the walls and patching holes. She dug out a can of sky-blue paint and transformed the space while music played in the background. Inspired, she found a can of white and added dabs.

The sun was lighting her windows when she finally plunked down on the floor and admired her work. Above her, surrounding her, was a bright sky filled with pillowy clouds that seemed to roll along the surfaces. It was fresh and beautiful.

Muscles unwinding, she leaned back on her hands. The music seemed to grow louder, as if someone had cranked up the volume. "Have I Told You Lately?" filled the air, and where the song had always made her cry, now she could only smile.

Thank you, Jack.

Warmth and peace wrapped around her, fortifying her for the last good-bye.

She rose and padded to her dresser where she pulled out a small spruce-green jewelry box nestled in a drawer. She opened it and stared at the large, smooth band that was the mate to her own. Her hands were steady, as though someone else's guided them, and she unclasped the necklace, placed it and her ring beside Jack's, and closed the box. Running her fingers over the box's worn edges, she whispered, "I'll always love you."

Hours later, Daisy rushed through the front door, Derek and Violet on her heels. Her daughter's gaze caught on the hallway, and she ran into it, her eyes widening as she turned a circle and looked up, down. Lily held her breath.

Daisy's gray eyes went to hers, and she broke out in a gorgeous smile that lit her sweet little face. "Momma, the sky is beautiful! Did you make this?"

Lily didn't realize she had any tears left in her well until fresh ones sprang to her eyes. "I did," she nodded. "Do you like it, baby?"

Daisy gasped. "Oh yes! Violet! Come see!"

Violet joined Daisy, and the girls chattered excitedly as they looked and touched.

Holding her breath once more, Lily turned to Derek. He raised an eyebrow. "You've been busy."

"I worked all night."

He nodded, seeming to take in her art project. "Looks it. I'd say you've performed an exorcism."

"It was very ... cathartic. What do you think, Der?"

He canted his head. "Does it matter what I think?"

"Actually, it does. He was your brother."

He pulled in a huge breath and averted his eyes. "He wanted me to look after you, Lil. He even came out and asked if I'd, uh, consider, maybe one day ..." he stammered. "Don't think I didn't consider it, but I just ... I'm sorry, but it didn't seem right. I mean, you're my sister. But I'll admit it also never seemed right for you to get together with another guy. Maybe that was me missing my brother. But now?" His eyes flicked to the hallway. "Yeah, you did the right thing."

Relief flooded her. "Really?"

"Really." He grasped her shoulders, one corner of his mouth twitching in a grin. "So. You and the hockey player?"

"His name's Gage."

He released her. "You and Gage."

"I'm not sure he's still in the picture, but if he is, can you get used to having him around?"

"I will if I have to."

"He plays guitar, you know. And he's pretty good."

His grin broadened. "See? I like him better already." He pulled her in for a quick hug "Honestly, Lil. Whatever you want. You deserve to be happy."

"I do, don't I?"

After Derek and Vi left, Lily checked her phone—something she'd been doing for weeks—and was disappointed with the same result. Nothing from Gage. Enough time had passed that she didn't know exactly how to bridge the breach. Awkwardness and embarrassment bobbed inside her, not to mention the worry that she'd jinx his awesome play. It was one thing to open herself up. It was another thing to convince him to give her another chance. Was he willing?

Only one way to find out.

She called Ivy. "I really screwed things up with Gage."

"And?"

"And I'm gonna need your help to unscrew them."

Chapter 36

THE HOLY GRAIL

For Christ's sake, another fucking party.

Gage groaned when he saw the text from Beckett Miller. Not only was it another party he wanted nothing to do with, but it was really going to chap his huevos. The wound from losing to Miller's team during the Western Conference Final was still raw. And damn if Arizona didn't go on to win the Stanley Cup! It was mid-June, a week after their victory, and Miller had one of the first turns with the trophy after announcing he was done. The big blowout was a nod to the Cup win, his retirement, and the birth of his second daughter.

As if the victory parade in Phoenix hadn't been celebration enough.

Yeah, it would be a rip-roaring time. *Whoopee!*

Sarah, who'd decided on a whim to spend a few days in Denver, was Gage's lone bright spot and his plus-one. As they strolled into Miller's backyard, Gage was bowled over by the sea of tents and balloons, a ridiculous number of children tearing around, and a stage butted up in a corner.

Sarah's mouth dropped open. "Wow! They really went all out."

"Might as well. It's his day with Lord Stanley's Cup. Party on," Gage said dryly.

He grabbed beers from one of the tents, and they ambled toward Miller, standing tall in a cluster of people. The guy was hard to miss—his smile alone was like a beacon, and a sharp pang of envy stabbed Gage. Next year, he promised himself, he'd get the holy grail of hockey and hold his own celebration with his mites and the sled team. *Yeah.*

Sarah tugged his sleeve. "There're Natalie and T.J."

They stood in the group surrounding Miller, intent on whatever was happening in front of them on the patio.

"What's going on?" Gage asked when they joined them.

"Oh, hey," Natalie said absentmindedly, giving them each a side-hug.

T.J. jerked his chin. "Nelsy." He leaned in and gave Sarah a brotherly squeeze.

"Baby Audrey is getting baptized in the Cup," Natalie whispered.

Gage glimpsed the little mush-ball of a baby actually *in* the Cup, all swaddled and looking like a drowsy dumpling. Miller, his arm anchored around his wife's shoulders, stood to the side while a guy in black shirtsleeves cradled the baby's head and recited something. On the other side stood people Gage guessed were their family members.

Miller's life was rich.

Gage focused on the Cup, and his breath hitched. It was beautiful, all silver and polished and gleaming, engraved with thousands of names of those who went before. What would it feel like to hoist it over his head on the ice? Kiss it? Hand it off to a teammate? Celebrate among friends and family?

The thought of having his own day with it was suddenly overshadowed by an ache he'd been living with for months. Lily and Daisy probably wouldn't be part of it—or anything else in his life—and his heart sank.

He hadn't talked to Lily since mid-April, though she'd dominated his thoughts every single hour of every single day. What would he say? *Hey, I know you want nothing to do with me, but wanna get together for pancakes and coffee?*

When the baptism was finished, he and T.J. shuffled toward the Cup, keeping a respectful distance. No way would either of them touch it. Not until they'd won it.

"Talked to Grims," T.J. said out of the side of his mouth.

"Yeah?"

"Says he'll be ready for training camp."

Gage gave the automatic answer. "Good."

What Gage didn't share with T.J. was that Grims had sent him a text apologizing for the quandary he'd put Gage in and acknowledging he had a long way back to earn Gage's trust. And respect. Yeah, Grims had lost a lot of chips. His use of PEDs had remained a tight-lipped team secret, so he hadn't endured the wrath of the league. No automatic suspension. No forced drug rehab. No public humiliation. Was that just?

Gage's opinion on the outcome was ambivalent at best—he was glad his teammates had remained oblivious, but he was still pissed at his captain. He was also busy beating himself up for his role in the whole mess, even though, in the end, no good answer had existed. This was a rare instance where Grandma had had it wrong. The right path *wasn't* always clear, whether you had a moral compass to guide you or not. No, this problem had bled all across the gray spectrum. Nothing about it was tidy, and answers weren't always easy or obvious.

Just like expecting Lily to do what *he* wanted and give Jack up might not have been so black-and-white either.

T.J. whacked him on the shoulder, jarring him back to Miller's backyard.

"Let's go congratulate the son of a bitch and get it over with." T.J. smirked.

After the obligatories were dispensed with, Gage glanced around. Sarah had disappeared, so he peeled away to scour the huge yard for her. In the far corner, the band had started up, but Sarah wasn't there either, so he continued his sweep. Where the hell was she?

A small movement in his hand startled him. When he looked down on blond curls and bright gray eyes, he realized what he'd felt was a small, familiar hand sliding into his.

"Hi, Gage." Daisy looked up at him shyly.

Emotions rushed up from his gut, jamming his throat. He dropped to a knee and yanked off his sunglasses so he could look into her luminous eyes.

His voice came out in a cracking warble. "Hey, kiddo. How've you been?"

Her body twisted from side to side. "Good."

"Is it okay if I give you a hug?"

Her answer was to throw her arms around his neck and cling tightly. It took every bit of restraint to keep him from picking her up and crushing her to him. Instead, he breathed in her sun-kissed hair.

When he finally unwound her arms from his neck, he peered at her. "You've grown. And you lost another tooth! What are you doing here?"

"Uncle Derek's band is playing." She turned and pointed to the stage.

He squinted, finally recognizing Derek's form. "Is, ah," he cleared his sticky throat, "is your mom here?" His heart started jackhammering at the thought.

"She's—"

"Right here."

He turned at the sound of Lily's voice and looked up from where he knelt. The sun shone from behind, outlining her shape and lighting sleek blond hair. As he rose, a tentative smile began curving her lips. His heart was now throwing itself against his ribcage in a bid to escape.

"What happened to your hair?" he blurted. *Oh, smooth!*

Her hand immediately reached up to run over it. "I used a flat iron." She let out a nervous laugh. His confusion must have shown because she added, "It's not permanent."

"I like," he said dumbly. His eyes traveled up her body and stopped at her neck. "Where's your necklace?"

Her eyes shimmered with something he didn't recognize but bored straight into his soul. "It was time to put it away."

A moment passed before the full weight of her statement registered. A puck-sized lump formed in his chest. His hopes wanted to climb, they really did, but he tethered them.

Eyes still trapped in her gaze, he swallowed hard. Neither of them moved, blinked, breathed.

"Mom?" Daisy piped up, shattering the spell.

Lily gasped a laugh, her palm pressing against her chest. "Yes, sweetie?"

"Your song is coming up."

To Gage, she shrugged an apology. "I'm singing a few songs. Will you be here for a while?"

A little voice told him he might be dreaming, so he drank her in. She wore a sundress with bright blue flowers, its hem just above her knees. On her feet, white sandals with straps that wound around her shapely calves. Simple. Beautiful. Heart-stopping.

Heart-aching.

He twirled his sunglasses. "What was the question?"

Another lilting laugh. "Are you sticking around?"

"Yeah. Yes. Sure." His sunglass-spinning was so vigorous that they flew from his grasp.

Daisy giggled and ran to pick them up.

"You look great," he whispered reverently.

"So do you, Professor." Lily's gaze swept from his face, over his T-shirt and board shorts, to his flip-flopped feet. He suddenly wished he'd worn something nicer.

"I owe you an apology." He shook his head. "For my mom. For being a selfish, possessive jerk. For ... lots of stuff."

Her smile grew wide, dazzling him. "It can wait. I have a few things to say to you too."

The air between them was charged, and his body felt like a high-voltage wire coursing with electricity. He needed to keep himself in check. After all, he had no idea if she'd removed the necklace for a new guy. Christ, he hoped like hell she hadn't. And if there wasn't a new guy, it didn't mean *he* had a place in her heart. She'd never told him she loved him—he'd been the doofus who'd put it all out there.

Daisy gave him his glasses, then tugged her mom's hand. "Come on, Mom."

Gage came to his senses and crouched down. "Hey, kiddo. Dance with me, and we'll watch your mom together, okay?"

Daisy beamed at him. Soon he was barefoot in the grass, swinging her arms as they swayed among a handful of people gathered in front of the stage. The band wrapped up their song, and Lily stepped up to the mic.

A crowd had filled in around them, including Sarah, T.J., Natalie, and the Millers rocking their daughters.

Mere feet away, Lily looked right at him, sending his pulse into overdrive, and in that sultry, torch-singer voice of hers, said, "This one's for the Professor." His mouth went dry.

She launched into "Love Sneakin' Up On You," sending chills dancing along his spine, raising the hair on his arms, his neck. Unlike her usual singing style, she didn't close her eyes. She kept them fixed on him.

His chest ballooned with possibility, but he quickly reminded himself she was performing. This wasn't real. He'd go with the flow, enjoy the moment, and wear the biggest damn smile he'd had in months.

When the song ended, the audience applauded and Lily breathed thank-yous into the mic. Then she looked at Miller. "May I?"

Smiling, he nodded back at her. "Go for it."

"I want to thank Beckett and Paige Miller for having us here today to celebrate not only Arizona's Stanley Cup win—" Hoots, whistles, and cheers interrupted her. "Not only the win," she resumed with a grin, "but Beckett's retirement and the birth of their beautiful daughter Audrey. Congratulations!" Lots of clapping now, along with ear-piercing whistles and various barky chants for the Colorado Blizzard.

Miller surveyed the crowd with a fake glare. "The beer's for Arizona fans only."

Lily laughed, and the crowd quieted. "I'd also like to thank them for allowing me to hijack the stage for a few minutes. As some of you may know, this band has been a Denver fixture for some time. I was fortunate enough to have been a full-time member back in the day, singing alongside my brother-in-law, Derek," she made a grand sweep of her hand as Derek bowed, "and his brother, my late husband, Jack."

"Yay, Uncle Derek!" Daisy clapped and bounced in place. "Yay, Mommy!"

Gage folded his arms over his chest, questions forming in his brain.

"When we lost Jack, I never thought I'd recover," Lily continued.

Someone elbowed Gage's arm, and he swung his head to the side, surprised to see Ivy and Parker next to him.

What in the actual hell is going on?

As if reading his mind, Ivy lifted her chin toward Lily standing on the stage.

"After Jack's death, I never imagined falling in love again." Lily began choking up. "I believed we only get one chance at finding 'The One.'" Gage jerked in place, all of him wanting to comfort her, and Ivy placed a hand on his arm.

Lily's eyes landed on him, bright with tears, setting off a chain reaction in him. Emotions jammed his throat, and tears stung his eyes.

"I was wrong," she said. "Some of us are fortunate enough to get a second turn. I didn't know it for a long time, and it wasn't until I pushed mine away that I realized I'd made the biggest mistake of my life. I should have never let you walk out that door."

Cartwheeling acrobats tumbled through his stomach. He jabbed his thumb at his swelling chest and mouthed, "Me?"

He could feel eyes burning into him even as a few tears spilled down his cheeks, but he didn't give a fuck. All his attention was focused on one person, one voice, and the one pair of eyes locked on his.

Lily nodded. "Yes, you. I want everyone here to know that you are the finest, most caring, loving man I know. I look at you, and my heart races as if it's going to jump out of my body. As your grandma so wisely says, life's too short, and I don't want to spend another minute without you. You're the love of my life, Gage Nelson. I love you, and if you—"

He sprang onto the stage—later he'd wonder how he did it—pulled the mic from her hands, and kissed her long and deep, savoring the taste of strawberries on her lips and the heady smell of jasmine and almonds. Someone slid the mic from his grip. Everything fell away until all that remained was the feel of her soft curves nestled against him and her fingers plowing through his hair. Whistling and clapping and cheering became dull noises in his foggy brain. He kissed her with all he had, afraid she was a dream he'd awaken from and lose.

"Get a room," someone laughed.

He couldn't have cared less that they were, literally, onstage putting on a show.

Finally, he registered Daisy's tiny voice. "I hope Gage is going to be my dad."

Me too, princess.

Lily pulled away, breathless, smiling through her tears. "I didn't intend on doing this in front of so many people."

"I don't give a shit about them." He was breathing hard. "Let 'em watch. Maybe they'll learn something."

She giggled.

He leaned his forehead against hers. "You love me?"

"So much. Do *you* still love *me*?"

"Absolutely." He thumped his palm against his chest. "Tell me again. I want to be sure I heard you right."

She placed her small hands on his cheeks and brushed away his tears. "I love you, I love you, I love you! Can you forgive me for being so blind?"

"I did months ago." Relief swam in her glistening eyes. "Can you forgive *me*?"

She nodded. "Did."

"So these are the good kind of tears, right?" He pulled his lower lip between his teeth and waited.

"Yes, Professor. The best kind of tears."

Lily floated on clouds so high she wasn't sure she'd ever come down. He still loved her. He still wanted her. He was hers. Gage lingered on the platform, grinning at her, holding her hand while she sang Bonnie Raitt's "Sweet Forgiveness."

When the song was over, they stepped offstage and joined family and friends eager to congratulate them.

Ivy hugged her tight. "You deserve this life with him, Lil."

More happy tears sprang to Lily's eyes. "Thanks, Ive, for everything. Especially for being tough enough to make me wake up."

“That’s what big sisters are for. And speaking of big sisters ...” Ivy introduced her to Gage’s sister, Sarah, a beautiful brunette with hazel eyes.

Sarah pulled her in for a hug. “I never would’ve guessed you were a hooker,” she laughed, instantly putting Lily at ease. “I’m so happy for my brother,” she added with a warm smile.

“I’m afraid your mom won’t be pleased.”

“Don’t you worry. We’ll get her there.”

The afternoon passed in a blur. Finally, Gage leaned in and kissed Lily’s temple. “What do you say we blow this Popsicle stand? Ivy said she and Parker will take Daisy tonight.”

“What about Sarah?”

“They didn’t offer to take her too.”

Lily smacked his chest. “You know what I mean.”

He laughed. “She wants to hang out for a while, so she’ll take my car.” He waggled his eyebrows. “Will you give me a ride?”

Lily fluttered her eyelashes at him. “I’d love to, Waffle-Butt.”

A look of horror came over his face. “Oh shit. She didn’t.”

She nodded. “Yes, she did. So how old were you when you made the brilliant decision to sit buck naked on a hot waffle iron, Professor?”

He groaned aloud, pulling his hand over his face. “Two.”

Lily’s eyebrows bounced. “Do you have a scar I missed? I think I need a closer look-see.”

His lips quirked. “On one condition.” He wove his fingers in her hair and tilted her head to the side. “You will never, ever tell *anyone*—especially my teammates.”

“Ooh, you might have to do a lot of kissing to shut me up.”

“It’s on.”

As they drove to her house, she took in his profile, and her heart stuttered. He wore a perma-smile, glancing at her periodically without saying anything. She’d had a lot of time to consider everything she loved about him, and she added that one to the list. He seemed to dial into what she needed and give it to her, even if it was utter silence. She’d never felt so in tune before, not even with Jack.

How had she almost let this man get away?

Gage's eyes roamed over her hair, and she was suddenly self-conscious. "Not a good look?"

"It's a *great* look, but so are the curls. Then again, you could be bald and you'd still be gorgeous."

The compliment, along with the heat in his eyes, flushed her cheeks with fire. She pulled into her drive and shut off the engine. Running a finger along her jaw, he chuckled. "I love this shade of pink on you, Goldilocks."

Locked inside her house, she gave him a moment to gawk at her revamped hallway before she tugged him into her bedroom and peeled off his clothes. He eagerly returned the favor. The sweetness in rediscovering one another had her heart on the verge of bursting, and she lost herself in their slow, torrid lovemaking.

Hours later, she lay curled against his body, walking her fingers lightly over his solid chest while his hand caressed her arm.

"There's something that has me a little worried," she began.

He craned his head and peered at her. "What's that?"

"After we stopped seeing each other, you played a lot better, and I'm just wondering if that means hanky-panky's off-limits during the season?"

"Hell no!" he laughed. "I'll give up hockey first." He kissed her head. "Seriously, I have off nights, like all players do. It happens. As for hanky-panky, we'll pace ourselves. If you can keep your hands off me, that is."

She smacked his very hard chest. "I can if you can."

"That," he laughed, "may be the tougher challenge."

They made love again, and as she snuggled against him afterward, she drifted and dreamed, bobbing contentedly among the clouds while "At Last" played in her head. Jack appeared, a quick flash where he waved and gave her a thumbs-up before he drove away in a sky-blue convertible.

Epilogue

Seven months later

Gage piled into the sleigh and spread a thick layer of blankets over Lily, who cuddled Daisy on her lap. He wrapped them both up in his arms, silvery moonlight setting the snow aglow as the snowcat lurched their contraption forward.

"Everyone nice and cozy?"

Daisy giggled. "My nose is cold."

"Of course it is." He shucked his glove and placed his hand over her frosty sniffer, getting another giggle out of her.

"You've had the giggles all night, baby girl," Lily declared as she gave her a little squeeze.

The all-star break was nearly over, and they were finishing up in grand style. Gage had been voted to go, but the coaches had kept him out to rest a banged-up shoulder. While he loved being selected by the fans, not going gave him a rare run of days to relax with his girls before the grueling end-of-season push toward playoffs.

Stanley Cup, here I come.

They'd seen the colorful ice castles in Dillon, explored Breckenridge, and were riding back to their retreat after dinner at Beano's Cabin. Their days in the mountains had been pure perfection. As a matter of fact, his *life* was pure perfection—except for one detail, which he planned to correct shortly. And that plan had his stomach gurgling. Maybe he should've stuck with soup for dinner.

Lily leaned her head against his chest. "We're gonna miss you when you go to the Bay Area."

The very last of his break would be spent in California catching up with family, seeing that they had everything they needed. He rested his cheek against Lily's soft beanie. "It's only a few nights. You could still come with me."

She raised her eyes to his. "Your mom wants you to herself this time."

"Grandma would love to see you again. I just don't know if she'd recognize you. I don't know if she'll recognize *me*." A band tightened around his heart. He hoped like hell his visit would fall on one of her good days. They were becoming a rarity.

"I'm sure your mom will be relieved."

"Hey, she's warming up. It's a cold thaw, but she's getting there," he chuckled. Even if it was by slow degrees, his mom was softening. She loved Daisy, and while she wasn't head over heels for Lily—yet—she was making the effort. One day, she'd "move on" and get over the fact Jessica would never become her daughter-in-law. As for Jess, he'd heard from Sarah that she was seeing someone, and he was happy for her.

"Yeah, I guess she is," Lily sighed, bringing him back to the present and what awaited when they reached the house. "I'm really glad you'll get to see them, especially your grandma. I just like having you around."

He gave her a quick kiss. "I like being around."

Daisy tilted her head back and grinned at them both. "You guys are mushy."

He wiggled his eyebrows and gently turned her face away. "Then stop watching." This earned him another giggle.

At their vacation rental, he took off their coats and hats, and the girls settled in front of the fireplace while he uncorked a bottle of Dom Perignon he'd stashed. He tapped his shirt pocket, opened a sparkling cider for Daisy, and filled champagne flutes.

Lily craned her head. "What's the bubbly for, Professor?"

"To toast the end of a perfect trip and the beginning of ... uh, a perfect year."

Her eyebrows bounced. "One that includes a Cup win?"

"Among other things. Hey, if I win the Cup, I can hire you to sing at *my* party."

"I'll always sing for you." She gave him a smile that had his nervous stomach beating a tattoo.

"I'm counting on it."

He handed out the bubbles, slid beside his girls, and clinked their glasses.

Daisy turned bright eyes on him. "Are you gonna play that song for Mom now?"

Lily's eyebrows scrunched. "What song?"

Setting down his champagne, he cleared his throat. "I've been practicing a song by Train."

Daisy began bouncing on the couch.

Showtime.

He picked up his acoustic guitar. "Daisy's gonna help me with this one. Ready, princess?" She bobbed her head, excitement gleaming in her eyes.

Lily's features reflected her growing bewilderment.

Heart thumping like the wheels of a freight train, he pulled in a few steadying breaths, and with a nod to Daisy, he began playing "Marry Me." After the first reedy notes, his plucking grew more sure and his voice stronger, and when he reached the chorus, Daisy's angelic voice blended with his.

Lily gasped and covered her mouth. Her wide eyes darted between Daisy and him, pooling with tears as the words inside him filled the room with the sweet serenade. Relief washed over him at the sight of Lily's quivering smile.

That's a good sign. Go with the flow.

When the song was over, tears streamed down Lily's cheeks. He set aside the guitar and stuffed his fingers in his shirt pocket, but his hand shook so much he couldn't grasp his prize.

"Daisy," he croaked, "help me out, kiddo."

She sprang from her seat, dipped nimble fingers into his pocket, and plucked out a diamond solitaire she triumphantly offered to her mother.

"Uh, I think I'm supposed to do that, princess."

Two pairs of wide eyes locked on him, and they all began laughing—*thank fuck!*—diffusing some of the tension in his body. Daisy handed him the ring with a broad smile and an encouraging pat, and he extended it to Lily. "Lily Everett, I promise to do my best to wear out the words 'I love you.' Will you promise to sing to me for the rest of our lives and do me the honor of—"

"Yes!" She launched herself into his arms, covering his face and neck with kisses.

"I like how you say yes," he laughed.

His fingers still held the ring, and Daisy took it from him while he encircled her mother in his arms and kissed her so she had no doubt how much he loved her. *My future wife.*

They broke apart, and Daisy wormed between them with the ring. "I helped pick out the ring, Momma! Do you like it?"

"Let's have her put it on first, princess." Gage took it from Daisy and slid it onto Lily's finger. "Well?" He held his breath.

Fresh tears sprang to her eyes. "I love it. I love you!" And she was back in his arms, Daisy squished between them.

It was perfect.

And only grew more perfect when, an hour later, Daisy was in bed, and they stood in his room looking out the window at the clear, moonlit sky. When they traveled, he always booked extra space to give Lily her own room for appearance's sake. Thank God that was coming to an end.

"How soon do you want to get married?" he asked as he began unbuttoning his cuffs.

"I don't know. After you win the Cup?" She moved away and plopped down on the edge of his huge-ass bed.

"Hmm ... three-and-a-half more months. Okay, but can we at least live under the same roof? I'm tired of waking up without you in my bed." He took a few steps toward her.

She sent him a wicked wink. "You do get to wake up with me."

He snorted. "Yeah, when we're super sneaky or get that rare night together. Sometimes I think it's just another one-night stand with you."

"The first one worked out pretty well, I'd say."

"You'll get no argument from me on that."

"I think living together can be arranged, Professor. But which house should we live in?"

He liked the sound of "we." "I don't care which house. I'll live wherever you want, as long as you and Daisy are there."

She tapped her finger against her temple. "Ooh, I can just picture the posts now. I'll have to spend some time planning it out so I maximize the splash factor for you."

"Oh hell no! We're not making a PR event out of this." He gave her what he thought was a goofy grin.

"Well, I'll have to do *something* so all your crazed female fans know you're taken and to *back the hell off*. By the way, whatever happened when Kathryn Tappen interviewed you during the playoffs?"

"Kathryn *who*?"

"Ooh, good answer, Professor! Seriously, did you get to talk to her personally?"

"Didn't want to, especially when my ideal woman was in Denver. Have I told you I love when you go all cavewoman?" he laughed. "Seriously, Lil, there are only two female fans I care about. And speaking of them ..." He sat beside her and took her hand in his. "I've been giving this a lot of thought ... what would you think of me adopting Daisy? And, maybe later this year, we could work on making a baby sister or brother for her? She's gonna be an awesome big sister."

Lily's free hand covered her heart, fresh tears pooling in her eyes.

Flustered, he stroked her upper arms. Maybe he shouldn't have sprung the idea on her so soon. "Ah, shit. All I seem to be doing is making you cry tonight."

"No," she choked out. "They're the good tears. I promise." She cupped his face and laid a gentle kiss on his lips. "I love the idea of you adopting her, and I love the idea of making a family with you." Her eyes mined his with a look so tender his breath hitched. "I adore you, Gage Nelson. I shudder every time I think I almost let you get away."

He pulled her hand from his face and kissed her soft palm. "I wasn't going anywhere. I would have let you stew until you came to your senses, then come right back to you. Remember what I said about setting my sights on something?"

She nodded, her bouncy curls catching firelight. "I do."

"Practicing our vows already?"

Soft giggles escaped her. "Speaking of vows, what would you think of my taking your name?"

"Lily Nelson? Hell yeah! Would you keep 'Everett' as Daisy's last name?"

"I'll leave it up to her, but I think 'Daisy Everett Nelson' sounds nice. And maybe she'll call you something besides 'Coach' or 'Gage'?"

"Yeah. 'Dad' sounds way better to me. And easier for her to say." Warmth settled in his chest.

Lily stood and sauntered to the fireplace on the opposite side of the bedroom.

"You're not going to your own room yet, are you?" he asked. "I was hoping ..."

"Hoping ...?"

"For a little cuddle time?" He waggled his eyebrows. She shot him a sultry look over her shoulder, then slowly unzipped her jeans and shimmied out of them, giving him an ass wiggle that shot a bolt through him, firing every nerve ending. She was sporting a lacy black thong he'd never seen before, and it brought his shirt unbuttoning to a dead stop and his cock to full attention.

She turned and, just as languidly, pulled her sweater over her head, giving him an eyeful of her curves gilded in the firelight's glow.

Fuck yeah!

She wore a matching bra of sheer black lace that left little for him to imagine—except taking it off of her. His cock was now begging to be set free.

Licking his lips, he swallowed hard and crooked his finger at her. "Lock the door and get your sweet little ass over here."

"Bossy. You're throwing your caveman weight around again." She tilted her head provocatively and struck her sassy pose, letting his eyes roam all over her. He just hoped his heart wouldn't seize.

"Come here, Goldilocks, and I'll show you caveman."

She took deliberate steps to the door, locked it, then turned and smirked. "What's in it for me?"

"Why don't you come over here and find out?" He patted the bed.

A devilish grin spread over her face, but she didn't budge.

"Chicken," he taunted.

"I'll show you chicken, caveman." She sprinted at him, closing the distance in the flutter of an eyelash. He barely had time to brace his arms and catch her before she crashed down on him. They tangled together like two people at the end of a game of Twister. Which was fine by him.

She covered his mouth with hers, her tongue dancing over his. While her mouth kept his busy, her fingers nimbly undid the rest of his buttons and tugged his shirt off—also fine by him.

"What are you trying to tell me, beautiful?"

She straddled him, pinning him on his back.

"You've been owning it on the ice, Professor. Now let's see you own it in the bedroom."

"Do your worst, your ladyship."

She unzipped his pants and worked him free. "Only my best for you."

His eyes rolled back in his head while his hands ran over her silky skin. God, he hoped he'd die like this.

But not tonight.

THE END

WANT MORE GAGE AND LILY? Download your bonus content on my website at www.griffin-brady.com and get a behind-the-scenes peek at the deleted moments from Gage and Lily's story.

SARAH CAN'T STAND QUINN. The feeling is mutual. When Mr. Smooth and Ms. Prickly shelter in place, not even his mansion is big enough to contain the fireworks. These two are sparks colliding with gas: combustible and explosive. Here's an excerpt from *The Winning Score*, Book 4:

A look of alarm spread over Quinn's features. "You weren't just planning on leaving her out there, were you?"

"Of course not! What do you take me for?"

His lips quirked. "Don't even get me started."

Sarah's mad-o-meter started to climb, and she narrowed her eyes at him. Why did this guy get to her anyway?

He took a step backward. "Whoa! What's with the stink-eye? Seriously, what did I ever do to you?"

She smirked. "It's not about what you did or didn't do. It's about what you want to do—well, not to me, per se, but to women in general—and what you want to do is completely controlled by that." She pointed at his crotch but kept her gaze fixed on his.

He gave her a cocky grin. "Well, at least you noticed I have one. Envious, toots?"

"You're such a tool."

He crossed his arms over his chest. "The more I'm around you, the harder it is to believe you and Gage are related. For one thing, I think you swear more than your brother does, and that's saying something considering he plays hockey for a living."

"Gage is the polite one."

"Yeah, I totally get that."

Arms still firmly crossed, he seemed to appraise her. His scrutiny made her insides squirm like tadpoles teeming in a pond.

Well, that and the modicum of guilt building inside of her for disparaging her brother's teammate.

"So tell me something," he drawled. "Did you acquire your sunny personality in engineering school, or do you come by it naturally?" His smirk deepened, making one dimple appear. She felt an overpowering urge to scrub it off his smug face.

"No, I learned it in common sense school—someplace you obviously didn't attend."

"Oh, ow. Burn, Sunshine." He covered his heart and laughed, then spun and headed toward his wing. With a backward glance, he said, "This has been fan-fucking-tastic. Let's do it again real soon. And yeah, I owe the swear jar five bucks for that. Totally worth it."

With that, he jogged down the hall. God, it was only her second day, and she wanted to throttle him even more than she had on day one. This wasn't going to work out. Suddenly, Daisy's bubble gum room was looking a hell of a lot better. Damn it, even Gage and Lily's couch held more appeal than Sarah's sumptuous suite if it meant not living under the same roof as Quinn "God's-Gift" Hadley.

Get your copy of *The Winning Score* at Amazon and find out if Quinn and Sarah can make it through quarantine together without throttling each other.

SEVEN PLAYMAKERS COUPLES unite for a winter wedding getaway, but there's trouble in Paradise. Claim your free copy of *Puck the Halls* at www.gkbrady.com/bonus-content/pth/ and see if they can find the spirit of Christmas—and each other—before it's too late.

Acknowledgments

First and foremost, the readers who have encouraged me throughout this process. This book wouldn't be possible without you.

To my beta readers and the Marbles, thank you for your time, your honest feedback, and your suggestions. I especially loved the "Gage wouldn't say that!" comments that made the story better.

To lovely Jenny Q, my editor, who spent a Friday afternoon brainstorming with me—and I do mean storm!—to make Gage's story what it is. Without you, it would have been vanilla.

Persnickety, always, for your impeccable i-dotting and t-crossing. Somehow you're able to see the minutiae and clean it up elegantly. Thank you for that talent and for making me look better.

And always, to my husband, Tim, who has labeled himself an author's widower. Thank you for talking through plot ideas with me, for framing my book covers for my birthday surprise, for making me dinners ... in short, for being Gage. I love you.

Author's Note

Thank you so much for reading *Gauging the Player*! I really wanted this good guy to get his own HEA, and who better than a sweet, beautiful, soulful singer?

If you enjoyed Gage and Lily's story, I would love it if you would leave a review on Amazon, BookBub, or Goodreads to help readers like you find the story. And if you do leave a review, I would love to read it! Email me the link at gkbrady@griffin-brady.com.

Stay up to date on upcoming releases, cover reveals, giveaways, and discount deals by joining my newsletter. Simply go to: www.griffin-brady.com/contemporary-romance/contact/

Trouble is brewing. Disaster strikes. Can they conjure a mistletoe miracle? Claim your free copy of *Puck the Halls* (Book 7.5), a Playmakers novella, when you join. Download it at www.gkbrady.com/bonus-content/pth/or scan this code:

The playlist for *Gauging the Player* can be found on Spotify.

Other Books

The Playmakers Series®

Book 0 - *Line Change*
Book 1 - *Taming Beckett*
Book 2 - *Third Man In*
Book 4 - *The Winning Score*
Book 5 - *Defending the Reaper*
Book 6 - *No Touch Zone*
Book 7 - *Twisted Wrister*
Book 8 - *Besting the Blueliner*
Book 9 - *Guarding the Crease*
Fall Novella - *Love Rinkside*
Winter Novella (Book 7.5) - *Puck the Halls*
Spring Novella - *Deking at Love*
Summer Novella - *Slapshot Summer*

The Fall River Series

Book 1 - *The Keeper*
Book 2 - *The Fixer*
Book 3 - *The Rescuer*
Book 4 - *The Harborer*

About the Author

Since childhood, all sorts of stories and characters have lived in G.K. Brady's imagination, elbowing one another for attention, so she's thrilled (as are they) to be giving them their voice on the written page.

A writer of contemporary romance, she loves telling tales of the less-than-perfect hero or heroine who transforms with each turn of a page.

G.K. is a wife and the proud mom of three grown sons. She currently resides in Colorado with her very patient husband.

Connect with her on these platforms:

 www.amazon.com/author/gkbrady

 www.twitter.com/GKBrady_Writes

 www.facebook.com/AuthorG.K.Brady/

 www.bookbub.com/authors/g-k-brady

 www.goodreads.com/author/show/19488321.G_K_Brady

 www.instagram.com/authorg.k.brady

 www.pinterest.com/gkbrady0993/

www.ingramcontent.com/pod-product-compliance
Lightning Source LLC
LaVergne TN
LVHW010601100826
845148LV00014B/2806

* 9 7 8 1 7 3 3 2 7 6 3 5 1 *